A Finer End

By the same author

A Share in Death

All Shall Be Well

Leave the Grave Green

Mourn Not Your Dead

Dreaming of the Bones

Kissed a Sad Goodbye

Deborah Crombie

A Finer End

MACMILLAN

First published in the United States of America 2001
by Bantam Books, New York

First published in the United Kingdom 2001 by Macmillan
an imprint of Pan Macmillan Ltd
Pan Macmillan, 20 New Wharf Road, London N1 9RR
Basingstoke and Oxford
Associated companies throughout the world
www.panmacmillan.com

ISBN 0 333 90195 9

Grateful acknowledgement is made to Samuel Weiser, Inc.
for permission to reprint material from *Glastonbury: Avalon of the Heart*
by Dion Fortune (York Beach, ME: Samuel Weiser, Inc., 2000).
Material used by permission.

1 3 5 7 9 8 6 4 2

A CIP catalogue record for this book is available from
the British Library.

Typeset by Intype London Ltd
Printed and bound in Great Britain by
Mackays of Chatham plc, Chatham, Kent.

Acknowledgements

Thanks to my writers' group once again for their unstinting support and patience: Steve Copling, Dale Denton, Jim Evans, John Hardie, Viqui Litman, Diane Sullivan, and Rickey Thornton. Added thanks to Diane Sullivan, RN, BSN, for advice on medical matters, and to Dr Davis Wortman, director of music, St Matthew's Cathedral, Dallas, Texas, for his advice on the complexity of Gregorian chant.

I am also indebted to Marcia Talley and Carol Chase for their suggestions and additional readings of the manuscript; to my editor, Kate Miciak, for making this a better book; and to my agent, Nancy Yost, for her encouragement.

And last but certainly not least, thanks to Rick and Katie, for providing me a firm foundation.

Part One

Chapter One

Imagination is a great gift, a Divine power of the mind, and may be trained and educated to create and to receive only that which is true.

Frederick Bligh Bond, from *The Gate of Remembrance*

The shadows crept into Jack Montfort's small office, filling the corners with a comfortable dimness. He'd come to look forward to his time alone at the day's end – he told himself he got more done without phones ringing and the occasional client calling in, but perhaps, he thought wryly, it was merely that he had little enough reason to go home.

Standing at his window, he gazed down at the pedestrians hurrying along either side of Magdalene Street, and wondered idly where they were all scurrying off to so urgently on a Wednesday evening. Across the street the Abbey gates had shut at five, and as he watched, the guard let the last few stragglers out from the grounds. The March day had been bright with a biting wind, and Jack imagined that anyone who'd been enticed by the sun into wandering around the Abbey's fishpond would be chilled to the bone. Now the remaining buttresses of the great church would be silhouetted against the clear rose of the eastern sky, a fitting reward for those who had braved the cold.

He'd counted himself lucky to get the two-room office suite with its first-floor view over the Market Square and the Abbey gate. It was a prime spot, and the restrictions involved in renovating a listed building hadn't daunted him. His years in London had given him experience enough of working round constraints, and he'd managed to update the rooms to his satisfaction without going over his budget. He'd hired a secretary to preside over his new reception area, and begun the slow task of building an architectural practice.

And if a small voice still occasionally whispered, *Why bother?* he did his best to ignore it and get on with things the best way he knew how, although he'd learned in the last few years that plans were ephemeral blueprints. Even as a child, he'd had his life mapped out: university with first-class honours, a successful career as an architect . . . wife . . . family. What he hadn't bargained for was life's refusal to cooperate. Now they were all gone – his mum, his dad . . . Emily. At forty, he was back in Glastonbury. It was a move he'd have found inconceivable twenty years earlier, but here he was, alone in his parents' old house in Ashwell Lane, besieged by memories.

Rolling up his shirtsleeves, he sat at his desk and positioned a blank sheet of paper in the pool of light cast by his Anglepoise lamp. Sitting around feeling sorry for himself wasn't going to do a bit of good, and he had a client expecting a bid tomorrow morning on a residential refurbishment. And besides, if he finished his work quickly, he could look forward to the possibility of dinner with Winnie.

The thought of the unexpected entry of Winifred Catesby into his life made him smile. Besieged by arranged dates as soon as his mother's well-meaning friends decided he'd endured a suitable period of mourning, he'd found the effort of making conversation with needy divorcees more depressing than time spent alone. He'd begged off so often that the do-gooders had declared him hopeless and finally left him alone.

Relieved of unwelcome obligations, he'd found himself driving the five miles to Wells for the solace of the evensong service in the cathedral more and more frequently. The proximity of the cathedral choir was one of the things that had drawn him back to Glastonbury – he'd sung at Wells as a pupil in the cathedral school, and the experience had given him a lifelong passion for church music.

And then one evening a month ago, as he found his usual place in the ornately carved stall in the cathedral choir, she had slipped in beside him – a pleasantly ordinary-looking woman in her thirties, with light brown hair escaping from beneath a floppy velvet hat, and a slightly upturned nose. He had not noticed her particularly, just nodded in the vague way one did as she took her seat. The service began, and in that moment when the first high reach of the treble voices sent a shiver down his spine, she had met his eyes and smiled.

Afterwards, they had chatted easily, naturally, and

as they walked out of the cathedral together, deep in discussion of the merits of various choirs, he'd impulsively invited her for a drink at the pub down the street. It wasn't until he'd helped her out of her coat that he'd seen the clerical collar.

Emily, always chiding him for his conservatism, would have been delighted by his consternation. And Emily, he felt sure, would have liked Winnie. He extended a finger to touch the photograph on his desktop and Emily gazed back at him, her dark eyes alight with humour and intelligence.

His throat tightened. Would the ache of his loss always lie so near the surface? Or would it one day fade to a gentle awareness, as familiar and unremarkable as a burr beneath the skin? But did he really want that? Would he be less himself without Emily's constant presence in his mind?

He grinned in spite of himself. Emily would tell him to stop being maudlin and get on with the task at hand. With a sigh, he looked down at his paper, then blinked in surprise.

He held a pen in his right hand, although he didn't remember picking it up. And the page, which had been blank a moment ago, was covered in an unfamiliar script. Frowning, he checked for another sheet beneath the paper. But there was only the one page, and as he examined it more closely, he saw that the small, precise script seemed to be in Latin. As he recalled enough of his schoolboy vocabulary to make a rough translation, his frown deepened.

Know ye what we . . . Jack puzzled a moment before deciding on *builded*, then there was something he couldn't make out, then the script continued . . . *in Glaston*. Meaning Glastonbury? *It was fair as . . . any earthly thing, and had I not loved it overmuch my spirit would not cling to dreams of all now vanished.*

Ye love full well what we have loved. The time . . . Here Jack was forced to resort to the dog-eared Latin dictionary in his bookcase, and after concluding that the phrase had something to do with sleeping or sleepers, went impatiently on . . . *to wake, for Glaston to rise against the darkness. We have . . .* something . . . *long for you . . . it is in your hands . . .*

After this sentence there was a trailing squiggle beginning with an *E*, which might have been a signature, perhaps 'Edmund'.

Was this some sort of a joke, invisible ink that appeared when exposed to the light? But his secretary didn't strike him as a prankster, and he'd taken the paper from a ream he'd just unwrapped himself. That left only the explanation that *he* had penned these words – alien in both script and language. But that was absurd. How could he have done so, unaware?

The walls of Jack's office leaned in on him, and the silence, usually so soothing, seemed alive with tension. He felt breathless, as if all the air in the small room had been used up.

Who were 'they', who had built in Glastonbury and who wrote in Latin? The monks of the Abbey, he supposed, a logical answer. And 'he', who had 'loved it overmuch', whose spirit 'still clung to dreams long vanished'? The ghost of a monk? Worse by the minute.

What did 'rise against the darkness' mean? And what had any of it to do with him? The whole thing was completely daft; he refused to consider it any further.

Crumpling the page, Jack swivelled his chair round, hand lifted to toss it in the bin, then stopped and returned the paper to his desk, smoothing the creases out with his palm.

Frederick Bligh Bond. The name sprang into his mind, dredged from the recesses of his childhood. The architect who, just before the First World War, had undertaken the first excavations at Glastonbury Abbey, then revealed that he had been directed by messages from the Abbey monks. Had Bond received communications like this? But Bond had been loony. *Cracked!*

Ripping the sheet of paper in half, Jack dropped the pieces in the bin, slipped into his jacket, and, sketch pad in hand, took the stairs down to the street two at a time.

He stepped out into Benedict Street, fumbling with unsteady fingers to lock his office door. Across the Market Square, the leaded windows of the George & Pilgrims beckoned. A drink, he thought with a shiver, was just what he needed. He'd work on his proposal, and the crowded bar of the old inn would surely make an antidote to whatever it was that had just happened to him.

Tugging his collar up against the wind, he sidestepped a group of adolescent skateboarders who found the smooth pavement round the Market Cross a perfect arena. A particularly fierce gust sent a sheet of paper spiralling past his cheek. He grabbed at it in instinctive self-defence, glancing absently at what he held in his fingers. Pink. A flyer, from the Avalon Society.

Glastonbury Assembly Rooms, Saturday, 7:30 to 9:30. An introduction to crystal energy and its healing powers, showing how the chakras and crystals correspond. Make elixirs and learn how to energize your environment.

'Oh, bloody perfect,' he muttered, crumpling the paper and tossing it back to the wind. That was the worst sort of nonsense, just the type of thing that drew the most extreme New Age followers to Glastonbury. Ley lines . . . crop circles . . . Druid magic on Glastonbury Tor, the ancient, conical hill that rose above the town like a beacon . . .

Although Jack, like generations of his family, had grown up in the Tor's shadow, he'd never given any credence to all the mystical rubbish associated with it – nor to the myths that described Glastonbury as some sort of cosmic mother lode.

So why on earth had he just scribbled what seemed to be a garbled message from some long-dead monk? *Was* he losing his mind? A delayed reaction to grief, perhaps? He had read about post-traumatic stress syndrome – could that explain what had happened to him? But somehow he sensed it was more than that. For an instant, he saw again the small, precise script, a thing of beauty in itself, and felt a tug of familiarity in the cadence of the language.

He resumed his walk to the pub, then a thought stopped him mid-stride. What if – what if it were even remotely possible that he *had* made contact with the dead? Did that mean . . . *could* it mean he was capable of instigating contact at will? Emily—

No. He couldn't even allow the idea of such a thing. That way lay madness.

A skateboarder whooshed past him, wheels clacking. 'You taking root, mister?' the boy called out. Jack lurched unsteadily on, across the bottom of the High Street towards the George & Pilgrims. As he reached the pub, the heavy door swung open and a knot of revellers pushed past him. An escaping hint of laughter and smoke offered safe haven before the wind snatched sound and scent away; and then, he could have sworn, he heard, faintly, the sound of bells.

The cats slept in the farmyard, taking advantage of the midday warmth of the pale spring sun. Each had its own spot – a flower pot, the sagging step at the kitchen door, the bonnet of the old white van that Garnet Todd used to deliver her tiles – and only the occasional twitch of a feline ear or tail betrayed their awareness of the rustle of mice in the straw.

Garnet stood in the doorway of her workshop, wiping her hands on the leather apron she wore as a protection against the heat of the kiln. She had almost completed her latest commission, the restoration of the tile flooring in a twelfth-century church near the edge of Salisbury Plain. The manufacture of the tiles was painstaking work. The pattern suggested by the few intact bits of floor must be matched, using only the materials and techniques available to the original artisans. Then came the installation, a delicate process requiring hours spent on hands and knees, breathing the dank and musty atmosphere of the ancient church.

But Garnet never minded that. She was most comfortable with old things. Even her work as a midwife – although it *had* honoured the Goddess – had not given her enough visceral connection with the past.

Her farm, a ramshackle place she'd bought more than twenty-five years ago, was proof of how little use she had for the present. The house stood high on the western flank of the Tor, its pitted stone façade in the path of a wind that had scoured down from the hilltop for years beyond memory. The sheep that grazed the grassy slope were her nearest neighbours, and for the most part she preferred their company.

At first she'd meant to put in the electricity and running water, but the years had passed and she'd got used to doing without. Lantern light brought ochre warmth and comforting shadows, and why should she drink the chemically poisoned water the town pumped out of its tanks when the spring on her property bubbled right up from the heart of the sacred hill? Enough had been done in this town to dishonour the old and holy things without her adding to the damage.

A cloud shadow raced down the hillside and for a moment the yard darkened. Garnet shivered. Dion, the old calico cat who ruled the rest of the brood with regal disdain, uncurled herself from the flower pot and came to rub against Garnet's ankles. 'You sense it, too, don't you, old girl?' Garnet said softly, bending to stroke her. 'Something's brewing.'

Once, long ago, she had caught that scent in the air, once before she had felt that prickle of foreboding, and the memory of the outcome filled her with dread.

Glastonbury had always been a place of power, a pivot point in the ancient battle between the light and the dark. If that delicate balance were disturbed, Garnet knew, not even the Goddess could foresee the consequences.

Glastonbury did strange things to people – as Nick Carlisle had reason to know. He'd come here for the Festival, part of his plan to take a few months off, see a bit of the world, after leaving Durham with a first in philosophy and theology. On a mild evening in late June he had rounded a bend in the Shepton Mallet Road and seen the great conical hump of the Tor rising above the plain, St Michael's Tower on its summit standing squarely against the blood-red western sky.

That had been more than a year ago, and he was still here, working in a New Age bookshop across from the Abbey for little more than the minimum wage, living in a caravan in a farmer's field in Compton Dundon – and trying to forget all that he had left behind.

He often came to the George & Pilgrims for a pint after work. A fine thing, when a pub did duty as his home away from home, but then his caravan didn't count for much – a place to put the faded jeans, T-shirts, and sweatshirts that made up his meagre wardrobe, along with the books he'd brought with him from Durham. The small fridge smelled of sour milk, and the two-ring gas cooker was as temperamental as his mother.

The thought of his mum made him grimace. Elizabeth Carlisle had raised her son alone from his infancy, and in the process had managed to make quite a successful career for herself penning North Country Aga sagas. She had managed her son's life as efficiently as she did her characters', and had then pronounced herself affronted by his resentment.

Furious at his mother's usurping of his responsibilities, he had convinced himself that he would be able to sort out his life as soon as he escaped her orbit. But freedom had not turned out to be the panacea he'd expected: he had no more idea what he wanted to do with his life than he'd had a year ago. He only knew that something held him in Glastonbury, and yet he burned with a restless and unfulfilled energy.

From his corner table, he surveyed the pub's clientele as he sipped his beer. There was an unusual yuppie element this evening, young men sporting designer suits, accompanied by polished girls in skimpy clothes. Nick could almost feel the rumble of displeasure among the regulars, clustered at the bar in instinctive solidarity.

One of the girls caught his eye and smiled. Nick looked away. Predators in make-up and Lycra, girls meant nothing but trouble. First they liked his looks, then, once they found out who his mother was, they saw him as a ready-made meal ticket. But he'd learned his lesson well, and would not let himself fall into that trap again.

Turning his back on the group, he found his attention held by the man sitting alone at the bar's end. The man was notable not only for his large size and fair hair, but also because his face was familiar. Nick had seen him often in Magdalene Street – he must work near the bookshop – and once or twice they had exchanged a friendly nod. Tonight he sat hunched over his drink, his usually amiable countenance set in a scowl.

Intrigued, Nick saw that he seemed to be writing or sketching on a pad, and that every few moments he raised visibly trembling fingers to brush a lock of hair from his forehead.

When Nick made his way to the bar for a refill, the blond man was staring fixedly at his beer glass, his pen poised over the paper. Nick glanced at the pad. It held neat architectural drawings and figures, and, scrawled haphazardly across the largest sketch, a few lines in what looked to be Latin. *It is for my sins Glaston suffered . . .* he translated silently.

'You're a classics scholar?' Nick said aloud, surprised.

'What?' The man blinked owlishly at him. For a moment Nick wondered if he were drunk, but he'd been nursing the same drink since Nick had noticed him.

Nick tapped the sketch pad. 'This. I don't often see anyone writing in Latin.'

Glancing down, the man paled. 'Oh, Christ. Not again.'

'Sorry?'

'No, no. It's quite all right.' The man shook his head and seemed to make a great effort to focus on Nick. 'Jack Montfort. I've seen you, haven't I? You work in the bookshop.'

'Nick Carlisle.'

'My office is just upstairs from your shop.' Montfort gestured at Nick's empty glass. 'What are you drinking?'

Montfort bought two more pints, then turned back to Nick. Now he seemed eager to talk. 'Working at the bookshop – I suppose you read a good bit?'

'Like a kid in a sweetshop. The manager's a good egg, turns a blind eye. And I try not to dog-ear the merchandise.'

'I have to admit I've never been in the place. Interesting stuff, is it?'

'Some of it's absolute crap,' Nick replied with a grin. 'UFOs. Crop circles – everyone knows that's a hoax. But some of it . . . well, you have to wonder . . . Odd things do seem to happen in Glastonbury.'

'You could say that,' Montfort muttered into his beer, his scowl returning. Then he seemed to try to shake off his preoccupation. 'You're not from around here, are you? Do I detect a hint of Yorkshire?'

'It's Northumberland, actually. I came for the Festival last year' – Nick shrugged – 'and I'm still here.'

'Ah, the rock festival at Pilton. Somehow I never managed to get there. I suppose I missed something memorable.'

'Mud.' Nick grinned. 'Oceans of it. And slogging about in some farmer's field, being bitten by midges, drinking bad beer, and queuing for hours to use the toilets. Still . . .'

'There was something,' Montfort prompted.

'Yeah. I'd like to have seen it in its heyday, the early seventies, you know? Glastonbury Fayre, they called it. That must have been awesome. And even that didn't compare to the original Glastonbury Festival – in terms of quality, not quantity.'

'Original festival?' Montfort repeated blankly.

'Started in 1914 by the composer Rutland Boughton,' Nick answered. 'Boughton was extremely talented – his opera *The Immortal Hour* still holds the record for the longest-running operatic production. All sorts of luminaries were involved in the Festival: Shaw, Edward Elgar, Vaughan Williams, D. H. Lawrence. And Glastonbury had its own contributors to the cultural revival, people like Frederick Bligh Bond and Alice Buckton . . . And then there was the business of Bond's friend Dr John Goodchild and the finding of the "Grail" in Bride's Well. That caused a few ripples . . .' Aware that he was babbling, Nick paused and drank the foam off his pint.

Looking up, he saw that Montfort was staring at him. Nick flushed. 'Sorry. I get a bit carried away some—'

'You know about Bligh Bond?'

The intensity in Montfort's voice took Nick by surprise. 'Well, it's a fascinating story, isn't it? Bond's knowledge was prodigious, his excavations at the Abbey were proof of that. But I suppose one can't blame the Church for being a bit uncomfortable with the idea that Bond had received his digging instructions from monks dead five centuries or more.'

'Uncomfortable?' Montfort snorted. 'They fired him. He never worked successfully as an architect again and, if I remember rightly, died in poverty. If the man had had an ounce of bloody sense, he'd have kept his mouth shut.'

'He felt he had to share it, though, didn't he? I'd say Bond was honest to a fault. And I don't think he ever actually claimed he'd made contact with spirits.

He thought he might have merely accessed some part of his own subconscious.'

'Do you believe it's possible, whatever the source?'

'Bond's not the only case. There have been well-documented instances where people have known things about the past that couldn't be accounted for otherwise.' Glancing at the paper Montfort had partially covered with his hand, Nick felt a fizz of excitement. 'But you're not talking hypothetically, are you?'

'This is' – Montfort shook his head – 'daft. Too daft to tell anyone. But the coincidence, meeting you here . . . I—' He looked around, as if suddenly aware of the proximity of other customers, and lowered his voice.

'I was sitting at my desk tonight, and I wrote . . . something. In Latin I haven't used since I was at school, and I had no memory of writing it. I tore the damned thing up . . . Then this . . .' He ran his fingertips across the scrawl on the sketch pad.

'Bugger,' Nick breathed, awed. 'I'd swap my mum to have that happen to me.'

'But why me? I didn't ask for this,' Montfort retorted fiercely. 'I'm an architect, but my knowledge of the Abbey is no more than you'd expect from anyone who grew up here. I'm not particularly religious. I've never had any interest in spiritualism – or otherworldly things of any sort, for that matter.'

Nick pondered this for a moment. 'I doubt these things are random. Maybe you have some connection to the Abbey that you're not consciously aware of.'

'That's a big help,' Montfort said, but there was a

gleam of humour in his bright blue eyes. 'So how do I find out what it is, and why this is happening to me?'

'Maybe I could help. You know it wasn't Bond who did the actual writing, but his friend, John Bartlett. Bond guided him by asking questions.'

'You want to play Bond to my Bartlett, then?'

'You said you came from Glastonbury. That seems as good a place to start as any.'

'My father's family's been in Glastonbury and round about for aeons, I should think. He was a solicitor. A large, serious man, very sure of where he stood in the world.' Montfort took a sip of his beer and his voice softened as he continued. 'Now, my mother, she was a different sort altogether. She loved stories, loved to play make-believe with us when we were children.'

'Us?'

'My cousins and I. Duncan and Juliet. My aunt and uncle had a penchant for Shakespeare. We always visited them in Cheshire on our holidays. It was a different world. The canals, and then the hills of Wales rising in the distance . . .'

Once more he fell silent, his eyes half closed. Nick was about to prompt him again, when, without warning, Montfort grasped the pen. His hand began to move steadily across the paper.

Nick translated the Latin as the words began to form. *Deo juvante . . . With God's help . . . you shall make it right . . .* Did that, he wondered, apply to him as well? Could he somehow set right what he had done?

In that instant, Nick knew why he had come to Glastonbury, and he knew why he had stayed.

*

Faith Wills rested her forehead against the cool plastic of the toilet seat, panting, her eyes swimming with the tears brought on by retching. She had nothing left to throw up but the lining of her stomach, yet somehow she was going to have to pull herself together, go out, and face the smell of her mother's breakfast.

It was a bacon-and-egg morning – her mum believed all children should go off to school well fortified for the day. They alternated cooked eggs, or porridge, or brown toast and marmite; and on this Thursday morning in March, Faith had struck the worst possible option.

A whiff of bacon crept into the bathroom. Her stomach heaved treacherously just as her younger brother, Jonathan, pounded on the door. 'You think you're effing Madonna in there or something? Hurry bloody up, Faith!'

Without raising her head, Faith said, 'Shut up,' but it came out a whisper.

Then her mother's voice – 'Jonathan, you watch your language,' and the crisp rap of knuckles on the door. 'Faith, whatever's the matter with you? You're going to be late, and make Jon and Meredith late as well.'

'Coming.' Unsteadily, Faith pushed herself up, flushed the toilet, then blew her nose on a piece of toilet tissue. Easing the door open, she found her mum waiting, hands on hips, and beyond her, Jon, and her sister, Meredith, all three faces set in varying degrees of irritation. 'What is this, a committee?' she asked, trying for a bit of attitude.

Her mother ignored her, taking her chin in firm

fingers and turning her face towards the wan light filtering in from the sitting room. 'You're white as a sheet,' she pronounced. 'Are you ill?'

Faith swallowed convulsively against the kitchen smells, then managed to croak, 'I'm okay. Just exam nerves.'

Her dad emerged from the bedroom, tying his tie. 'How many times have I told you not to leave studying until the last minute? And you know how important your A levels—'

'Just let me get my books, okay?'

'Don't take that tone with me, young lady.' Her dad jerked tight the knot of his tie and reached for her. His fingertips dug into the flesh of her bare arm.

'Sorry,' Faith mumbled, not meeting his eyes. Tugging free, she escaped to the room she shared with her sister and, once inside, leaned against the door, praying for a moment's peace before Meredith came back. It was a child's room, she thought, seeing it suddenly anew. The walls were covered with posters of rock stars, the twin beds with bedraggled stuffed animals. Her hockey uniform spilled from her satchel; the sheets of music for that afternoon's choir practice lay scattered on the floor. All things that had mattered so much to her – all utterly meaningless now.

She wouldn't be fine, she realized, closing her eyes against the tide of despair that swept over her. Nothing would ever be fine again.

And she couldn't tell her parents. In her mother's perfect world, seventeen-year-olds didn't start the day with their heads in the toilet, and her dad – well, she couldn't think about that.

She had promised never to tell, and that was all that mattered.

Faith hugged herself, pressing her arms against the new and painful swelling of her breasts. Never, never, never. The word became a litany as she swayed gently.

Ever.

Chapter Two

Glastonbury is the one great religious foundation of our British forefathers in England which has survived without a break the period of successive conquests of Saxon and Norseman, and its august history carries us back to the time of the earliest Christian settlement in Britain.

Frederick Bligh Bond,
from *An Architectural Handbook of Glastonbury Abbey*

On a soft evening in late June, Gemma James stood beside Duncan Kincaid in the pew of St John's Church, Hampstead. They had come to hear Kincaid's neighbour, Major Keith, sing in the choir at St John's evensong service.

Brought up in the spare tradition of Methodist chapel, Gemma had not learned to feel at ease in the Anglican Church. She watched Kincaid closely, standing when he stood, kneeling awkwardly when he knelt, and envying the ease with which he made his responses. Her mum would be horrified to see her here, she thought with a small smile; but Gemma was used to her mother's dismay, given her choice of career.

The music, however, made up for her discomfort with the order of service. Gemma avidly followed the programme in her leaflet: first the lovely opening prayer, then a psalm, then the Magnificat and Nunc Dimittis.

Then, with a rustle of movement, the choir rose again and began to sing, the voices coming in one after another, each more joyous than the last. The sound struck Gemma with a force almost physical; so rich was it, so full, that it seemed as if it displaced the very air. She shivered, blinking back tears.

Kincaid glanced at her, eyebrow raised, and put his arm round her shoulders. 'Cold?' he mouthed.

Shaking her head, she found the piece in her leaflet. *Ave Maria*, by Robert Parsons. '*Hail Mary, full of grace; the Lord is with thee: blessed art thou among women, and blessed is the fruit of thy womb*,' read the English translation.

Gemma closed her eyes, letting the soaring, pulsing sound carry her with it, and the rest of the service passed as if in a dream.

'You all right?' Kincaid asked as they filed out afterwards. The sun, low in the sky, cast the gnarled trees in the sloping churchyard into deep shadow.

'The music . . .'

'Lovely, wasn't it? Good choir at St John's.' He whistled under his breath. 'I promised the Major we'd buy him a drink. The Freemason's Arms, you think? It's a nice enough evening to sit outside.'

Gemma gazed at him in consternation. Tall, slender, his unruly chestnut hair falling over his forehead, looking down at her with an expression of interested enquiry – he made a picture of the perfect sensitive man. So why did she suddenly feel they might as well be from different planets?

How could he take such music for granted? Had he not felt that the glory of it was almost beyond bearing? The gap between their perceptions seemed immense.

'I – I promised Toby I'd be home for bath and story time tonight.' But she lied. The truth was she needed time to absorb what she'd heard, and that she felt too burdened by what she hadn't brought herself to tell him to make small talk. 'I'll take the tube,' Gemma said. 'You wait for the Major. Give him my best.'

'You're sure?' Kincaid asked, his disappointment visible for an instant before he schooled his expression into pleasant neutrality.

'I'll see you at the Yard in the morning.' Slipping her hand round the back of his neck, she kissed him quickly, a silent apology. Before she could change her mind, she turned and strode away.

But before crossing Heath Street to the Underground station, positioned at the very top of Hampstead High Street, she paused. The view from these upper reaches, south over the rooftops of London, never failed to inspire her. She loved to imagine Hampstead as the village it had once been, a green and leafy retreat, its air free of the noxious fumes and fog that choked London below.

That vision made a startling contrast to the bowels of Hampstead tube station, the deepest in London. Gemma found a seat on the crowded train and did her best to ignore the hygienic deficiencies of the man next to her, letting the echo of the choir reverberate in her head. So intense had been the demands of the past few months that even half an hour on a train was welcome time to gather her thoughts.

The death of Kincaid's ex-wife two months before had left him with an eleven-year-old son whose existence he had not previously suspected. His struggle to deal with the complexities of that relationship, as well as the guilt he felt over the death of the boy's mother, had put considerable strain on his relationship with Gemma. Then, just when she'd begun to think they'd regained their equilibrium, she'd been faced with a particularly difficult case and her deep sense of connection to one of the suspects.

In the end, she'd been unwilling to give up the bond she and Kincaid had forged, but the episode had left her feeling unsettled. She sensed change in the offing, and it made her want to dig her heels into the present and hang on.

She left the tube at Islington, walking slowly through the familiar streets towards her garage flat as the summer evening faded towards twilight. Hazel, her landlady, looked after Gemma's son, Toby, and the arrangement had given Gemma as idyllic a year as a single, working mum could possibly wish.

Letting herself into the garden by the garage gate, Gemma thought she might find her son and Hazel's daughter, Holly, still playing outside. But the flagged patio showed only signs of hastily abandoned toys, and from an open window she heard a squeal of laughter.

'Am I missing a party?' she teased, peeping in the kitchen door.

'Mummy!' Toby slid from his chair at the table and darted to her, throwing his arms round her thighs.

She picked him up for a hug and a nuzzle, noticing that it seemed to take more effort than it had a week ago. 'I do believe you've been eating stones,' she laughed, pinching him and setting him down with a make-believe groan.

'We made play-dough,' Hazel explained, coming in from the sitting room. 'Flour, water, and food colouring. Non-toxic, thank goodness, as I think they've eaten more than they've modelled. Supper? There's cheese soup and fresh-baked bread.'

Hazel Cavendish was one of those women who made everything look effortless, and Gemma had long ago given up envy for unadulterated admiration. 'Cheese soup's my favourite,' she said, 'but' – she glanced at the children, Toby insisting that his mottled green lump was a dinosaur, Holly claiming just as adamantly that it was a cat – 'they seem content enough for a bit. Would you mind if I practised my piano first?'

'Take a glass of wine with you,' commanded Hazel, pouring her something chilled and white from the fridge.

Glass in hand, Gemma made her way into the cluttered sitting room. The piano stood at the back, amid the scattered games and toys and squashy, well-worn furniture. It was old, and not in terribly good condition, but Gemma was grateful just to have something to play. There was certainly no room for an instrument in her tiny flat, even had she been able to afford one.

She slid onto the bench, pushing a strand of hair

from her cheek, and poised her fingers over the keyboard. In some small way, she could attempt to reconnect with the feeling she'd had in the church. Her music book stood on the rack – Bosworth's *The Adult Beginner*, or 'the green book', as she thought of it – open to Prelude in C. She played each note carefully – right hand, left hand . . . louder, softer – then the last two staves, both hands together. Coordination was still a struggle, but each time she practised it got easier. Her teacher was pleased with her progress, and Gemma guarded her Saturday lesson time fiercely.

She continued through her exercises, stretching out the brief minutes in which her mind held nothing but the order of the notes and the way they resonated in the air. But all too soon she'd finished, and she knew she'd only been avoiding thinking about the problem she'd been wrestling with for months.

In the two years since she had become Superintendent Duncan Kincaid's partner, their personal relationship had sometimes strained their working relationship. But it had also enriched it – they *knew* each other, could anticipate one another's ideas and reactions, and their partnership had evolved into a finely tuned and creative entity, the sum greater than the parts.

All this Gemma realized, and she also was aware of how much it had meant to both of them to spend their days together, to share their lives so intimately.

But she hadn't joined the force to be a career sergeant. She was due for promotion, and if she didn't make a move soon, she'd be considered a non-starter.

Sidelined, her career shot before her thirtieth birthday, all her ambitions come to naught.

A simple enough conclusion, put in those terms. But promotion to inspector would mean a new duty assignment, possibly with another force, and the end of her partnership with Kincaid. And she hadn't been able to bring herself to tell him what she'd decided to do.

She stood, closing the lid on the piano keys with a thump. It wouldn't get easier, so she might as well stop making excuses and get on with it. Tomorrow, first thing, she would take him aside and say what she must. And then she would face the consequences.

From where Andrew Catesby stood, on the summit of Wirral Hill, he imagined he could just make out the estuary of the River Brue, the slight dip in the land that marked the gateway to the sea. To the north rose the Mendips, to the south the lesser Polden Ridge, and to the west, between him and the sea, stretched the wide, flat expanse of the Somerset Levels. Just when, he wondered, had he lost all joy in the prospect? Was there nothing safe from the anger that seemed to seep from him, staining all it touched?

Beside him, Phoebe, his spaniel, tugged at her lead, and Andrew freed her for a brief run before the light faded altogether. He turned, looking down at the lights of the Safeway on the Street Road, and beyond it the rising flank of the town itself, and behind that, the ever-present shadow of the Tor. Glastonbury was not really an island, of course; it had not been one within the span of human memory. It was a peninsula, linked to the higher ground to the east by a neck of layered limestone. But there had been many times when Glastonbury must have seemed an island to those travellers arriving from the west – even now, with the seawater contained by extensive seawalls and deep-cut rhynes, heavy rains could bring the waters lapping once more at the foot of Wirral Hill. Andrew much preferred that appellation to the more commonplace Wearyall Hill, a direct reference to the Joseph of Arimathea myth. Below him on the slope grew the famous Glastonbury Thorn – a dubious tourist attraction, in his opinion.

After the Crucifixion, according to legend, Joseph brought twelve companions by sea to Glastonbury. The long, humped back of the hill proved the travellers' first sight of land, and as a grateful and weary Joseph climbed ashore, he planted his staff of hawthorn in the earth of the hillside. The staff took root and a flowering tree burst forth, a sign to Joseph and his companions that here they should build a temple, the first Christian church in England.

Of course, the original thorn had long since died, replaced by a spindly, windswept shrub Andrew had difficulty believing could inspire awe in the most gullible pilgrim. But then, he dealt in facts, not fiction; he preferred things that could be measured, sampled, and recorded.

It seemed to him that the history of Glastonbury was so rich that it needed no embellishing with myths and questionable fables, and that the archaeology of the area provided an endless – and verifiable – source of discovery. The casual way his students accepted the blatant rubbish circulated about Glastonbury infuriated him. If it was drama they wanted, he'd give them the savage execution of the last abbot of Glastonbury, Richard Whiting, hanged on the Tor by Henry VIII's henchmen. As soon as Whiting was dead, his head was struck off and his body cut into quarters, one to be displayed at Wells, one at Bath, one at Ilchester, and one at Bridgwater. His severed head the king's men placed over the great gateway of the Abbey itself.

Whiting had been a kindly old man, an unlikely candidate for fate to choose as a martyr to a king's greed, but the abbot had gone to his death with quiet dignity. Andrew never climbed the Tor without thinking of Richard Whiting's execution, and he resented bitterly those who would make a theme park of one of Glastonbury's most sacred spots.

In this he had his sister Winifred's support. As an Anglican priest, she found the New Age marketing of Glastonbury as difficult to deal with as he did. Of course, both town and abbey had a long history of embellishment, ending with the scam of all time, the digging up in 1191 of King Arthur's and Queen Guinevere's supposed bones from the Abbey churchyard.

Winnie, always one to see the best in people, insisted that the Abbey monks had acted in good faith, but Andrew was more cynical. After the devastating fire of 1184, the Abbey had been in dire need of funds for rebuilding. The 'newly' discovered relics meant pilgrims – and therefore revenue. Human nature had not changed that much in eight hundred years, he thought grimly.

Realizing it was almost fully dark, Andrew whistled for Phoebe and reclipped her lead as he turned to retrace their path down the hill. Phoebe picked her way through the tussocky grass, and as Andrew followed he considered the lecture he needed to prepare for tomorrow's sixth-form history class. Sixth-formers were always difficult – full of their own importance as they neared freedom and university – but he had hopes for one girl in particular, a scholar with an interest in archaeology, but then he had been disappointed before. It didn't pay to invest oneself too deeply in adolescents.

Winnie teased him about his students, saying he'd been born in the wrong century. According to her, he'd have made a perfect nineteenth-century gentleman archaeologist, surrounded by rapt disciples, but Andrew thought it unlikely that the coterie of scruffy graduate students who usually staffed his digs could be described as 'rapt'.

He and his sister had enjoyed an unusual rapport since childhood. Having lost their parents quite young, they'd become particularly close and when, after five years in London, Winnie had been given a parish near Glastonbury, he had felt his life complete. He supposed he'd taken for granted that things would go on as they were indefinitely – in fact, he'd even considered selling his house on Hillhead and moving into the vicarage with Winnie. They had always shared interests, particularly their love of music, and it had been their custom to spend their free time together.

But all that had changed since Winnie had become involved with Jack Montfort last winter.

In Winnie's company, Andrew had been content –

with his teaching, his archaeological work, and his activism in the community – but now these once-beloved things seemed pointless.

The Thorn loomed ahead of him, its twisted silhouette a darker shadow against the dusk, and soon afterwards he reached the stile where the path intersected his street. Winnie loved the house on Hillhead, with its sweeping vista of the Somerset Levels, and she had helped him decorate it in a spare style that enhanced the view. Here they had spent many a winter evening in front of the fire, and in summer had lingered past dusk on the terraced patio.

As Andrew entered the house, its emptiness seemed to mock him. He hung Phoebe's lead neatly on the hook beside the door, then scooped her evening portion of food into her bowl. But after a quick perusal of the fridge, he lost any enthusiasm for the preparation of his own meal.

Instead, he poured himself a solitary glass of red wine and took glass and bottle into the darkened sitting room. Through his uncurtained windows, he could see faint lights twinkling in the plain below, as remote as the stars pricking through the velvet expanse of the southern sky.

His life seemed as if it were collapsing around him, forming a dark, cold weight in his chest that gnawed at him like a tumour. He'd tried seeking solace elsewhere – a mistaken attempt with consequences so disastrous he strove to put the incident from his mind.

Never had he dreamed that anything – or anyone – could separate him from his sister, or that he would find her absence so devastating. If ever he had shared

Winnie's faith, this blow would have shattered it – how could any god inflict such loss upon him, after what he had suffered? Nor would any god right it, he thought as he poured another glass of wine. That, he could see clearly now, was entirely up to him.

Fiona Finn Allen had awakened that morning with the smell of her childhood lingering from a half-remembered dream. Crisp and piney-green as the air of a summer morning on Loch Ness, the scent stayed with her throughout the day, tickling the edge of her awareness. It filled her with a deep, almost physical longing to paint, but she resisted the impulse.

In the past few months, whenever she'd touched brush to canvas, she had painted the same thing – a child's face, a little girl perhaps four or five years old. Where the image came from, or why it persisted, she did not know, but its occurrence left her feeling head-achy and ill, and she'd begun to suspect that something was terribly wrong.

Kneeling in the heavily mulched rose bed, she ruthlessly deadheaded the spent blooms and tried to shake off her malaise. Soon she'd go in and put the last touches to her vegetable soup. Her friend Winnie Catesby was coming to lunch.

It was an odd friendship. She had never been able to accept the primary tenets of the Christian faith and Winnie was an Anglican priest, but their relationship was one Fiona had come to treasure in the year since she and Winnie had met at a council meeting. Winnie had the rare gift of making others feel as if they truly deserved her attention, and the time spent in her company had helped Fiona deal with the grief that had coloured her life for so long.

That pain not even her husband had been able to heal, although he had given her much joy in other ways. Sitting back in the sun-warmed earth, she thought of how beautiful Bram had been when they had first met, and she smiled.

Even now, with the once-golden locks cut short and thinning, and the inevitable slight softening of the fine features, she found him irresistible.

How fortunate she was that fate had seen fit to bring them both, like ancient pilgrims washed ashore, to the first Pilton Festival – Glastonbury Fayre. She and Bram had found their destiny in Glastonbury, and had never looked back. Bram had sold her first few canvases on the street. Their success had enabled him to find gallery space for her work. It was not long before he owned the gallery, and in the years since, he'd developed an international clientele for her work and that of other painters he had taken on.

They'd made a good life for themselves, she and Bram, built on their mutual efforts and their love for each other. But sometimes in her dreams she saw that life for the fragile thing it was, and she would wake with a start of fear.

Jack stood, hesitating, before the Glastonbury Assembly Rooms, an ugly square block of a structure built in the 1860s, partly from stone salvaged from the Abbey precincts. Nor was the alleyway that led from the High Street to the building prepossessing in the dusk – it smelled of damp and cat urine, and the tattered shreds of posters pasted to its doors madc a sad collage.

But the poster advertising that evening's event had not yet suffered the ravages of time and weather. Simon Fitzstephen's ascetic face was familiar – Jack had seen it often enough on Fitzstephen's book jackets since he had started browsing in Nick Carlisle's New Age bookshop. An Anglican priest who had given up active ministry to pursue his studies, Fitzstephen's books were at the more conservative end of the shop's offerings – the author was a local man, and a respected authority on the early Church and on Grail mythology. What would Fitzstephen think, Jack wondered, if he knew about his correspondence the past few months with a dead monk?

Like a jewel set in the greensward the Abbey lay . . . a city sufficient unto itself. We entered through the eastern gate . . . gone now . . . all gone . . .

My father, always sharp in his dealings, meant to make one less mouth to feed and yet cheat the Abbey of his gift, for I was a sickly child and he foresaw I would not reach my manhood. My mother lamented, but my father would not hear her . . .

The Abbot blessed me, his hands upon my head. Then they stripped me, washed me, clothed me in the rough brown habit. I was pledged to God, yet I knew nothing . . .

So today's script had read, the first in several weeks. Although it had been almost three months since the strange writings had begun, Jack had yet to tell Winnie about the communications from Edmund of

Glastonbury. He feared she'd be appalled by something that smacked of spiritualism – and he felt guilty over the fact that he'd been unable to silence the nagging hope that somehow, sometime, this strange gift would put him in touch with his dead wife.

Tonight, he told himself, he had come here merely to satisfy his curiosity – to ask, for instance, when the Abbey's east gate had fallen into disuse; or when the Church had discontinued the practice of accepting children into the Order as gifts.

But he knew there was more to it than that. He needed to forge a connection with the past: to see the Abbey as the monk Edmund had seen it, to imagine the universe in Edmund's terms.

Still, he hesitated. This seemed to him a public declaration of intent, as if he were crossing the line that separated sceptic from fool, and if he took that step he could no longer keep his experience secret from all but Nick.

Then he thought of the last line from his pen that day:

I did not weep.

He climbed the steps and pulled open the Assembly Rooms' door.

Chapter Three

The one test is the quality of the message, whether it be truthful or otherwise, edifying or lacking in helpful qualities.

Frederick Bligh Bond, from
The Gate of Remembrance

Life, thought Winifred Catesby, has a way of delivering the perfect one-two punch when you're least expecting it. She was thirty-six years old and single – and it had been at least a decade since she'd seriously contemplated any alteration to that condition. Although Anglican priests could marry, not many men were willing to play second fiddle to God, or even second fiddle to the demands of her job, for that matter. And as Winifred was not beautiful, and she had never been blessed with the gift of flirtation, she'd thought herself fairly well reconciled to celibacy and the comfortable routine she had established with her brother, Andrew.

And then she'd found herself sitting beside Jack Montfort in the choir stall of Wells Cathedral, and nothing since had been the same.

On this June evening they were meeting for dinner at the Café Galatea in the High Street, a cheerful restaurant with a decidedly hippie ambience and surprisingly good food. Although Jack teased her good-naturedly about the vegetarian fare, which he referred to as 'bird food', the café seemed to have become their regular spot to meet after work.

Coasting to a stop at the Street Road roundabout, she gave herself a swift inspection in the rearview mirror. Hair okay, lipstick okay, nose could definitely be a bit more patrician . . . Oh, well, it would have to do, as would her serviceable skirt and jumper, and the clerical collar.

She'd come straight from a meeting with the archdeacon, and she was running late. It had been an even more taxing day than usual, arranging to cover the obligations of two parish vicars who were away. But she had been fortunate, young as she was, and a woman, to be appointed rural dean, over and above the duties required by her own parish of St Mary's, and she reminded herself of that whenever she was tempted to whinge.

She slowed as she passed the Abbey, gazing through the wrought-iron fence at its grounds. As a child she'd felt a secret inclination towards the cloistered life; even now, a breath of the Abbey air made her feel strangely peaceful. Had the pilgrims come by the thousands hoping for a dispensation to save their souls, or because a glimpse of the Abbey itself was as close as they might get to paradise?

Turning into the High, she was lucky enough to spot a parking place on the street a few doors past the Galatea. She swung the Fiat into the space, then walked back to the café, stopping to peer into the window.

The café's door stood open to the air. Jack sat at their usual table, halfway towards the back, reading something intently. Free to study him for a moment, Winnie tried to consider him dispassionately. A large, solidly built man with a shock of fair hair, and a rugged, hook-nosed face, he had the most piercingly blue eyes she had ever encountered. He might have played rugby – certainly he was not the weedy vicar type she had always found attractive. The thought made her smile, and in that instant, Jack looked up and saw her.

By the time she reached the table he had shuffled his papers out of the way. 'Long day?' he asked, giving her a swift kiss. 'You look a bit knackered. I've ordered some wine.'

'You're a dear,' she replied, relaxing into her chair with a sigh as he poured her a glass of the burgundy already open on the table. 'We had more than the usual squabbling and backbiting in the Deanery chapter meeting.'

Jack studied her with the intense gaze she still found disconcerting. 'I can tell. You've that strained look about the eyes.'

She took a sip of the wine already waiting, let it linger on her tongue, then nodded towards his briefcase. 'Working?'

'Mmmmm,' he answered non-committally. 'Hungry?'

'Ravenous. All that fresh air.'

'Don't tell me you've come on that dreadful bike?' he asked, grinning.

'No, more's the pity. It would have been a lovely

day for it, but I had to go too far afield.' They had an ongoing disagreement about her bike, which he considered a threat to life and limb. But she loved the old thing, and after her London parish she cherished the freedom she felt as she made her daily rounds on it. There were times, however, when the weather or the distance of her calls forced her to use the serviceable Fiat that had come with the job. She narrowed her eyes, giving him a mock glare. 'I've no intention of giving it up, you know, no matter how much you nag me.'

'Then we had better build up your strength,' he replied wryly as the waitress arrived at their table.

Over dinner, they chatted companionably about their respective days, but Winnie soon sensed that in spite of his solicitousness, Jack was distracted. As he waited for her to finish eating, he lapsed into silence, and she was seized by a sudden fear that he had tired of her and couldn't quite bring himself to say so.

Well, if that was the case, there was no point putting it off, she scolded herself. Gripping the stem of her wine glass tightly between her fingers, she asked, 'Jack, is something wrong?'

He gave her a startled glance; his gaze strayed to the briefcase he'd left on the table. He frowned. After a moment's hesitation, he said, 'No. Yes. I don't know. There's something I haven't told you.'

Winnie's heart sank, and she braced herself for bad news.

Jack, however, seemed unaware of her discomfort. 'Something very odd has been happening to me these past few months, Winnie, and I don't know what to make of it. I haven't said anything because . . . well, I was afraid you'd think I was a bit mad. And because it seemed somehow that telling you would give it a credence I wasn't willing to acknowledge.'

'What *are* you talking about?' Winnie asked, now utterly baffled.

'I suppose you hear all sorts of odd things . . .'

'Mostly ordinary things, really. People worried about their families, illness, debt . . . Jack, are you in some sort of trouble?'

'Nothing like that. Although that might be easier.' He hesitated a moment longer, then reached for his briefcase and removed a sheet of paper. 'Read this.'

She took it curiously. It was an ordinary sheet of foolscap. On it a few Latin phrases had been penned in a small, square hand. Beneath that were parts of sentences scrawled in English, in a hand she recognized instantly as Jack's.

At night the candles shone forth from the windows of the Great Church as stars from the heavens . . . Our voices rang round roof and cloister . . . the gargoyles shouted praises to Our Lord. This you know . . . That which was hidden will . . . out. Out of a thought will come truth. Fear not . . .

'What is this?' she asked, looking up at Jack. 'Are you translating something?'

'You might say that. Only, I wrote it. Both parts.'

'You wrote the Latin? But that's not your handwriting. I don't understand.'

'Neither do I.' He leaned forward, elbows on the table, pushing his wine glass aside. 'The first few times it happened I had no awareness of it at all – just had to assume I'd written it because there was no other explanation. I had a few stiff drinks after that, I can tell you.

'But now . . . especially today – with this one' – he touched the page with his fingertip – 'it's like I'm watching myself from a distance, but I feel disconnected from what's happening.'

'But you understand what you're writing—'

'No. Not until afterwards. And then I struggle a good bit with the translation.'

Winnie stared at him. 'But surely you can control it if you want—'

'It doesn't occur to me. You *do* think I'm daft, don't you? I can see it in your face.'

She made an effort to collect herself. 'No, I . . . of course I don't. But you should see a doctor, have a check-up. Maybe there's something—'

'A brain tumour?' He shook his head. 'No other symptoms. Nor of any other physical ailment I've been able to find. Believe me, I've tried.'

'Then—'

'I suppose I could be suffering from some sort of mental breakdown, but I seem to be coping well enough otherwise. Wouldn't you say?'

'Of course,' Winnie hastened to reassure him. He seemed as normal and as capable as anyone she had ever met, and that made his story all the more disconcerting.

'Good. That's something, anyway,' he said with the ghost of a smile. 'Having ruled out physical ailments, I started to research. There are parallels to something that's happened before.'

Realizing she was still clutching her wineglass, Winnie relaxed her fingers and took a sip, forcing herself to be silent, to let him tell it his own way.

'Does the name Frederick Bligh Bond ring a bell?' Jack continued.

'Didn't he have something to do with the Abbey? Sorry. That's all I can come up with.'

'Bond was an architect, like me, and an authority on early church architecture. But he was also an amateur archaeologist, and when the Church of England bought the Abbey from private owners in 1907, Bond got the commission to excavate the ruins. He made some marvellous discoveries, including the existence of the Edgar Chapel. All very respectable, all very above board, until several years into the excavations, when he revealed that his finds were due to instructions from former monks of the Abbey – and that the monks had communicated with him through automatic writing. He was fired, his reputation in ruins, and he never recovered.'

'But if he was familiar with the history of the Abbey, he was most likely just dredging up stuff from his subconscious,' Winnie protested.

'Oddly enough, Bond never claimed otherwise. He believed individual consciousness was merely a part of a transcendent whole – a cosmic memory – and that every person has the power to open a door into that reality. There was a spiritual revival going on in Glastonbury at the time, particularly after the First World War. It attracted all sorts of notables – Yeats, Shaw – Dorothy Sayers even attended one of Bond's sessions. So the general climate was not averse to Bond's ideas.'

'So he thought he was tapping into this collective memory as well as his own subconscious?'

'It was Bond's friend, a Captain John Bartlett, who did the actual writing, but Bartlett knew very little about the Abbey or archaeology—'

'But surely Bond prompted him?'

'Bond asked specific questions,' Jack corrected. 'Bartlett's first few episodes had occurred spontaneously, then Bond suggested that this . . . conduit . . . might be directed in a specific way. But often enough they got something completely unexpected.'

Jack's blue eyes were alight with passion, and Winnie had a sudden chilling thought. He'd never talked about his dead wife – she knew only what had been repeated round the town, that his wife had died in childbirth, along with their infant daughter, only a few months after he'd lost his mother to a prolonged illness and his father to a heart attack. 'Jack . . . you're not thinking that you can . . . direct this? That you might . . . contact . . . Emily?'

He regarded her, unblinking. 'I had considered it,' he answered at last. 'And I have to admit the idea that the dead are perhaps . . . not so far away is . . . comforting. But it's not that simple, Winnie. I think it's a case not of what I want from him, but rather what *he* wants from *me*.'

'Him?'

'It seems to be a "he". "Edmund". A monk of

Glastonbury Abbey, although I haven't been able to pinpoint the exact time frame.'

'That's why you were interested in Simon Fitzstephen,' Winnie exclaimed.

'I went to hear him speak the other night. If I could arrange to meet Fitzstephen, give him specific details, perhaps he could help me.'

'Jack—' Winnie didn't want to encourage his association with Simon Fitzstephen, but couldn't think of a concrete objection that wouldn't require her to expose her past dealings with the man.

Misinterpreting her hesitation, Jack said, 'I can't blame you for being sceptical. I don't know what the explanation is – only that it's not going away. If you feel you can't go on seeing me—'

Winnie took his hand, holding it tightly in both of hers. 'Now you *are* talking daft. Of course I'm not going to stop seeing you. And I'll do whatever I can to help you. You know that.'

'Even if I'm crazy?'

'You're not crazy.' She spoke vehemently. 'You *will* find an explanation for these writings. May I read them?'

'Would you?' The thought seemed to please him. 'You might see some clue I've missed.'

'Well,' she said slowly, wondering if she had completely taken leave of her senses, 'have you tried simply *asking* Edmund what he wants?'

This, thought Bram Allen as he looked round his gallery, was what a church *should* be like. The plush carpeting muffled both voice and footfall, the illuminated paintings on the hessian-covered walls glowed as if they were stained-glass windows lit from within, and bells chimed musically with each swing of the door. It seemed an impenetrable sanctuary . . . and it was the only place he felt truly safe.

There were some, he knew, who were made uncomfortable by the fierceness of the creatures in Fiona's paintings, but he had always found them strangely reassuring, as if that very quality might hold evil at bay.

What did concern him was the fact that the number of Fiona's paintings on the gallery walls was steadily decreasing. Although his other artists sold well, it was Fiona's work that provided the backbone of the business, and it had been months since she'd produced anything she was willing to let him display. Not that he *wanted* to hang those recent paintings – God forbid! What on earth had possessed her to paint *that* face?

Fiona's gift was not something that could be subjected to a rational analysis – or so he'd always assumed. But now he wondered if there was some external factor at work, something that had changed in their lives? Or in Fiona's life?

As he gazed out of the gallery window, the bell began to toll for Evensong at St John's, just across the street. That was his signal to close for the day. Automatically, Bram tidied and switched off lights. Then, as he locked the door to the last peal of the bells, it came to him. Something *had* changed in Fiona's life this past year. She had become friends with Winnie Catesby, who had begun counselling Fiona to express the grief she felt over her childlessness. Was this what had triggered Fiona's visions?

But that still didn't explain why she should paint that particular child. Had Winnie somehow managed to loosen a fragment of memory lodged in Fiona's subconscious? Or did Fiona know more than he had always believed?

Bram realized he was sweating and wiped a hand across his brow. One thing was certain – he must find a way to stop Winnie Catesby's meddling before it destroyed them all.

The kitchen of the Dream Café smelled strongly of cabbage, but Faith didn't mind. Her morning sickness seemed to have improved at last – and the food odours did help disguise the ever-present smell of damp that permeated the place.

The café was built right into the base of the Tor, and condensation coated the limestone walls with a slick sheen. The front room held tables; the rear was divided into a small shop on the left and the kitchen on the right, separated from the eating area by a serving bar. Not that they served much – the menu consisted of hot soup, tea (herbal or otherwise), and a vegetarian special of the day. Faith, who had barely boiled water at home, had become quite adept at concocting the soups and hot dishes, and this morning she would have everything ready by opening time. Humming as she put the final dusting of paprika on the day's cauliflower bake, she imagined what her mum would say if she could see her handiwork. But the thought brought a stab of homesickness and a prickle of tears behind her eyelids.

It had been almost three months since that day in early April when she'd run away from home. She would never have believed she could miss her beastly brother and sister so much – or her parents. So many times she'd been tempted to go back, to invent a story they would accept – she'd say it had been a boy in her class . . . but, no, that wouldn't be fair . . . a stranger, then, passing through on a pilgrimage to Avalon . . .

But she had known instinctively that lies wouldn't wash, that they'd demand the one thing she couldn't give them – the truth. So she'd managed as best she could; begging friends to let her climb in their bedroom windows for a dry night's sleep, then, when their hospitality wore out, she'd slept rough wherever she could find a spot, taking handouts from the local charities.

School seemed a distant universe, and sometimes she missed that, too, with an ache so fierce it surprised her. But things were better, now, since she'd met Buddy and got the job at the café. She'd been leery at first, but the offer had turned out to be no more than the kindness it seemed. After a few weeks she'd begun volunteering to open and close the café. If her boss knew she spent the nights in the tiny upstairs room, he'd never let on. And if it spooked her sometimes – the must of damp oozing from the walls, the strange dreams that kept her restless and sweating . . . she'd known it was better than the alternative.

There was a toilet and washbasin at the top of the stairs, so she'd been able to keep herself clean, and to wash out her few items of clothing. But everything was getting tight now, stretching across her swelling belly.

She didn't think about how she would manage when the baby came.

You just did one thing at a time, and right now the soup needed stirring. It was a rich mixture of cabbage, tomatoes, and caraway seed – *Schii*, Buddy said it was called, a recipe from his German grandmother who had emigrated to the Texas Hill Country. She tasted it, reached for the salt, then felt the oddest sensation in her abdomen. A flutter, almost a tickle – there it was again.

She was standing, spoon in one hand, salt in the other, mouth open in surprise, when the door opened and a woman came in. Dark, silver-streaked hair in a plait down her back, a worn face, dangly earrings, long Indian cotton skirt – Faith recognized her as a regular customer and a friend of Buddy's, but she'd never really spoken to her.

'Are you all right?' the woman asked, coming up to the serving counter.

'I – I just felt something . . . I think the baby moved.'

'First time?'

Faith nodded. Putting down salt and spoon, she pressed her palm carefully against her abdomen.

'Good. That's normal, you know. Nothing to worry about. Before you know it she'll be kicking you like a footballer.' The woman looked Faith over, assessing her with what seemed a professional eye. 'Do you have a midwife?'

Faith shook her head.

'Have you been to an antenatal clinic?'

'No.' All those things meant registering with the social services, giving name, address, parents . . .

The woman studied her a moment longer. 'Like that, is it? How old are you?'

'Seventeen. Old enough to be on my own.'

'Your parents know where you are?'

'Don't want to know,' Faith replied, struggling to keep her voice steady. 'And I don't see why it's any of your business.'

'How about making me a cup of tea?' the woman said, apparently unfazed by Faith's rudeness. 'I'm Garnet, by the way. I live up the hill.'

Faith complied, glad of the opportunity to collect herself, while Garnet stayed at the counter, watching her.

When Garnet had her tea, she said as if continuing a casual conversation, 'Not very comfortable, sleeping in that old boxroom upstairs, I shouldn't think. Not the best thing for a girl in your condition, either – all that damp.'

Faith's heart raced with panic. 'But . . . how did you—'

'Buddy and I have been friends for a long time. He's worried about you.'

Flushing with embarrassment at her own stupidity, Faith stammered, 'But I thought he didn't—'

'Don't let the drawl fool you. He's a sharp old bird, and more kind-hearted than he'd like anyone to know. He thought I might have a spare room. It's nothing fancy,' Garnet continued, 'but it's warm and dry, and there's a real bed.'

'But I—'

'You could pay me a little rent, and help out with the shopping. Buddy says you're turning into a pretty good cook.'

'But why would you do this for me? I don't understand.'

Garnet gestured at her belly. 'You're going to need care, girl, and I can give it to you. I was a midwife, once, and those things you don't forget.'

'That's still not why,' Faith said stubbornly. 'Are you in the habit of taking in strays?'

Garnet smiled. 'Only cats.' Shrugging, she added, 'I'm not sure I can give you a better reason. I hadn't made up my mind until I saw you again. There's something . . . I don't know. Let's just say I have some old accounts to settle.'

'I couldn't pay much,' Faith said slowly.

'You'd better come and see the place before we talk about that,' Garnet said, businesslike again. 'Go straight up Wellhouse Lane. It's the old farmhouse on the right, just past the junction with Stonedown. If you come after work today, I'll be there. And you'd better look to your soup.' Finishing her tea, she handed Faith her empty mug and turned away.

It was only when the door had jingled shut behind her that Faith realized the woman had referred to her baby as 'she'.

Winnie had never quite learned to quell the depression engendered by Jack's house. Although the detached, orange-brick Victorian villa was massive and respectable in the way of its kind, it seemed dwarfed by the shadow of the Tor looming above it. Adding to that unprepossessing beginning, the shrubbery was overgrown, last winter's leaves still littered the garden path and covered porch, and even on this sultry July afternoon, the interior was bone-numbingly cold.

Rubbing at the goosebumps on her bare arms, she followed Jack through a dining room filled with massive and unrepentantly ugly Victorian furniture, and into the kitchen-sitting area. This was the snuggest room in the house, with a leather armchair drawn up to a television, an oak table bearing evidence of Jack's hastily cleared tea, and warmth radiating from an Aga.

Jack switched on the red-shaded lamp over the table. 'Like a cuppa while we wait?' he offered as Winnie took a seat. 'Nick rang; he's on his way.'

Refusing Jack's offer of tea, Winnie asked, 'However did Nick manage to get an invitation to Simon Fitzstephen's for drinks?' The author was reputed to protect his privacy fiercely and did not often lend his presence to social events.

'Fitzstephen came into the bookshop for a signing. Nick took the opportunity to lay on some judicious flattery.'

Winnie was not looking forward to seeing Simon Fitzstephen, but she had no intention of letting Jack go without her. 'It would take a dyed-in-the-wool curmudgeon to refuse Nick. He has such an irresistible air of earnestness,' she said lightly, while wondering how her former mentor would react to her unexpected appearance.

And what sort of reception would their story get from Simon? He had made his reputation by documenting the history of the Grail legends, but Winnie had always suspected that for Fitzstephen the Grail study was an exercise of pride rather than heart.

From Jack's inability to sit still tonight, she gathered he was nervous about the meeting as well. 'You don't have to tell Fitzstephen anything, you know, if you don't feel it's right.'

'I know,' Jack said as he sank restlessly into a chair beside her. 'But then I'll feel an ass for having wasted his time.'

'Nonsense,' she reassured him. 'It's a friendly social occasion.'

'Right.' He acknowledged her effort with a grin, then pulled a folded piece of paper from his jacket pocket. 'But I do have something more concrete to go on.'

'This came today?' Taking the sheet, Winnie added, 'That makes it sound as if it came in the post.' In truth, the communications were sporadic, the connection sometimes tenuous. Often the message would stop in mid-sentence, then take up again a week or two later in exactly the same place, as if there had been no interruption.

It was a bit like putting together a jigsaw puzzle – a piece here, a piece there, trying to make sense of it as you went along.

Aethelnoth was abbot then, and made us the poorer for it. Tender as a willow shoot, I was, but sturdy. Sturdier than my father had foreseen. He did not count on the ministrations of Brother Ambrose, the infirmarian, who kept me in when the wind blew from the north and fed me with herbs and warming broths. There I grew into my calling, and my heart rejoiced. But all that was before . . . brought God's wrath upon us . . .

She looked up. 'That's all?'

'Yes. But the name of the abbot gives us a date. Aethelnoth was the last Saxon abbot, from 1053 to 1078. I hope Fitzstephen can tell us more.'

There was not going to be any way round telling Jack the truth about Simon; she could see that. And the longer she waited, the worse it would be. Winnie steeled herself for a confession. 'Jack, there's something I ought—'

'There's Nick.'

Rescued by the sound of a motorbike, Winnie thought as Jack stood, giving no evidence of having heard her faltering words. Breathing a sigh of relief as she followed him to the door, she promised herself she *would* tell him, at the very first opportunity.

Leaving Nick's motorbike in the drive, they took Jack's car for the short drive to the village of Pilton. The evening light slanted across the rolling landscape, and behind them the Tor rose in silhouette against the setting sun.

As the road made the sharp left-hand bend into the village, Nick navigated from directions scribbled on a scrap of paper. 'It's below the church. You take the turning signposted "The Old Vicarage".'

Pilton had to be one of the most charming of the Somerset villages, running down steeply wooded hillsides into a meandering stream valley. It was also a maze of twisting switchback and dead-end lanes. Their turning took them downhill, past the lovely church of St John the Baptist, then another sharp turning to the left brought them into a steep lane barely wide enough for the Volvo. 'Just on the right,' Nick called out, pointing. 'Riverside Cottage.'

Jack followed the lane to its end, pulling the car up in a grassy space where a stone bridge crossed a rocky stream. They got out and took their bearings. The light was a liquid green under the thick canopy of trees; the silence was broken only by water gurgling over the rocks. The cottage stood before them, divided from the lane by a low stone wall; inside the wall a smooth expanse of lawn ran down to the stream, and a flagstone path led from the gate to the arched front door.

Following the men, Winnie paused, her hand on the gate. She felt suspended in the strange, breathless atmosphere, and wondered if she might, at the very last instant, change her mind.

Then Jack turned, waiting for her, and she knew that whatever transpired that night, there could be no going back.

Simon Fitzstephen stacked the dishes from his cold supper in the sink for Mrs Beddons, his housekeeper, to wash in the morning. They had reached a comfortable arrangement over the years: Mrs Beddons came in the mornings, fixed his breakfast, did the chores, and made him a hot lunch; then before she left for the day she put together a salad or cold meats for his evening meal.

Although the royalties from his books would have allowed him to live on a grander scale than Riverside Cottage, he had no desire to leave Pilton. The village was not only beautiful, it was one of the oldest possessions of Glastonbury Abbey, a gift from the Saxon king Ine sometime early in the eighth century. Fitzstephen traced his own family's links to the Abbey only as far back as the twelfth century, when an ancestor had acted *in loco abbatis* for King Henry II, on the death of the previous abbot.

These associations of place and family gave Simon Fitzstephen an integral sense of connection to his work, at which he had been gratifyingly successful. He had not imagined, when he left active ministry to pursue his study of the Grail, that his books would be so well received by the public. The only drawback he had been able to discover to his minor celebrity was the tendency of his readers to an uncomfortable degree of familiarity. He was by nature a reserved man; he'd found his one speaking tour in America an excruciating experience.

At least the young man who had wangled an invitation this evening was English, and seemed quite civilized. He was also quite astonishingly beautiful and seemingly unaware of it.

The thought made Simon glance at his watch. Nicholas Carlisle and his architect friend would be arriving soon. He should finish the preparations for his guests.

By chance, Simon had run into his old friend Garnet Todd that afternoon, and he had invited her along as well. She was knowledgeable and sharp-witted: surely she'd add a bit of spice to the evening's gathering.

He set glasses, mixers, gin, and whisky on the round drawing-room table. Inlaid with walnut burl and set round its circumference with two rows of drawers, it had been used by the lords of Pilton Manor for collecting rents. With a vase of full-blown garden roses set in its centre, it did justice to the room, his favourite in the house. Three gothic-arched windows stood open to the lawn, and the green silk on the walls brought the garden in. Ornately framed sepia photographs hung everywhere, generations of Fitzstephens. But Simon was the last of his branch of the family, and childless. His name would have to live on through his books, a prospect which did not distress him, except for the fact that lately the well of his creativity seemed to have run dry. What could he say about the Grail that he had not already said, and said well? And yet he had another book under contract to his publisher, and he could not stall much longer.

Returning to the kitchen, he fetched the silver dishes of olives and salted almonds Mrs Beddons had left ready. Just as he had everything assembled, the bell rang. He swiped a hand through his thick hair and went to greet his visitors.

Nick Carlisle stood on the doorstep with his friend, a large, fair-haired man – and, much to Simon's shock, Winifred Catesby. What was she doing here?

Nick introduced Jack Montfort first, giving Simon a chance to recover as he shook Montfort's hand absently. When released, Simon forestalled Nick's second introduction.

'Winifred.' He bent to kiss her cheek, his lips meeting air when she turned her face away at the last moment.

'Hullo, Simon.'

'You know each other?' Montfort asked.

'Simon taught a few of my classes in theological college,' Winifred replied coolly. 'It's been a long time.'

'Yes, hasn't it?' Simon responded drily. He ushered them into the drawing room, very much aware of her bare arms and her sleeveless, blue silk dress.

The bell rang again just as he had them seated, this time heralding Garnet Todd and an unfamiliar companion. Garnet wore her usual Romany attire, which amused Simon almost as much as her staunch vegetarianism; once, in a moment of indiscretion, she'd revealed to him that she was a butcher's daughter from Clapham.

'I hope you don't mind, Simon,' said Garnet. 'I brought my boarder. This is Faith.'

The girl was tall and slender, with a long neck and short-cropped hair that set off her delicate features. She was also, Simon realized as she moved past him into the entrance hall, quite visibly pregnant, and not much more than a child. 'Faith?' he repeated. 'Just Faith?'

'Just Faith.' The girl turned serious dark eyes on him, with no hint of a smile. What, Simon wondered, had Garnet got herself into?

And if he had had any doubts about young Nick Carlisle's sexual preferences, they were resolved the instant Faith walked into the drawing room. Both men rose, but Nick was clearly riveted. The girl seemed unaware of her effect, regarding them all with the same solemn gaze.

As Simon introduced Garnet, Winifred said, 'Garnet Todd, the ceramicist? I love your work! I've been hoping one day to have you restore the tiles in my church.'

'Your church?' Garnet's worn face creased in a smile.

'I'm vicar of St Mary's, Compton Grenville,' Winifred answered, and they were soon deep in discussion of the church's tile work.

Trust Garnet to monopolize the conversation, Simon thought acidly as he served drinks. When he could get a word in edgeways, he said, 'Nick tells me you have a particular interest in the history of the Abbey, Mr Montfort?'

'You might say that. Call me Jack, please. And I understand that you're the expert where the Abbey is concerned. I'm especially interested in the eleventh-century period and in Aethelnoth's abbacy.'

'Aethelnoth? That's not a name most people know. Not exactly a shining star in the Abbey's history, that one.'

'I wondered what happened in his time that the monks would have seen as bringing God's wrath upon their House?'

'Among other things, Aethelnoth removed the gold and silver from the Abbey's holy books and sold it for his own profit, and he appropriated Church lands. His rather disreputable career ended when he was formally deposed and sent into confinement at Christ Church, Canterbury.

'In fact,' Simon continued, warming to his subject, 'neither of the last two Saxon abbots was anything to write home about. Aethelweard, Aethelnoth's predecessor, hacked up King Edgar's remains and tried to stuff them in a reliquary, after which he became incurably insane – small wonder – then fell and broke his neck. But I don't know that any of their misdeeds was worthy of calling down God's wrath upon the Abbey.'

Montfort and Nick Carlisle exchanged a look of disappointment. 'Those sorts of things were fairly common, I take it?' Montfort asked.

'Unfortunately. Abbatical election usually had more to do with political astuteness than religious vocation, but those two lacked either quality. Of course, Frederick Bligh Bond came up with a much glorified version of Aethelnoth through his automatic writings, but in this case I'm inclined to believe the historians.'

'Bligh Bond?' Nick echoed huskily, then cleared his throat. Again he and Montfort exchanged a loaded glance.

'You're familiar with Bond?' Simon asked.

Montfort's reply made it clear that he was. 'Are you saying that you accept Bond's . . . um . . . *received* information in other cases?'

'Do I believe that Bond had a direct line to former monks of the Abbey?' This was turning out to be a good deal more interesting than Simon had anticipated. 'Not likely. But Bond's knowledge of the Abbey's history and architecture was extensive. I think it highly probable that he communicated it somehow to his friend, Captain Bartlett.'

'Oh, really, Simon!' broke in Garnet. 'Why not say "telepathy" if you mean "telepathy"? And if you're willing to admit that possibility, why rule out the idea that Bond – and Bartlett – might have tapped into some sort of collective memory? You certainly know the importance of collective memory to the Celts—'

'That's an entirely different matter. Their collective – and racial – memory was based on the transmission of myth and tradition through highly stylized story-telling, ritual, and ceremony.'

'And it was an extremely powerful force, in ways we can't even begin to understand,' Garnet challenged, reddening. 'Why is it impossible that there are other things that operate beyond our understanding?'

'What are you talking about?' asked Faith, speaking for the first time. 'What's automatic writing?'

Jack Montfort gave her an encouraging smile. 'It's when someone writes things down without being consciously aware of what they're writing, or knowing where the information originates.'

'You mean like ghosts? Or a seance?'

Wincing, Montfort said, 'Not necessarily. It could be the person's subconscious seeking . . . well, I suppose you could call it an unusual outlet.'

'Is that what you think happened to Mr Bond – whoever he was?'

'It was Bond's friend who actually did the writing,' Simon said tersely. 'So whether the information came from Bond's subconscious or another source, he still had to transmit it in some way to Bartlett. Unless, of course, the two were total charlatans, and that I *don't* believe.'

'It seems odd, don't you think,' Montfort mused, 'that the one question no one ever asked was "Why John Bartlett?" Bond's connections to the Abbey were obvious – was Bartlett chosen simply because of his friendship with Bond, or was there something more? Bartlett was a retired military man, intelligent and fairly well educated, but there was nothing to indicate a natural facility for automatism.'

'When you say Bartlett was "chosen", I take it you favour the collective-memory hypothesis?'

'I'm inclined to, yes,' Montfort answered with what sounded suspiciously like a sigh. 'Speaking from my own experience, I find anything else highly improbable.'

There was a moment of surprised silence, then Garnet said, 'Your own experience? Do you mean you've done automatic writing?'

Montfort hesitated, then with a glance at Winifred, pulled a folded sheaf of papers from his inside jacket pocket. 'All these since March. And I knew very little about the history of the Abbey, just the ordinary schoolboy stuff.'

Curiosity battling against disbelief, Simon reached for the papers. He had always been intrigued by the story of Bligh Bond's experience – what if he'd been wrong in assuming that Bond himself was the source? He read, fascinated, from the first halting script. As he finished each page Garnet reached eagerly for it, then passed it in turn to Faith.

As he read, a strong sense of personality began to emerge. Simon glanced at Jack Montfort, who sat cradling his drink in his hands. Montfort seemed an unlikely candidate for a hoax, nor could Simon imagine that some repressed part of Montfort's personality sought expression as a medieval monk. And as an architect, the man certainly had nothing to gain by revealing such a thing – it could, without a doubt, seriously damage his career.

Simon felt the beginnings of an excitement he hadn't experienced in years. Suppose there was the remotest possibility that these communications were genuine, that it was somehow possible to establish a living link with the past. What would that mean for his own studies, to have direct access to history? There could be a book in this that would take his career in an entirely unexpected direction.

He had reached the last page. *Seek one goal and ye shall win*, began the monk who signed himself as Edmund. *Work at that which comes. Take others as ye find, for the task is great, ere ye shall join the Company. We are those who watch, and we are ever with you.*

Garnet took the sheet from him almost before he'd finished reading it. She skimmed it, then read it again more slowly, her lips moving. Wide-eyed, she looked up at Montfort and breathed, 'The Company of Watchers. They've chosen you.'

'What are you talking about?' asked Winifred. 'Who – or what – is the Company of Watchers?'

'The Watchers are those who are tied to Glastonbury by a bond not even death could sever. They guard the spiritual heart of Britain – Logres – and some even say they watch over King Arthur, waiting for the day when he will rise again.'

'Britain's hour of greatest need?' scoffed Simon. 'Surely no one believes that old chestnut?'

'Six months ago I wouldn't have given it the time of day,' Montfort answered slowly. 'But now . . . after all this . . .'

Garnet fingered the Celtic pendant she wore at her throat. 'This is a time of conflict, so near the Millennium–'

'Your paranoia's showing, my dear,' Simon said sharply. Then he looked at the pages gathered in Faith's slender hand and wavered.

'And the task?' asked Faith.

'I don't know,' answered Montfort. 'That's one of the things I hoped to learn when I came here today.'

'*Take others as ye find*,' Faith read, then she looked at each of them, her gaze intent. 'Don't you see? *We* are the others. Whatever it is, it can only be accomplished if we work *together*.'

'All for one and one for all,' said Simon, still half mocking, but finding himself strangely drawn to the idea. 'What do you think, Winifred? I doubt the Church would approve of your dabbling in the paranormal.'

'They didn't much care for Bond's methods, either, and yet he gave us invaluable information about the Abbey. Can't we judge the material on the basis of its historical validity, rather than its source?' She looked at Jack Montfort, as if for confirmation; with an unpleasant jolt it dawned on Simon that they were a couple.

Garnet's face was alight. 'That's why we're here tonight, Simon. And that's why Faith came to me. We were all drawn together for this purpose. I'm sure of it! You could interpret the material in historical terms–'

'And you have the resources and the skills to trace any possible connection Jack might have with Edmund,' Nick Carlisle interrupted. 'Perhaps we all have something to offer, even if we're not sure what it is at this point.'

Simon read dismay in Winifred's expression. It was that, as well as the thought of his own possible gain, that prompted him to say, 'Just how exactly would we go about this . . . investigation?'

Perhaps they *had* been brought together for a purpose, and if that meant Winnie Catesby would have to put up with seeing him on a regular basis, then it bloody well served her right.

Chapter Four

The water meadows are of that emerald green only to be seen where the subsoil water is near to the surface. Travelling through parched lands at mid-summer, one knows that Avalon is near by the greenness of the earth.

Dion Fortune, from
Glastonbury: Avalon of the Heart

Kincaid could not imagine a more perfect day. The heat and mugginess that so often characterized late August days in the south of England had been swept away by a westerly wind that cleared the sky and brought a hint of autumn crispness to the air. Strangers passing in the street nodded, smiled, said, 'Fine day,' and, for once, the English obsession with talking about the weather seemed justified.

He and Kit had spent the morning battling the machines in the Leicester Square video arcade, and by the time they emerged into daylight the temperature had climbed into the region of shirtsleeve comfort. 'Ready for lunch?' Kincaid suggested, knowing the question was rhetorical.

'Um . . . do you think we could go to the Hard Rock

Café?' Kit asked with the tentativeness that still marked most of his requests.

'Why not? I think I could manage to eat a tourist or two for lunch. Tube?'

Kit hesitated, watching the crowds surging across the pavement in the bright sunshine. 'Could we walk?'

In Kincaid's opinion, walking through the heart of the West End on a Saturday in August was akin to forcing one's way through the mob at a football match in riot gear, but he nodded. 'Go for it, sport.'

They set off towards Piccadilly Circus, picking their way through the warren of streets. Kit dodged oncoming pedestrians in order to stay beside him, his shoulder brushing Kincaid's arm in comfortable contact. Kincaid thought of the time just a few short months ago when the precariousness of their relationship had made every word or touch a potential hazard. There was still the occasional minefield, but they'd come a long way.

As he looked down at his son's fair head, he realized that one day soon he would no longer be able to look down at Kit, full stop. As yet, Kit had not outgrown childish things, and for that Kincaid was eminently grateful. Kit's friend Nathan Winter had given the boy a microscope for his birthday, and their agenda for the morrow was collecting pond-water samples on Hampstead Heath. Girls and rock music would intervene soon enough; in the meantime, Kincaid had a lot of making up to do.

His marriage to Kit's mother had ended stormily and abruptly, and it was not until a few months ago that Kincaid had learned Vic had been pregnant when they separated. She'd been having an affair with one of her professors and had subsequently married him, passing the child off as his. It must have been obvious to her very early on that the boy was not Ian McClellan's son, but Kincaid's. Whether she'd meant to confess as much when she'd contacted him last spring, Kincaid would never know.

She had been killed just a few weeks after she'd asked his help in the investigation of another death, leaving him with the sense of much unfinished between them.

Now as he looked at Kit matching him stride for stride, he realized it no longer shocked him to see a younger version of himself. Nor did the boy's resemblance to Vic – her smile, her gestures, her mannerisms – cause him as much pain as it had in the first weeks after her death.

In due course, they reached Piccadilly Circus and from there made their way down Piccadilly towards Hyde Park. As they walked, some of Kit's excitement infected Kincaid and he remembered how glorious he'd found the city when he'd first come to London two decades earlier. Kit met his eyes and they shared a smile of sheer delight in the bustle and colour of it all.

By the time they reached the Hard Rock Café, they were warm and ravenous. They emerged from the café an hour later, replete with cheeseburgers, French fries, and chocolate milkshakes, and with Kit in possession of a much-coveted T-shirt proclaiming the London Hard Rock as the Original.

Across Piccadilly, Green Park beckoned, and they

soon found a choice spot to stretch out in the grass. People sprawled on blankets or in awning-striped deckchairs, making the most of summer's end. Although Kincaid usually found it difficult to relax in a public place, the sun soaked into his skin like a drug and his eyelids began to droop.

He came awake with a start when Kit rolled over on his stomach and declared, 'I wish we could have brought Tess.' Kit gestured at the number of dogs walking or trotting beside their masters, chasing frisbees or just panting happily in the sun.

'We couldn't have done the videos, then,' Kincaid reminded him, rousing himself.

'I know. I'm not complaining. It's just nice here, that's all.' Kit chewed a blade of the springy grass meditatively. 'It's sort of like wanting it to be just the two of us, but at the same time missing Gemma and Toby.'

'That's why Zen philosophers teach concentrating on the moment. Otherwise you miss now because you're too busy wanting other things.'

'Are you good at that – what did you call it?'

'Concentrating on the moment? I don't do it half as well as I'd like. But you've helped me be better.'

'Me?'

'When I'm with you, I don't want to think about stuff like work. So when something niggly crops up in my head, I just think, *Go away*. And usually it does.'

'But it doesn't stop you missing Gemma, does it?'

The question caught Kincaid like a punch. He stared at his son. Kit usually approached emotional issues with crablike self-protectiveness. 'No,' he said, surprised into honesty. 'It doesn't.'

'I don't understand why she had to go away.'

'She's off on a training course, Kit. You know that.'

'But why'd she have to put in for a promotion? Why couldn't she just leave things the way they were?'

Why indeed, Kincaid thought bitterly. Oh, he knew all the rational arguments – he had even given them lip-service – but in his heart he felt as abandoned and unhappy as Kit. She had left him, and days on the job without her company seemed interminable. The succession of temporary assistants only made him more irritable. At least when Gemma returned from Bramshill they'd have some off-duty time together, depending on her posting, but there would be no replacement for their partnership. 'It's something she needed to do,' he said, hearing the lack of conviction in his voice.

Kit scowled at him, unmollified. 'So why can't you just get married, and we could be like a . . . you know, a normal family?'

'That's not in the cards,' Kincaid said, more sharply than he'd intended. Gemma had made that quite clear, and he'd done his best to be content with what they had. Neither of them, after all, had made a success of marriage the first time round, and now that Gemma had separated herself from him so deliberately, he felt even less certainty about their future.

But what had got into Kit? Their relationship as father and son was still a touchy subject, and this was the first time he'd heard Kit directly acknowledge that they were – or could possibly be – family. 'Is something going on with Ian, Kit?' he asked, studying the boy's averted face. Kit spent the week with the man he had known for almost twelve years as his father, Ian McClellan, and most weekends with Kincaid.

Kit chewed his lip, his eyes half shielded by the wayward lock of hair that fell across his forehead. 'I'm not supposed to know. But I saw the letter, and I've heard him talking on the phone.'

'What letter?'

'The one from the university in Quebec. Offering him a job. " . . . his academic career, more opportunities, blah, blah . . ." What they mean is more money.'

'And you think Ian means to accept?'

'He's been dropping little hints. "*Wouldn't you like to learn to ski, Kit? How's your French coming, Kit?*" '

Kincaid felt a rush of panic. After everything that had happened, all that they had been through, he would *not* lose Kit now. As calmly as he could, he said, 'You don't want to go?'

Kit glanced at him, then away, with studied nonchalance that didn't quite come off. 'I want to stay here. With you.'

'It would mean leaving Grantchester and living here in London.'

'I know. Would the Major mind Tess having a run in the garden sometimes?'

Kincaid smiled. 'I think you might persuade him.' Trust Kit to think of the ragamuffin terrier first, rather than new schools, friends, and all the other logistics that boggled the mind. And nothing, of course, would be possible without Ian's consent; he was still Kit's legal guardian.

Ian McClellan's behaviour had never been predictable. First he had left Kit's mother to run off to France with a graduate student; after Vic's death he'd refused to take any responsibility for Kit. Then, a few months ago, he had come back from France, determined to make amends, and moved Kit back into the cottage in Grantchester. Now it seemed the man was itching to be off again. How would Ian feel about leaving Kit behind?

For that matter, how would *he* fare as a single parent? It would further complicate things with Gemma, he could see that, but he knew Kit had to come first.

'Would you . . . You wouldn't mind, would you? If I came to stay with you.' This time Kit met Kincaid's eyes.

'There is nothing,' Kincaid answered truthfully, 'that I would like more.'

Winnie made it a point to have lunch with Fiona Allen at least once a month, sometimes at the Vicarage in Compton Grenville, sometimes at Fiona's home on Bulwarks Lane, below the Tor. Today they'd chosen Fiona's house, due to Winnie's commitments in Glastonbury, and Fiona had set out a *salade niçoise* in her pale Scandinavian kitchen.

'I hate August in Somerset,' groaned Winnie, sliding into a chair and pulling her sticky blouse away from her damp skin. 'It's like living in soup.'

'You can't fuss as long as you insist on riding that bike,' admonished Fiona as she laid plates on the table.

'You sound just like Jack. At least I get a breeze on the bike. The car's a travelling oven.'

'You're incorrigible.' Fiona shook her head, smiling. 'How is the *supposedly* delicious Jack? I'm beginning to think you're conspiring to keep me from meeting him, so that I can't judge for myself.'

'I'll give a dinner party. Soon, I promise. It's just that all our spare time seems to vanish these days.'

'The automatic writing? How is that going?' Fiona was the one person outside the group in whom Winnie had confided.

'It's fascinating – the material itself, I mean.'

'This can't be comfortable for you.'

'Ghosties and ghoulies and things that go bump in the night?' Winnie teased in a fair parody of Fiona's Scottish brogue. Then she continued more soberly. 'You know, it's odd, but somehow Edmund seems too real to be a ghost. Too human. And I suppose I've got used to it.'

Fiona raised an eyebrow. 'Then what's giving you the pip?'

'Too much experience with committees gone sour, I suppose,' Winnie said with a sigh. 'The group dynamics seem to be changing, and that doesn't bode well.'

'I thought it was all sweetness and light and save-the-world enthusiasm.'

'It was, in the beginning. But we've not had any luck finding out just what it is that Edmund wants, so all that energy is finding other outlets. Nick – the young man from the bookshop – is besotted with Faith—'

'Your pregnant teenager.'

'Right. Faith, on the other hand, seems totally oblivious. The girl has something about her that inspires devotion. She's quite self-contained in a way I've never seen . . . and yet there's something vulnerable about her.'

'Family trauma?' mused Fiona.

'I don't know. I'd like to help her, but I haven't been able to find a chink in her armour.'

'There's more,' Fiona prompted, nibbling on a shiny black olive.

'Nick is terribly jealous of Simon – understandably so. I think Nick saw himself as a necessary part of the equation; then Nick introduced Jack to Simon Fitzstephen—'

'And now Jack's spending more time with Fitzstephen than Nick, and Nick feels abandoned.'

'Classic, isn't it? Damn Simon. I suspect he's playing up Jack partly out of spite towards me and you can bet that whatever other motives he has aren't unselfish. I don't trust him as far as I could throw him. And then there's Garnet—'

'Garnet Todd?' Fiona's hazel eyes widened. 'You didn't tell me Garnet was part of your group.'

'Didn't I? Do you know her?'

'Who doesn't? Garnet's a fixture round here. She always had a talent for stirring things. I take it that hasn't changed?'

'She seems to have taken a dislike to Nick,' admitted Winnie.

'And you end up as peacemaker?'

'Not very successfully, obviously. But what bothers me most is Jack. His obsession with this seems to be growing. You'd think he'd be discouraged by our lack of progress, but it seems to have the opposite effect.

It's as if he feels there's a clock ticking. And I can't hear it.' As Winnie spoke she realized just how alone that made her feel.

'Don't be too hard on yourself. Here you've tumbled into this unexpectedly wonderful relationship, then he goes and gets into bed with a rival you can't even see.'

'It's not like *that*!' Winnie protested, then laughed at her own discomfort. 'Well, maybe it is, a little. Tell me about you,' she added, eager to change the subject.

'Not much to tell, unfortunately.'

Winnie studied her friend's face. 'You look a bit transparent round the edges.'

Fiona shrugged. 'It's not that I expect to control what I paint – that's never been the case – but nothing like this has ever happened before.'

'You're still painting the little girl, then?'

'They're so dark, these paintings. There's no happiness in them. I've begun to dread the urge to paint. And Bram hates them; I can tell—'

The banging of the back door silenced her.

'Sorry I'm late, Fi,' Bram Allen said, coming into the kitchen and kissing his wife's cheek. 'Waiting on an international call. Winnie,' he added, favouring her with a perfunctory nod. 'Good to see you.'

As Fiona readied her husband's meal, Winnie watched the couple with a stirring of envy. Married more than twenty-five years, they still seemed as devoted as newlyweds. Did she and Jack have such a future ahead of them? Or would Jack's involvement with Simon lead him down a path she couldn't follow?

She had been happily self-sufficient until she'd met

Jack Montfort, unaware of any void in her life. So why, now, did the thought of a future without him fill her with such desolation?

They had made themselves comfortable in Jack's kitchen – Winnie and Jack, Nick, Garnet Todd, Simon, and the girl, Faith. The heat wave that had plagued southern England for weeks had abated, and there was a crispness that presaged autumn in the breeze that blew through the open windows. From where Winnie sat, she could see the slope of the Tor rising beyond the neglected back garden, a solitary sheep grazing in the green grass.

Lazing over cups of tea, they indulged in the sort of desultory chat associated with warm summer afternoons. Jack sat with a notepad ready.

Suddenly, his pen began to move across the paper. Jack continued his conversation with Simon, seemingly unaware of the actions of his own hand. As often as Winnie had experienced the phenomenon, she still found it uncomfortably eerie, and, in spite of herself, the word *possession* came to mind.

As soon as Jack stopped writing, Simon began to translate.

Brother Francis has given me my own carrel. We work on the north side of the cloister where the light is best, and my carrel is near a window, a much-coveted spot. Brother Francis has set me the Abbot's own missal to copy, as I have learned so quickly, but warns me against the sin of pride.

Simon looked up from the page, frowning. 'Then

there are a couple of lines I can't make out at all – then something . . . something . . . *meadowsweet*, I think. *The scent of meadowsweet.* Then . . . *much rain . . . Glaston rises from the flooded plain . . . an island in the mist. Supplies come by boat from Abbey holdings further afield, but our visitors are few, and this suits me well.*'

'Have you noticed he's suddenly giving us the present tense?' asked Winnie.

'I don't know that linear time means much to someone in Edmund's . . . uh, condition,' said Jack.

'Really, Jack, there's no need to spare Winifred's sensibilities by avoiding the word *ghost* or *spirit*,' said Simon. For once, Winnie had to agree with him. Who was she to quibble over dogma, if Edmund, who had been a Catholic monk, seemed to have no objection to *being* a ghost?

'Winnie's right,' said Garnet. 'It is a change – it's as if the past has become more immediate to him. Is there anything more, Simon?'

Simon glanced round the table, but Nick was watching Faith, who was gazing at Garnet. Clearing his throat, he waited until he had their attention, then took up the notepad again.

Nothing interrupts the rhythm of our days, long in the summer twilight. Down the night stairs for Matins, the stone cool under our feet. We sing the Office in that state between sleeping and waking . . . then are we closest to God.

The times are now ripe for the glory to return. You must strive to restore all that was lost . . . It was my sins brought such misfortune upon us . . .

'That's all.' Simon looked up, and Winnie came back

to the present with a start. For a moment, she had seen the Great Church, illuminated by candlelight, and heard the voices raised in worship. The longing she felt for this vision was so intense she found herself blinking back tears.

Had the others felt it too? Faith's face was luminous. Their eyes met, and an acknowledgment passed between them.

'What exactly is it that we're supposed to strive to restore?' Jack sounded exasperated. 'Not to mention how to go about it, *if* we knew what it was.'

Winnie said hesitantly, 'I – I might have an idea . . .' They all turned to stare at her. Would they think her barmy? But she knew it didn't matter.

'I don't understand how . . . But he . . . Edmund . . . I could feel his joy, and a sense of – I guess you would call it complete harmony. I don't know how else to describe it. Everything felt right with the world and with God. I think that's what he wants you to know – that this is possible.'

Garnet leaned forward abruptly, raking them all with her intense gaze, and a sudden air current lifted the sheer curtain behind her. 'And nowhere is this more true than in Glastonbury, one of the sacred power centres of the earth. Edmund has opened a window for us, a channel, a way to pull that energy into the present.'

'But how?' Jack frowned. 'And that still doesn't explain why it should come through me.'

'I know Simon hasn't found a direct family connection,' mused Winnie. 'But I can't help feeling there *must* be a genetic component.'

Jack rubbed his chin as he thought, an unconscious gesture that Winnie always found endearing. 'My father's family does go back in these parts as far as anyone can remember. But I don't have the foggiest idea how to follow it from my end.'

'If there's a connection, Simon *will* find it,' insisted Garnet. 'I know it's hard to be patient–'

'You can't expect us to sit round waiting for Simon until Doomsday,' snapped Nick. 'He's not the only one with access to genealogical records–'

'No one's suggesting we leave avenues unexplored,' Jack broke in, forestalling outright hostilities. 'I've some elderly relatives I could have a word with. That seems as good a place to start as any, don't you think, Simon? More tea, everyone?'

Winnie hesitated, glancing at her watch. She felt a great need to block out the emotional undercurrents of the group so that she could absorb what she had just experienced. 'I think I'll go to Wells for Evensong. Jack?'

'Sorry, darling, I can't. I'm meeting some clients at six.' He touched her arm lightly. 'You're sure you won't stay?'

'I'd like to come with you, if that's all right,' offered Faith, much to Winnie's surprise.

'Of course,' Winnie said with genuine pleasure. She'd been hoping to have a word with the girl without appearing too much the interfering priest, and she had just been handed the perfect opportunity.

Historically, Wells had long been Glastonbury's rival,

with much building at the Abbey spurred by progress at Wells, and vice versa. As the west front of the cathedral came into view across the green, Winnie tried to imagine that the Abbey had once looked very like it, but it seemed impossible to superimpose the magnificent front and towers of the intact cathedral against the ruins that remained at Glastonbury.

'The ladders are my favourite thing.' Faith stopped to look up at the carved stone saints climbing to heaven.

'Mine too,' Winnie agreed. 'You've been here before, then?'

'Lots of times.'

When Faith didn't offer anything further, Winnie glanced at her watch. 'I think we've time for a cup of tea in the refectory, if you'd like. Are you hungry?'

Faith gave her a shy smile. 'Always.'

As they entered the main doors of the cathedral, Winnie felt a lift of delight, as she always did, at the sight of the great scissor arch supporting the towers. Some historians theorized that Glastonbury had once had an arch like that, and it suddenly occurred to Winnie that they might ask Edmund – a sure sign that she was becoming as batty as the rest of them.

They turned right, passing through the gift shop and into the refectory, where Faith accepted a cheese roll and insisted on herbal tea. 'Garnet says I mustn't have any caffeine,' she explained. 'It's bad for the baby.'

'Do you get on well with Garnet?' Winnie asked when they were settled at a table overlooking the quiet green square of the Cloisters.

'She's been brilliant. And she knows ever so much

about everything. Have you seen her tiles?' Faith took an enormous bite of roll.

'Yes, in several of the churches I visit. They're beautiful.'

'She knows all about the Old Religion, too, and about how Goddess worship was incorporated into the Christian Church as worship of the Virgin Mar—' She stopped, giving Winnie a horrified glance, as if suddenly realizing Winnie might not approve of these views.

'I dare say she's right,' Winnie interposed gently. 'It's an interesting idea. You said you'd come to Wells often?'

'I sang in the choir at school,' Faith explained. 'We came to hear other choirs, and once we were even invited to sing ourselves.'

Did she detect a wistful note in the girl's voice? 'You must miss that.'

'It was . . . It made me feel sort of . . . outside myself, I suppose.' Faith gave a small shrug, as if embarrassed by her admission.

'Like today? You felt it, too, didn't you?'

Faith nodded. 'It was really weird – like I was there, in the church, and I could hear them singing.'

'I don't think the others had the same experience.' Winnie drank her tea, which had gone lukewarm, while she thought. 'I can't explain it. I'm not even sure I believe this whole thing.'

'Maybe you needed convincing.' The look in Faith's dark eyes brooked no dissembling.

'Maybe I did. But what about you?'

Touching her belly, Faith said, 'I think it might

have something to do with this. Since the baby – it's like the world's more *intense*. I see better, hear better – everything seems to have another layer.'

A hormonally boosted increase in perception? Winnie wondered. Or something more? 'Faith, about the baby – do your parents know where you are?'

The girl pushed away her empty plate and cup. 'My dad— They said they never wanted to see me ever again. That I was a disgrace to them.'

Oh, dear God, thought Winnie. 'People often say things in anger that they don't mean. I'm sure your parents have spent the last few months regretting every word, and that they're worried sick about you.'

'I can't go back. Not after that. You don't know my dad. And my place is with Garnet now.'

Winnie thought she'd glimpsed a hint of tears in Faith's eyes, but the girl's chin was set in a stubborn line. She wouldn't push her luck, but perhaps she could at least open negotiations. 'Would you let me talk to them?'

Faith started to shake her head before Winnie had even finished her sentence.

'I wouldn't tell them where you were,' Winnie continued. 'I wouldn't tell them anything you didn't want me to – only that you're all right.' Seeing Faith waver, she added with a grin, 'You can trust me to keep a promise – it's part of my job description,' and was rewarded with a hesitant smile.

'Could you – could you tell my sister and my brother that I miss them? And my mum?'

'Of course. You give me the address and I'll go and see them first chance I get.' Looking round, Winnie realized the refectory was almost empty. 'We'd better go, or we'll miss the service.'

Returning to the front of the cathedral, they made their way down the left-hand side of the nave to the rope that blocked entry to the choir until it was time for the service to begin. There was a sizeable crowd waiting, and after a moment the verger released the barrier and ushered them into the stalls.

There was a visiting choir that evening, as the cathedral choir was on August holiday, and Winnie saw with pleasure that they were singing the Bach Magnificat, then Parry's 'Songs of Farewell', two of her favourites.

After the usual rustle and shuffle of people adjusting positions and shedding belongings, a hush fell as the choir processed in and took their seats.

Surrounded by the rich, dark wood of the stalls and the glow of lamplight, Winnie felt shielded from the outside world, sealed in a nucleus that rendered time and space meaningless. As the music rose about them, she glanced at the young woman beside her. Faith's countenance was suffused with such joy and longing that Winnie's heart ached, and she knew that this child was one innocent she would protect with all the weapons of her calling.

Chalice Well Gardens lay in the gentle valley between Chalice Hill and the Tor. The gardens rose, level by level, until the last, an enclosed, leafy bower that housed the well itself. Water the colour of blood filled the five-sided well chamber, then flowed through an underground pipe into the Lion's Head pool below at an unceasing twenty-five thousand gallons a day and a constant temperature of fifty-two degrees Fahrenheit.

Nick sat on a bench near the well, waiting for Faith, who had promised to meet him for a half-hour before they both had to be at work. He contemplated the well's intricate wrought-iron cover, designed just after the First World War by Frederick Bligh Bond; funny how old Bond kept cropping up, once you'd made a connection with him.

The carving was an ancient symbol called the *vesica piscis,* two interlocking circles said to represent the interpenetration of the material and immaterial worlds, or the yin and yang where the conscious and unconscious meet.

It was also said to represent the blending of male and female energy . . . perhaps a propitious sign for this meeting, but he wasn't getting his hopes up. He told himself often enough that it was utterly stupid to be in love with a pregnant schoolgirl; he of all people should know better. But it made no difference. And what did he think he would do if she *did* return his feelings? Marry her and take care of mother and infant? Absurd. He barely managed to feed himself and pay the rent on his caravan.

But there was something special about Faith, some quality of inner stillness he had never before encountered. Once or twice he thought he'd glimpsed a spark of possibility in her eyes, before she withdrew again into that calm silence he could not penetrate, and this kept him from giving up.

Impatiently, he stood and paced the confined area

of the garden, stopping again at the well. The cover was pulled to one side, enabling him to peer down into the chamber itself. There was said to be a grotto set into one of the walls, large enough for a man to stand in, but he could see no sign of it. Dropping to his knees for a closer look, he didn't hear Faith coming until she opened the gate to the well garden.

'Don't fall in,' she teased, coming to stand behind him. 'Garnet says it's the Goddess's well, and I doubt She'd like some big bloke splashing about in it.'

Faith wore a striped football shirt beneath denim dungarees, and her cropped hair and delicate features looked all the more feminine for it. *Bugger Garnet*, Nick thought savagely, but he didn't say it aloud. 'I was duly worshipping. Hands and knees, see?'

'Nick, don't joke. It's a sacred place.'

Rising, he returned to the bench and patted the seat beside him. 'No offence intended. Come and sit; you stand all day.'

She obeyed, but kept a chaste distance between them. His desire for her was driving him to distraction, but he didn't dare cross the boundaries she'd set, for fear of destroying the friendship they'd forged over the past months. Yet the thought that she had crossed those barriers with someone else was maddening, and it was all he could do not to ask her who . . . or why she continued to protect him.

Not that he had much opportunity to be alone with Faith. Garnet Todd had become both mother hen and fierce watchdog, and she'd made no effort to conceal her disapproval of Nick's interest. On the few occasions he'd ventured up to Garnet's farmhouse to see Faith after work, he'd sat uncomfortably in the primitive kitchen with the two of them, feeling like an unwelcome Victorian suitor. Hence this morning's tryst in the garden.

'Some people think this is the garden Malory meant when he wrote that Lancelot retired to a valley near Glastonbury,' Nick mused, stretching his arm across the bench top, an inch from Faith's shoulders. 'Do you suppose this very place is where Lancelot lived out his days, dreaming of Guinevere in her nunnery? They died within months of one another – did you know that?'

Faith shivered. 'That's too sad. This garden isn't meant to be sad: it's a healing place.'

'I suppose it was a sort of healing for Lancelot, if he came to terms with his love for Gwen and for Arthur in the time he had left. And if he had been denied the Grail, perhaps living by a spring said to flow with the blood of Christ was some compensation.'

'I can see him here,' Faith said dreamily, tilting her head back until her hair brushed his arm. 'With his little hut in the woods, and the spring flowing out of the hillside.' Her face darkened. 'But the other spring would have been always below him, reminding him of the darkness to come.'

'The White Spring?' It flowed from the base of the Tor itself, and if the Red Spring represented the female element, the White Spring was said to represent the male.

'Garnet says it's the entrance to Annwn, the home of Gwyn ap Nudd, Lord of the Underworld. And I can feel . . . something there . . . it's a dark place.'

'Oh, bollocks, Faith.' He touched her chin with his fingertips, turning her face towards his. 'You don't really believe that, do you? It's just a fairy story.'

'How do you know?' She twisted her face away and sat up straight. 'The Druids were in tune with the earth itself, and there's nothing more powerful.'

'But it's myth, Faith! Symbolism. It was their way of explaining the world. No one's meant to take it literally.'

'Is what's happened to Jack a myth? Do you not believe that's real?'

'Yes, but—'

'If Edmund can speak to us across nine hundred years, how can you set limits on what's true?' Faith stood and faced him, her eyes bright with anger.

'But that's different—'

'Is it?'

'Of course it's different. Glastonbury Abbey was a real place, and monks really did live there. Edmund was a real person—'

'Can you prove it?'

'I don't need to prove it. I've experienced it.'

'Then how can you say other people's experiences aren't valid?' she shot back.

He stared at her. This was not going at all the way he'd intended. 'Look, Faith, meet me tonight. We can talk about it, but right now we're both going to be late for work.'

'I can't. Garnet wants me to study.'

'Study what? The Old Religion?' He heard the loathing in his voice.

Faith's chin went up defensively. 'The *first* religion.

You know the Christian Church just built on what went before. Even Simon says so.'

'That's not the point. You need to be doing normal, ordinary things. Finishing school. Taking your exams. Thinking about what you're going to do with your life – and how you're going to take care of your baby. You need to go home, Faith.' As he said it, he knew it was a mistake, and worse, if she were to take his advice he would very likely lose her altogether.

'Don't patronize me, Nick Carlisle,' she spat at him. 'And don't tell me how to live my life. I've done all right—'

'Only because Garnet took you in, and I suspect she had her reasons—'

'You don't know what you're talking about! Garnet understands me, and she knows I have something to do, something important – I just can't see what yet. So just bugger off, okay?' She spun round, opening the gate and clanging it shut behind her.

Jumping up, he called out, 'Faith, I'm sorry—' but she ran down the path, away from him.

Chapter Five

We also had to meet with a certain amount of jealousy from that section of the community which regards all positive happiness as tending to evil, and all beauty as an endowment of the devil; for it did undoubtedly happen that the young things that studied with us acquired a liveliness and a physical carriage that marked them out from their fellows.

Rutland Boughton, from
The Glastonbury Festival Movement

Having given Faith chamomile tea and tucked her in bed for a nap, Garnet walked down the hill towards the café, for once oblivious to the beauty of the mild afternoon. Buddy had sent the girl home after lunch, insisting that she take the afternoon off, and Garnet needed to know exactly what had transpired that morning.

She was thankful to find the café empty and Buddy cleaning tables after the lunch rush. When she entered, he smiled and motioned her to a seat with a flourish of his cloth.

'You're a sight for sore eyes, darlin'. It's been a bugger of a day.' His Texas drawl had never faded, although it was regularly interspersed with English slang.

'And you're culturally confused,' Garnet replied. There was something about Buddy's lanky frame and greying ponytail that still made her think of the Wild West, although he swore his only contact with cows had been on a plate and that he wouldn't know what to do with a horse if it bit him.

'Tea?' he asked. 'You look like you could use the real thing.'

'Yes, please,' Garnet said gratefully, and waited until he'd made two mugs and brought them to the table.

'How is she?' he asked, sitting across from her.

'Sleeping, I hope. What happened this morning, Buddy?'

'Hell if I know. She came in five minutes late – first time she's ever done that – puffy-eyed and silent as a newt. Dropped things all morning like her fingers had been greased, then I found her crying in the soup.' He shook his head. 'Anybody could see the poor girl wasn't fit to work, so I sent her home. She didn't like it, though.'

Garnet sighed. 'I never thought I'd be looking after a teenager, and a pregnant one at that. She left the house early this morning; I just assumed she was coming in to help you.'

'Think she met someone? But who?'

'Nick Carlisle would be my guess, damn him. Although I've never seen Nick get her in such a state.'

'Maybe it was someone else. What about the baby's father? Has she ever said anything to you?'

'Not even a hint. But I wonder . . . Faith told me

last night that Winnie Catesby intends to talk to her parents. It may be that's what has her so out of sorts.'

'The priest?'

'You make it sound as if Winnie has a disease, Buddy.' Garnet laughed in spite of her worry. 'She means well.'

'Then let her send the girl home to her mom. It'd be a burden off you.'

'I can't.' Garnet said it flatly.

'And why the hell not? Sounds like the sensible solution to me.'

'It would be, except that it's not safe.'

'Not safe?' Buddy frowned. 'You think her dad would hurt her?'

'I don't know. She's never said so, not flat out. But there's something not right in that family.'

'Anybody laid a hand on that girl'd have me to answer to, dad or not.' Buddy bristled.

'You're a good man, Buddy, not like some. But it's not as simple as that.' Garnet tried to gather into words what she felt with such certainty. 'Faith is a pivot, a magnet, for forces much more powerful than her father. She and her baby are in dire peril – I'm more sure of that than anything I've ever known. Faith has to stay with me – it's the only way I can protect her.'

'And the boy you're so riled up about – Nick? Is he part of this danger?'

'I don't know. But he is a distraction, and that's something Faith can't afford right now.'

Buddy fidgeted with his mug, then reluctantly met her eyes. 'Are you sure you're not . . . overreacting?'

'I don't *want* to be proved right, Buddy. And I don't

care what anyone thinks. I'm not willing to risk Faith if I can help it. Are you?'

'No . . . I . . . well, I've gotten used to having her around, if you want to know the truth. If anything happened to her . . .'

What a pair they were, thought Garnet. Childless, never married, no family. And this slip of a girl had come into their lives and pierced them like an arrow.

'Just look after her, Buddy, when she's with you. Promise me that.'

It was the best she could do . . . But she was terribly afraid it would not be enough.

Faith's family lived in the town of Street, just two miles from Glastonbury across the sluggish trickle of the River Brue. Whenever Winnie drove across the bridge, she found it hard to imagine that it was here King Arthur was said to have seen a vision of the Blessed Virgin; perhaps in those days it had been a more prepossessing spot.

Street was home to the Clark Shoe Company. One of the more enlightened of Victorian employers, Clark's had provided good working conditions and comfortable housing for their factory workers, and the town had carried that air of forward-looking prosperity into the present. It was quite a contrast to Glastonbury's ragtag appeal, but it was Glastonbury that Winnie preferred.

Faith had admitted reluctantly that her name was Wills, and had given Winnie an address in a comfortable housing estate near the Street police station. At half past five Winnie stopped her car in front of the Wills house. It sat at the end of a quiet close of similar brick, semi-detached homes that looked as if their owners had participated in a 'tidy garden' contest. There was neither an untrimmed shrub nor a weed to be seen, and Winnie found it vaguely depressing. Nor was there any sign of life: no bicycles, no roller skates, no one digging in a well-manicured flower bed.

As she neared the front door, however, she saw signs of neglect that had not been visible from the street – weeds sprouting in the beds, parched petunias and begonias that had been allowed to wither. Winnie rang the bell, and after a moment a woman of about her own age opened the door. The woman wore smart business clothes, and would have been pretty had she not looked drawn with worry or exhaustion.

'Mrs Wills? Could I speak to you for a moment?'

'I'm sorry, but we've already donated at our church.' She started to close the door.

'Mrs Wills, it's about your daughter.'

The woman stared at her, her hand flying to her throat in the classic gesture of shock that Winnie had seen too often.

'She's all right, Mrs Wills,' Winnie hastened to reassure her. 'May I come in, please?'

Mrs Wills moved back like a sleepwalker, then sank onto a sofa in the small, formal front room. There was a faint smell of cooking potatoes in the air. 'Is she . . . is the baby—'

'Faith is as healthy as a horse, and hasn't had any difficulties or complications with the pregnancy.' Winnie sat in a nearby chair. 'My name's Winifred

Catesby, Mrs Wills, and Faith asked me to come and see you.' That might be stretching the truth a bit, but Winnie didn't see any harm.

'Where – where is she?' Mrs Wills started to rise, as if to go to her daughter that instant.

'It's Maureen, isn't it?' said Winnie as she laid a gently restraining hand on her arm. 'Maureen, Faith wanted you to know that she was safe and well.'

'But she's coming home? She is coming home, isn't she?'

Winnie had known this would be difficult. 'Not just now, Maureen. She seems to be content where she is for the present, but she wanted you to know that she misses you, and that she misses her brother and sister.'

Maureen Wills put her face in her hands. 'You don't know – you can't imagine what it's been like,' she choked out. 'Losing your baby, not knowing if she's alive or dead. And Gary – Gary won't even allow us to speak her name— It's been terrible for Meredith and Jon . . .' She raised her face, blotched and tear-streaked. 'How could she do this to us?'

'Maureen, kids make mistakes. We all make mistakes, but this one isn't easy to put right. I'm sure Faith never meant to hurt any of you.'

'Then why is she so stubborn? If she'd just told us what happened, who the father is, or if she'd just been reasonable about having an—' Maureen broke off abruptly, with a glance at Winnie's collar. 'I never thought . . . when Gary told her she was legally an adult, that if she was going to disrespect us that way, she could fend for herself, I never thought she'd go.'

Winnie listened, nodding encouragingly, knowing

how badly Maureen Wills must have needed to say these things to someone.

'And then, when I found her gone, that was terrible enough. But I never thought she'd stay away. Every minute, every hour, I thought I would hear the door. Or she would ring and ask me to come and get her. Sometimes I'd find myself thinking I had to pick her up from football practice, or choir, and then I'd realize . . .'

'She told me she sang in the choir. It seems to have meant a lot to her.'

'She was at Somerfield. We were so proud of her.'

'Faith is very special, Mrs Wills – Maureen. What's happened doesn't change that. I've seldom seen a girl her age with such courage and self-reliance.'

'I want to see her, please. Can't you take me to her?'

The tearful supplication was hard to resist, but Winnie shook her head. 'I can't betray Faith's wishes. But I'll tell her what you've said, and I'll do my best to arrange a meeting. I think that's all we can hope for just now.'

'But where is she? How is she managing? Is she eating? Does she attend your church?'

'I came to know Faith as a friend, not in my official capacity,' Winnie explained. 'She has a job, and a safe place to live, and a number of people who are concerned for her welfare.'

'But how will she manage, once the baby's . . . When is it . . . ?'

'Late October, I believe. As for what she'll do then, I don't know, but we've some time to find a solution. If you'll just—'

There was a sound from the back of the house and Maureen Wills froze, holding up a hand to silence Winnie. 'It's Gary and the kids. I don't want him to— It'll be better if I talk to him. Could you—'

The woman looked so terrified that Winnie quickly handed her the card she'd taken from her handbag and rose. 'Here's my number. Ring me.'

She patted Maureen's trembling hands, and was out of the front door as a man's furious voice called out, 'Maureen, where are you? The damn chips are burned to a crisp! *Maureen?*'

Winnie drove home with hopes that she had made some progress in reconciling Faith with her family, although perhaps a goal of physical reunification was unwise if Mr Wills was as intimidating as he seemed. It seemed obvious that he was the real stumbling block. Winnie had seen this a number of times in her years of counselling parishioners – men often took a daughter's pregnancy as a personal affront, and even in the more well-balanced families there seemed to be an element of jealousy involved. What she did find curious was the lengths to which Faith had gone to protect a boy who apparently had shown no further interest in her.

The next challenge would be arranging a meeting between Faith and her mother on neutral ground. As she neared home, she decided that her study at the Vicarage would provide the ideal setting.

The Vicarage was on the Butleigh Road, south of Glastonbury, in the village of Compton Grenville. Winnie had come to love her parish in this gentle countryside, with its view of the Levels to the east, and to the west the Hood Monument at the top of wooded Windmill Hill.

The house was the epitome of the draughty Victorian pile, but in five years Winnie had come to regard its eccentricities with a profound affection.

Of course, to do the place justice would have taken a small fortune, but Winnie had done the best she could with diocesan funds, and she had used a bit of the small inheritance she and Andrew had had from their parents. She had made the front parlour her office, and had turned the large old kitchen into a combination sitting/eating area.

She turned into her drive with the pleasure she always felt. She and Jack had no plans for that evening; for once she had no pastoral obligations, and she was rather looking forward to a quiet evening spent working on her sermon. Then, to her surprise, she saw Andrew's car pulled round near the kitchen door.

Andrew had been dropping in unannounced rather frequently of late. While Winnie adored her brother, she was aware that his concern was much more likely to be for his welfare than for hers. Andrew had come to depend on her, perhaps too much, and she had tried to reassure him that her feelings for Jack wouldn't change things between them – although if she were honest with herself, she'd have to admit they already had.

Stopping the car, she retrieved the shopping she'd picked up for her supper from the boot and let herself in at the back door. Andrew sat at her kitchen table, the *Observer* spread out before him, a half-empty glass of red wine in his hand. He looked up with an impish smile.

'Hullo, darling. I brought you a nice bottle of Burgundy, and thought I'd stay to do the honours.'

'I can see you already have.' She gave him a fond peck on the cheek as she set her shopping on the table. The cheerful kitchen was her favourite room in the house. Roman blinds in tomato-red canvas covered the windows, so that the morning sun filled the room with its own sunrise, and she'd slip-covered the old sofa and chair in the small sitting area in a combination of prints in the same red and apple green.

Now in the evening light the rich colours were muted, the room cool and welcoming. Andrew examined the contents of the shopping bag. 'A loaf of bread, a hunk of cheese – farmhouse Cheddar, no less – apples, and a bar of Cadbury's chocolate. Planning a romantic dinner?'

'No, a working one, actually, so I'd better go easy on the wine. But I will have a glass and put my feet up for a bit before I dig in.' Winnie fetched a glass from the cupboard and sat down beside Andrew, slipping out of her shoes with a sigh of relief.

She had often been told that they resembled one another, but she'd always thought that Andrew had got the better part of the deal. He was taller, slimmer, and on him her pleasant features and untidy brown hair were refined to quiet good looks. His tortoiseshell wire-rimmed spectacles added just the right touch of distinction. *Perfectly professorial*, she thought as she filled her glass, and smiled.

Raising an eyebrow, Andrew queried, 'Had a good

day, then? You look as though you've been impressing the bishop.'

'Tougher than that.' She hesitated. How much might she tell him about Faith's situation without compromising the girl's trust? Without mentioning names, she briefly outlined her efforts to negotiate a reconciliation.

Andrew swirled the wine round the rim of his glass, then took a swig and studied her over its edge. 'Winnie, don't you think you've gone beyond the pale here? This girl is not a member of your congregation, or even C of E as far as you know. No one has asked you to intercede – or interfere, as the case may be – and it seems to me you're likely to do more harm than good.'

She stared at her brother, astounded. 'It's my job to minister to people, parishioners or not. You know that. And I would never have gone to see the girl's parents without her permission. She's seventeen years old, for heaven's sake, and she misses her home and her family!'

'You don't have a clue what girls are like these days! Or teenagers, for that matter. They're lazy and they expect the world handed to them on a platter, and this one probably deserved her predicament—'

'That's absurd—'

'Not to mention the fact that she's already got a strike against her if she's involved with these batty friends of yours. And what makes you think this girl's told you the truth about anything?' Andrew shook his head in disgust. 'Since you met Jack Montfort, you seem to have lost all common sense.'

'Andrew, what on earth has got into you?' Then

realization dawned. 'This isn't about my work at all! This is about Jack, isn't it?'

For a moment she thought he would deny it, then he met her eyes. 'Glastonbury is a small town, Winnie. People talk. I went to a council meeting last night, and you and Jack Montfort were a great source of speculation. Montfort may have some justification for going off the deep end, but I can't see that you have any excuse for plunging in with him. I'm surprised that your bishop hasn't had a discreet word with you about associating yourself with blatant spiritualism—'

'That's enough!' She pushed back her chair and stood, her bewilderment turning to icy fury. 'You're being bloody offensive, and you don't know what you're talking about. I think you'd better go home.'

Andrew stood too, a little unsteadily, and leaned towards her. 'How do you think *I* feel, being *gossiped* about? I've worked for years to build my reputation in this town – you know how hard it is to get project funding – and now people snigger when they see me and make comments about my sister's raging hormones causing her to take leave of her senses. They all want to know if you're sleeping with him – are you sleeping with him, Winnie?'

For the first time since she was nine years old, Winnie raised her hand and slapped her brother across the face as hard as she could.

'Inspector James . . .'

Gemma said the words aloud as she drove, trying out the sound on her tongue. Heady things, titles. They tempted you to think you were a different person, when in reality the changes were more like the layers of accretion on a pearl. A little more irritation gained you a little more lustre, another layer of knowledge, of experience.

Or perhaps she'd wanted the title to make her into a different person – one whose sense of accomplishment wasn't tempered by her sense of loss. She'd been so busy worrying about how Kincaid would deal with her decision that she'd failed to take her own response to their separation into account. And in spite of her excitement, and the intensity of her focus on her training, she'd felt a constant ache that seemed only to grow more profound with time. She'd come to think of it as the equivalent of the phantom-limb syndrome – she found herself carrying on imaginary conversations with him throughout the day. It was as if their thought processes had become permanently intertwined. Even when they'd been apart in the course of a job, investigating different avenues on a case, she'd been constantly filing away mental references to share with him.

Kincaid had reacted the way she'd expected, his initial dismay turning quickly to angry bewilderment. 'Doesn't our partnership mean anything to you?' he had asked, and her justifications had sounded weak in her own ears. He'd pulled himself together, of course, had even tried to be understanding and supportive – but he had withdrawn from her. During her last weeks of training in Hampshire, she'd rung him a few times and their conversations had consisted of pleasantly distant chat. Returning to London yesterday, she'd found her new duty assignment awaiting her, and she knew she must tell him about it in person.

He'd been away from the Yard on a case, so she'd gone home, fed Toby his supper, then tucked him up at Hazel's and headed for Kincaid's Hampstead flat. She should have rung – he might still be out, he might have other plans, he might not want to see her – and perhaps it was fear of the last that had prompted her to go unannounced.

The traffic was light as she drove through Camden Town, the September evening warm enough to allow her to drive her new car with the windows down. The Ford Escort, whose colour went by the romantic and improbable name of Wild Orchid, had been a much-needed gift to herself on her promotion. The increase in her salary had made it feasible, but more than that she had needed some sort of visible symbol of her achievement. And Kincaid had not seen the car yet, which gave her an excuse for showing up on his doorstep.

When she reached Hampstead the glitterati were out in force, strolling and positioning themselves to see and be seen in the pavement cafés, mobile phones permanently attached to their ears.

Turning into Carlingford Road, she saw Kincaid's old MG Midget parked in front of his building, covered with its tarpaulin, but that didn't necessarily mean he was at home. The Major's ground-floor flat was quiet, as was the stairwell of the building, nor was there any sound of telly or stereo from Kincaid's flat when she reached the top floor. Her hopes sank, but she knocked, and after a moment he opened the door.

'Gemma! I didn't know you were back.'

She absorbed the details as if it had been months rather than weeks since she'd seen him: unruly chestnut hair, jeans and a cornflower-blue T-shirt that brought out the indigo in his eyes, bare feet, and the smile that always made her catch her breath.

'Late yesterday,' she answered as she followed him into the flat. 'I'm not interrupting anything, am I?'

'Not unless you count drinking a beer and sitting on the balcony.' Going to the fridge, he retrieved a lager and held it out towards her, one eyebrow raised questioningly.

Nodding, she accepted the cold bottle and looked round the flat with pleasure. He had managed that rare thing: comfortable masculinity. The small but functional kitchen was separated from the sitting room by a lamplit island that served as the flat's depository for keys, the day's mail, and the usual household odds and ends, but the clutter was well organized.

In the sitting room, the furniture was upholstered in rich reds, blues, and greens – stained-glass colours, he called them – the walls held his collection of vintage London Transport art, and every spare nook and cranny was filled with books. But the true focus of the room was the view, first of the balcony with its colourful pots of flowers (contributed by the Major) and, beyond that, the panorama of London rooftops limned by the evening light.

'Join me outside?' he asked, and as she stepped out through the French doors she laughed aloud.

'You've made Sid a platform!' Sid, the black cat Kincaid had inherited from his late friend Jasmine

Dent, turned and gave her an unblinking emerald stare from a cat-sized perch attached to the balcony railing.

'I got fed up having heart failure every time he jumped up on the railing,' Kincaid explained, running his hand along the cat's back. 'He's already used up a couple of his nine lives – and I'd hate to think what the Major would do to me if Sid plummeted three floors into one of his prize rose bushes.' He settled in one of the lawn chairs, stretching out his long legs and resting his feet on the railing. 'I can't take credit for the platform, though. It was Kit's idea.'

Gemma sat beside him, very much aware of his physical nearness. 'How is Kit?'

Kincaid frowned. 'Ian's thinking of taking a job in Canada. Kit wants to stay with me if Ian goes, but I haven't been able to get a commitment out of Ian either way. The last thing Kit needs is to be uprooted. And I want him here.'

'But how would you manage?' she asked, thinking of the conflict with the job – and of the changes it would mean in her relationship with him.

'How much more difficult could it be than the weekends he spends here now?'

A good bit, she thought, but aloud she said merely, 'What if Ian won't agree?' She had never trusted McClellan's sudden desire to make things up to Kit.

'We'll deal with that if it happens. It's not even positive about the job yet.'

Gemma sat forward and peered down into the garden. The roses were lush with late summer's passion, but the rectangle of lawn was as primly tidy as ever. 'Where *is* Kit tonight? I thought he'd be with you for the weekend.'

'In Grantchester, getting Tess ready for an obedience trial tomorrow. I'll go up in the morning.'

Gemma felt suddenly excluded, as if they'd done a perfectly good job of carving out a life without her. And yet she knew that was unreasonable – wasn't she the one who had chosen to go away? 'I thought I'd see you at the Yard today,' she said, striving for firmer ground. 'Tough case?'

'Wrapped up today, barring the paperwork, and that I've turned over to my sergeant.' He gave her a wicked grin. 'Serves him right for being such a bloody eager beaver.'

'Wasn't I?'

'Not like this. He's a public-school boy – Eton, no less – and full of do-gooder's enthusiasm for the job. Hasn't learned he can't change the world yet.'

'What's his name?' she asked casually. Surely it was ridiculous to be jealous of this young man who had taken her place.

'Doug Cullen. He's not a bad chap, really, and I think he'll make a decent copper once he's seasoned a bit. At any rate he's intelligent, and that's an enormous improvement over the last two they assigned me.' He took a sip of his beer and studied her. 'You'll be bossing sweet young things about yourself, any day now. How does it feel?'

She heard the distance in his tone and said awkwardly, 'Don't know yet, really.' He'd given her an opening, and the longer she waited to take it, the more difficult it would be. Abruptly, she said, 'I've got my duty assignment. Notting Hill.'

For a moment he didn't respond, then, without taking his gaze from the garden, he said softly, 'Your old stomping ground. Good. That should make things easier for you. Congratulations,' he added, but she could see it took an effort.

'This has been harder than I expected.'

'Gemma, I've no doubt you can do the job—'

'No, that's not what I meant. I feel so . . . displaced . . . without you. It's like half of me's missing. I never realized . . .'

He stared at her, then said lightly, 'And I thought you'd come to give me a "Dear Duncan" send-off in person. *I met this terrific bloke on my Criminal Behaviour course . . .*'

'Fat chance, that!' she exclaimed, laughing.

He moved his bare foot along the railing until it touched hers. 'I've missed you too.'

The wave of desire that washed over her from that small contact was so intense it left her shaken. She closed her eyes and held quite still, struggling to convince herself that every nerve ending in her body hadn't suddenly migrated to the left side of her left foot.

When she opened her eyes, Kincaid was watching her. 'Gemma? You okay?'

Tentatively, she said, 'Just exactly how much did you miss me?'

He brushed her cheek with a fingertip. 'Are you angling for a demonstration, Inspector?'

Her pulse leapt. 'Yes, sir, guv'nor, sir.' The lights

blinked on in the house opposite, as if to signal the coming of night. 'You can't make a case without evidence, you know.'

'Oh, I think that could be obtained easily enough, don't you?' He stood, and she caught the flash of his grin as he held out his hand to her. She slipped her fingers into his, and willingly gave herself up.

Chapter Six

There are times in the history of races when the things of the inner life come to the surface and find expression, and from these rendings of the veil the light of the sanctuary pours forth.

Dion Fortune, from
Glastonbury: Avalon of the Heart

She lay beside him, listening to his soft breathing, with the slight whistle on the exhalation that might easily become a snore. That she found tolerable, much to her surprise, even though she had slept alone for so many years.

Not that Winnie felt entirely comfortable with the fact that she *was* sleeping with Jack, and she knew the excuse that the transgressions of a number of Anglican priests far surpassed hers was no justification. But she also knew that it felt right, blessed, and she could not believe that God would find such joy offensive. God had more to worry him than a bit of out-of-wedlock love-making . . . as did she.

Easing out of bed, she fumbled for slippers and dressing gown, then remembered that she had not meant to stay and that her clothes lay in a heap on the floor. That meant borrowing Jack's dressing gown from the bedpost and slipping on thick socks.

She had learned her way round this room, which had been Jack's parents', well enough to navigate in the dark. The first time she had stayed the night, Jack had admitted rather shamefacedly that he had been using the small single bed in his boyhood room, unable to bear the thought of taking over the mahogany four-poster in which his parents had slept for almost fifty years. But the single bed had not been big enough for two, and together they had made the transition to the larger bedroom.

If she had thought the house cold on bright summer days, now that October had arrived it was frigid. Winnie sometimes fancied that it was the shadow of the Tor that kept it so, but that was absurd. It was merely, she told herself, shivering, that the house was old and the central heating inadequate.

As she shuffled down the stairs, hugging the banister, she indulged a moment's fantasy in which she and Jack were snuggled up cosily in her warm room at the Vicarage. But she knew that no matter how discreet they were, tongues would wag eventually, and she did *not* need more gossip just now. Her archdeacon, Suzanne Sanborne, had already expressed concern over rumours circulating about Winnie's 'dabbling in the paranormal', and this Winnie suspected had been instigated by Andrew.

Andrew had apologized to her after their row, and she'd made every effort to smooth things over, but there remained a wedge of discomfort between them that she feared might never be healed. His criticism had hurt her deeply, and she was finding forgiveness difficult. 'Practise what you preach, Winnie,' she whispered as she reached the kitchen.

Switching on the light over the table, she opened the fridge and filled a mug with milk, then popped it in the microwave.

Jack could teach her a thing or two about forgiveness, she thought as she retrieved her drink and breathed in the sweet, comforting smell of scalded milk. Once she'd finally worked up the nerve that evening over dinner to tell Jack about her past relationship with Simon Fitzstephen, he had merely said gently, 'I never believed you were a saint, Winnie. I hate to think you've been worrying over this for months.'

'You don't mind?'

'The thought of you with another man does give me a twinge,' he admitted. 'But it was a long time ago, and I don't see how it affects us now.'

'I haven't told you why I broke it off.' Winnie hesitated, piecing together a story that she'd kept to herself for more than a decade. 'There was another student, Ray, a protégé of Simon's. He was killed in a car accident.'

'You were friends?'

'Yes. He'd have made a good priest – a very compassionate man, with a real gift for pastoral care. But he was a scholar as well, and he worshipped Simon. If Ray had lived, I think he'd have outgrown it in time, but he wasn't given the chance.'

Frowning, Jack said, 'Tragic, but I don't see how this reflects on Simon.'

'Ray was working on a research project under Simon's tutelage, an exploration of an obscure thirteenth-century Grail legend. When Ray was killed, Simon published the paper as his own.'

'But surely there was some mistake—'

'No mistake. A few months after Ray's death, his family asked me to sort through his things. I found the original. When I confronted Simon, he said the work was his, that Ray had merely been transcribing it for him.'

'Of course, that would be it,' Jack said with evident relief.

'But Ray left notes, extensive ones. There was absolutely no doubt that he had done the research *and* written the paper.'

Digesting this, Jack asked, 'Did you tell anyone?'

Winnie felt herself flushing. 'No. Simon said he'd make a fool of me to the bishop, that he'd say I was acting out of spite because he'd rejected me, and that he'd make sure I never got a good living. He had the influence to do it too. So I convinced myself that it was a minor academic point, nothing that really mattered to anyone – and I've hated myself for it ever since.'

Jack covered her hand with his. 'You were young, inexperienced—'

She shook her head. 'There's no excuse for what I did. I know that. But I also know that you can't trust Simon Fitzstephen. He would betray you in an instant if it was to his advantage.'

'But there's nothing to betray,' protested Jack. 'What could Simon possibly have to gain by helping me?'

'I don't know. But promise me you'll be careful.'

She had had to be content with that. Jack had insisted on giving Simon the benefit of the doubt, and she realized she wouldn't choose to change that about him – it was one of the reasons she loved him.

If only her brother was as generous, Winnie thought, finding herself back at the problem that had initially kept her from falling asleep. She could see no way to mollify Andrew other than to give up seeing Jack, which she was not willing to do, or to convince Jack to give up his communication with Edmund, which he was not willing to do – even if it were possible. This rift in her relationship with her brother nagged her like a toothache.

Sipping her milk, she thought of Faith Wills, and Andrew's criticism of her intercession in Faith's affairs. Andrew had been vindicated, in a sense, as things had certainly not turned out as Winnie had hoped, but she still felt strongly that she had done the right thing. Faith had agreed to see her mother, had even set a time to meet at the Vicarage, then had abruptly changed her mind. Winnie had not been able to budge the girl from her decision, and Faith had offered no excuse. The closer Faith came to her due date, only a few weeks away now at the end of October, the more concerned Winnie became about her.

Although Garnet had assured her that Faith was doing well and the pregnancy seemed normal, Winnie sensed that Garnet was holding something back – and that both Faith and Garnet were avoiding her. Had she unwittingly alienated them by her efforts to reunite Faith with her parents?

Nor had the tension between Nick and Garnet abated, as their mutual concern for Faith only seemed to increase their antagonism.

And as far as Winnie knew, no one in the group seemed to have gained any true understanding of what it was that Edmund wanted of them.

Sighing, Winnie set down her empty cup and rubbed her face. Tired, but no closer to sleep, she couldn't shake the feeling that things were building to some sort of climax, and she found no comfort in the passage from Ephesians that came suddenly to mind. *For our struggle is not against enemies of flesh and blood . . . but against the cosmic powers of this present darkness, against the spiritual forces of evil in the heavenly places.* Could there be some truth in Garnet's dire forecasts of doom and dark forces?

No, surely not. That was absurd. But whatever the cause of the foreboding she felt, she must protect Jack as best she could – and she could only do that if she knew exactly what she was up against.

As much as she disliked the idea, it was time she had a confrontation with Simon Fitzstephen . . . and she mustn't let herself forget that it was she who held the upper hand.

With a decision made, she rinsed her cup in the sink, switched off the lamp, and climbed the stairs. Diving under the covers, she snuggled up to Jack's solid warmth and fell instantly into a deep and dreamless sleep.

*

We who watch . . . rue the day of Thurstan's coming . . . Darkness came upon us then . . .

Simon Fitzstephen sat next to Jack Montfort at the round table in Fitzstephen's sitting room, translating aloud what Montfort had just scrawled on the page in his notebook. A fire crackled in the grate, John Rutter's arrangement of William Byrd's *Miserere mei* played softly on the stereo, and they had drawn the heavy velvet curtains against the coming of evening.

Having invited Jack on the pretext of continuing their genealogical research, Simon had encouraged him to try asking Edmund for information once more. Fitzstephen was convinced that the presence of the others in the group hampered the automatic-writing process: it looked as though the results of this session might prove him right.

Thurstan had been the first Norman abbot at Glastonbury, brought from Caen in France by King William after the Conquest to succeed Aethelnoth. By Simon's reckoning, Edmund must have been in his early teens when Thurstan became abbot in 1077.

Jack's hand again moved across the paper. *The church was never finished . . . it was cursed. One day the Abbot went into the Chapter House and spoke against the monks. He sent for his men and they fell upon us fully armed. We scattered in terror. Some fled into the church, thinking to be safe there. But evil . . . that day . . . the Frenchmen broke into the choir . . . Some shot arrows towards the sanctuary so that they stuck in the Cross that stood above the altar. Many . . . monks were wounded . . . three were killed. Blood came from the altar on to the steps, and from the steps onto the paving stones . . .*

'Where were you?' Simon asked softly.

I hid in the scriptorium, among the books. But I saw . . . afterwards. I washed the bodies of the dead . . . and wept for them. I weep still for what the Abbot stole from us that day.

'What was that? What did the abbot take?'

But Jack's hand rested unmoving on the paper, his fingers slack, and after a moment he blinked.

'Get anything?' he asked, laying down the pen and stretching.

'See for yourself.' Simon paced while Jack read, for while Jack's translations had improved, he still didn't think as easily in Latin as Simon did.

Jack came to the end of the page and looked up. 'There's something here I don't understand. Why did Thurstan "speak against" the monks? Had they done something wrong?'

'No. Although Thurstan was a godly man, and a builder, like all the Normans, he made the monks stop the Gregorian chant that had been part of the Abbey's tradition from time immemorial, substituting a French chant by William of Fécamp. When the monks protested, Thurstan attacked them. You must understand that this substitution was no minor thing to the monks – the chant was part of the very fabric of their daily lives.'

'And Edmund witnessed this . . .' Jack mused. 'Maybe it was even more than that . . . Do you remember when Winnie said that as she listened to Edmund's description of the monks' service she felt an immense sense of joy and harmony? She told me later that she had seen a vision, that she'd been in the church and heard them singing . . .'

Would wonders never cease? thought Simon. The pragmatic Winifred Catesby was the last person he'd have expected to have a vision. Aloud, he said, 'She heard them singing . . . Do you suppose . . . Could it be the *chant* that Edmund wants us to restore?'

'It sounds a bit far-fetched. The chants must be well documented—'

'No, wait.' Something nipped at Simon's memory. He went to the bookcase and ran his finger along the spines until he found the volume he wanted, but the mere act of touching it triggered his memory and he held the book, unopened. 'There's a Celtic tradition that Joseph of Arimathea brought with him to Britain a twelve-part chant that had been secretly passed down through the centuries from pre-Christian temple priests in Egypt. Although no one is certain what they sang at Glastonbury, some sources say it was the one place where this chant was maintained in its purest form by a perpetual choir . . . What if it was *this* chant that Thurstan forbade?'

'And the monks would have risked their lives for this?' Jack's doubt was evident.

'Perhaps if they thought that the survival of their society depended on it. The word *enchantment* is derived from "chant". The ancients believed that music was the strongest magic, that it kept man in tune with the cosmos and in harmony with one another. Music was almost always the province of the priesthood, and in some cultures, it was considered so powerful that music that deviated from the prescribed rituals was strictly forbidden.

'A twelve-part chant was part of Celtic magic as well,' Simon continued, 'and the two traditions may have blended together over time, increasing in significance and importance.'

Standing, Jack went to warm his hands at the fire. 'If you're right, how could we possibly restore something like that? I wouldn't have the foggiest idea where to begin.'

'There might have been a written record,' Simon said thoughtfully. 'That could be where your family comes into it.'

They had been able to trace Montforts as far back as the thirteenth century, but had not been able to find a link between that Montfort – a Glastonbury wool merchant – and Edmund, twelfth-century monk of the Abbey. When they'd questioned Edmund directly, he'd merely said, '*Blood helps the link, sometimes . . . oftentimes it obscures . . .*' Over the months, Simon had become aware of distinct personality traits apparent in their otherworldly correspondent, and this was Edmund at his cagiest.

Jack rocked on his heels, a mannerism that should have been clumsy on so large a man, but was not. 'Do you seriously think something like that could have survived intact all these years?'

'Abbey deeds were found in a parish church fairly recently.' Simon made an effort to keep his voice calm. To discover an untouched fragment of the past, hold it in his hands—

'But say we did find this chant, then what would we do? We couldn't sing it ourselves—'

'Let's not put the cart before the horse here,' Simon soothed. 'We may not even be on the right track. It is interesting, though, that most of us – including your Anglican friend – have a strong interest in church music.'

'Winnie! Bloody hell! I'm supposed to be at the Vicarage for dinner in a quarter of an hour. I completely forgot. And Winnie's invited the Archdeacon and her husband, and her brother – a peacemaking attempt of sorts – so there'll be hell to pay if I'm late. I'd better fly.' With that, he grabbed his coat from the peg by the door, and was gone.

Simon followed him to the porch and stood for a time, ignoring the cold, gazing up at the patch of starlit sky visible through a gap in the foliage above his garden. Did Jack Montfort have any idea of the significance of what they'd just learned? Or of its inherent possibilities?

Perhaps, decided Simon, it was just as well he did not. They had gone beyond parlour games now, and it was time to test allegiances. He went inside for his car keys, and set out to pay a visit.

It seemed to Faith that every day it got harder to walk up the bloody hill. The steep incline of Wellhouse Lane was made more treacherous by the slimy mat of dead leaves coating the tarmac, and if she fell she'd be as helpless as an overturned tortoise. The baby's feet were lodged firmly in her diaphragm, and the pressure of its head on her sciatic nerve sent pain shooting down her thigh – at least that was what Garnet had told her, and Garnet would know.

Faith stopped, panting, pressing her palm into the small of her back and wiggling feet already swollen from a day of standing behind the café's counter. She could hear the trickle of water beneath her feet. These hills were honeycombed with water – it ran in the culverts laid under the tarmac; it leached from the verges and sprang from every nook and cranny.

Wood smoke lay heavy on the still, damp air. Garnet would have the stove lit, and Faith imagined the smoke rising from the chimney, spilling down the hillside like a cloak, hiding everything beneath it from mortal sight. But then she had been thinking strange things of late, and her dreams were stranger still.

It was odd that the nearer she came to having her baby, the more she missed her own mother. Often now, she dreamed she heard her mother's voice calling her name – sometimes she even felt her mum's hand on her brow, stroking back her hair – and then she would wake in the silent, cold room, the only living presence the calico cat curled on the foot of her bed.

Stepping carefully on the slippery tarmac, she began the uphill trudge again. To her left rose the massive cone of the Tor, blotting out the sky. When she had first come to live with Garnet, she'd liked to climb up to the head of the spring above the farmhouse and gaze out over the Levels, imagining centuries past and the land below her covered with water, Glastonbury an island in the Summer Sea.

But now the pull of the Tor was too strong – she

carried it with her, waking and sleeping. Was this feeling of oppressive power bound up with what Jack and the others were trying to do? Or was it something else entirely, something so old and dark it stretched beyond memory?

She wished she could talk to Winnie about it. Winnie listened without judging, without trying to make you see things her way. But she was no longer sure she could trust Winnie, after what Garnet had told her. That saddened her, as did her decision not to see her family. As much as she missed them, that was not her path. Faith knew that as surely as she knew she held two lives in her hands.

The smell of smoke grew stronger as she reached the farmyard gate. The yard was a pool of shadow beneath the peaked slate roof of the house. But as she clicked the gate latch, the door opened. Garnet stood outlined against the kitchen's warm glow, looking anxiously out into the dusk, and Faith hurried to meet her.

Other than Andrew Catesby, Jack had not met Winnie's guests before.

Archdeacon Suzanne Sanborne, Winnie's immediate superior, was a woman in her forties with short, dark, silver-streaked hair that curled about her square jaw. She had a forthright manner and a talent for putting people at their ease, and Jack knew that Winnie both liked and admired her.

The Archdeacon's husband, David Sanborne, was a physician with a busy practice in Street. His mild demeanour made an interesting contrast to his wife's more forceful personality.

Both Sanbornes seemed well acquainted with Andrew Catesby, as was Winnie's friend Fiona Allen and her husband, Bram. The two women listened to Andrew with rapt attention, laughing at his stories on cue, and it seemed odd to Jack that a man so attractive to women had never married. Andrew did a good job of excluding him from the general conversation, but no one else seemed aware of it, and Jack was content to observe until Winnie called the party in to dinner.

Winnie had painted the dining room the colour of aubergines, which made the large space seem smaller and more intimate. Above the table, she'd hung a Victorian chandelier she'd found in a junk shop, polishing the brass until it gleamed and filling it with candles. The effect was lovely. And Winnie looked lovely herself in the candle glow, in a dress of midnight-blue velvet that set off the blue of her eyes and the creaminess of her skin. Was it Jack's imagination, or was Andrew watching his sister even more intently than usual?

As they started on the first course, David Sanborne addressed Andrew: 'Any new projects on the archaeological front since I saw you last?'

'There are always projects – it's the funding for them that's scarce.' Andrew's smile was acid. 'It's not newsworthy, is it, digging for shards of sixth-century pottery? But then you have chappies calling themselves Pendragon and digging up the High Street for treasure with a bulldozer, and that makes the front page.'

Suzanne chuckled. 'That did cause a bit of a stir in the town council. Mr Pendragon would probably rate as a genuine English eccentric.'

'I can testify to that.' Bram Allen smiled. 'It happened right in front of my gallery, so I had a ringside seat. Right out of King Arthur, he was, with flowing white hair and a star-covered robe. Had to be forcibly removed, poor chap, and the police impounded the bulldozer.'

'Certifiable, if you ask me,' Andrew said too loudly. 'All these mumbo-jumbo followers are loony, spouting off about dreams and visions.'

Fiona Allen went very still, and into the awkward silence Winnie said, 'The Biblical prophets might take exception to that view, wouldn't you say, Suzanne?'

The conversation moved on as they progressed through poached salmon with dill sauce and new potatoes, but there was a distinct feeling of unease at the table.

After the salad, Winnie served a lemon roulade that she readily admitted was shop-bought. 'I don't have the patience for puddings,' she said. 'They're too fiddly – all that measuring and sifting.'

'Why bother when you can buy things like this?' Fiona took the last bite of her portion with a contented sigh. 'Mind you, I'll expect this the next time I come for lunch.'

'Not too soon, I hope,' her husband said. 'Or my gallery walls will be bare. Fiona's been doing more lunching than painting lately.'

'Painter's block, would you call it?' asked David Sanborne with interest.

'Something like that,' Fiona replied tersely, casting an injured glance at Bram.

'Coffee, anyone?' Winnie said brightly, and received a relieved-sounding chorus of affirmatives.

'I'll help, shall I?' Andrew offered as they rose to return to the drawing room.

'Jack and I can manage,' Winnie shot back, and the look Andrew gave Jack could have drawn blood.

Returning to the drawing room after he had helped Winnie clear the table, Jack made an effort to ignore Andrew. He slipped Handel's 'Dixit Dominus' in the CD player, and as the conversation flowed around him, he thought of what he and Simon had discussed. Was it possible that they were right in thinking it was the Abbey's lost chant Edmund wanted them to find?

Winnie's recent warning about Simon crossed his mind, but he dismissed it easily enough. Surely Winnie had been mistaken – perhaps overly zealous in defence of her dead friend. And if not – if Simon had done such an unscrupulous thing, Jack could not believe it was more than an isolated incident that Simon had later regretted.

Hoping for a moment alone with Winnie, he went back into the kitchen. She stood at the worktop, her back to him, stacking cups and saucers on a tray. He placed his hands on her shoulders and bent to kiss her exposed shoulder just above the neckline of her dress. She relaxed against him, and he wrapped his arms round her.

But before he could speak he felt a prickling at the back of his neck, and a small current of air. Turning, he saw Andrew Catesby standing in the doorway, watching them.

'Oh, good, Andrew – you can carry the coffee,' said Winnie, as if nothing were amiss, but Jack had seen the venom in her brother's eyes.

With a forced smile, she handed Jack the cheese tray, and as he left the kitchen he heard Andrew say, 'Not very fitting behaviour for a priest, fawning all over him like a common tart.'

Winnie snapped something in reply that Jack couldn't quite make out. He'd turned back, determined to intervene, when Winnie came out of the kitchen, cheeks flaming.

'Winnie—'

'Later. We'd better serve the guests.'

They returned to the drawing room, and when Andrew had joined them, David Sanborne said, 'Nice choice, the Handel. I believe that's what the Somerfield choir is doing at Christmas this year – am I right, dear?' He glanced at his wife.

'Our Nigel's hanging on to his soprano part by a hair, I'm afraid. We're all praying his voice will hold another few months.'

'It must be frustrating for boys that age, being neither fish nor fowl,' said Winnie, her colour still high. 'And then just when they've got themselves sorted out, grown a bit of hair on their chests, they have to move up and deal with Andrew.'

'I do what I can,' Andrew said. 'Vile, back-stabbing little buggers, most of them. Your son excepted, of course.' He nodded at the Sanbornes.

David Sanborne grinned. 'Sixth-formers shaping up this year, are they?'

'As well as they ever do, meaning it would take a miracle to make historians out of them.' He gave Jack a malevolent glance. 'Montfort here is an amateur historian of a sort – why don't you tell them about your interest in the history of the Abbey?'

The bastard, thought Jack, groping for an acceptable answer. 'Just a bit of local genealogy, really. It's odd, but with both my parents gone, I suddenly realized I wanted to know more about my family. I've been able to trace Montforts in Glastonbury as far back as the twelve hundreds, but earlier than that it gets fuzzy.'

'Montfort's a French name, surely,' said Fiona, who had been quiet since her husband's dig about her painting. 'If your ancestors didn't arrive until after the Conquest, that would explain why the trail disappears.'

'Any relation to Simon de Montfort, the reformer?' asked Bram.

'An interesting idea,' Andrew mused, 'but that de Montfort came to a very bad end. His revolutionary zeal got him gutted on the battlefield, I believe.'

'Simon Fitzstephen's been remarkably helpful,' Jack said as he saw Winnie blanch. 'I'm sure if there was a connection, he would have found it.'

'Yes, but would he have told you?' murmured Suzanne. Then, seeing all eyes turned on her expectantly, she shook her head slightly. 'Oh, that was out of turn. Too much wine, I expect. It's just that Simon's been known to withhold information when it suited him. Church politics can be surprisingly vicious, and Simon was a master player.'

David Sanborne stood. 'I think I'd better take you home, my dear, before you become indiscreet. And I've got early surgery tomorrow – you know what they say, farmers and doctors never get a lie-in.'

'We'd better be going too,' said Bram Allen. 'Fiona needs her rest. It's been an interesting evening, Winnie. Unparalleled, you might say.'

As they made their farewells, Fiona took Jack's hand. With a glance at her husband, she said softly, 'I *am* glad to meet you.'

It was a fine, crisp night, with stars hard and bright in a clear sky, and when the two couples had left, Andrew remained on the porch, shifting from one foot to the other. Winnie moved closer to Jack, slipping an arm round his waist.

'Well, I'll leave you two young lovers to it, shall I?' Andrew spat, then turned on his heel, and strode away. A moment later his car sped out of the drive.

Guiding Winnie by the shoulder, Jack stepped inside and shut the door. In the brighter light of the hall, he could see that her eyes were swimming with unshed tears.

'He was beastly,' she said. 'Absolutely beastly.'

'I'm sorry, love. It's my fault for getting you into this—'

'If it's anyone's fault it's mine, for not seeing this coming – but there's no excuse for his behaviour.'

'Winnie, he's jealous! And I think he's terrified of losing you.'

'No, there's something wrong, really wrong, but he

won't talk to me. We were best friends for most of our lives, and now I seem to have become the enemy.'

'Let's not think about Andrew right now.' He pulled her to him and stroked her hair. 'You're cold. Come in by the fire – I've something to tell you.'

Pushing the chair back, Gemma stretched, yawning, then sipped at the dregs of cold tea in her mug. The clock on the cooker in her tiny kitchen alcove read half past eleven, and if she didn't get to bed she'd be struggling at work tomorrow. Giving the papers on the tabletop a half-hearted shuffle to straighten them, she stood and padded into Toby's room in her stocking feet.

Although it was one of the first cold nights of the autumn, he'd kicked off his small duvet and lay spread-eagled on his stomach. It wouldn't be long before he outgrew his junior bed; how would they would fit anything larger into what was essentially a boxroom?

Giving the covers a last pat, she turned away with a sigh. They would just have to manage. She wasn't willing to contemplate leaving the garage flat just now – one change at a time was enough.

The adjustment to the new job had been more difficult than she'd expected. Although she'd been a rookie at Notting Hill, she'd just had her own bit of turf to worry about in those days. In the past two months she'd discovered that the reality of command was a different beast altogether, and with it came a mountain of paperwork that was never finished – hence her midnight stint at the table with cold tea. Added to that was the lingering sexism demonstrated by both her chief inspector and some of the male officers under her command. Only now did she realize how much she had taken her working relationship with Kincaid for granted, and how much it had insulated her from active prejudice.

These problems were complicated by her enforced separation from Kincaid; between their schedules they were lucky to snatch a few hours together in a week. She told herself daily that she *had* made the right decision, that things would get easier, that she wouldn't let herself whinge over changes that had been her own choice. But more and more often she found herself awake and restless long past a sensible hour, wondering just exactly what it was she wanted from her life.

She poured the remains of her tea down the sink and rinsed the cup, then wandered round the room, turning down the bed and picking up stray toys and books. She found the routine comforting, for although she was physically tired, she didn't feel ready to sleep.

Rummaging in the trunk that served her as a wardrobe, she found the ancient flannelette nightdress she hadn't worn since the previous winter. For a moment, she held the fabric to her face, feeling the softness against her skin and inhaling the scent of her mother's rose sachet. The nightdress had been a much-coveted Christmas gift from her parents while she was still at school. She had never quite managed to part with it, even during her marriage to Rob, although he'd hated it with a passion he usually reserved for rival football teams.

She slipped out of her clothes and put the nightdress on, then found a pair of heavy socks. Armed against the chill, she went into the bathroom and brushed her hair until it crackled, then washed her face and cleaned her teeth. She saved using the loo until last, as a good-luck charm of sorts, but when she checked the loo paper, there was no trace of pink.

The panic that welled up in her left her shaking, nauseated. But there was really no need to worry, she told herself – she was only a few days late – and there was certainly no need to tell Kincaid. Not yet.

Chapter Seven

> *So many holy men have prayed and died at Glastonbury that the spiritual atmosphere is alive and aglow. Their dust, mingling with the earth, sanctifies the very ground beneath our feet.*
>
> Dion Fortune, from
> *Glastonbury: Avalon of the Heart*

It rained heavily during the night. After Jack left, Winnie had tossed and turned, drifting in and out of a fitful sleep in which the sound of water falling was ever present. But the day dawned clear and freshly washed, and she woke feeling surprisingly lucid and serene, considering her interrupted night and the task she had set herself that day.

She had put off too long her visit to Simon, and what Jack had told her last night made it imperative that she talk to him. But first, she said her Morning Office; then, when she had dressed and breakfasted, she wheeled her old bike from the garden shed and cycled the two miles into Glastonbury. She reached the Abbey at half past nine, just as the gates were opening. Here she would be able to collect herself, to work out just what she meant to say.

Stowing her bike in the rack, she paid her admission and pushed through the turnstile. The museum exhibits were artfully done and informative, but she passed them by and exited through the glass doors that led to the Abbey grounds.

There, she stood on the step, transfixed. The sky was a perfect robin's-egg blue, the emerald grass sparkled with moisture from the night's rain, and the stone walls of the Abbey ruins shone golden in the morning sun.

This was why she had come. Once she was inside the Abbey precinct, the very air and light seemed different. It was as if she had stepped into an illuminated page of a manuscript, and the sweet, unlikely scent of apple blossom filled the air. It came to her that for a short while she might, if she chose, transcend time *and* season.

Winnie stepped down into the grass, unmindful of the damp that immediately began to soak into her shoes. Before her lay the exquisite Lady Chapel, its moss-grown walls casting lengthy black shadows on the grass.

But that was not what she had come to see. The Lady Chapel dated from just after Edmund's time, and she was searching for a physical, concrete link to Edmund. She turned to the east, with the orchard on her right. There, ridges in the grass marked the monks' kitchen; a fragment of a wall, the refectory. In her mind, Winnie began to restore it. Stone by stone, the walls went up, the long oak tables filled with brothers in their coarse brown robes. They ate in silence. From a raised lectern at one end of the hall, a monk read to them, so that their minds might be nourished as well as their bodies.

Winnie moved on, into the square depression in the grass that had been the cloisters. There, the monks were busy at their tasks, and on the north side, where the light was best, the copyists and illuminators worked in their carrels. And there, that was Edmund, bent over a page of vellum, inking the glowing design of a capital with a fine and steady hand. Had he been tall and fair, like Jack? Had his hands ached from cramp and cold as he worked through the brief winter days? For a moment, she imagined that he might look up and meet her eyes, and know her, but the image faded and she saw only the windswept grass.

From the cloisters she entered the nave of the Great Church, drawn, as she'd known she would be, towards the Choir. Passing through the ruined and jagged buttresses of the north and south transepts, she saw it as it had been. Here it was that a great scissor arch had thrust skyward, supporting the vault. The weathered stone of the remaining walls gleamed with gilt, the gaping windows glittered with the jewel colours of glass, stalls of rich, dark oak filled the empty greensward. And in the stalls, monks, possessors of a chant kept secret through centuries.

It was their voices she could hear, lifted in praise, weaving a tapestry of joy more real than the stones that surrounded them.

In that instant, she knew the chant for what it was. She knew why the monks had been willing to die for it, and she knew, too, why Edmund and those like him had reached out across the centuries in an effort to restore it.

For centuries people had searched for a *thing*, a cup – had even claimed to have found it here in Glastonbury, secreted away in the *holiest eyrth in England* – not realizing that the Grail was only a symbol of something too immense to contain in a physical vessel.

Winnie sat in the Café Galatea, her icy hands wrapped round a mug of steaming tea. She had no recollection of leaving the Abbey, but she must have, for here she was, and with her old bike propped against the front window. She felt oddly detached from herself, as if she had been ill for a long time and forgotten how to use her limbs. Her vision had already begun to fade and she wanted desperately to hold on to it as tightly as she clutched the cup in her hands, but at some level she knew this was not possible. It was too much for an ordinary person to bear for any length of time – after all, hadn't Galahad died from the rapture of it? And he had been prepared for miracles.

She had an image of herself glowing so fiercely from the inside that any sudden movement might split a seam and release the radiance within. This made her laugh aloud, and the waiter – a man with a ponytail and a round, freckled face – looked at her and smiled. He probably thought she was tipsy, and as if to prove it, she hiccupped. Smiling back at him, she rose and left coins on the table to cover tea and tip.

Jack! She must tell Jack what she had seen. But he

had gone to Bath that morning on a commission for a client. She would have to wait, then, and in the meantime she had pastoral calls to make, and it was more important than ever that she should see Simon Fitzstephen.

Simon's visit the previous evening had been both unexpected and perturbing. There had been a time when Garnet would have welcomed the attention, would have been excited – aroused even – by the chance to learn from him. But she had soon discovered that the knowledge Simon possessed was all intellectual, not instinctive – and if there was any passion in it, it was for his reputation alone. How could someone who had studied the Grail so thoroughly not be moved by the power and wonder of the tales, or sense the awesome truth behind the legends?

And what had he wanted of her?

She slid the flat end of the long wooden paddle beneath the row of newly fired tiles in the kiln. Carefully, she lifted the paddle and stepped back, until the tiles were free of the confines of the oven. But as she turned to place the tiles on her worktable, her grip on the paddle faltered and it tilted, sending the row crashing to the barn floor.

Garnet stared down at the wreckage in horror. How could she have done something so clumsy? Now hours' worth of work were gone to waste, and she was already behind schedule on this commission.

Hands trembling, she set the paddle aside and sank onto her stool. The dreams – it must be the dreams . . .

They had begun again in the past few months, haunting her with faces she'd thought long forgotten, tormenting her with a sense of urgency she only vaguely understood. Added to that was her worry over Faith and the rapidly approaching birth of Faith's baby, and the growing fear that the two things were somehow connected.

Believing knowledge to be the best weapon against powers that affect the mind, she had tried to teach Faith how to defend herself without frightening her, and without communicating her own unease.

But more and more often she found herself snapping at the girl, even when she knew the real target of her anger was her own sense of inadequacy. She'd stopped Faith climbing the hillside above the farmhouse; between them she and Buddy kept an eye on her as best they could; and yet every day Faith seemed to feel the pull of the Tor more strongly.

What else could she do to protect this child who had come to mean so much to her? She had thought about enlisting Winnie Catesby, but no – that way was closed to her now. If Winnie knew the truth about the child, she could not be trusted, and if not, Garnet could not tell her.

That left her one option: she must try to set right the sins that had haunted her for so long. Perhaps that would stop the build-up of forces whose unleashing could only result in another tragedy.

Her ruined tiles forgotten, Garnet gathered her cloak from its hook and set off to pay a call on an old friend, knowing that her visit would not be welcome.

*

Winnie wheeled the bike to a stop in front of Jack's house and gazed down the drive. His Volvo was nowhere in sight. She felt an instant's rush of disappointment, then chided herself. Surely he would be back soon – it was almost five o'clock. She'd get herself some tea and have a word with Faith while she waited.

Hopping back on the bike, she cycled round the corner into Wellhouse Lane. She left the bike against the ribbon-decorated tree in the café's forecourt and went inside. There were no other customers, and for a moment she thought the small kitchen empty as well. Then Faith's shorn head appeared above the serving bar as she said, 'Sorry. Can I – Winnie!'

'How are you, dear? Can a person get a cup of tea in this place?' Winnie asked cheerfully, hoping she hadn't let her shock show. Gone was the rosy bloom Faith had exhibited through most of her pregnancy. The girl looked utterly exhausted, and her skin had an unhealthy pallor. 'Why don't you make yourself a cuppa and sit down with me? Where's Buddy this afternoon?'

'Gone to the superstore for supplies. He didn't like to leave me – you'd think I couldn't manage the place by myself.' Faith turned and busied herself with kettle and mugs. When she had the tea ready, she came round the bar and set their mugs down at the table. The girl looked ungainly now, Winnie saw, her arms and legs too thin in contrast to her distended abdomen.

'Are you feeling all right, Faith?'

'I'm not sleeping too well these days.' Faith attempted a smile. 'The baby presses on my diaphragm when I lie down – makes me feel I can't breathe.'

'Have you been to the clinic, had a check-up?'

The girl shook her head adamantly. 'Garnet says it's perfectly normal. And I've only a few weeks to go now.'

'But—' Winnie saw Faith raise her chin in the familiar stubborn gesture, and subsided into silence. She took a sip of her tea, then tried again. 'We've missed you. You haven't come to see us lately.'

'Is there anything new . . . with Edmund?' Faith asked eagerly, her eyes alight.

'Oh, yes. We've made progress at last. Yesterday, Jack and Simon learned that Edmund was there when Thurstan, the first Norman abbot, had some of the monks murdered in the church itself. The one place they were assured sanctuary, and their own abbot . . .' She shuddered. 'I can't imagine how terrible it must have been.'

'We learned about that when I did archaeology at school,' Faith said, frowning. 'It's the only time blood was shed in the history of the Abbey – unless you count Richard Whiting. But then Whiting was executed on the Tor, wasn't he?' For a moment the girl seemed far away, wrapped in something Winnie couldn't see, then she looked up and met Winnie's gaze again. 'But I can't remember why Abbot Thurstan had the monks killed.'

'It was the chant. The monks refused to give up their sacred chant. We think—'

The bells hung on the café door chimed as it swung open, and Faith sloshed her tea, startled. Garnet Todd stood in the doorway, wrapped in a long cloak.

'Hullo, Winnie,' Garnet said with a pleased smile;

then it seemed to Winnie that a shadow fell across her face. She stepped down and strode across the damp flagged floor, her cape streaming behind her. She, too, looked drawn and tired – what on earth was wrong here?

'I was just telling Faith we've missed you both.' Winnie tried to mask her concern. 'Why don't you come to Jack's with me? We could catch up on our news while we wait for him to get back from Bath.'

'I—' Garnet seemed to hesitate, then shook her head. 'I wish we could, but I've an appointment – a delivery. Soon, though, we'll all get together.' She put a hand on Faith's shoulder. 'But just now I'd better run Faith home. It's too hard a climb up the hill for her these days.'

'And I've got to lock up,' said Faith, rising awkwardly. 'Then I've some studying to do.' Faith cleared their tea things without meeting Winnie's eyes, and Winnie knew then the rapport of moments ago had shattered.

Shrugging, she said, 'Right. Soon, then.' At the door, however, she turned back. 'You will take care, won't you? Both of you?'

Once outside, she stood her bike upright, then paused. There was a sharpness to the air that matched the clarity of the magenta sky above the Tor, and from somewhere she could have sworn she heard the faint thread of pipes. She felt again the temporal dislocation that Glastonbury sometimes engendered, as if the centuries had eased their boundaries and bled into one another.

Then the sensation passed, and the images of the

morning rushed back into her mind with such force that she felt breathless. She must talk to someone about what she had experienced. With sudden resolution, she began pushing her bike up the lane towards Fiona's house.

Nick Carlisle struggled to conceal his impatience with the elderly woman who couldn't make up her mind between a book on the Glastonbury Zodiac and one proclaiming the *Return of the Goddess.* In the end, having spent half an hour dithering, she put down both books and smiled beatifically at him, saying, 'I think I'll come back another day, dear.'

Nick summoned a smile and locked the door after her. It was already well past closing. He might have sold her the Goddess book if he'd pushed a bit, but he had no stomach for such things these days.

He wandered towards the back of the shop, checking the tables for out-of-place material, stopping only when he reached the small nook that held Dion Fortune's books. Running his fingertip along the spines, he frowned.

Fortune had acknowledged the old gods, but she had understood the need for balance between the Christian and the pagan, the Abbey and the Tor. What would she have thought of the pagan revival creeping through Glastonbury like a stain?

Lately, there was a darkness in the more bizarre fringe in Glastonbury, an underlying rumble of destructiveness that made him apprehensive. It didn't do to place too much credence in rumours in

Glastonbury, but there had been hints of rituals, a whisper of sacrifice and of a growing desire to unleash old energies long held in check. If this was the Old Religion Garnet Todd was teaching Faith, the latter could be in grave danger.

It had been weeks since he'd seen Faith. Garnet kept her sequestered in that old wreck of a farmhouse, and when he had tried to see her at the café, Garnet had turned up as if she had radar. Or second sight.

He'd thought of going to the police, but Faith was legally an adult, living with Garnet by choice, and if he told them he thought she was being hypnotized, or coerced by dark magic, he'd merely make himself look barmy.

Although Winnie Catesby had refused to give him Faith's parents' address, he'd found it easily enough on his own. One day in the café, when Faith had been talking to Buddy in the shop, Nick had glanced at the student card in her wallet.

He had traced her family to Street; he had even sat at the top of the close, watching the house, looking for some trace of Faith in that sterile cul-de-sac. He could go to her parents now, tell them where Faith was, but they had no power to make her come home. And Faith would know he had betrayed her. That would surely end any hope he might have of continuing as her friend.

Nothing in the past few months had turned out the way he'd imagined – not with Faith, nor with Jack.

Simon Fitzstephen seemed to take up all Jack's free time – and what had Nick Carlisle to offer Jack compared with the renowned Fitzstephen? The bitterness of it burned in Nick's throat, but he knew there was more to his unease than that. The excitement of discovering Jack's gift, the sense of adventure, of mission, had given way to a tension, a foreboding, that made him feel almost physically ill.

He'd thought about chucking it all in, leaving Glastonbury, getting a proper job. Once he'd even got so far as stuffing his meagre belongings into a duffel bag . . . and once, on a very bad day, he'd even thought about going home to Northumberland and facing the music.

Lifting a Dion Fortune book to slot it back into the shelf, he glanced at her photo on the dust jacket. She had understood the power of evil, and had faced it with strength and good sense. If only there were someone like Fortune he could talk to, someone who would not instantly dismiss what he sensed about Garnet, or attribute it to a maladjusted childhood. A priest, perhaps—

Winnie Catesby, of course! It had been right under his nose all along, but somehow he'd never thought of Winnie in her professional capacity. How could he have been so blind?

He would talk to Winnie, tell her the suspicions he had hardly dared to formulate. Then together they could confront Faith, get her to agree to leave Garnet before the baby came. She wouldn't have to go back to her parents; he and Winnie could find a safe place for her.

Locking the shop behind him, he retrieved his motorbike and headed south through the dusk towards Compton Grenville. His heart lifted when he saw

Winnie's small car parked in the gravel drive of the Vicarage.

But there was no answer at the front door, nor did his knocking at the kitchen door bring any response. The house remained dark and silent, and he shivered with more than the chill of evening. He knew, with a sickening sense of urgency he could not explain, that he must find Winnie Catesby, and soon.

'You all right, Fi?' Bram Allen looked up from the remains of his supper.

'Bit of a headache,' she said. He had always seemed to know, with some uncanny sixth sense. 'I think I may be . . . painting . . . when you get back from your council meeting.' She did not acknowledge her hope that this time it might be different. A few days ago, she had asked him to hang some of the recent canvases in the gallery. He had done so under protest, and the resulting awkwardness between them had not been improved by his comments at Winnie's the previous evening.

'Do you want me to stay?' he asked.

'No. I'll be fine.' They both knew that the onset of her visions could be unpredictable, but even as a child Fiona had taken up crayons, then paints, as a means of dealing with it. If she transferred what she saw to paper, the visions no longer terrified her.

Fiona wandered down the corridor to her studio. Bram had built it for her, a glass-walled room on the back of the house, overlooking the deep hollow of Bushy Coombe. Fiona turned on the small lamp that lit only her blank canvas and her palette. She opened her paints and took up a brush.

The voices were clamouring now in her head, and when she looked up the shapes were thronging outside the glass – luminous, winged, half-human creatures; they beckoned to her, and the night sky beyond the glass had become a deep and iridescent blue.

Images began to take shape on the canvas, faces impossibly radiant and severe, and in their midst, the child. At some point Fiona sensed Bram's presence as he stood watching from the doorway, but he did not disturb her, and when she looked round he had gone.

Then all her awareness of things beyond brush and canvas vanished. The tumult of sound had become more distinct, as if someone had fine-tuned a radio, and she realized the voices were singing, singing to her, and the clear melody soared and leapt inside her until she feared her head would burst.

The last colour faded from the sky and wisps of fog began to form in the dips and hollows beneath the Tor. A dilapidated white van hurtled by Winnie – Garnet's, with Faith in the passenger seat, heading up the hill towards the farmhouse.

Rather than allaying her worry, Winnie's visit to the girl had only increased her concern. She would have to manage a word with Garnet in the next few days about Faith's health; perhaps Garnet could shed some light on her emotional state.

And why had Faith seemed suddenly to shut her

out, back in the café, refusing even to meet her gaze? Was it something she'd said?

As Winnie went back over their conversation, something odd struck her. Faith had said she'd done archaeology at Somerfield, which meant she must have been one of Andrew's students. But in that case, why had he never mentioned her? Surely the disappearance of a bright student, a girl in her final year and destined to go on to greater things, would have concerned him? But then lately he had seemed to scorn all his pupils – what had happened to his love of teaching?

Reaching the entrance to Lypatt Lane, Winnie pushed the bike into the narrow opening. The lane would take her into Bulwarks Lane, which overlooked the steep fall of Bushy Coombe, and at its end lay Fiona Allen's house. The sky made a paler channel between the hedges rising high on either side of the lane. A bit of azure lingered in the west, but above her the first brittle stars had appeared. She switched on her bicycle lamp, but it flickered wanly, then went out.

As she picked up her pace, Winnie continued to puzzle over Andrew's odd behaviour. It occurred to her for the first time that perhaps she didn't know her brother at all. The thought alarmed her, and she suddenly longed for Jack's company, for his calm and common-sense response. Surely he would be home by the time she reached Fiona's; she'd ring him from there and ask him to come and collect her.

She reached the little bend where the footpath that ran round the back side of Chalice Hill met Lypatt Lane. Beyond the bend the track became Bulwarks

Lane, and she felt an unexpected stirring of relief that she had almost reached her destination.

Pausing, she checked automatically for oncoming traffic, even though she could not have failed to hear a car on such a still night. The lane was dark as a tunnel now, visible only by the layer of mist that had settled near the ground.

She stepped out, pushing the bike, and a light came out of nowhere, dazzling her, blinding her. Throwing up her arms as she heard the roar of an engine, she sensed a rush of movement towards her.

Just before impact, some tiny fragment of her consciousness noted that there had been no squeal of brakes.

Part Two

Chapter Eight

> *. . . it yet raises the little limited self to the consciousness of a possibility, awful and beautiful, of a contact with something greater than itself, and yet akin; and to the dignity of a mystical fellowship in which isolation ends, and Past and Present are seen as parts of a living whole; points in the circumference of a circle whose radius is Life beyond these limitations.*
>
> Frederick Bligh Bond, from
> *The Gate of Remembrance*

The music changed, slowly; the joyous melody faded, softening, until it became a lament. Fiona sensed an immense sorrow for a passing, an ending, of something precious beyond human understanding, but more than that she could not tell.

At last there was only a hollowness in her head, and beyond the glass there was nothing but darkness and the faint lights of the town across the Coombe. She put down her brush, exhausted. She had no idea of the time – she never kept a clock in the studio – but she could tell by the cramp in her hand and the ache in her back that she'd been painting several hours.

Stepping back, Fiona surveyed the canvas. She,

herself, never named the creatures that came to her, but the critics referred to them as sprites, spirits, or sometimes, angels. Tonight, to her surprise, she had painted them within a framework of greensward and ruined stone walls – the gates of the Abbey itself – and for the first time, the spirits seemed to hold the now-familiar little girl within their protection.

It was only blocked in, of course. She would finish it tomorrow, if there were no more visions. Now she needed rest; but first, a walk, to clear her head.

The house was quiet, breathing in its midnight rhythm, and when she peeped into the bedroom she saw the humped shape of Bram's body under the duvet.

Grabbing an old Barbour off a peg, she let herself out of the front door and stood for a moment, breathing the frosty air. To her left lay Wick Hollow; to the right Bulwarks Lane gave an open view of the Coombe to the west. Threading her way through the garden, she turned to the right, and when she had passed the house a break in the canopy of leaves above her gave a view of the stars.

As she walked, she became aware of movement in the woods, an agitation more intense than the usual nocturnal shufflings of badgers and rabbits. Fiona stopped, listening, wondering what could be disturbing the woodland creatures on such a calm and beautiful night. 'What is it?' she whispered, but there was no response. Feeling uneasy, she continued onwards, but more cautiously.

When a tendril of wind moved down the lane, disturbing a bit of rubbish, she started, then chided herself. It was only a supermarket carrier bag, and as she watched it blew a few more feet, lodging against something larger in the road, a dark shape, perhaps a fallen branch, and beside it a longer, more solid object. Drawing closer, she saw that the more solid shape was oddly human. Another trick of perception, she decided. Her steps slowed until she came to a halt beside the thing.

Not until she knelt and touched the form was she convinced that what she saw was real. It was a woman, her upturned face a pale smudge, and beside her not a branch, but a fallen bicycle. Fiona pulled her small torch from the pocket of her jacket, then gasped as it lit the woman's face.

Jack Montfort came to a halt a yard inside the intensive-care unit, overwhelmed by the sight of the machines and tubes surrounding Winnie's slight, still form. Why hadn't they told him she would look like this – alien, and frail beyond hope? A tube ran into her nose, another into her mouth, and on a shaved strip of her scalp the angry edges of a wound were held closed with clips.

'You're here to see Winifred, aren't you, dear?' a soft Irish voice said beside him.

Jack turned, barely registering a uniform, a friendly smile, and a name badge that read 'Maggie'. He nodded, not trusting his voice.

'You're her "friend," I take it? Her brother came in a bit ago. Took one look, turned green, and bolted, poor man.'

'Did he?' Jack's resolve not to do the same strengthened, as he suspected she had intended.

'It's all these high-tech doodahs give people the willies. But don't let them frighten you. They're just keeping her comfortable, and letting us know how she's doing.'

'How – how is she?'

'We've got her warm and toasty now, and resting quite comfortably. She was hypothermic when they brought her in, and her heart was a bit dicky, but she's stable now—'

'Heart?' A fresh jolt of fear shot through him.

'A bit of cardiac arrhythmia, due to the warming process. All perfectly normal. She's a lucky girl, your Winifred. Do you know where she was found exactly?'

'In Bulwarks Lane, below Glastonbury Tor.'

'On the tarmac itself? Probably saved her life, then. The tarmac would have held the day's heat. A few feet either way into the grass or the ditch . . .' Maggie shook her head ominously.

It had been Suzanne Sanborne who had rung Jack in the early hours of the morning. He had been increasingly uneasy about Winnie – it wasn't like her not to let him know her whereabouts – but he had told himself that she must have had an emergency. He had, in fact, imagined her sitting at the bedside of an ill or dying parishioner. That was an irony too painful now to contemplate.

In a daze, he had driven the thirty miles to the hospital in Taunton. While Andrew Catesby acknowledged him with a tight-lipped nod, Suzanne told him that the police believed Winnie must have been on her way to visit her friend Fiona Allen when she had been struck by a hit-and-run motorist. It had been Fiona who had found her, rung for the police and medical help. Fiona had then rung Andrew, who in turn had called Suzanne. How like Andrew, thought Jack, not to have rung him.

By daybreak, they had still not been allowed to see Winnie, and Suzanne had been unable to stay longer. Left alone with Andrew Catesby, who glared at him from across the waiting room, Jack had left the hospital and driven to police headquarters in Yeovil. There he had seen Detective Inspector Alfred Greely, the officer who had taken the call on Winnie's accident. Greely, a phlegmatic man with a farmer's face and a West Country burr, held out little hope that the driver of the car could be traced. There were no witnesses, and little, if any, possibility of forensic evidence on the bike – their only avenue lay with Winnie herself, if she should awaken and remember something vital.

Now, looking down at her smooth face, calm in a repose more profound than sleep, Jack asked Maggie, 'Can I speak to her? Will she know me?'

'Of course you can, dear, and the more the better. And it's a good bet that when she wakes up, not only will she remember that you've been here, she'll remember everything you've said to her.' Maggie fetched a hospital chair that looked too insubstantial to support Jack's large frame and placed it next to the bed. 'She'll need you to anchor her, give her consciousness a focal point. Talk to her, touch her, hold her hand. Tell her what's happened to her.'

When Jack took Winnie's hand between both of

his, it felt cool and unresponsive. 'Winnie, it's me, Jack,' he began awkwardly. 'You've had a bit of a bump on the head, but you're going to be fine, love.'

'You just keep talking to her,' Maggie instructed when he paused, 'and I'll give you a few more minutes.' She moved away to attend to another patient, her face impassive.

Jack fumbled in his pocket for the prayer book the hospital staff had found in Winnie's handbag and began to read, hoping the familiar and comforting words would somehow reach her. *'O Lord our heavenly Father, Almighty and everlasting God, who has safely brought us to the beginning of this day: Defend us in the same with thy mighty power; and grant that this day we fall into no sin, neither run into any kind of danger; but that all our doings may be ordered by thy governance . . .'* His voice broke; he bowed his head and closed the small leather-bound book with its gilt-edged pages. It was Winnie's, a gift from her parents upon her confirmation, she had told him once. They had been killed in a boating accident shortly afterwards, and the book had become one of her treasures.

How had she managed to survive such grief whole? he wondered. He whispered to her, rubbing her hand between his, telling her he loved her, that she was strong and that he would let nothing – nothing – take her away from him.

Maggie reappeared at his side with a soft touch on his shoulder. 'You'll have to go now, I'm afraid, but you can come back in a couple of hours.' As Jack stood, regretfully letting go Winnie's hand, she added, 'Did I hear someone say that Winifred was a vicar?'

'Of St Mary's, in Compton Grenville.'

'If she likes music, you might bring something for her to listen to. Music can be a very strong trigger for some people, especially if it's an important part of their daily lives.'

'Can I leave this with you?' Jack held out the prayer book. 'In case you have a chance to read to her? Or if she wakes . . .' He looked up, desperately meeting Maggie's hazel eyes. 'What if she wakes up while I'm gone? Or . . .'

Maggie dug a piece of paper and a pen from her pocket. 'You have a mobile phone?' Jack nodded. 'Give me your number, and I'll ring you if there's any change at all.'

Jack thanked her and, with a last look at Winnie, went out into the waiting area. It was then that he sank into the nearest chair, shaken by the realization that he could not bear to lose her, could not bear to go back to the desert that had been his life after Emily's death.

Nor could he bear to sit idly by, waiting. There were too many unanswered questions. What would Winnie tell them *when* – he refused to consider the possibility that it might be *if* – she woke? Why had she been going to see her friend Fiona at that time of evening? Where had she been before that? Why hadn't she rung him? And what had she seen before the car struck her?

There must be something he could do. The police had certainly not shown much interest in investigating the accident. Winnie was much too level-headed to have cycled blindly into the path of an oncoming vehicle. But how else could this have happened, unless someone had deliberately hurt her? And that was unimaginable.

He would go and see Fiona. Perhaps Winnie had rung her, told her something that would explain her unlikely appearance in Bulwarks Lane.

And there was one other person he could call; someone he could trust to tell him if he was completely mad.

Kincaid returned the phone to its cradle on his desk just as his sergeant came into his office with a sheaf of papers in a folder.

'Report from forensics,' Douglas Cullen said, sliding the folder across the desk and pulling up a chair.

'Any joy?'

Cullen shook his head regretfully. 'No, sir. Nothing, zilch, nada.'

Kincaid raised an eyebrow. 'I see you've been watching American telly again.' He suspected that Cullen liked to imagine himself a tough, *NYPD Blue*-type detective – a harmless enough fantasy as long as it didn't get in the way of his work – but surely no one could look a less likely candidate. With his fair hair, spectacles, and rosy-cheeked, schoolboy complexion, Cullen was the very image of the traditional English bobby.

For the past two weeks, they'd been working on a case that looked disturbingly as if it might be the beginning venture of a serial killer. The victim, the owner of an antiques stall in Camden Passage, had been found on her own premises, and so far they had not turned up a smidgen of useful evidence. Kincaid had begun to think that the killer had worn a hermetically sealed suit, and been invisible to boot.

As he opened the folder, his mind wandered to his recent – and unexpected – phone call from his cousin Jack Montfort and the dilemma it had presented him.

How long had it been since he'd seen Jack? He had been away on a case when Emily and the baby died . . . It would have been his aunt's funeral, then, but he had done little more than shake Jack's hand and offer his condolences before rushing back to London.

If there was anyone who'd had more than his share of tragedy, it was his cousin. But now it seemed Jack's new love was lying in hospital and he seemed distraught, fearing that the hit-and-run might not have been an accident. Hesitantly, Jack had urged, 'You could come for the weekend, just see what you think.'

'But I'd have no jurisdiction,' Kincaid had protested.

'It doesn't matter. I just . . . It would be good to see you.'

His mother and Jack's had been close, and the families had spent extended time together in the summers when the children were small. Jack had been a rather solemn but likeable boy, always ready for an adventure, and he had grown into an engaging and generous man. Kincaid's memories of the holiday Jack had given him in his Yorkshire time-share had been marred by Emily's death so shortly afterwards, but the thoughtfulness of the offer had been typical of Jack.

'I'll let you know if I can work something out,' Kincaid answered, ringing off. As much as he regretted letting Jack down, he had no real intention of driving to Somerset for the weekend.

There was no way he could leave London; something might break on the case, and Doug Cullen wasn't experienced enough to handle it alone. And he and Gemma had managed little enough time together lately – he'd been hoping to make the most of Kit's plans to spend the weekend with friends.

He shuffled papers resolutely, determined to focus on the matter at hand. But as he read through the disappointingly negative report, he couldn't quite forget the desperation he'd heard in Jack's final words. His cousin needed his support, and Kincaid suspected how dearly it had cost Jack to ask for it.

'Sir?'

'Oh, sorry, Cullen. Afraid I was wool-gathering.'

'You've not heard a word I've said.' Cullen sounded a bit injured. Kincaid gazed at his sergeant speculatively. He was a sound lad; perhaps it was time he had a chance to sink or swim. And Gemma . . . If her touchiness the past few weeks was anything to go by, Gemma badly needed a holiday. The question was whether he could convince her to take it.

He smiled at Doug Cullen. 'Think you could manage on your own for a few days, Sergeant?'

When Jack rang him at the bookshop with news of Winnie's accident, Nick felt a sharp jolt of relief. Cold, hunger, and common sense had driven him back to his caravan the previous evening, but he'd not been able to rid himself of a gnawing feeling of foreboding.

'How – how is she?' Nick asked.

'Unconscious, but stable. They'll let me in to see her again soon,' Jack told him.

'Is there anything I can do?'

'Let the others know, if you can. I'll ring you if there's any . . . change.' Jack's voice had wavered and Nick sensed the control it took him to keep it steady.

'Right. I – I'm sorry, Jack.' Unable to find anything more adequate to say, Nick hung up. He stood, then flipped the sign on the shop door and locked it as he left. He would tell Faith, but not on the telephone.

He found her ladling pumpkin soup into bowls, the scent of cinnamon and spices combating the dankness in the café. Next door in the shop, Buddy was on the phone, the murmur of his voice an underlying accompaniment to the Gregorian chant playing over the sound system.

When Faith had served her customers, Nick leaned over the bar and whispered urgently, 'Have you heard about Winnie?'

For the first time since he'd entered, Faith looked at him directly. Colour drained from her already wan face. 'Winnie?'

'She was on her bike last night, in Bulwarks Lane. Someone hit her. She's in hospital, unconscious.'

'Wh-what?' Gripping the serving bar, Faith gave a dazed little shake of her head. 'That's not possible. She was here— Oh!' Her eyes widened. 'We saw her, after. I could've sworn she said she was going to Jack's, but she was pushing her bike *up* the lane.'

'We?'

'Garnet and I. On our way home. Winnie was turning into Lypatt Lane—'

'It must have happened right afterwards, then. You didn't see anything – or anyone else, did you?'

'No,' whispered Faith. 'But Garnet – Garnet went out again, in the van. Maybe she . . . when she came back . . . she was . . .'

'She was what?'

'I don't know. Odd. She didn't want to talk to me, or help me study. She went into her office and closed the door.'

Nick's heart began to race. 'Faith.' He leaned over the bar until his face was inches from hers. 'Go home as soon as you can. Check the bumper on the van. But don't let Garnet see you do it.'

'What are you talking about? Why should I—' She stared at him, two bright spots of colour flaming on her pale cheeks. 'You don't think Garnet had something to do with Winnie's accident? You're crazy. Nick! I won't! I won't even think such a thing!'

Several customers looked up from their meals at the sound of rising hysteria in her voice.

'It's only taking logical precautions,' he whispered. 'You must see that. What can it—'

'Get out, Nick!' she shouted at him. 'I'm not listening to you, so just get the bloody hell out!'

Flushing under the fascinated stares of the café's diners, Nick had no choice but to leave.

Garnet heard about Winnie from a customer, the vicar of the church on the edge of Salisbury Plain. The ecclesiastical community was a small one, and news travelled fast. She had finished installing her tiles, then driven back to Glastonbury and the sanctuary of her workshop, her mind working furiously all the while.

Winnie was lying in hospital, more likely to die than live, if the vicar's information were correct.

In spite of the heat radiating from the wood-fired kiln Garnet was shivering with cold, and the midday sun falling in a bright block across the threshold of the barn door beckoned. Taking her stool, she moved it into the sun and sat there gratefully.

The weight of regrets, past and present, lay heavily upon her. There were so many things she had meant to do, so many things she had hoped to accomplish; now suddenly she saw the years remaining to her dwindling to a pinpoint, then blinking futilely out – as had a child's life, so many years ago.

But Faith – and Faith's child – had given her an unlooked-for chance at redemption.

By her calculations, Faith would give birth on Samhain, 31 October, All Hallows' Eve, the day when the veil between the worlds was at its thinnest. The Tor had drawn the girl from the beginning – that was why she had come to the café, and to Garnet. Such a birth in such a place would open a gateway, unleash ancient powers that could wreak havoc beyond imagining. Once, Garnet had thought she could use that force, control it, but cruel experience had taught her otherwise. The Old Ones had never been gentle gods, and they had never been concerned with human welfare.

The path was set, the signs unmistakable; Faith

could no more turn from it than she could will herself to stop breathing.

Garnet knew that only she had the knowledge necessary to halt the gathering storm. And if last night she had failed in the task she had set herself, she must bear that burden as well.

But she would not fail again.

Chapter Nine

> *Glastonbury is the gateway to the unseen . . . The long road from London spans the breadth of England and leads from one world to another.*
>
> Dion Fortune, from
> *Glastonbury: Avalon of the Heart*

'Jack!' Fiona Allen opened her door wide. 'Is Winnie all right?'

'She's still unconscious. But they let me see her for a bit, and the nurse says she's doing well.'

Motioning him inside, she said, 'Sit down, please, and let me get you something to drink.'

Jack sank into a chair and rubbed at the stubble on his jaw. 'No, I'm fine, really.' He found himself grateful for a few moments' respite, and Fiona Allen's very ordinariness was a comfort.

The house, too, was welcoming, its interior a contrast from the unassuming stone façade and the proper cottage garden. Spare and open, the sitting room had polished oak floorboards and clean-lined furniture covered with batiked prints. There were books, and a few strategically placed wooden carvings and masks, but not a painting anywhere in sight.

Perching on a rattan ottoman, Fiona said, 'I've rung the hospital a dozen times, but they won't tell me much. *Resting comfortably* is a terrible euphemism.'

'Head injuries are very unpredictable, apparently.' He tried to banish the image of Winnie, motionless in her hospital bed. 'I wanted to see you, Fiona - see if there was anything you could tell me about last night. Do you have any idea what Winnie was doing in your lane?'

'It does seem odd, doesn't it? She must have been coming to see me. There's no one else along here.'

'If you hadn't found her—' Jack stopped, embarrassed by the sudden sting of tears.

'But that's odd too,' Fiona said thoughtfully. 'I don't usually go for walks at that time of night. But I'd been painting and I needed the air.'

'Coincidence?'

'Probably. But—' Fiona gazed at him, then seemed to change the subject. 'I want to show you something.' She stood and led the way towards the back of the house.

Baffled, Jack followed her through the open sitting area and into a corridor, where she opened a door and entered a glass-walled studio.

Beyond the glass the ground dropped away, so that the room seemed to hang in space, suspended over the Coombe with its white puffs of sheep in the green grass, like a child's drawing of clouds in an emerald sky. Canvases were stacked neatly against the walls, but face-inwards, as was the canvas on the easel. 'You don't display your paintings?'

'I don't need to see them,' Fiona said baldly. 'But

this one . . . this one was different.' She turned the canvas on the easel round.

Jack felt his mouth go dry. He'd seen the paintings in magazines, and occasionally in a gallery window in Glastonbury, but he hadn't been prepared for the power and immediacy of such an intimate exposure. 'They're . . .'

'Don't you dare use the *F* word,' said Fiona, when he hesitated.

'*F* word?'

'Fairies.' She scowled. 'Like Tinkerbell. Victorian. Silly, fluffy things.'

Jack shook his head. 'No. They . . . I was going to say they frighten me. They remind me of Blake's visions. Beautiful. And terrible.'

'Exactly.' Fiona met his eyes. 'But this one– Oddly enough, in the twenty-some-odd years I've lived here in Glastonbury, I've never painted the Abbey before. So why paint it now, on this particular night?'

The creatures, some winged, some not, with their severe asexual faces, thronged round the familiar silhouette of the ruined Great Church, hands extended in supplication. Behind them, the sky was a mottled bruise reflecting the setting sun, pierced by the dark shape of the Tor.

Fiona turned back to the canvas. 'And there was something else. They sang to me. I can't describe it. It was' – she shrugged – 'it was the most beautiful thing I've ever heard, and yet the saddest. I'd give anything if I could recreate it, even in my head, but I can't. That's not my gift.' Her voice was filled with regret.

Slowly, Jack said, 'Did Winnie ever speak to you about what we were doing?'

'The automatic writing? A bit.'

'You didn't think it odd?'

Fiona smiled. 'What's *odd* to me? I've lived with oddness since I was a child. Is your expression of a voice from the past any more strange than my ability to see things that other people can't?'

'I suppose not. We've guessed all along that Edmund communicated with me for a reason, but now we think it may have something to do with the sacred chant that was banished from the Abbey after the Conquest.' He gestured at her painting. 'It seems more than coincidence that you should paint this, and hear singing, on a night that Winnie was coming unexpectedly to see you.'

'If only she'd rung me first . . .'

'Do you know of anything that might have been worrying her?'

Frowning, Fiona ran a finger along the edge of her canvas. 'I know she was quite distressed by Andrew's behaviour. I suppose a rift was inevitable when Winnie formed a strong attachment to someone else – Andrew had taken her for granted for too many years – but I wouldn't have expected him to go so far off the rails.'

'Do you think he would hurt her?'

'Hurt Winnie? I shouldn't think so.' Fiona sounded less than confident. 'But after the dinner party, I'd think *you* should watch your back.'

'Did you see or hear anything – or anyone – unusual last night?'

'I was painting. I didn't even hear Bram come in. But . . . I've been thinking about it since . . . There was something, before I found Winnie . . . The woods seemed unsettled . . . as if there was violence lingering in the air.' She shot him a sharp glance, then turned away, gazing down into the Coombe, where the gathering clouds made flying shadows on the grass. '*If* someone did this to Winnie . . . has it occurred to you that, having failed, they might try again?'

Surely Winnie was safe as long as she was in hospital, Jack told himself, but his foot seemed to press harder on the accelerator of its own accord.

He was returning from Compton Grenville, where he'd scoured the Vicarage for things he hoped might comfort Winnie. Her favourite nightdress, her hairbrush, a small CD player, and discs of the music she loved most.

In moments he'd reached Ashwell Lane. A quick wash, a change of clothes, and he would be on his way back to Taunton.

Leaving the car in his drive, he nudged the accumulated leaves from the front doorstep with his foot and let himself in. The house felt cold, neglected, his only welcome the red light flashing on his answering machine. He switched on the kitchen lights and pressed the play button.

Faith's voice filled the room. '*Jack, I heard about Winnie. Ring me at the café, please. Please.*' She sounded frantic, in tears.

Concerned, Jack rang the café, but when a harried

Buddy answered, he said he'd sent Faith home after lunch, as she wasn't feeling well.

As soon as Jack disconnected, the phone rang. He snatched it from its cradle, fearing bad news. 'Jack, Nick rang me about Winifred,' Simon Fitzstephen said. 'I'm so sorry. How is she?'

'No change as far as I know. I'm just on my way to hospital again now. Simon, could you do something for me? I'm worried about Faith. She left a message for me, but I can't reach her at the farmhouse, and I haven't time to go up there now.'

'Blast Garnet for not having a telephone,' said Simon. 'But I'll check on the girl. Don't worry.'

Jack hesitated, torn between the desire to make a stop at the farmhouse himself and his need to get away to Taunton, then said, 'Right.' He would let Simon take care of it.

Having found the café closed, Nick put his motorbike into first gear for the climb up the steep incline of Wellhouse Lane. If Faith wouldn't look at Garnet's bumper, he'd do it himself, and then he'd show her what he found. He'd make her see the truth.

But to his dismay, when he reached the farmhouse the yard was already in deep shadow. Garnet's van was parked with its nose inside the gloom of her shop; there was no way he could examine the bumper without a torch. Well, then, he would talk to Faith again, convince her to see reason.

When the sputter of the bike's engine died away, the yard was hushed except for the squeaking of a flock of black birds passing overhead. A butter-coloured cat lay curled against the door, as if it had given up seeking entrance. As Nick climbed the steps and rapped on the door, the cat gave him a baleful glance and slunk away.

There was no response, but he could see the glow of an oil lamp through the curtained kitchen window. He knocked again.

The door swung open and Garnet Todd stared at him without speaking.

'I want to see Faith,' Nick said.

'She's not here.'

'I don't believe you.'

'I'm telling you, she's not here.' Garnet started to close the door.

Nick stepped forward, jamming it with his shoulder. 'Where else would she be? The café's closed, and she never goes anywhere else, does she? You can't stop me seeing her.'

'You're trespassing. This is my house,' protested Garnet, but gave way a step.

Nick's anger surged with his small victory. Why had he let this witch bully him – and Faith – for so long? 'What are you going to do, ring the police? You don't have a telephone.' Another step and he was in the house, shutting the door behind him. He looked round the kitchen for some sign of Faith, then called out her name.

'I've told you, she's not here.'

'Then where is she?'

'I don't know!' There was an edge of panic in Garnet's voice. 'When I went to fetch her from work she was gone, and she hasn't come home.'

'You're sure she's not in the house?'

'Why don't *you* look, then, if you don't trust my word.'

Nick turned away without replying and left the kitchen, but once in the corridor he realized the folly of his gesture. There was no electricity, and dusk had invaded the house. Well, he bloody well wasn't going back to ask Garnet for a candle or a lantern – he'd just have to navigate the shadows as best he could.

Downstairs, first. He went through the dark hall into the parlour at the front of the house, a musty, disused room, filled with tatty furniture. There was no sign that it had been recently disturbed.

Next, the room that served Garnet as an office, with its rolltop desk and ancient wooden filing cabinets. A glass-fronted case against the far wall held a collection of dusty bird's nests and shells . . . relics of Garnet's childhood hobbies, perhaps, now long forgotten.

Returning to the hall, he found the cold and primitive bath beneath the stairs. In the dim light, he made out a bottle of shampoo on the shelf beside the tub – Faith's. When he opened it, the pear scent evoked her so strongly that she might have been standing beside him.

What if she *had* come home and confronted Garnet over Winnie's accident? Would Garnet have silenced her?

But he'd sensed a real fear behind Garnet's assertion that Faith hadn't returned to the farmhouse – and if that were true, where could she possibly have gone?

Home to her parents in Street? Not likely. Or – and

this was the thorn that Nick never quite managed to dislodge – had she gone to the baby's mysterious father? For all Faith had given away about him in the past months, the child might as well be the result of immaculate conception. But could Faith have been driven to seek the father out?

Suspicions roiling, Nick climbed the straight flight of stairs. First, he tried the bedroom on the left, immediately recognizable as Garnet's. An open wardrobe held her gypsy clothes; a dressing table, a collection of combs, brushes, hair slides, and a pretty etched-glass oil lamp. With the matches he kept in his pocket for lighting candles in the bookshop, Nick lit the lamp. Shadows danced on the walls and ceiling as the light illuminated a carved, four-poster bed draped with a lace coverlet. It suddenly occurred to him to wonder if Garnet had ever shared it with anyone.

He took the lamp into the bedroom on the right. This room held little other than a narrow iron bedstead, and beside it a plain deal table. Pegs on the wall organized Faith's few clothes. A white nightdress and a worn plush rabbit were arranged tidily against the pillow. On the bedside table lay the copy of T. H. White's *The Once and Future King* he had brought her. There was nothing to indicate where she might have gone.

Returning the lamp to the bedroom, he went back downstairs to the kitchen. Garnet sat in the chair by the stove, rocking slowly, but her knuckles were white where she gripped the chair arms.

'Satisfied?' she demanded.

'I'll find her. And if anything's happened to her—'

Leaving the threat unspoken, Nick let himself out of the door.

The night creatures had begun to venture out of their burrows, but Faith lay still, curled in a nest of leaves beneath the hedge. At last, a bird shrieked nearby and she woke, conscious at first only of the cold and of the stiffness of her limbs. As she moved, a branch scratched her face and awareness seeped back.

At Buddy's insistence, she'd left work early. A customer had given her a lift up the hill and dropped her at the farmhouse gate. Immediately, Faith saw that Garnet was home – the van stood in the yard, its wheels mud-caked.

She hadn't meant to look. But she couldn't avoid passing the van on her way to the house, and before she could stop herself she'd swivelled round and stared. The bumper was smudged and smeared, with one wide swipe that could have been made by an impact with a large, solid object – a body?

Oh, God. She felt a surge of nausea. Nick couldn't be right – he just couldn't. But why had Garnet been so strange when she'd come back last night? And all that time Winnie had been lying nearby, injured and unconscious . . .

Faith blinked back tears. Garnet had done so much for her . . . How could she even think her capable of such a terrible thing? But what if – what if Nick were right? Fear clutched at her. She couldn't go into the house – couldn't face Garnet. Not yet. She had to think.

Turning away, she walked out of the yard, into the lane. The pull of the Tor drove her up the hill. As she climbed, tendrils of pain began to radiate from her pelvis round her abdomen, but she picked up her pace, ignoring them. The sun had formed an enormous red ball hovering on the horizon – if she didn't hurry she'd have to climb in the dark. Her sense of urgency increased. She knew she must get to the top of the Tor, although she couldn't quite formulate why. Then, as she came in sight of the entrance to the north path, a cramp caught her, doubling her over in pain and surprise.

She stopped, panting, took another step, stopped again. The pain worsened, squeezing at her. She had to get off her feet, just for a little while, make it stop. Then she would go on.

Looking round, she had seen the gap in thc hedge, just big enough for her body, and when she'd crawled inside, she'd fallen instantly into a deep and dreamless sleep.

Now, fully awake, she cupped her hands round her abdomen, felt the gentle flutter of the baby turning. The pain had gone, and she realized that whatever had driven her had dissipated as well. Although it still tugged faintly at the edges of her consciousness, it was not as powerful as her desire to go home. She knew now what she had to do.

She could not betray Garnet without giving her a chance to explain herself.

Easing herself from the hedge, she looked up, letting her eyes adjust to the darkness. The sky was overcast, starless, and her only orientation was the deeper blackness of the hedges. Slowly, she made her way down the hill, watching for the glow of oil lamps that would mark the farmhouse.

But it was the white shape of the gate she saw first. Only then was she able to make out the house, a darker shadow against the Tor's flank. There was no sign of Garnet's van in the yard, and when Faith let herself in the unlocked back door, only the cats came to greet her.

It was fully dark by the time Jack reached the hospital. He hurried through the car park, head down against the damp, chill wind, assuring himself that no news from Maggie meant that Winnie's condition remained stable.

But the first person he saw when he entered the ICU waiting area was Andrew Catesby, sitting with his head in his hands.

'Andrew,' he said sharply. 'What's wrong? How is she?'

Andrew looked up, dropping his hands from his face with apparent reluctance. 'I don't know. They won't tell me anything.'

Jack swallowed, making an effort to keep his panic in check. 'Have you seen her?'

'No. I—' Andrew shook his head. 'I couldn't bear it.' He stood, so that their eyes were on a level, and Jack saw that his face looked sallow and pinched, as if he was utterly exhausted. No trace remained of the boyish charm Jack had seen him display with Suzanne and Fiona.

'I've been here for hours,' Andrew continued. 'Suzanne came, and Simon Fitzstephen, and the bishop. They all wanted to know where you were, as if her life depended on *your* presence. But I know the truth.' He jabbed an accusing finger at Jack. 'She wouldn't be here if it weren't for you. You and your daft ideas, and your daft friends – you've done this to her. We were happy on our own before you came. We had a good life. And now – now nothing will ever be the same. Maybe she'd be better off dead.'

'Andrew! You can't mean that!'

'Can't I?' Andrew turned and disappeared through the swing doors.

Jack stared after him. The man was utterly mad.

Shaken, he rang the bell for admittance to the ICU. It was not Maggie who answered his summons, but an older, heavy-set nurse whose name badge read 'Joan'.

'You're here to see Winifred?' she asked.

'How is she?'

'Her heart's still playing up a bit, and that's causing her blood pressure to drop.'

'But she'll be all right? Can I see her?'

'We seem to have got her settled down again for the time being.' Joan glanced at her watch, then said kindly, 'Fifteen minutes. Then I'll throw you out on your ear.'

Jack eased himself into the chair by Winnie's bed and took her hand. It seemed to him that it felt cooler than it had that morning. He spoke to her quietly, stroking the soft skin on the inside of her wrist, telling her about his day and his visit to Fiona. 'You've had a good many visitors,' he continued, 'and Andrew was here when I—'

Was it his imagination, or had her fingers moved? He gripped her hand more tightly and gazed at her face. There! Surely her eyelids flickered, surely he felt an infinitesimal change in her breathing. 'Nurse!' he called, and Joan came immediately from the next cubicle.

'I was talking to her – I think she moved her hand, and blinked.'

'Good, that's very good,' said Joan, checking the monitors. 'She knows you're here, and she wants to respond. She's just not quite there yet.' The nurse scrutinized Jack with a professional eye. 'And I'd say you're about done in. Why don't you go get yourself a bite to eat in the canteen, then come back for another little visit? Are those her things you've brought?' She nodded towards the carrier bag beside Jack's chair.

Joan helped him set up the small CD player beside the bed, and as he left he heard the opening bars of the Palestrina 'Agnus Dei' he had chosen – one of Winnie's favourite pieces.

In the canteen, he ate his sandwich mechanically. He couldn't get Andrew Catesby's words out of his mind. Why would Andrew think that someone Winnie had met through Jack would want to hurt her? And how could he possibly say that Winnie would be better off dead than with him? Were Andrew's feelings for his sister even more twisted than he had suspected?

A horrifying thought struck him. Had it been not his voice that had triggered Winnie's brief response a few moments ago, but his mention of Andrew's name?

Jack . . . Jack's voice . . . deep, smooth, a river of sound . . . Telling her– No, she had lost it. She tried to speak, to tell him she heard, but she seemed to be at the bottom of a well . . . Couldn't reach the surface. Her heavy limbs wouldn't respond. Or did they belong to someone else? There was a light . . . Somehow she knew that. Was she dead?

But there was pain. Hers, she was sure, although it was distant, quite separate from her. Not dead, then.

But where? And how had she got here?

Andrew – it had to do with Andrew. Something bad about Andrew. Something she must do . . .

Weary . . . too weary . . . Jack's voice faded to nothingness, and she drifted away once again, untethered . . . except that she heard, as if from a great distance, the sound of singing.

By the time he left the lights of Taunton behind, Jack knew he was too exhausted to drive safely. He should have taken a hotel room near the hospital, stayed the night, but he couldn't summon the energy to turn round.

All his senses seemed heightened, raw, and the headlamps of the oncoming cars seemed unnaturally bright. He found himself squinting – once even closing his eyes, which terrified him so much he spent the remainder of the journey wide-eyed, gripping the wheel.

As he turned into his drive, his lights caught a flash of something white within the shelter of the porch. It took a moment to register that it had been a human face. He got out of the car with some apprehension, calling out 'Hello?'

He heard a thread of sound in reply, perhaps a whimper. His alarm increasing, he went forward. He had to kneel to be sure of the identity of the huddled shape against his door.

'Faith?'

'I didn't tell,' she whispered urgently through chattering teeth. 'But she left – left me . . . shouldn't have . . . I wouldn't have told.'

Jack touched her cheek. The girl was burning with fever.

'Who left?'

'She never goes out, not that time of night, not in the van . . . I didn't tell, did I?' She peered beseechingly up at him.

He lifted her to her feet and held her, shivering, against his chest. 'Of course you didn't. We've got to get you inside, ring for the doctor—'

Faith tugged away. 'You've got to find her, before it's too late—'

'Find who, Faith?'

'Garnet. They've taken her away.'

'Who has?'

Making an obvious effort, she looked round, as if

afraid someone might overhear. Then she rested her cheek against his chest and whispered, 'The Old Ones. But it was *me* they wanted.'

Chapter Ten

. . . to the great Spirit and Fountain of life, all things, in both space and time, must be present . . . action, once begun, never ceases . . . thus the past is always present, although, for the purpose of fitting us for this mortal life, our ordinary senses are so constituted as to be unperceptive of these phenomena.

Catherine Crowe, from
The Night-Side of Nature

The miles fell away under a leaden sky. Traffic had been fairly light on the M4 since they'd left Reading, allowing Gemma to relax enough to enjoy driving. Beside her, Kincaid dozed, head tilted back against the headrest. They had left London before seven, hoping to avoid the worst of the morning rush hour.

He'd rung her the previous afternoon with the invitation to spend a long weekend in Glastonbury. Her first response had been an adamant no, she had too much pending at work. Kincaid had patiently reminded her that she had the authority to delegate, and that she hadn't taken a full weekend off since she'd started the new job.

Bristling, she'd pleaded a meeting and hung up.

But afterwards, sitting at her desk in the brief after-lunch lull, she wondered if Kincaid were right. When she'd first been promoted, he'd warned her that the biggest danger in command was thinking oneself indispensable – had she unsuspectingly fallen victim to that delusion? Her team was competent, and although they were working on a number of ongoing cases – a string of petty burglaries in the Portobello Road; a serial rapist who posed as a good Samaritan – there was nothing they couldn't manage on their own for a few days.

And staring into the cold cup of coffee that had made up her lunch, she had to admit she was exhausted. She wasn't eating right, nor sleeping well. Maybe a weekend away would give her a chance to recoup.

She'd rung Kincaid back and accepted. Before he could respond, she'd added, 'I'll drive. You're daft if you think I'm riding all the way to Somerset in your rattletrap of a car.'

Now, as she glanced at his relaxed form beside her, she realized that perhaps there had been more than duty involved in her overwork the past few weeks – she'd been avoiding spending time with Duncan as well.

What a coward she was! To confirm what she suspected she had only to go into the nearest chemist and buy a test. But then she would have to deal with her choices – and with Kincaid's reaction, should she decide to go through with the pregnancy.

Would he be pleased? Horrified? Although they had smoothed over the rift caused by her leaving Scotland Yard, she knew the hurt was still there, beneath the surface, and it had left their relationship on shaky ground. Not to mention the fact that he had just begun to adjust to the acquisition of a twelve-year-old son. How would he cope finding himself abruptly saddled with her, Toby, and another child on the way? Not that she couldn't manage on her own, she'd proved that, but just now the thought of it seemed overwhelming.

Oh, Lord, how could she have been so careless, with so much at stake on the job? She was at a point in her career when a maternity leave was the last thing she needed. And how would her new superiors respond to a pregnant and unmarried detective inspector?

Blinking back tears, she concentrated on overtaking a lorry, then slid the Escort back into the centre lane. She'd done too much of that lately: crying at the drop of a hat. A bad sign. Out-of-control hormones mixed with a healthy dose of self-pity. She snorted at the irony of the whole situation, and beside her Kincaid blinked and stretched.

'Sorry. Was I snoring?'

'Actually, you were sleeping quite gracefully. I could do with a map check, though. I think our exit's coming up soon.'

He retrieved the large-scale AA map book from the rear seat and glanced at the open page. 'Exit seventeen, towards Chippenham, Bridgwater, and Taunton.'

'We passed sixteen a few miles back.' Rain spattered against the windscreen and Gemma turned the wipers on. 'It's getting darker by the minute.'

'Not a bad omen for the weekend, I hope,' Kincaid said, grinning. 'Want me to drive the last leg?'

'I'm fine.'

'You just don't want to give up possession.' Kincaid patted the car's dashboard. 'Now aren't you glad I gave you an excuse to take it out on the motorway?'

'I'm looking forward to meeting your cousin,' she quipped back. 'So he can fill me in on all your embarrassing childhood exploits. Seriously, though,' she continued, glancing at him, 'it sounds as if he's a bit paranoid, thinking someone may have run his girlfriend down deliberately. I hope you're not getting into something awkward.'

'Jack's the last person I'd have described as nervy. But I haven't seen him since Emily's death. He may have changed.'

His wife *and* baby, Kincaid had said. Gemma shuddered. It didn't bear thinking of. 'How long since they died?' she asked.

'A couple of years now. It was just about the time we started working together.'

How green she had been, thought Gemma. And how little she'd anticipated what had developed between them.

'Will we stay with him?' she asked.

'He didn't say. As I remember it, the house is a great Victorian pile of brick, built right against the side of the Tor.'

'The Tor?'

'You'll see,' he answered cryptically. 'When I was a kid I found it fascinating and a bit frightening, but Jack seemed oblivious. Home ground, I suppose.'

Intrigued by this unfamiliar aspect of his childhood, Gemma said, 'Did you visit them often?'

'Only a few times. Usually they came to us. I don't think my aunt Olivia ever gave up being homesick for Cheshire.'

'Your mother inherited the family home, then?'

He laughed. 'You make it sound like some sort of grand country estate. It's just a rambling old farmhouse, a bit leaky round the edges. I'll take you for a visit sometime. And Kit.'

'I'd like that,' Gemma said carefully, unwilling to pursue it further. Instead, she asked, 'How did Kit mind our going away for the weekend?'

'He already had plans with the Millers. A dog show in Bedford.'

'Any word from Ian about the Canadian job?'

'No. He's still hedging. I don't know why.'

'Maybe he wants the job but feels guilty about taking it.'

'He's got to make his mind up before the beginning of spring term.' Kincaid's exasperation was evident. 'I don't want the transition to be any more difficult than necessary for Kit.'

'Aren't you making rather a big leap, assuming Ian won't insist on taking Kit to Canada with him? He does have the right.'

'Yes, but I can't see him doing it. It would cramp his style too much. Right now he's getting mileage with the ladies by playing the grieving widower with child, but in a new setting Kit might prove more hindrance than help.'

'Oh, that's cold.'

'But true.'

Gemma had to agree, having heard enough snippets from Kit about Ian's 'tutorials' behind closed doors in what had been Vic's office.

They fell silent as they reached their exit from the motorway, and soon they were heading due south, with the plains of Wiltshire on their left and the rising hills of Somerset on their right. At Trowbridge they picked up the A361 towards Shepton Mallet and Glastonbury, and the sky began to lighten in the west.

'It may clear up,' Kincaid said hopefully, and by the time they'd passed through the hillside village of Pilton, a few miles east of Glastonbury, his prediction proved correct. The heavy overcast sky had broken up, leaving a milky blue streaked with wisps of cloud.

Concentrating on the road, Gemma caught a fleeting glimpse of a strange, cone-shaped hill before it disappeared round another bend. 'What on earth was that?'

'Glastonbury Tor.'

The hill came into view again, this time staying on the horizon. It looked artificial, a man-made mound with the squat shape of a building perched on the summit like a Christmas cracker paper crown. 'Did somebody make it?' Gemma asked.

'No. The hill itself is a geological formation. The contouring of the sides could possibly be man-made, but if so, it's so old that no one knows who did it, or why.'

'And the building on the top?'

'St Michael's Tower. All that's left of a twelfth-century church, destroyed by an earthquake. The remains of the last Christian stance against the pagan, legend has it.'

'You don't believe that?'

He shook his head. 'I've been up there. The wind blows through the tower like a knife, and that stone is colder than death. I doubt anything Christian ever stood a chance on that hill.'

'Are you sure you won't go in and sit with her for a few minutes?' Suzanne Sanborne asked. 'I think it would help you—'

'No!' At the startled glances of the other visitors, Andrew lowered his voice to a snarl. 'You don't understand. Our parents—' He stopped, unable, even after so many years, to relate the horror of being made to stand at his unconscious mother's bedside. She'd been in the water too long before they'd fished her body from the wreck of their sailing boat off the Dorset coast. And now Winnie . . .

'Then you've got to get some rest. You're not doing Winnie any good by getting yourself in such a state.'

'I can't sleep.' Andrew clasped his hands between his knees to stop their obvious trembling. They sat in the visitors' area outside the ICU, waiting for the nurses to allow Suzanne another ten-minute stint by Winnie's bedside.

'Then go to the surgery and have David prescribe you some tablets. I'll stay here with Winnie until Jack comes. There's no need for you to—'

'What right does *he* have to be here?' The rage that had been eating at him for months burned in his throat like acid. 'Arranging your schedule, ordering the nursing staff about—'

'Jack's here because Winnie would want him to be.' Again the light touch of Suzanne's fingers on his arm, and the direct gaze he couldn't meet. 'Andrew, we've been friends for a long time. Jack's a good man: he cares for your sister very deeply. What more could you want for her?'

'Someone who wasn't a crank,' he replied bitterly. He had read the papers she left lying about the Vicarage, as if communications from a dead monk were nothing to be ashamed of. Oh, he knew all about their little Arthurian group, and it sickened him.

But that wasn't the whole truth. He had never wanted to share his life with any woman other than his sister, and Jack Montfort had stolen that from him. The rhythm and pattern of their days together had provided him with an anchor, a touchstone, and her absence had left him adrift.

And as if that weren't enough, he thought as he took his leave of Suzanne, he knew now that Montfort had brought Winnie too close to things she had never been meant to know . . . things that must be kept from her, no matter what the consequences.

After a morning spent at home, lingering over coffee and newspapers, Bram Allen could no longer put off going into the gallery, but he disliked leaving Fiona on her own.

If he'd been at home yesterday afternoon, he might have prevented Jack Montfort from stirring up the horror of Winnie Catesby's accident all over again. Why did it have to be Fiona, of all people, who'd found

Winnie lying in the road? And why had Winnie been coming to see Fiona – if indeed that were the case – without warning or invitation?

Frowning, he buttoned his crisply pressed shirt, chose a tie, and went to find his wife.

She was in her studio, sitting on her stool, but to his relief her easel was empty and her hands idle in her lap.

'All right, darling?' he asked, slipping his arms round her. He had thought, once, that he had the makings of an artist. Then he'd met Fiona, seen canvases come to glowing life beneath her brush, and he'd known that gift would never be his. So he'd nurtured her work as best he could, shielding her from life's vicissitudes and taking a vicarious pride in her achievements – until she'd begun to paint the one thing he couldn't bear to see.

Fiona sank back against his chest. 'It's just . . . there's this tension in things. I thought when I started painting it would dissipate; then when I found Winnie I felt sure it had been in anticipation of that. Precognition of a sort, perhaps. But the feeling's still there.'

'Maybe it's just stress, system overload. Try not to fret, darling.'

'I'm sure you're right,' murmured Fiona, but he was not at all convinced she meant it.

Bram held her more tightly. 'I love you, Fi. You know that, don't you?'

'Of course I do. How could you think otherwise?' She patted his hand. 'Go on. I'll be fine, I promise.'

With that he had to be content.

*

Jack carefully cracked open the door to the spare bedroom and peered in. Faith lay on her side, her hands curled into fists under her chin. The innocence of her face, relaxed in sleep, tugged at his heart. She could be his child, he thought, his little Olivia, if she had lived to grow up.

Turning away, he closed the door quietly and returned to the kitchen. Not knowing who else to call, he had got David Sanborne out of bed the previous night to check on Faith. Exhaustion, stress, a chill from exposure, David had pronounced – nothing that a hot water bottle and plenty of rest wouldn't cure, but the girl had better stop such silliness if she didn't want to induce labour prematurely.

But once Jack had got a fairly coherent story from her, Faith had continued to fret about Garnet until he'd agreed to ring the police. The duty officer in Yeovil informed him that they couldn't report Garnet Todd missing until at least twenty-four hours had passed. Jack had left a message for Detective Inspector Greely, and only then had Faith fallen into a fitful sleep.

After a few hours' sleep himself, Jack had spent the morning fielding phone calls and checking with the hospital. Winnie's condition remained stable, and Suzanne Sanborne had offered to spend the morning with her.

In the meantime, he waited for his cousin's promised arrival. Duncan had rung the previous evening to say he would be coming for the weekend. Although relieved, Jack had begun to worry. How was he going to explain the events of the last few months? Would Duncan think him as mad as the police obviously did?

It didn't matter, he told himself. He *must* convince Duncan that Winnie was in danger; and now he'd begun to fear for Faith too.

How much of the girl's rambling last night had been delirium? Nick had rung this morning, saying he believed Garnet had struck Winnie with her van – but why would Garnet Todd do such a thing? And if it were true, where was Garnet now?

Filling the kettle from the tap, Jack spooned loose tea into his mother's old brown teapot. Hadn't he read once that tea stimulated one's mental processes? If that were the case, he should be competing with Sherlock Holmes after another cup, but he was no further along in finding answers.

He'd just poured boiling water over the fresh tea leaves when the doorbell rang. Jack hurried to the door and swung it wide.

As he grasped his cousin's hand, he saw that Duncan had lost the hollow-eyed look he'd remarked on when he'd seen him last. But who was the pretty redhead with him?

She held out her hand and gave him a warm smile. 'Jack, I'm Gemma James. I take it Duncan didn't tell you I was coming?' The look she cast at his cousin was affectionately withering. 'Your manners, love, leave something to be desired.'

They had got the awkwardness of their accommodation out of the way first. Jack had apologized profusely, explaining that he'd just put someone in the room fitted out for guests, but he'd move his things into his old room and give them the master bedroom. Encouraged by Gemma's well-placed kick at his ankle under the kitchen table, Kincaid had demurred, saying they'd find a nearby B & B, and Jack had recommended an establishment near the Abbey.

Gemma had breathed an inward sigh of relief. She found the dark old house with its ugly Victorian furniture depressing, and the mass of Glastonbury Tor rising from the back garden made her feel unexpectedly claustrophobic. It was as if the hill might lean over and swallow the house at any moment.

Over cups of tea, Jack had haltingly recounted his experiences with the automatic writing, his meeting with Winnie Catesby, the gradual involvement of the others in the group, and the disappearance yesterday of Garnet Todd.

If Kincaid felt any surprise at his cousin's story, he didn't show it. His expression remained neutral and sympathetic, a demonstration of his listening skills, and Gemma realized how acutely she missed working with him.

'Can you do it on demand?' Kincaid asked when Jack paused. 'The automatic writing.'

'I – I don't know. I've done it often enough with Nick or with Simon Fitzstephen, but—'

Kincaid leaned forward, his eyes alight with interest. 'What do you have to do?'

'Just have pen and paper, and empty my mind. Talk about something inconsequential, or listen to someone reading the paper, for instance. Sometimes it works and sometimes it doesn't.'

'Let's give it a try, then. I'll be your assistant.' The

look Kincaid gave his cousin was challenging. What sort of mischief had he beguiled Jack into in those long Cheshire summers? Gemma wondered.

She watched them as they sat opposite her at the table in Jack's cluttered kitchen, Kincaid reading an incomprehensible financial article aloud from the *Guardian* while Jack sat in a relaxed posture, pen and paper ready. Jack Montfort was larger, fairer, and more blunt-featured than his cousin, but the resemblance was there if you looked. What was more readily apparent was the easiness between them, the sense of long-established trust and camaraderie. And the man certainly seemed rational and well balanced, in spite of his worries. Could this bizarre tale he'd told them possibly be true?

Lulled by Kincaid's voice and her own drifting thoughts, Gemma starred violently when Jack's pen suddenly began to move across the paper. He wrote without pause, and without looking at the script. His eyes, half closed, seemed fixed somewhere in the distance.

He filled several pages, then set the pen down. 'Success, I see,' he said, looking at the scattered pages.

'You mean you don't know what you've written?' asked Gemma.

'I suppose I'm aware of it at some level, but I don't process it – it's like static on a radio.'

Kincaid touched a page. 'What does it say?'

'I'll have to translate, so if you'll bear with me . . .

'O Lord, forgive me, for I have sinned grievously against Thee. Though my days of the flesh are but a

distant memory, still I feel her skin, soft as goose down, and the round fullness of her breasts . . .'

Frowning, Jack stopped and cleared his throat, and Gemma found it endearing that he had coloured slightly.

'Sixteen and yet a woman, Alys she was called, the daughter of the stonemason come to repair the damage to the church. She found me comely and would wait for me when I went to the spring. There was little speech between us . . . we came together in need and pleasure as the beasts do.

'The work was finished when Alys found she was with child. She begged me for herbs . . . To my shame I did her bidding . . . for my cowardice as well as my lust I have brought misery on us all . . .

'From Brother Ambrose, who had befriended me, I stole the necessary potion. With it I gave her what was most precious to me . . . a bond between us stronger than death. Alys and her father left the Abbey then. Such sorrow I had never known, it tethers me to this place still . . .'

Jack looked up, his eyes wide with surprise. 'This woman – Alys – she meant to abort their baby. Don't you think that's what he means?'

Gemma, intensely moved by this recounting of the girl's predicament, said, 'I – I suppose it's possible. They were very skilled in using herbs, and her position would have been untenable, wouldn't it? Edmund couldn't have married her.'

'I suspect it would have been thought she'd sinned against the Church, as well, in seducing Edmund, rather than the other way round,' Kincaid offered.

'But what if Alys changed her mind? Or the herbs didn't work?' demanded Jack. 'We've searched for months for a blood connection – perhaps a niece or nephew – as we suspected there might be a genetic component to the link.'

'An illegitimate child?' Kincaid mused. 'In that case there wouldn't have been any record.'

'I must tell Simon. This gives us a new angle' – Jack grimaced – 'although I don't know that trying to trace an eleventh-century itinerant stonemason's daughter will get us much further forward.' Glancing at his watch, he added, 'And in the meantime I've got to get to hospital. When I rang Nick this morning, he said he'd come at midday and look after Faith. I didn't like to leave her on her own, with Garnet still—'

'You've not found her, have you?'

Startled, they all turned towards the doorway. How long had the girl been there, listening? Gemma wondered. Her short hair stood on end, as if she had just slipped out of bed; her cheek still bore creases from the pillow. As she entered the room, Gemma saw that her slender body was made awkward by the weight of the child she carried.

Jack was the first to collect himself. 'No, I'm afraid we haven't. Faith, this is my cousin Duncan and his friend Gemma. They've come to help.'

'I don't think anyone can,' Faith said softly, and her dark eyes held the glint of tears.

'Sit down,' soothed Jack, rising and arranging a chair for her, 'and let's get you a cup of tea. I'm sure Garnet's fine—'

The doorbell rang. 'That must be Nick, now,' Jack

said hastily, and disappeared towards the front of the house.

But there was an unmistakable tone of the official in the low-voiced response to Jack's greeting, although Gemma couldn't quite make out the words. Kincaid had caught it as well – he was up and moving swiftly out of the room. With a quick look at Faith, who had sunk into the chair Jack provided, Gemma followed Duncan.

As she reached the door, Kincaid was showing his warrant card to a burly, tweed-jacketed man with thinning red hair. 'Duncan Kincaid, Scotland Yard,' he said, shaking the man's hand. Turning to Gemma, he added, 'Inspector James.'

She saw Jack's surprise as she in turn shook the man's hand – earlier, she hadn't introduced herself by rank.

'Alfred Greely, Somerset CID.' Greely's voice was thick with a West Country burr, and his look was unabashedly appraising. 'Is there somewhere we could have a chat?'

'We'll go into the kitchen,' Jack replied. 'Is this about Winnie – Miss Catesby?'

'I'm afraid not. Mr Montfort, I understand you rang up last night and reported a Miss Garnet Todd missing.'

Once inside, Jack nodded towards Faith. 'This young lady is staying with Miss Todd. She came to me last night when Garnet didn't come home.'

When Greely switched his gaze to Faith, she seemed to wilt further into her chair. 'I'm afraid we've found Miss Todd,' he said. 'A gentleman taking his morning constitutional round the Tor thought a farmer's gate an odd place to abandon a van and investigated.'

'Garnet's?' Faith's pallor was ghastly.

'I'm afraid so, miss. And her inside it.'

'Dead?'

'Yes. I am sorry.'

Faith's eyes were enormous in her pale face. 'She killed herself, then,' she said with what Gemma could have sworn was relief.

'Oh, no,' Greely replied, watching her intently. 'I very much suspect Miss Todd was murdered.'

Chapter Eleven

> *So it is, we are told, with the Company of Avalon, a group of souls who are impregnated with the devotional ideal which was translated into an architectural symbol by the Benedictine brethren of old time.*
>
> Frederick Bligh Bond, from
> *The Company of Avalon*

Kincaid stood in the thick, nettle-filled grass at the edge of Basketfield Lane, watching two crime-scene technicians dust the outside of Garnet Todd's van for fingerprints.

When he'd asked DI Greely if he could have a look at the scene, Greely had given him a sharp glance, saying, 'You don't get enough murders in London? Funny way to spend a holiday, if you ask me.' But he had not objected, and Kincaid had followed him in Gemma's car, down the end of Ashwell Lane and up to the right. They were only a few hundred yards from Jack's house, but the narrow, hedge-enclosed lane seemed a different world.

Through the low-lying trees Kincaid could just make out the steep eastern side of the Tor, and the snaking queue of climbers making their way up its zigzag path. As still as it seemed in the lane, he could see the wind whipping at the climbers' clothes. It would be cold at the summit.

A few yards away, Greely slipped his mobile phone back into his jacket pocket, then came to join Kincaid. 'The doc's on his way now,' he said, adding, 'Old Doc Lamb has a busy practice, so sometimes we have to wait a bit. But he's the best there is – been at it since before I joined the force.'

The coroner's van had already arrived. The driver had pulled it tightly into the nearest passing spot, and he and the attendant sat inside, eating sandwiches and sharing a newspaper.

'Funny your cousin's young friend should assume the woman killed herself.' Greely chose a dry stem of grass, and breaking it off, chewed it meditatively.

Watching him, Kincaid wondered if city boys ever learned to chew grass in quite the same way. 'You from around here?' he asked.

'Born in Dorset, just across the border. But I've lived within twenty miles of the Tor, near enough, since I was a lad.'

'Tell me what you've got so far, if you don't mind.' Kincaid nodded at the van. 'Why are you so sure she *didn't* commit suicide?'

'Van was locked, no keys. Of course, she could have locked herself in, rolled down the window, and tossed them, but in that case she had a throwing arm like a cricket bowler. We've had a good look about and there's no sign of keys. Doesn't make sense anyway,' he mused, moving the grass stem to the other side of his mouth. 'I can see her locking herself in, but what good would it do to toss the keys?'

'And the cause of death?'

'Don't know for certain yet. Nothing obvious. No slit wrists; no sign of the usual pill-induced vomiting; no exhaust hose run through the window. And she was in the back – looks as if she was dumped there. No attempt to make herself comfortable for her last few minutes on earth.'

'Mind if I have a look?' Kincaid asked, his curiosity growing.

Abandoning the grass stem, Greely gave a phlegmatic nod. 'Suit yourself.'

Kincaid made his way to the van, careful to use the same path as the crime-scene technicians. The rear doors stood open. Flies buzzed in the van's interior, and the familiar odour of death wafted out to meet him. The woman's body lay wedged in a clear space to one side, and some smudged sections in the dust made him think she had been pushed into place among the odds and ends of tiles and equipment on dusty rubber flooring. Her feet, clad in old-fashioned black boots, were towards him. She wore a wool cape that had fallen back to reveal a bright, multicoloured skirt. Her thick dark hair had come loose from its plait; it covered her face like a curtain.

Kincaid borrowed a pair of gloves from one of the techs and inched inside the van for a better look at the body. Lividity was fairly pronounced, indicating she'd been dead some hours, and when he lifted her eyelid he saw the red spots in the eye indicative of asphyxiation. There was no noticeable bruising on throat or neck, however.

With a fingertip, he moved the thick hair away from her face. She had worn long, dangly earrings; the left one was missing.

Garnet Todd's eccentricities had gone deeper than costume, according to the brief account Jack had given him, Kincaid mused as he crawled out into the welcome fresh air. But what cause had the woman given someone to murder her? If it had been she who struck Winnie Catesby, as the girl, Faith, suspected, her death made even less sense.

Greely had not managed to get much more out of Faith after his announcement that he believed Garnet Todd had been murdered. She had begun to cry – not a storm of sobs, which might have offered some possibility of consolation, but slow, despairing tears that ran down her face unchecked. Jack had protested then, and Gemma had shepherded the girl back upstairs to her room.

Gemma had offered to stay with her so that Jack could go on to the hospital, and he had accepted gratefully. Knowing Gemma's aversion to being designated as handholder, Kincaid had given her a questioning glance, but she'd reassured him with a nod. Method? Or sympathy? he wondered – or perhaps a bit of both.

There came the sound of a car climbing the gradient, then the crunch of tyres on gravel as an ancient Morris Minor appeared round the bend and rolled to a stop. A balding, bespectacled man climbed out, medical bag in hand. It seemed the police surgeon had arrived.

'I see you've made it a point to interrupt my lunch, Alf,' he said to Greely by way of greeting, but his jovial tone matched his pink, cherubic face.

'A lack I'm sure you'll make up, Doc.' Greely gave a pointed glance at the doctor's paunch, visible evidence of a weakness for good living.

'Too true. I shall have to take up slimming one of these days, if I can just convince Carole to give up cooking. What have we got here, Alf?'

'Woman found this morning locked in her van, keys missing. We were hoping you could tell us a bit more. This is Superintendent Kincaid, *visiting* from London.' Greely's ironic emphasis on the verb was unmistakable.

Meeting the doctor's eyes as they shook hands, Kincaid saw that, despite the jolly-elf exterior, it wouldn't do to underestimate the man.

'All right, let's have a look.' Lamb took off his jacket, handing it to Greely, then pulled a pair of gloves from his trouser pocket and slipped them on.

Greely stepped away and Kincaid followed suit as the doctor climbed into the van. 'Sharp old bugger,' Greely said. 'But he gets tetchy if you get in his way. Not that I've ever much enjoyed watching the poking and prodding part.'

They waited in silence while the doctor made his examination. Kincaid gradually became aware of the bustle of activity taking place in the hedgerow as birds searched for tasty berries and insects, and of the inappropriate rumbling of his own stomach. He had forgotten all about lunch.

'One odd thing,' Greely offered meditatively,

providing Kincaid with a welcome distraction from his hunger. 'The walker who discovered the body this morning was a bloke called Bram Allen – the husband of the lady who discovered Winifred Catesby in the lane.'

Kincaid raised an eyebrow. 'Coincidence?'

'He said he walks round the Tor every day – could be his wife's experience made him nervy – that, and the flies buzzing round the van.'

'Did he know the victim?'

'According to Mr Allen, everyone in Glastonbury knew Garnet Todd. Seems the woman was a genuine eccentric.'

Dr Lamb reappeared, rear end first as he backed out of the van. He removed his gloves, brushed off his knees, and rolled down his shirtsleeves before accepting his jacket from Greely.

'All right, Doc, you've kept us in suspense long enough,' Greely said, and Kincaid suspected the pair had a well-developed routine.

'Well.' Lamb brushed a twig from his lapel. 'I'd say she's been dead at least twelve hours, maybe a good bit longer with last night's drop in temperature. Lividity is well established, but there's some slight staining in other areas that indicates she may have been moved after death. There's no sign of sexual interference that I can see.'

Grudgingly, as if he knew it was expected of him, Greely asked, 'Cause of death?'

'Well, now, that's the most interesting thing. There are indications of asphyxiation, but no ligature marks or bruising on the throat or neck area. I have my suspicions, but I'm not going to say any more. You'll have to wait for the autopsy.'

Greely groaned. 'I can't see that we're much further along. Can we move the body, then?'

'Mmm.' The doctor nodded. 'Ask the pathologist to give me a ring when he's finished, would you? Satisfy my curiosity.' He turned to Kincaid. 'Staying long, Superintendent? You might find this one interesting.'

'Just the weekend,' Kincaid answered. He shook the doctor's hand and watched as he climbed back into his decrepit Morris and chugged up the hill.

Greely signalled to the mortuary attendants. They transferred the corpse onto a white sheet to preserve any trace evidence, then moved it from one van to the other. The doors clanged shut with metallic finality and the van pulled away. The crime-scene technicians were still busy at Garnet Todd's vehicle, while two uniformed constables painstakingly searched the surrounding area.

Casually, Kincaid asked, 'Any leads?'

'Absolutely sod all – except for the young lady your cousin, Mr Montfort, seems to have taken in. We'll have to interview her, you know, and the sooner, the better.'

'Did you find any evidence that Garnet Todd's van was involved in Miss Catesby's accident?'

'A few smudges on the front bumper. Could have been caused by a close encounter with a hedge. There was not much vehicular damage to Miss Catesby's bicycle, mostly scrapes and dings from the road. And there was no bleeding from Miss Catesby's injuries—'

'So no hope of blood on the vehicle,' Kincaid said grimly. 'What about fibres?'

'We're checking now. But' – Greely shrugged – 'it's a snowball's chance in hell, if you ask me, and we've nothing to link the two incidents other than the girl's story.'

As he wondered if Gemma had managed to coax anything more from Faith, Kincaid realized how easily they, too, had fallen into their old routine.

As anxious as he was about Winnie, Jack felt he must take the time to let Simon Fitzstephen know about Garnet's death – and not by telephone. Simon and Garnet had been friends for too long for an impersonal notification.

At least he could feel sure that he'd left Faith in good hands. Duncan's Gemma had a quiet authority that inspired confidence, and she had succeeded in calming Faith where he had failed.

So they were colleagues as well as lovers, he thought, wondering how long they'd been together, and if Duncan had finally managed to lay his troubled marriage to rest. Jack had been sorry to hear of Vic's death the previous spring, but had done nothing more than send Duncan a brief note – such things still struck too close to home.

And now he found himself the apparent custodian of a pregnant young woman who might deliver her child at any moment. The prospect terrified him.

He found Simon on his knees in front of his perennial border, snipping the dead stalks from bloomed-out plants. 'Dreary time of year, isn't it?' Simon rose, wincing, and as he came across the lawn Jack saw that he was limping. 'And digging in the dirt may be good for the soul, but it plays hell with my bad knee.'

'Old injury?' Jack asked.

'Climbing accident. Slipped in the scree years ago and tore a few ligaments. Just let me wash my hands and I'll put the kettle on.'

'No, really, I can't stay. I just came – Simon, I'm afraid I have some bad news.'

Simon went very still. 'Not Winifred?'

'No. It's Garnet Todd. She's dead. I thought you should know.'

'Dead?' Simon groped for the weathered wooden bench beside his front door and sank onto it. 'But she can't— I don't understand . . . Was there an accident?'

'No. The police seem to think she was murdered.'

'But – but that's absurd! Surely there's some mistake. Why would anyone want to kill Garnet?' There was a quaver to Simon's voice, and his skin had taken on an unhealthy hue. 'Did someone break into the house?'

'No. She was found in her van, round the other side of the Tor. I'm afraid that's all the information I have. I am sorry. I know you were old friends.'

'Friends . . . yes. Lovers, once. An odd woman, Garnet. I never understood how she became who she was, after such an ordinary beginning . . . And now she's gone. I can't quite believe it.' Simon gazed into the garden as if he had forgotten Jack's presence.

'Simon, I'm sorry, I'm afraid I'll have to go – but

there was something I wanted to show you if you feel up to it.' Jack pulled the pages he'd scribbled that morning from his pocket.

Simon took them abstractedly, but once he began to read, Jack could see his interest quickening. 'So that's the connection. An illegitimate child. We should have guessed.'

'Is there any possibility we could trace the woman – the daughter of a stonemason who worked on the cathedral at the time Edmund gives?'

'That would be a tall order. But I've some resources that might be helpful . . . I'll see what I can do.' Simon's voice was stronger, and it seemed to Jack that his colour had improved. 'Do you mind if I keep these? It would help me to have the details.'

'Of course you may. But I hate to leave you—'

'Don't be daft, man. I'll be fine. It's Winifred who needs your attention. But these' – he tapped the papers in his hand – 'we mustn't let things go too long. There seems to be an urgency to this, a reason Edmund wants us to recover this chant now. We mustn't risk losing the energy, breaking the connection – and without Garnet . . . things may be more difficult. She was a strong force.' He stopped and cleared his throat.

'Are you sure there's nothing I can do?'

'I'll be fine.'

'I'll ring you, then.' Jack turned away, but stopped and looked back when he reached the gate. Simon still sat on the bench, his eyes closed.

'Simon,' Jack called out. 'Thanks for going to see Winnie yesterday. It was kind of you.'

Simon opened his eyes and smiled. 'She'll be all right, you know. She's a fighter, that young woman.'

She had tucked Faith back into bed and sat with her until the tears stopped. Examining the bedroom, Gemma saw that someone had made an effort to counteract the darkness of the northern exposure and the heavy furniture. The walls were papered in a spring-like yellow and green sprigged pattern, and the coverlet on the fruitwood bed picked up the same pale yellow. But the landscape over the chest of drawers was dominated by the brooding presence of the Tor, and through the window, she could see its rock-strewn slope beyond the neglected back garden.

Faith blew her nose, then eyed Gemma over the wad of tissues. 'What are you doing here? Did you come to arrest Garnet?'

'We came because Jack was worried about Winnie, and Duncan wanted to help. That's all.'

'They're cousins?'

'Their mums were sisters.' Gemma surveyed Faith critically. 'How long has it been since you've eaten?'

'I don't remember.' Faith's hands, still clasping the tissues, were trembling. 'Yesterday morning at the café, I think. Before I heard about Winnie—' Her eyes filled again.

'Lunch, then,' Gemma said briskly. 'You stay right where you are and I'll bring it to you.'

Downstairs in the kitchen, she eyed the contents of fridge and cupboard with dismay. Eggs, a bit of cheese, a half loaf of slightly stale bread. A typical man's kitchen, but she could put together cheese omelettes and toast. That and a pot of tea would do.

Once the omelettes were done to perfection and the tea and toast ready, Gemma assembled a tray and carried the simple feast upstairs. Perhaps, she thought, some of Hazel's domestic skills were rubbing off on her.

She found Faith sitting up a bit straighter in the bed, dry-eyed, watching her with alert curiosity. The girl tucked into the food with concentration, and Gemma wondered if a portion of her emotional fragility had been due to simple hunger.

When they had both finished, Gemma asked, 'Better?'

Faith smiled. 'Yes. I didn't realize how hungry I was.'

'Good. Now we need to talk. I want you to tell me about your friend Garnet.'

Faith pinched her lips together. 'I don't know what you mean.'

'Start from the beginning. How did you meet her?'

'She came in the café– Oh, my God. I've got to go to work. I never even thought. And Buddy won't know about Garnet–'

Gemma eased her back down. 'I'll ring him – Buddy, is it? Is that your boss?'

'Yes. They were friends. That's how Garnet knew about me.'

'So Garnet had heard about you before she ever met you?'

'I was sleeping in the boxroom above the café. I thought Buddy didn't know. Garnet offered me a place to live for just a bit of rent. And she knew about babies. I was so scared then – there hadn't been anyone to ask. She . . . I'd never met anyone like her. She seemed so free. Not like my parents at all. And she knew about magic. Women's magic . . .'

'That must have been fascinating – and just frightening enough to be irresistible.'

'That's exactly how it was.' Faith sounded surprised, and Gemma gave herself a point for hitting the right note. 'But I didn't know, then . . .'

'Know what, Faith?' Gemma prompted.

'Old stuff. Dark stuff.' Faith shook her head. 'After a while it wasn't fun. Garnet said I had to learn, that ignorance wouldn't protect me. And she worried about me.'

'How could you tell?'

'The last couple of months, she didn't want me to go anywhere, or see anyone. Especially Nick.'

The classic signs of an abusive relationship, Gemma thought, and Faith would have been such a vulnerable target. Pregnant, homeless, friendless.

'Did Garnet have something in particular against him?'

'She and Nick rubbed each other up the wrong way from the very beginning. She thought he meant to turn me against her.'

'Garnet didn't like that.' Gemma made it a statement.

'No. But there was more to it, her worrying, I mean. It was like she knew something she wasn't telling me. And all the time the pull got stronger . . .'

'What pull?'

'Can't you feel it?' Faith shuddered. 'I did, even before I met Garnet. The Tor . . .'

Gemma thought of the odd feeling she'd had that morning when the Tor had first come into view. 'What about the Tor?'

'Last night . . . it was so strong. I couldn't stop. Then the pain came. I had to rest, and when I woke up it was gone.' Faith seemed to read Gemma's confusion. 'The force. The pull.'

'What does it want you to do, this force?'

'It's not like that. There aren't any words. I just have to climb.' She plucked at the sheets again and said, almost querulously, 'Where's Nick? Jack said Nick was coming.'

'It's only just lunchtime. Don't worry,' Gemma soothed her, wondering just exactly how Nick fitted into the equation. Was he the baby's father, perhaps?

She poured Faith another cup of tea from the old brown teapot, much loved by someone, if the chips and crazing in the glaze were any evidence. It occurred to her that she'd given up tea entirely when she was pregnant with Toby, and that she wasn't at all sure she'd have the discipline to do it again.

'Tell me what happened yesterday,' she said. 'Why were you so worried about Garnet?'

'Nick said . . . When I told him Garnet had gone out after we saw Winnie pushing her bike up the hill, he said he thought Garnet had hit Winnie with the van. I was so angry . . . but when I went home I looked at the van and I saw a smudge . . . I was afraid.'

'Then what happened?' Gemma asked it gently.

'I – I couldn't face her. I was so ashamed for even

thinking such a thing. I climbed the Tor. When I came back, she was gone. I never saw her again. If I'd only gone into the house—'

'You can't know what would have happened,' interposed Gemma. 'No one can.'

'But if she went looking for me, and someone—'

'I'm sure it had nothing to do with you,' said Gemma, not sure at all. 'And there's no point in speculating. What we have to do now is look after you. Jack said the doctor wanted you to go to the antenatal clinic for a check-up today—'

'No!'

Gemma jerked back in astonishment at the violence of Faith's response.

'I won't go,' the girl insisted. 'I can't. Garnet – Garnet promised to take care of me . . . how could she leave me like this?' She began to cry again, her shoulders heaving.

Gemma slipped her arms round the girl, holding her and murmuring, 'It's all right, it's all right,' just as she would with her own son. Faith was still a child, after all, and she had just lost the woman who seemed to have been in some powerful sense a substitute mother.

After a bit, Faith's sobs subsided, but she kept her face buried in Gemma's shoulder, sniffing occasionally. Gemma stroked the short, damp hair back from the girl's forehead.

Faith smiled sleepily, whispering, 'You're nice. Like my mum,' as her eyes drifted closed. In moments she was asleep, and not even the loud buzz of the doorbell disturbed her.

*

It amazed Jack how quickly sitting at Winnie's bedside, stroking her hand, and talking to her as if she could understand, came to seem normal. He told her that his cousin had come to visit, and that Faith was staying with them for a bit. He said nothing about Garnet's death.

His thoughts strayed to Duncan. What had he found when he accompanied Detective Inspector Greely? How had Garnet died? And how had his cousin – the boy who had gone white with distress at every injured bird or dead fox in the road – grown into a man who took death so easily in his stride?

When Maggie, who was back on duty today, motioned him that it was time for a break, he went reluctantly to the hospital canteen and had a sandwich. Suzanne Sanborne had told him that Andrew had been there most of the morning, but had not gone in to see his sister.

She'd added, 'I don't want to worry you, but Andrew's behaving quite oddly. He seems so irrational . . . Just watch yourself, okay?'

Jack walked back to the ICU, mulling it over. He'd been concerned about Andrew for Winnie's sake, but not his own. Andrew was a schoolteacher, he reminded himself – an academic unlikely to have bloodied a nose even in primary school. If Andrew wanted to have a go at him, then let him.

'She's been restless since you left,' Maggie informed him as soon as he reached the ward. 'Encourage her to wake up, to talk to you, to let you know she can hear you.'

Jack pulled his chair as close to the bed as he could,

and when he reached out to stroke Winnie's cheek, he saw that his hand was trembling. 'I hear you missed me,' he said, trying for a light touch. 'I always knew I was irresistible.' He took her hand in his and kissed it. 'I won't leave you unless I must – you know that. But I need you to wake up, to talk to me. I miss you, Winnie, and I need to know you can hear me. Wake up, darling, please. Talk to me.'

Had he felt her hand move? Winnie's eyelids had fluttered, he was sure of it. Then she blinked, once, twice, and opened her eyes. He saw awareness flood back into her gaze, then she focused on his face and he knew that she knew him.

So intense was the rush of relief that his throat tightened and his eyes brimmed. He bowed his head, and in that moment felt her hand grip his convulsively.

When he looked up, her eyes were wide with panic. She turned her head from side to side, reaching up with her free hand to scrabble at the tubes.

Maggie was there in an instant, restraining her, calming her. 'We'll get the breathing tube out in a tick, dear. You won't be needing it now you're awake. Now take a deep breath and breathe out when I tell you.'

Jack tightened his hold on Winnie's hand as the nurse slipped the tube out on Winnie's exhalation.

'I know it hurts,' said Maggie. 'I'm going to give you a little sip of water and that will help.' She fetched a cup and held the straw to Winnie's lips. 'Not too much at once, now, dear. When we see you're handling your liquids well, we'll take out the stomach tube.'

Winnie released the straw and sank back into the pillow, closing her eyes.

'Just rest, darling,' Jack said, his voice still unsteady. 'You're going to be fine.'

But after a moment she opened her eyes and tried to speak. When no sound emerged, she touched her throat and tried again. 'What . . . happened?' Her voice was the barest whisper. 'What time is it?'

Jack looked at Maggie, who nodded. He said gently, 'You had an accident. On your bike. You've been in hospital for two days.'

'Days?'

'You've had a bump on the head, but you're going to be fine.'

'I can't remember . . . I was going somewhere – something I had to do . . .'

'Don't worry. You will. But now you have to rest.'

With an obedience that moved him deeply, Winnie closed her eyes. Soon her breathing became slower and more regular.

'She's not—' Jack asked Maggie, panicked. 'She hasn't gone under again, has she?'

Maggie smiled. 'It's just a normal nap. That's a good thing. She's going to be very weak at first. But she's over the hump.'

'But will she remember the accident, or what happened before?'

'The human brain is a funny thing. Sometimes the gaps never fill in. We'll just have to wait and see.'

'Jack?'

Winnie had opened her eyes.

'Yes, darling. I'm here.'

'You came to dinner . . . Andrew was there . . .

There was something I had to tell you about Andrew. Why can't I remember?'

With a quick glance at the cardiac monitor, Maggie interposed. 'That's enough for now. You need to rest, dear, and your Jack will be waiting just outside for you to wake up.'

Jack took his cue, kissing Winnie's cheek gently before he left the ward. He sank into the nearest chair in the waiting area and gave himself over to a flood of profound relief and gratitude.

But after a moment, he stiffened, frowning. What hope did they have of finding out exactly what had happened, and why, when Winnie had clearly lost a day?

Chapter Twelve

So Glastonbury sank into the darkness of the Middle Ages, but Avalon lived on in the hearts of men and the Arthurian legends wove about her ancient history. Here came the knights who sought the Graal. They crossed the little River Brue by Pons Perilis, and watched all night in the little chapel at the foot of Wearyall Hill, overlooking the water, where dark temptations came to try the soul.

Dion Fortune, from
Glastonbury: Avalon of the Heart

The young man looked as if he were a Greek sculpture come to life. Tall and slender, with square shoulders balancing a graceful neck, he had classically moulded features and a perfectly shaped head covered with a tight cap of dark curls.

Gemma decided instantly that no one so beautiful could be entirely trustworthy. 'Hullo,' she said. 'You must be Nick.'

He nodded. 'Who are you?'

'I'm Gemma. My . . . um, friend . . . is Jack's cousin. We've come to help out.'

'Where's Jack? I need to talk to him.' He pushed past her.

Following him into the kitchen, Gemma replied, 'Gone to the hospital to see Winnie. He waited for you as long as he could.'

'Faith—'

'Upstairs. She's just gone to sleep. Please don't wake her.'

Nick had already turned towards the hall, but the firmness of her tone stopped him mid-step. For the first time, he seemed to really look at her, and in doing so lost a little of his momentum.

'She's had a very difficult morning, and she's exhausted,' Gemma said, taking full advantage. 'Why don't you sit down?'

Reluctantly, he came back to the table and pulled out a chair. 'I'm sorry. I didn't mean to be rude. It's just that I've been frantic all day.'

'Faith was worried about you.'

'As soon as I could get away from work, I went looking for Garnet. I drove by the farm, but there was no sign of her van. Then I checked all round Glastonbury. I thought if I could tell Faith that Garnet was all right—'

'I'm afraid that's not going to be possible,' Gemma said.

'What? Why not?'

'Garnet was found in her van this morning. She's dead.'

Nick gaped at her. 'But – I suppose she killed herself?'

That makes two, thought Gemma. 'Why would you say that?' she asked quietly.

'Well, it seems obvious, doesn't it? If she tried to kill Winnie, and then she felt guilty . . . or maybe she was afraid Faith would find out what she'd done . . .'

'Would that have mattered to her so much?'

'She seems obsessed with Faith—'

'In a sexual way?'

'I – I don't know. I don't think so. But she is insanely jealous of her.' He scowled at Gemma, tapping his fingers on the table. 'If you don't mind me saying so, you ask a lot of questions.'

'Sorry. Bad habit.' He would find out soon enough that she was a copper, but until then she might as well make the most of her temporary anonymity. 'Do I take it Garnet wasn't fond of you?'

'Not particularly, no.' He didn't seem eager to pursue the subject. 'How did Faith take the news?'

'She was quite upset, but she's doing better now. We do need to get her into the antenatal clinic for a check-up, though, and she won't even consider it. I don't suppose you have any influence . . .'

'Not likely.' Nick sounded bitter.

'Have you any idea why she's so set against it?'

'I always supposed it was because Garnet discouraged it. A power thing.'

If it had been Garnet's intention to make Faith dependent on her care, she seemed to have succeeded, mused Gemma. 'Faith told me you thought Garnet had struck Winnie with her van. Why were you so sure of that?'

Nick fidgeted. 'Faith said Garnet went out about

the time of Winnie's accident, and when she came back she was behaving oddly.'

'That's not much to go on, is it? Why would Garnet have done such a thing?'

'Maybe she thought Winnie was going to convince Faith to go back to her family. Or maybe – maybe Winnie found out something that Garnet didn't want known.' This hypothesis seemed to please the boy. 'Winnie's good at talking to people. Maybe Faith told her something . . .'

'Something about Garnet? But what?'

'I don't know.' Nick answered a little too abruptly. 'Now that Garnet's . . . gone, has Faith said what she means to do?'

'No. I just assumed she'd stay here for the time being. She certainly has no business being on her own.'

'She'll need some of her things, then.' He pushed his chair back from the table with an air of relief. 'I'll just nip up to the farmhouse—'

'No,' Gemma interrupted. 'I'll go. Faith will want to see you if she wakes, and I could use the exercise. Just give me directions.' She didn't mention that the place would be crawling with police by now, and she could at least plead official status. Besides, she had to admit she was increasingly curious about Garnet Todd.

'Okay,' Nick said at last, and gave her terse directions. Glancing critically at her shoes, he warned, 'It's a good climb, though.'

'I'll be fine, don't worry,' she answered, amused. Her new shoes had a slightly higher heel than she usually wore on the job, but her feet were veterans of abuse. As she gathered up her handbag and jacket, she remembered the promise she'd made to Faith. 'The café where Faith works – is it near here?'

'Halfway up the lane to Garnet's farm. You can't miss it.'

At the door, Gemma turned and made a last entreaty to Nick. 'You will try to convince Faith about the doctor, won't you?'

He snorted. 'Trying to get Faith to do something she's made up her mind against is like trying to move the damn Tor. I don't know how Garnet managed to make her so biddable.'

'Hypnotism, maybe?' Gemma said lightly.

'Or something worse,' Nick muttered darkly, but when she raised an eyebrow, he shook his head and said, 'Never mind.'

Gemma hadn't realized how much the atmosphere of Jack's house oppressed her until she was outside it. Most of the houses along the way were massively Victorian, like Jack's, but a good many showed obvious signs of modernization and redecorating. Odd that Jack's mother had done so little to make the place more liveable.

On the right, the slope of the Tor rose from the back gardens, while beyond the houses on the left side of the road, the land dropped steeply away to a flat, level plain.

Soon she came to the sharp turn Nick had indicated and began the climb up Wellhouse Lane. Immediately, she saw the bough-entwined entrance of the footpath that led to the Tor's summit. She found the prospect strangely tempting, in spite of the uneasiness the hill engendered in her, but she resolved to put off the climb until another time.

A bit winded by the time she reached the Dream Café, Gemma paused to examine the charm-and-ribbon-bedecked tree in its courtyard. It occurred to her that Winnie had come to the café on her bike, perhaps leaning the bicycle on that very tree.

The interior of the café was dim and damp. Van Morrison's 'Moondance' played on the cheap sound system, and a few customers sat eating at wooden tables. Beyond them, a lanky man with a greying pony-tail worked in a small kitchen behind a serving area.

'Are you Buddy?' Gemma asked, reaching the counter.

'One and the same.' His smile was friendly, his accent vaguely American. 'What can I do for you?'

'My name's Gemma. I'm a friend of Jack Montfort's, visiting from London—'

'Is it Winnie? Not—'

'No, Winnie's condition hasn't changed. Faith asked me to come and see you; she's staying at Jack's.'

Buddy looked relieved. 'I didn't know, when she didn't show up for work this morning. I thought the baby . . .' Then his brow creased as he sorted out the implications. 'Why isn't Faith with Garnet? Is Faith all right?'

'Faith is fine. It's Garnet. I'm very sorry to say she's dead.'

'Dead?' Buddy stared at her. 'You're joking, right?'

'I'm sorry,' Gemma repeated gently. 'I know you were friends.'

'But – she can't be dead! Not Garnet! There must be some mistake.'

'Faith got worried when Garnet didn't come home last night. She went to Jack, who called the police. They found her in her van this morning.'

'In her van? But . . . I don't understand.' He seemed lost, the cheerful bonhomie extinguished. 'Was there an accident? Was she ill?'

'No one knows for certain, yet. But Faith wanted me to tell you.'

'Faith . . .' Buddy seemed to focus on Gemma with difficulty. 'Who's going to look after Faith now? I promised – promised Garnet I'd keep her safe . . . Look. I appreciate you doing this. But if you don't mind . . .' He looked ill, and his eyes had filled with tears.

'Of course. There should be someone at Jack's, if you want to ring up later.'

Buddy nodded, and Gemma left him to his solitary grief.

As she continued her climb, she wondered what other lives had intersected with Garnet Todd's. The woman had certainly inspired strong emotion in those close to her – surely not a bad epitaph?

The muscles in the backs of Gemma's calves began to ache as the lane grew steeper. She was paralleling the northward rise of the Tor, moving closer to the ruined church on its summit. The climbers milling about the structure were clearly visible now, if disproportionately antlike.

At last she saw the landmark Nick had given her, the fork of Stonedown Lane to the left and, fifty yards beyond it, a solitary and dilapidated farmhouse. Much to her surprise, there were no police cars. Only a Volkswagen saloon stood before the closed farmyard gate.

As Gemma drew closer, she saw a man in the yard, and something in his movements struck her as furtive. He peered into the barn, then walked towards the back door of the house. A few feet from the porch, he halted, as if unsure what to do next.

Reaching the gate, Gemma hailed him. 'Hullo, there. Can I help you?'

The man spun round, and for an instant she had the impression he might bolt. But she stood between him and his car, and by the time she'd let herself through the gate and crossed the yard, he seemed to have thought better of it.

'I'm looking for Garnet Todd,' he replied, planting his feet firmly as if he had every right to be there. 'I want to consult her about some tile work. This *is* the right place?' he added, smiling, and it occurred to Gemma that he was quite attractive.

'Yes, it's the right place. But I'm afraid Miss Todd won't be able to help you.'

'But I've heard she's the best—'

'I'm sorry. I should have explained straight away. Miss Todd won't be helping anyone. She died sometime last night.'

'Died?' he echoed blankly. 'But— Oh my God, but that's dreadful! What was it, a sudden illness?'

'I don't think so. The police are investigating.'

The man paled, and for an instant Gemma could have sworn she saw swift calculation in his eyes. Then his brows drew together in concern and he said, 'I'm sorry. That's even more horrible. Are you a relative of Miss Todd?'

'Not exactly,' Gemma equivocated. 'Did you know her well?'

'Oh, no. I'd never actually met her.' The man glanced at his watch. 'Look, I've got to go. So sorry to have bothered you.' He flashed her an apologetic smile, then made his way swiftly across the yard and out of the gate. Gemma watched him curiously, making a mental note of the car's registration, until he had reversed and driven away.

How very odd, she thought, then turned her attention to the farmhouse. First, a look in the barn – obviously Garnet Todd's workshop. The tools and materials were all neatly organized, and there was no sign of any struggle or disturbance.

She crossed the yard again and, using her handkerchief, eased open the back door to the house. A chorus of pitiful mewling greeted her. The daylight coming in through the filmed windows was sufficient to illuminate three furry, protesting shapes on the kitchen table. It seemed no one had fed Garnet's cats.

Although not wanting to incur DI Greely's ire by contaminating what might prove a crime scene, Gemma carefully searched the primitive kitchen until she found a tin canister filled with dried cat food. Garnet's disdain for modern conveniences had apparently not extended to cat food. Gemma filled a stoneware bowl and put out fresh water as well. She watched with satisfaction while the cats ate, but after a moment she shivered as the room's chill began to penetrate. The wood-burning stove had long since gone out, and the room had the dank smell of cold ashes.

She tried to imagine choosing to live as Garnet Todd had, and failed. How difficult must it have been for a suburban child like Faith, weaned on television and instant gratification? The thought gave her a new respect for the girl's perseverance.

Fastening her lightweight jacket, she looked round the kitchen with unabashed curiosity. There was a good supply of staples on the open shelves, but no perishables that she could see other than milk, cheese, butter, and eggs. Garnet would have been a vegetarian, no doubt, and had probably done her shopping daily. The table held a casserole dish carefully covered with tinfoil. Using the handkerchief again, Gemma peeled back a corner, looked, and sniffed. A cheese and vegetable dish of some sort, still fresh.

There were no dirty dishes in the deep, old-fashioned farmhouse sink, and the washing up had been carefully left to dry on a tea towel. It looked as if Garnet had prepared their evening meal as usual, but then what? Had she gone out, expecting to come back and share the casserole with Faith?

The rumble of an approaching car startled her out of her ruminations. She nudged aside the faded curtains just in time to see Kincaid pull her Escort into the yard. As he got out, Gemma had the momentary pleasure of watching him unobserved. Relaxed in jeans and his old leather bomber jacket, the wind ruffling his chestnut hair, he moved with a grace unusual in a tall man.

Coming back across the yard after closing the gate,

he stopped abruptly and peered at the ground. Curious, Gemma went out to join him.

Kincaid looked up at the sound of the door and flashed his quick grin. 'So you are here. Good. But I see Greely's men haven't made it yet.'

'You must have been back to the house.'

'Um-hmm. And met Jack's young friend Carlisle. Did you happen to notice his motorbike?'

'Vaguely. Why?'

'I used to have a bike like that, before I came down to London. I was the terror of the countryside, and my parents were certain I was going to end up glued to a tree. The thing is' – he knelt and touched a finger to the rutted surface of the yard – 'I'd recognize those tracks anywhere.'

Gemma looked more carefully at the ground. Of course, he was right. The tread marks were too narrow for a car, much less a van, and they were recent. She shouldn't have missed them. 'Bloody hell. How fresh are they, do you think?'

'We'll have to find out when it rained, but I'd say these tracks were probably made this morning or yesterday.'

Their eyes met. 'When I spoke to Nick he said he had driven by this morning. He didn't mention coming into the yard.'

'I'd say that puts him right in the frame for Garnet's murder.'

Gemma picked up his thought. 'In which case, maybe it wasn't such a good idea to leave Faith alone with him. We should go back – but I meant to pick up a few of Faith's things, if I can do it without disturbing the scene.' She turned back to the house and Kincaid followed. She heard his snort of surprise when he stepped through the door.

'I don't suppose Garnet had any Y two K worries. Talk about off the grid.'

The cats, sated now and prone to view Gemma as their saviour, rubbed madly about her ankles, purring, until she let them out. 'I'll just see what I can turn up upstairs.'

Leaving him, she made her way through the dim passage and up the staircase. She found Faith's room first, as comfortless a retreat as she had ever seen. The sight of the folded nightdress and the teddy bear on the pillow moved her almost to tears.

Suddenly she wanted desperately to hold her son, to feel his small body warm against hers and rub her nose in his silky hair. Gathering a few meagre things for Faith, she left the room quickly.

However, she couldn't resist a peep in the bedroom across the hall. On the threshold, she stopped in surprise. The room was unexpectedly feminine, considering the rest of the house. The high four-poster bed was neatly made, and the room as undisturbed as the kitchen. There had been no struggle here.

When Kincaid pulled the Escort into Jack's drive, Jack's blue Volvo stood in its usual spot and there was no sign of Nick Carlisle's motorbike. 'An unexpected changing of the guard?' Kincaid asked. 'Let's see what's up, shall we?'

They found Jack in the kitchen, on the telephone,

saying, 'Right. I'll ring you then. Cheerio.' Smiling widely, he motioned them in as he hung up the phone.

'Good news?' Kincaid asked.

'She's awake. Winnie's conscious! I've just rung the Archdeacon, and Fiona Allen.'

'That's terrific, Jack.' Kincaid clapped his cousin on the shoulder. 'Did you see her?'

'I was there when she opened her eyes. She knew me right away.' Jack turned away and made rather a big fuss over filling the kettle and warming the teapot, and Kincaid suspected that he was fighting to keep his emotions under control.

'The bad news is that she doesn't seem to remember anything past the evening before her accident. The nurses tell me she'll probably regain the missing bits, but there's no guarantee.'

'Did she say anything at all that might give us a clue as to what happened?'

'She seems to be worried about her brother. But that may be because her last clear recollection is Andrew's abominable behaviour at her dinner party.'

'How much longer will they keep her in the ICU?' Kincaid asked.

'As soon as they see she can handle liquids on her own, they'll move her into a room.'

'At that point, you might want to make sure that someone you trust is with her at all times.'

Paling, Jack tended to the boiling kettle. He brought the tea things to the table and sat down heavily. 'Somehow I'd managed to convince myself that we were over the worst.'

'It *is* wonderful news,' Gemma reassured him. 'And

cause for celebration. Let's drink a toast.' She raised her cup.

'Wait.' Jack rose and fetched three glasses and a bottle of twelve-year-old Macallan. He splashed a bit in each glass and pushed theirs across the table. 'We'll do it properly. Here's to Winnie.'

They all raised their glasses, and although Kincaid and Jack downed theirs, Kincaid noticed that Gemma took the merest sip. Lately she'd been ordering orange juice in the pub, and leaving her after-work glass of wine almost untouched. Was she slimming and had not bothered to tell him?

Now she sipped demurely at her tea, asking, 'How's Faith?'

'Still sleeping,' Jack told her. 'Nick said she never stirred.'

'Have you checked on her?' Kincaid heard the unintended sharpness in his voice, and Jack gave him a puzzled look.

'Yes, before Nick left. Sleeping like a baby. Why?'

'Has it rained recently?'

Jack stared at him. 'Yesterday morning. A brief shower, but heavy. Duncan, what on earth are you getting at?'

'Would you say Nick is trustworthy?'

'Of course I would! What is this about?'

'Nick's been to the farmhouse in the last day, something he very carefully neglected to mention.'

'I'm sure he was looking for Faith last night,' Jack protested. 'He said he'd searched everywhere for her. The farmhouse would have been the obvious place to start.'

'Then why not say so?'

There was an uncomfortable moment of silence as the implications sank in, then Jack said, 'Look. I'm sure it's simply a matter of miscommunication. Nick's a good kid, and he'd do anything for Faith—' Too late, he seemed to realize where that avenue was leading.

'We'll have to tell Inspector Greely. You do see that.'

'Duncan, I can see the difficult position I've put you in by asking you to get involved in this. But I have obligations as well, and Nick is my friend. Talk to him first, before you turn it over to Greely. Surely that can't hurt.'

Kincaid weighed this, then glanced at Gemma, who nodded. 'Fair enough. Where can we find him?'

'When he left here he said he was going home. I know he lives in a caravan in Compton Dundon, but I've never been there. You could ask at the bookshop where he works. On Magdalene Street, just across from the Abbey gates. But first you'll want to get settled in at the B and B.'

'It would be nice to unpack and freshen up. With all that's happened, it seems as if we've been here for days rather than a few hours.' Gemma gathered up her bag and carried her cup to the sink. 'Oh, by the way, there was a man snooping round Garnet's house when I got there. He said he wanted some tile work done, but it didn't quite ring true.'

'What did he look like?' asked Jack.

'Tall, slender, glasses, dark hair. Mid-thirties. Nice-looking in a bookish sort of way. He was driving a silver Volkswagen saloon.'

Jack had paused with his glass halfway to his

mouth. 'How very odd. That sounds like Andrew Catesby, but I can't imagine what he'd be doing at Garnet Todd's.'

'Poor Jack,' said Gemma as she slid behind the wheel of her car. 'I don't think he was prepared for the idea that someone he knew and liked might be involved in Winnie's accident – or Garnet Todd's murder.'

Kincaid buckled up and opened a guide to Glastonbury that Jack had provided. 'Go west, then bear left at the first roundabout,' he instructed, then added, 'And I don't think he's realized that Faith has no alibi after she left work yesterday afternoon. What did she tell you?'

'She said she couldn't stop herself looking at the van's bumper, then she felt so ashamed of her suspicions that she couldn't face Garnet. She tried to climb the Tor, but when she started to have pains, she curled up in a hedge and went to sleep.'

Kincaid's raised eyebrow shouted his scepticism. Irritated, Gemma said, 'So what are you proposing? That this nine-months-pregnant girl went home, had an argument with Garnet, killed her somehow or other, then dragged her body to the van?'

'Asphyxiated, it looks like,' Kincaid said placidly. 'Although the doctor was a bit cagey about the method.'

'Even if Faith were physically capable of strangling or suffocating Garnet, why would she do such a thing? Maybe someone killed Garnet to keep her from hurting *Faith*.'

'Nick, for instance?' Checking the map again,

Kincaid directed, 'Right at the next roundabout. The B and B should be just along Magdalene Street.'

Gemma made the turn and slowed, searching for the B & B's sign. 'I'd like to know what Winnie Catesby's brother was doing poking about Garnet Todd's place.'

'I suppose we could have a chat with Mr Catesby as well. There!'

Gemma swung the car sharply into the gravel drive of a square, well-kept Georgian house, red brick with white paint. Kincaid got out and rang the bell, and soon returned with a pleasant young man who opened the security gate for them and directed Gemma where to park.

The young man informed them that their room was in the coach house, and while the men removed the bags from the boot, Gemma looked round with pleasure. The coach house stood at the end of the drive, separated from the main house by a formally landscaped garden, and protected from the noise and traffic of the busy street.

Inside proved as delightful as the exterior, and as Gemma followed the men up a graceful staircase, she was thankful not to be spending the night in Jack's dark house beneath the Tor. 'The Acacia Room,' the young man told them when they'd reached their room, and Gemma's first thought was that 'Rose' would have been more appropriate, for it was done up in soft shades of that colour. A bay window on the front looked over the drive.

As Kincaid thanked the young man and closed the door, Gemma went to the north window and pulled aside the lace curtain. Below her was a square pool with a fountain, canopied by a tree with the most beautiful bark she had ever seen. Patterned in shades from the palest green to deepest russet, it reminded her of an abstract painting.

'The tree – what is it?' she asked as Kincaid came to stand beside her.

'An acacia. Lovely, isn't it?' He put his hands on her shoulders and she leaned back against him. Her gaze travelled upward, over the garden wall, and she gave an involuntary gasp of surprise. 'What is that?' She pointed at the view of rolling, emerald-green grounds and, just visible through the trees, a round stone building.

'It's the Abbey,' he replied, sounding amused. 'You didn't know?'

'Right in the centre of the town?'

'Mm-hmm. The Abbey came first, and the town grew up around it.'

'And that?' She gestured at the round structure.

'The Abbot's Kitchen. It's the only intact building in the precinct, saved – if I remember correctly – because after the dissolution the Quakers used it as a meeting house. See the four chimneys, large enough that the Abbot could roast whole pigs or oxen for his guests.'

'Doesn't sound a very religious life, throwing big parties.'

'*And* they drank a lot of wine. It was a very political life. If an abbot wanted his establishment to prosper, he had to butter the right bread.'

Gemma laughed. 'I think you've mixed your metaphors. How is it that you know these things?'

'I was an annoyingly curious child. It's a good thing I found an outlet for it as an adult, or I'd very likely have come to a bad end.' He wrapped his arms round her for a moment, then released her. 'I've got to make some calls before we go out again, if you want to unpack.'

'Nick's bookshop is just down the street, isn't it? Why don't I see if I can turn up his address, then meet you back here. That way we'll save a bit of time.'

She started up Magdalene Street, eager to see more of the Abbey, but after a briefly tantalizing glimpse through an iron railing, her view was blocked by the public toilets, then a hideous public car park. Past that, she glimpsed the tunnel-like entrance to the Abbey and, on the opposite side of the street, Nick's bookshop.

She accomplished her errand at the bookshop quickly. The shop's owner informed her that Nick wasn't on the telephone, but told her how to find his caravan in Compton Dundon.

Thanking the woman, Gemma went back out into the street. She crossed to the paved area surrounding the Market Cross, where Magdalene Street met the High Street, and looked up the High, taking stock of the town. It seemed pleasant but unremarkable, except for the high incidence of New Age shops offering candles, artwork, crystals, clothing, and every sort of healing imaginable.

Turning away, she walked back the way she had come. This time when she reached the Abbey entrance, she turned in. At the end of the flower-lined passage she found a separate gift shop as well as the entrance to the Abbey museum and grounds. Posted signs directed her past the museum's exhibits and the brass-rubbing station, and at last she stepped through the door that led to the Abbey ruins.

Directly across the sweeping expanse of lawn lay the Abbot's Kitchen and, nearer to her, a partial ruin whose shape made her think of a cauliflower. But it was to the left that she was drawn, past the smaller, more complete church and the discreet sign that designated it as the Lady Chapel, towards the twin towers whose silhouette seemed as familiar to her as the shape of her hand. The grass seemed greener, the sky bluer, than any she had seen before, and there was a quality of stillness to the air that she had never experienced.

She walked slowly, the grass springing beneath her feet, past the single standing wall of the nave, until she reached her destination. The 'North Transept', and the 'South Transept', the signs read. This had been the great central aisle of the church, not the entrance, as she had initially thought. She gazed up, marvelling at the human ingenuity that had constructed such things.

She had no sense of time passing, or of anything other than the immediate moment. It seemed nothing could disturb the peace within the precinct walls, and with a newly comprehended horror, she thought of the story Jack had told them of the monks murdered by their own abbot.

It was only when she reached down to touch the stone of what had been the High Altar that she chanced to see her watch. An hour had gone since she entered the Abbey gate. To her it had seemed only minutes. Kincaid would think her lost, or kidnapped.

As she hurried back towards the entrance, it occurred to her that perhaps those alternatives were no stranger than the truth – but how could she tell him that she had been spellbound?

Kincaid had long since finished his phone calls and given up peering out of the front window. Although he was tempted to go looking for Gemma, he stuck by his rule of staying put when separated. Perhaps she'd found Nick Carlisle at the bookshop after all and taken the young man for a coffee.

Instead, he stretched out on the bed and mulled over the unanticipated events of the hours since their arrival. He had expected to spend a couple of days reassuring his cousin over the matter of his girlfriend's accident. What he had got instead was a murder; a likely attempted murder; the possibility that Jack's friend Nick might be the prime suspect in the murder inquiry; and the bizarre phenomenon of Jack writing out messages from a monk dead more than eight hundred years. The complications arising from any of these items were mind-boggling.

He should have known better. If it turned out that Nick Carlisle was guilty of murder, and he participated in bringing him to book, then his relationship with his cousin might be irreparably damaged. He'd seen similar situations too often. The job didn't mix with friends and family.

And there was the matter of Gemma's apparent

rapport with the girl Faith. Already Gemma seemed inclined to defend her, and Kincaid suspected that if Carlisle had indeed murdered Garnet, Faith had been an accessory to some degree. Gemma had been touchy enough lately without adding emotional involvement to what should be a professional matter.

But he could hardly turn tail and go back to London at this point, especially if there were any chance that Winnie Catesby might still be in danger.

That left Jack. His cousin had never been given to flights of fancy, and he certainly seemed normal enough now, except for the automatic writing. And as Kincaid had no logical explanation for what he had seen with his own eyes, for the time being he supposed he would have to take communications from Edmund of Glastonbury at face value.

Glancing restively at his watch, Kincaid thought that unless Gemma *had* found Carlisle, they would be looking for his caravan in the dark. Just as he swung his legs off the bed and stood, he heard quick footsteps on the stairs.

'What on earth happened to you?' he demanded as Gemma came in. She looked flushed and dishevelled, as if she'd been hurrying.

'Oh – I was . . . I stopped at the Abbey, just for a bit.' She went to the dressing table and, unfastening her hair, brushed it out. 'I've got the directions, such as they are. Just give me a second, then we'll go.' She replaited her hair with a speed he always found amazing, then turned to him with a smile. 'Ready?'

*

'That's Wearyall.' Kincaid pointed at the long, humped hill on their left as they left Glastonbury. 'According to the legend, it was the first land sighted by Joseph of Arimathea after his voyage from the Holy Land.'

'This was under water?' Gemma asked, surprised. They were heading west, towards the larger town of Street, only two miles away, then south to the village of Compton Dundon.

'Almost the entire area. That's why they call it the Isle of Avalon. At one time, Glastonbury Tor must have been the only thing above water for miles. And that,' he continued as they crossed a sluggish little stream, 'is the River Brue. I was devastated as a child when I learned that this was the site of the Pons Perilis, the bridge where King Arthur had his vision of the Virgin Mary.'

'Doesn't look like much, does it?' Gemma agreed. They were coming into Street. The town seemed both more prosperous and more suburban than Glastonbury, if less charming. As they quickly left it behind, a ridge of hills rose to their left, lit by the western sun.

'It's pretty country,' Gemma said a bit wistfully.

Kincaid gave her an amused glance. 'Don't tell me you're turning into a country girl. I never thought I'd see the day.'

'I wouldn't go that far. It's just—' She stopped, having no idea how to explain the sudden longing that had swept over her for the peaceful, rolling landscape. Instead, she shrugged. 'Maybe I just needed a break, that's all.' But, for the first time, she wondered how much Kincaid had missed his native Cheshire.

'Carefully, now,' he said, glancing at the map. 'It's this side of Compton Dundon.'

She nodded, slowing, and soon found the turning – and a mile or two up the lane, in a farmer's field, the caravan. The latter had seen better days, and looked forlorn with only a few scraggly sheep for company. Nick Carlisle's motorbike was parked near the door.

'Let's leave the car by the road and walk, shall we?' Kincaid suggested. 'That field looks a bit treacherous.'

Gemma found a wide spot in the verge to park and they picked their way across the rutted, mucky ground. 'Rain must have been heavier here,' she said softly, then fell silent as they approached the caravan. There was no sound of music or telly, and Kincaid's rap on the door shattered the air like a gunshot.

Nick opened the door quickly, paling when he saw them. 'What is it? What's happened? Is Faith—'

'No, she's fine,' Gemma hastened to reassure him.

'Then what—'

'We just wanted a word. Can we come in?'

'Oh. Sorry.' He stepped back, holding the door for them. 'My humble abode. And it *is* humble.'

Not only humble, but untidy, thought Gemma as she surveyed the space. It was essentially one room, with a kitchenette at one end, a sleeping area at the other, and a partition at the back that must house shower and toilet. Dishes were piled on the draining board and clothes strewn on the floor, but the majority of the clutter consisted of books. They filled every available space. There were even a few stacks that appeared to be permanently installed on the bed, as if Nick arranged himself around them when he slept.

Nick looked tired and rumpled; he gazed at them, then looked round the room with a perplexed expression, as if unsure what to do with visitors.

Kincaid gestured towards the small table. 'Perhaps we could sit down?'

'Oh. Right.' Nick hurried to clear two of the chairs of books and papers, dumping them unceremoniously on the floor, then pulled out the chairs with an air of triumph. 'Tea?'

Gemma averted her eyes from the kitchen. 'No, no, we're fine, really. We just wanted to have a chat about yesterday.'

Nick flipped the third chair round and straddled it, watching them warily. 'Okay. Chat away.'

'You said that you looked everywhere for Faith yesterday afternoon and evening,' Kincaid said easily. When Carlisle nodded confirmation, he continued, 'But you didn't go to the farmhouse?'

This time the young man's nod was less assertive.

'That's a bit odd, isn't it?' Gemma asked. 'It would seem the obvious place to start.'

'I – I promised Faith I wouldn't go there. Garnet didn't like it when I did.'

'But you were obviously worried about Faith,' said Kincaid. 'And you'd told her to look at Garnet's van. If it had been me, and I thought Garnet might have been responsible for Winnie's accident, and then Faith disappeared, I'd have turned that place upside down looking for her.'

'I—' Nick hesitated. Then his resolve seemed to

harden. 'Look. I know you're Jack's cousin, but I don't see that this is any business of yours. Why are you asking me all these questions?'

'Because a woman is dead, and fresh tracks from your motorbike are all over her yard,' Kincaid replied sharply. 'And because Jack asked us to have a word with you before we brought that to Inspector Greely's attention. Jack was sure you'd have a good explanation.'

Nick looked from Kincaid to Gemma, dismay written on his face. 'Oh, shit. I didn't think of that.'

'You were there.' Gemma made it a statement.

'I was worried about Faith. I went to the farmhouse to talk to her, even though I knew she'd be furious with me.'

'Did you see Garnet?'

Nick nodded. 'She said Faith wasn't there, but I didn't believe her. I searched the house.'

'And then?'

He bridled. 'And then I kept looking. I even went to Street and had a look at her parents' house, just in case she'd been desperate enough to go back, and to the Vicarage, in case she'd gone there.'

'If you left Ms Todd alive and well, why not tell the truth?' Kincaid asked him.

Nick shrugged. 'When I heard Garnet was dead, I started to think . . . you know, it looked bad. And how was anyone else to know I'd been there? Pretty stupid of me, I suppose.'

'Quite,' Kincaid agreed dryly. 'You'll have to talk to the police, and I'd recommend you do it before they come looking for you. You do realize you may have been the last person to see Ms Todd alive?'

Colour stained Nick's face. 'No. I hadn't . . .'

'How did you leave things with her?'

'I'll sound a right prat . . .' When Kincaid merely raised an eyebrow, Nick stumbled on. 'I told her that if anything had happened to Faith, she'd be sorry. But I didn't mean – you can't think – Good Lord, I never wished her *dead*!'

'No one's saying you did,' interposed Gemma. 'Did you see anything to indicate she was expecting someone? Or that she meant to go out?'

'No, I can't say that I did. But . . . there was something . . . she seemed different. I was surprised that she actually let me in the house, for one thing. And she seemed really worried about Faith. I think that's what convinced me that she hadn't done something horrible to her.'

'You didn't see anyone hanging about the place?'

'No. I suppose it would be better for me if I could say I had.'

'And you didn't know what had happened to Faith until you heard from Jack?'

'He rang me at the shop first thing this morning. As soon as I could get away, I went looking for Garnet. And I did go back to the farmhouse, to see if she'd come home.'

'Did you go inside?'

Nick nodded uneasily. 'The door was unlocked. I didn't search the house, though. Just stood in the kitchen and called out.'

'Had anything changed since the previous afternoon?'

'Not that I could see.'

Kincaid stood. 'Well, if you want my advice, Nick, the sooner you talk to DI Greely, the better for you.' He handed him Greely's card. 'Why don't you take this number down.'

While Nick rummaged for pen and paper, Gemma had a chance to examine some of the books he had moved to make room for them. There was a preponderance of volumes on Druids, Goddess worship, and ancient magic. Lifting one, she said, 'Nick, what did you mean when you said Garnet might have done something worse than hypnotize Faith?'

'Did I say that? Must have been talking off the top of my head. I've no idea.' Nick scooped up an armload of books and dumped them on the far side of the table.

'Garnet Todd seems to have been quite knowledgeable about such things.' Gemma gestured at the books. 'Did she see Faith as a disciple?'

'If she did, she wouldn't have confided in me,' Nick said bitterly.

'There's something I'm not sure I understand, here. Why was Garnet so determined to shut you out of Faith's life? Surely as the baby's father—'

'I'm not the baby's father!'

'But I thought—'

'No. Faith was pregnant when I met her.'

'But then who—'

'Faith won't tell. No one has a clue. Unless . . .' Nick frowned.

'Unless Garnet knew,' Gemma finished for him. 'It would make sense, if Faith confided in anyone, it would have been Garnet. I wonder . . . What if someone made sure Garnet wouldn't reveal the father's secret?'

Chapter Thirteen

Glastonbury is not only deep-rooted in the past, but the past lives on at Glastonbury. All about us it stirs and breathes, quiet, but living and watching.

Dion Fortune, from
Glastonbury: Avalon of the Heart

What?' Kincaid demanded. 'Have I got jam on my face?'

'No.' Gemma smiled. 'Crumbs. You look quite fetching.'

He set down his croissant, used his napkin, then poured them both another cup of coffee. They were lingering over a continental breakfast in the B & B's dining room. The room was elegant and comfortable, the food delicious, and he had refused to rush. They were, after all, at least nominally on holiday.

Gemma looked more relaxed than he had seen her in months, dressed for a casual day in russet-coloured linen trousers, a pale yellow jumper, and boots.

Nevertheless, he was convinced something was worrying her. She had tossed and turned in the night, mumbling in her sleep, and lately he had been catching her watching him – as he had just then – with a pensive expression he couldn't fathom. Each time he'd asked her what was wrong, she'd brushed his enquiry off with an inconsequential reply.

'What's first on the agenda?' Gemma leaned back in her chair. 'I'd like to know how Faith's doing this morning.'

'I'll give Jack a ring, see if I can catch him at home before he leaves for the hospital.' He had just pulled the phone from his pocket when it rang, earning him a dirty look from the couple at the next table. 'I should keep the damned thing on vibrate,' he muttered as he answered.

'Duncan?'

'Speak of the—'

'The police have taken Nick in for questioning this morning,' his cousin interrupted. ' "Helping them with their inquiries," Greely called it. You said all Nick had to do was tell the truth.' He sounded as though he felt betrayed.

'Jack, there's never anything to gain from lying to the police. Look, I don't imagine they have enough to keep him more than a few hours, but I'll give Greely a ring. I'll call you back.'

'They've picked up Nick,' Gemma guessed as he disconnected.

'And Jack thinks I've led them both up the garden path.' Kincaid grimaced. 'Bloody hell. I suppose I'd better find out if Greely knows something we don't.'

He dialled the mobile number Greely had given him, identifying himself when the detective answered. 'I hear you've pulled in Nick Carlisle.'

'I thought Mr Montfort would be speaking to you,' Greely answered, sounding amused. 'The boy's prints are on record, and we also found them all over the farmhouse when we dusted it yesterday.'

'Well, they would be if he did what he claims,' Kincaid observed mildly. 'Any luck with the van?'

'No prints except Todd's and the girl's.'

'Anything wiped?'

'No. Our killer must have worn gloves. There are quite a few smudged places on the steering wheel and door handles.'

'Somehow our lad doesn't strike me as the calculating type.'

'Maybe not,' said Greely, 'but he's the best thing we've got at the moment.'

'You don't have enough to charge him.'

'No. But it never hurts to shake the bottle a bit. We'll send him on his way this afternoon if nothing else turns up, keep an eye on him. Maybe the girl helped him, and she's the one that thought to wear gloves.'

Not a bad hypothesis, Kincaid thought, and of course in Greely's position he'd think – and do – exactly the same. 'How'd the lad get himself a record?'

'Some university fracas in Durham. Too much beer ending in a punch-up, is my guess. Oh, and thanks, by the way, for having Carlisle deliver himself. Saved us a bit of work.' Greely sounded quite pleased with himself.

Glancing up, Kincaid saw that the couple at the next table were now listening to him with undisguised curiosity.

'You'll keep me posted?' he asked Greely, reluctant to say more.

'Right. Oh. One more thing. We begged and bullied the pathologist into performing the post mortem this morning. You're going to like this one.' Greely plainly relished keeping Kincaid in suspense.

'And?'

'It seems as though Todd drowned. Fresh water, untreated. So it didn't come from a tap.' With that, Greely rang off.

'What's he—' began Gemma, when Kincaid jerked his head towards their eavesdropping neighbours. She fell silent, toying with the flakes of pastry on her plate, while Kincaid sipped at his coffee, his mind busy with speculation.

After a few unrewarding minutes, the couple gave up and left the room. Kincaid grinned. 'Short attention spans.' He then repeated Greely's side of the conversation.

'I don't believe Faith helped murder Garnet, or that she's calculating,' Gemma said stubbornly when he'd finished. 'For heaven's sake, she's still a child.'

'You know all too well that's no guarantee. And she did show up in hysterics at Jack's around the time Garnet was killed, with no real explanation for where she'd been.'

'I still don't buy it. Greely says Garnet drowned? What are Nick and Faith supposed to have done – held her under in the tub? That's ridiculous. And I don't think it's any more likely that they enticed her to go somewhere where they could do it more conveniently.'

'If it's any comfort, Greely wouldn't dare charge Nick at this point unless he had a confession, and he says Todd drowned in fresh water.'

'Did the pathologist estimate time of death?'

'I didn't have a chance to ask. But if Nick's telling the truth, it has to have been later than five o'clock.'

'That gives Jack a fairly watertight alibi, I should think.'

Kincaid stared at her. It had not even occurred to him that the local coppers might consider his cousin a suspect in Garnet's murder. And it was obvious – if Jack had thought Garnet responsible for Winnie's brush with death, who would have had better motive?

'That's if you consider Faith a reliable witness from the time Jack reached Glastonbury,' he mused, thinking it through.

Gemma pushed aside her coffee cup with decision. 'So what do we do now?'

'I'd say we give Greely another suspect.'

Written sources connected the 'island' of Beckery with Glastonbury Abbey from 670, when a charter of dubious authenticity granted it to Abbot Berthwald. But oral tradition cited Beckery as a religious community as far back as 488, when it was supposed to have been visited by the Irish saint Bridget.

Andrew had never been inclined to accept such stories at face value, but excavations did indicate that the community had been occupied at least since early Saxon times.

Between Beckery and the mass of Wirral Hill, less than a kilometre to the south, lay what had once been Wirral Park, the ancient deer preserve of the abbots of Glastonbury – now home to a hideous complex of supermarkets and car parks.

Standing atop the mound at Beckery, Andrew surveyed this modern encroachment with a disgust that bordered on hatred. They ruined everything, money-grubbing fools with no foresight and no appreciation of the past.

He had walked from Hillhead with his spaniel, along what was left of the sluggish river. It was one of their frequent Saturday-morning excursions, and he was usually able to put aside his anger as he poked about the excavations. But on this day his rage seemed uncontainable, seeping like bile into every nook and cranny of his mind.

He didn't know which was worse – the developers or the crackpots. Even here at Beckery, which had never been more than an unassuming community, the crackpots had been at work. There had been a spring, most likely one of the main reasons for the founding of the monastery on that spot. By the middle of the nineteenth century it had degenerated into little more than a muddy pool, known thereabouts as Bride's Well, after St Bridget. Then, in 1885, a doctor named Goodchild had brought home a bowl he'd found in a shop in Italy and, instructed by a vision, placed it in Bride's Well.

Goodchild then cast hints in appropriate ears, and eventually two young and virginal ladies – also instructed by visions – had chanced to recover the dish. There followed much intense debate in exalted circles as to whether this bowl was the Holy Grail, although Goodchild later insisted that he had never claimed so.

This incident had, in Andrew's view, precipitated the entire business of the Glastonbury Revival – including the absurd claims of that charlatan, Frederick Bligh Bond.

Andrew struck violently at a tussock with his walking stick, startling Phoebe, who looked up at him reproachfully.

'Sorry, girl,' he muttered, yet swung at the next with equal force. Dead monks, for Christ's sake! Who could possibly have believed such nonsense? And now Montfort had perpetuated it. And worse, had dragged his sister into it.

It must have been the clever references to music that had hooked Winnie so easily. Music was a love they had shared since childhood, one of the bonds that had sustained them after their parents' deaths. Now that, too, had been stolen from him.

Had he brought this disaster upon himself by his own actions, a ludicrous parody of some hero in a Greek tragedy?

Brooding, Andrew continued his circuit of the excavation site, Phoebe at his heels. Over the centuries, three successive chapels dedicated to St Bridget had been built at Beckery, each around the confines of the previous one, at the highest point on the peninsula. According to medieval references, a hole had existed in the south wall of the earliest chapel, and all who passed through it had obtained forgiveness for their sins. How unfortunate for him, Andrew thought bitterly, that no such option now existed.

Or would he have been buried face-down in the cemetery on the north side of the chapel, the fate of six out of the sixty-three bodies found there? It was the position the pagans had used to bury criminals and evildoers, and the custom had most likely been adopted by the early Christian settlement. It certainly left no question as to who – or what – a man had been in life.

Andrew looked back to the east, past the town with the Abbey at its heart, to the Tor rising into a grey bank of cloud. Could he face such exposure? Ruin? The loss of everything he valued? He had never wanted to do anything but teach, and that would no longer be possible.

Worse, his sister would despise him, and that above all he could not bear.

Since Jack's visit the previous afternoon, Simon had combed minutely through copies of the Abbey accounts. A record of the produce from the Abbey's many estates had been an important part of Abbey life, and information noted for a particular year included such notations as '7,000 eels from the fisheries at Martinsey', 'honey from the mead-maker at Northload', or '30 salmon from the cellarer for the monks' feast'.

But the Abbey's expenditures had been recorded, too, and it was in such an account that Simon discovered something in the tiny, faded script. He sat up, rubbed his eyes, and read it again.

In the summer of the year 1082, Abbot Thurstan

had paid a mason named Hamlyn for repairs done on St Dunstan's Church.

There was no mistake. He had probably read that particular entry a dozen times these past few months without paying it any attention – but he had not possessed the knowledge to make a connection.

He was making a number of assumptions, of course: that Edmund would have still been in his teens when he succumbed to Alys's charms, that only one mason was hired to do repair work during that period, that Hamlyn might have had a daughter called Alys.

Trying to keep his excitement in check, Simon began to search his sources for any mention of her. It was almost noon when he found it, and it amazed him that he had not seen it before when he had looked for references to Jack's family. Herluin, who succeeded Thurstan as abbot in 1100, had been determined to regain lands lost to the Abbey during the Conquest and to increase the Abbey's wealth. The abbot had required an extensive accounting of the Abbey's possessions, and in one such record it was noted that Alys Montfort, née Hamlyn, had given a gift of fine cloth to the church, with the stipulation that it be recorded in her name.

So Alys had married, and it looked to have been a good marriage at that. But what had happened to the child? If it had lived, contrary to Edmund's expectation, Jack might be a direct descendant of Alys Montfort. Her husband's Christian name wasn't given, but surely there couldn't have been many men called Montfort in that time period, especially with professions that would have allowed his wife to make such a generous gift to the church.

Edmund might provide the answers, but not only was Jack focused on Winifred's recovery at the moment, Edmund's information tended to be very capricious. And as it seemed Edmund was capable of intense emotions concerning past events, it was possible that the subject of his lover's marriage might still be painful to him.

Was it guilt that drove Edmund to communicate across the centuries? The monk seemed to feel that his dalliance with Alys Hamlyn, and his help in her attempt to abort her baby, had in some way been responsible for the loss of the chant, and that only the music's return would expiate his sins.

Simon perused the last communication from Edmund. What did he mean when he said he'd given Alys what 'was most precious to him'? Suppose, just suppose, that when Alys left the Abbey, Edmund had given her a copy of the chant for safe keeping?

Edmund had been both musical and literate – a scholar, by his own admission. Was it unreasonable to think that the monk might have written down a version of his beloved chant?

And if that were the case, might Alys have given it to her child? For eight centuries, might it have been passed down through the family, unremarked?

Gemma and Kincaid had decided to walk the short distance from the B & B to Hillhead Lane. But by the time they neared the address Jack had given them for Andrew Catesby, halfway up the eastern slope of Wearyall Hill, Gemma was breathing hard. She gazed at the Tor rising behind them. 'It doesn't look so daunting from here, does it?'

'A trick of height and distance, my dear. This hill is a good climb, but nothing compared to that one.'

She hadn't strictly meant the climb, but she continued her upward progress without clarifying her words.

'This looks the place,' Kincaid said after a few more yards, nodding. The house just ahead was a pleasant, pale-peach stucco, with an arched entrance that gave the building a vaguely Spanish air. 'Ready?'

A dog barked loudly as Gemma knocked, and a moment later Andrew Catesby opened the door. Seeing his expression of neutral query change swiftly to recognition, she smiled and said, 'Mr Catesby? We met yesterday at Garnet Todd's house. My name's Gemma James.' She flashed her identification at him. 'We'd like to have a word with you, if you don't mind.'

Before Catesby could offer an objection, Kincaid introduced himself, and as they stepped forward, Catesby gave way.

'I suppose you'd better come in, then,' he said, and favoured Gemma with the quick smile she'd seen yesterday.

The dog, a liver-and-white spaniel, was sniffing enthusiastically at Gemma's ankles. Gemma knelt and fondled her silky ears. 'She's lovely. What sort of spaniel is she?'

'Springer,' Catesby replied. 'Phoebe, leave off,' he scolded affectionately. The spaniel went resignedly over to a cushion near the front door and curled up with a sigh, head on her paws.

Gemma turned her attention to the house. The hall opened to a simple kitchen and, ahead, a living area with a glass wall that gave on to the southern view. Here Catesby led them, gesturing towards the leather sofa.

'Lovely view of the Levels,' Kincaid said as he took the proffered seat. 'You must enjoy it.'

'Yes, of course,' Catesby answered pleasantly, but Gemma caught the scent of fear, and her pulse quickened.

'When I saw you yesterday at Ms Todd's farmhouse, you were hoping to commission some tiles. Yet you said you'd never met her. Did someone recommend her to you?'

Catesby hovered restlessly near an armchair, but couldn't seem to bring himself to sit. 'I'm an archaeologist – amateur, you know, summers and holidays – and everyone knows she's the best there is at tile restoration. Was, I mean. She was.'

'You were interested in having her do some work on an archaeological project?'

'She took on personal commissions as well. It was my kitchen. It needs doing up. I thought some tile work . . .'

'Quite.' Kincaid nodded with such apparent sincerity that Gemma almost smiled. 'So you went to her house. Did you by any chance happen to go inside?'

'No. No, of course I didn't. There was no answer when I knocked. I was sorry to hear of the woman's death, but I'm not sure I understand why you're asking me all these questions.'

'You might have seen someone poking about,' offered Kincaid. 'Murderers do sometimes come back to the scene.'

'Murder? Garnet Todd was murdered? But you said – you said she was *dead*.' Catesby's shock seemed genuine. 'And I thought – a heart attack. Or an accident.'

'Yes, we believe she was murdered,' Kincaid informed him evenly. 'And that requires us to go through a process of elimination. If we know, for instance, that you didn't touch anything, we don't have to worry about your fingerprints.'

'But I've told you – I never met the woman, and I never went inside her house.'

'Then you won't mind telling us where you were on Thursday evening,' said Gemma.

Catesby took a breath as if to protest again. Then, shrugging, he said, 'I was at home all evening, marking exams. And no, there's no one that can verify that.'

'And the evening of your sister's accident?'

'My sister? What the devil does my sister have to do with any of this?'

'An accident and a murder, on consecutive days and in the same area; the victims both women who knew one another . . . It only seems logical that there might be some connection.'

'But Winnie—' Catesby sat down for the first time. 'But it *was* an accident. She was struck by a car, for God's sake.'

'A car that didn't stop and render aid; a location in

which the car would have had to make an effort to get up enough speed to do any damage; and as I understand it, Mr Catesby, your sister is too sensible a woman to have walked out in front of a vehicle if she had heard it approaching.'

'But . . . it's preposterous to think anyone would deliberately hurt Winnie, of all people!'

'Nevertheless,' said Gemma, 'there may be a connection.'

Kincaid returned to his original question. 'The evening of your sister's accident, Mr Catesby – where were you?'

'You can't possibly think . . . You can't actually think *I* had something to do with Winnie's accident?' Catesby stared at them.

'No, of course not,' Gemma reassured him. 'It's just routine, really. We have to ask.'

'I had a parents' consultation at school. Then I was home – alone – for the rest of the evening.'

'What time did your consultation finish, Mr Catesby?'

'About half past six, I think—'

'Can the parents you met confirm this?'

'You're not serious? You can't involve parents of my students in this! Do you realize what something like that would mean? When you teach at a public school, you can't afford a breath of scandal. Something like that would go round the board of trustees like wildfire. I'd be finished!'

'No one's accusing you of anything—'

'Even the possibility of involvement is enough. Please, you must understand.'

'Mr Catesby—'

'I won't tell you their names.'

'But—' Gemma stopped. There was no point pushing him. If they needed the information, they could easily get it from other sources. Instead she took another tack. 'I understand your sister has regained consciousness, Mr Catesby. That's wonderful news.'

'I— Yes, isn't it?'

'You've seen her, then?'

He gazed at her blankly. 'No. No, I haven't. I'd thought of going to hospital this afternoon.'

'Perhaps she'll remember something that will help us trace the person responsible for her injuries.'

'Yes, I suppose that's a possibility.'

'Did you see your sister at all that day?'

'No, not after the dinner party she gave on the previous evening.'

'And you've no idea why she was in Bulwarks Lane?'

'Obviously, she must have meant to visit Fiona Allen, but I've no idea why.'

Kincaid stood and handed Catesby one of his cards. 'You've been very helpful. If you think of anything else, just ring my mobile number.' He started towards the door, then stopped and peered into the kitchen. 'I've just refitted my kitchen recently. It was bloody hell, so you have my sympathy. What did you have in mind?'

Catesby looked from Kincaid to the kitchen as if trying to decipher a foreign language. 'Oh – I – everything. Start from scratch. I'd thought tile worktops, but now . . .'

Good recovery, thought Gemma, stopping to give Phoebe a last pat as they said their goodbyes.

When they reached the street, Kincaid took her arm. 'Shall we climb to the top of the hill before we start back, since we've come this far?'

Gemma nodded and, when they had continued upwards for a few yards, said quietly, 'What would you bet that Andrew Catesby had never given a thought to his kitchen before this morning?'

Kincaid grinned. 'I'd need damned good odds. But if that's the case, what did he want with Garnet Todd?'

They reached the stile that gave access to the Wearyall Hill footpath, and he gave her a hand over. The west wind tore at their hair and clothes, and sent ripples like waves through the long green grass on the slope.

'Is that the famous Thorn?' asked Gemma, spying a small, twisted tree enclosed by a circle of chicken wire. 'It seems so forlorn.'

'So would you be, if you were stuck on this hillside and whipped by this bloody wind day in and day out.'

When they reached the summit, they found they could lean against the full force of the wind as if against a wall.

'Are you okay?' Kincaid asked, knowing how much she disliked heights.

'It's all right as long as I don't get too near the edge – lovely, in fact. I feel right on top of the world.'

Kincaid pointed to the west. 'There – see where the land dips right at the horizon? That must be the Bristol Channel.'

Squinting into the wind, Gemma gazed into the

grey-blue distance, but failed to make out anything that might be the sea. Then she rotated slowly and looked out across a low, flat landscape criss-crossed by a grid of straight, silvery lines. 'What are those?'

'They're called rhynes. Drainage ditches. That's what keeps this area from reverting to marshland, but it still floods when the rains are heavy.'

Gemma turned once more, knowing what she would see. To the east, the southern edge of the town nestled in the valley between Wearyall and the Tor. The Tor seemed to float above the red tile rooftops, its humped shape and well-defined contours giving it the look of an alien leviathan. Kincaid followed her gaze.

'It is a very odd thing, isn't it?'

'Surely those terraces are man-made—'

'If they are, it was so long ago that there's not even an oral tradition to explain them. Although some people claim it's a maze, or a labyrinth, used for ritual magic, I don't know that there's any historical evidence to support it.'

Gemma thought of Faith's tale of being drawn to climb the Tor. As absurd as it sounded, she had been convinced that the girl was telling the truth - or at least what she believed was the truth. She shook off a chill of unease.

'Let's go back,' she told Kincaid.

He gave her a concerned glance. 'You've been working too hard, and not looking after yourself properly.'

Unwilling to pursue the topic, Gemma started downhill. 'What's next, then?'

Kincaid walked in silence for a few minutes,

apparently mulling over their progress. 'Have you noticed how everything seems to revolve round Winnie Catesby?' he said at last. 'I think it's time we paid a visit to hospital.'

Jack had protested at the idea of their visit when Kincaid rang him on his mobile, saying, 'I don't want her upset. She's still weak—'

'She's going to have to know these things – that someone may have tried to kill her, and that Garnet Todd's dead,' Kincaid had interrupted. 'And for her own safety, you must tell her as soon as possible.'

At that, Jack had given in, albeit unhappily. When they reached the hospital and found the proper ward, Jack joined them in the corridor with an anxious expression. 'She's dozing again.'

'How is she today?' asked Gemma.

'She seems more clear-headed, but fragile . . . You really think this is necessary?'

'I do, if we're to get any further with this. I rang Inspector Greely again, by the way. They've had to release Nick Carlisle, but if they can turn up the least bit of concrete evidence, they'll charge him in a heartbeat.'

'I don't believe Nick had anything to do with this.' Jack said it so fiercely that Kincaid wondered if he were convincing himself.

'Then we had better find out who did,' Kincaid replied reasonably. 'Why don't we wait out here, and you let us know when Winnie starts to stir. Any sign of her brother, by the way?'

'No. He hasn't shown up since I've been here, and he hasn't rung to check on her, as far as I know.'

They had struck up a conversation with the nursing sister in charge of the floor when Jack reappeared a quarter of an hour later. As Jack motioned them inside, Kincaid realized he was looking forward to meeting Winnie Catesby with a good deal of curiosity.

As he entered the room, his first thought was that the woman in the hospital bed was plain. Of course, she had been ill, but even making allowances for that, she seemed quite ordinary; her features certainly lacked the distinction of her handsome brother's.

Then she looked up at him and smiled, and all thoughts of conventional beauty fled his mind. It was instantly apparent why Jack had fallen in love with Winnie Catesby.

'Jack's been telling me all about you,' she told Kincaid. She seemed oblivious to the fact that her head bore an unsightly shaved spot, with the edges of a wound pulled together with a clip.

'Has he mentioned all the times I got him into trouble when we were kids?'

'More than once. But I don't believe he was as innocent as he makes out,' Winnie replied, with a mischievous glance at Jack.

She greeted Gemma, then, when they had chatted for a few moments, Kincaid pulled a chair up close to the bed.

'Winnie, did Jack tell you *why* he asked us to come?'

She focused all her attention on him, her face

grave. 'No. I just assumed he needed a bit of moral support . . .'

'Have you remembered anything about your accident?'

'Sometimes there are . . . flashes. Did you ever catch a glimpse of something out of the corner of your eye – a glimpse so fleeting that you not only weren't sure what it was, but whether you really saw anything at all?'

Kincaid nodded encouragingly.

'That's what it's like. I know something's there, but I can't grasp it long enough to put words to it. I'm sorry.'

'Don't worry,' he reassured her. 'I'm sure it will come back to you in time. You *do* know that someone struck you with a car and knocked you off your bike?' She nodded. 'Jack thought it was odd that the person didn't stop to help you, and the circumstances of the accident were a bit strange as well. So he rang and asked me to come down, just in case there was something dodgy going on.'

'And is there?' asked Winnie, frowning.

'We think it's possible. Your accident was on Wednesday night, just round the corner from Ms Todd's house. On Thursday, when Faith heard what had happened to you, she was afraid that Ms Todd might have been responsible.'

'Garnet?' Winnie looked utterly astonished. 'That's impossible! Why on earth would Faith think such an absurd thing?'

'Faith said you stopped at the café,' explained Jack. 'When Garnet ran her home a few minutes later, they saw you pushing your bike up the hill. Then Garnet went out alone, and when she came back, Faith said she seemed terribly upset. This would have been just about the time you were struck.'

'Well, I'm sure she must have had a perfectly good reason that had nothing to do with me. What did she say when you asked her?' In the silence that followed her question, Winnie's expression of mild exasperation swiftly changed to alarm. 'What aren't you telling me?'

'Darling.' Jack took her hand. 'I'm afraid Garnet's dead.'

'Dead?'

'I'm sorry,' Kincaid said gently. 'Ms Todd was murdered the evening after your accident.'

'Oh, no . . .' She sank back into the pillow, as if that blow had used up her fragile reserves. Tears leaked from beneath her closed eyelids.

'Surely that's enough for now,' protested Jack. 'Let her—'

Winnie's eyes flew open. 'Faith! What about Faith? Is she—'

'She's fine,' Jack reassured her. 'She's tucked up in the spare room at my house.'

'And have you any idea who could have done such a thing to Garnet?'

'The police have been questioning Nick,' Jack answered reluctantly.

'Nick! Nick wouldn't hurt a fly! I don't believe that for a minute!'

'It's all routine,' Kincaid said hastily. 'The police have to ask these things. But Carlisle did go to the farmhouse the afternoon before Ms Todd was killed.

He may have seen someone, or something, that will prove helpful.'

'Winnie,' said Gemma, 'when I went to pick up Faith's things yesterday, I ran across your brother at the farmhouse. Do you know of any connection your brother might have had with Garnet?'

'Andrew?' Under the sheet, Winnie's chest rose with the sharp intake of her breath. 'No. No, none at all.'

'Has Andrew mentioned anything to you about having his kitchen redone?'

'Andrew?' Winnie said again, this time with a snort. 'It would never occur to him – the poor man can hardly boil water.'

'And was Andrew aware that *you* knew Ms Todd?'

'I – I don't know.' Winnie seemed suddenly uncomfortable. 'I might have mentioned her at some time. Why?'

'Just more routine,' Kincaid reassured her. 'I know this is hard for you. Just one more question, then we'll let you rest. Jack's told us that you visited Faith's parents. It's occurred to me that they had very good reason to be angry with Garnet—'

'But I never told them where Faith was!'

'No, of course not. But it's possible they found out some other way. We should talk to them, if only to eliminate the possibility. If you could just give us Faith's surname and address—'

'I'm sorry.' Winnie's voice was bitingly firm. 'Those are things Faith told me in confidence, and I simply can't reveal them without her permission. You'll have to find some other way.'

Chapter Fourteen

Prove all things, and hold fast that which is true.
Frederick Bligh Bond, from
The Gate of Remembrance

Faith insisted she didn't mind staying on her own. Jack had offered to take her with him to visit Winnie, but there were too many things she couldn't face talking about just yet. Not with Winnie, when she still didn't know how much Winnie knew, or if Garnet were responsible for her accident. And now Garnet was dead.

Dead. Alone in Jack's house, Faith repeated the word to herself, desperate to make sense of it. Garnet had been alive – she had sung to the cats in the morning when she thought no one could hear; she had put courgettes in everything she cooked, even though she knew Faith loathed them; she had read tattered copies of *National Geographic* in the loo; she had kept a doll collection wrapped in tissue paper in a box in her bedroom cupboard.

And now she was *not*.

She spent the first hour after Jack's departure watching some mindless comedy on the old telly in the sitting room, but when the snow on the screen began to give her a headache she gave it up. She had asked Jack once why he hadn't kept any of his own things when he came back to Glastonbury, and he'd replied that they'd absorbed too many memories, like emulsion on film. He'd sold everything in a job lot.

Would Garnet's possessions bear her imprint? Faith had watched her in her workshop, handling her tools with such delicacy. Those she had loved, and her books, and her cape and colourful clothes.

Faith wandered about the house, running her fingertip through the layer of dust on the furniture, her thoughts skittering. She felt as if someone had taken her apart and put the pieces back in the wrong order.

Without conscious decision, she climbed the stairs, slowly, one hand supporting the weight of her belly. She had not been in any of the upstairs rooms except the one Jack had put her in. Now she opened each door along the corridor, peering inside. Hers came first, then a tiny room that bore traces of boyhood occupation. The large room near hers had a high four-poster bed and smelled of Jack and, faintly, Winnie. The other two rooms were filled with boxes, stacks of books and papers, and odd bits of furniture.

What had it been like to grow up in this house? she wondered, recalling her parents' cheerful suburban semi. That brought a pang of intense homesickness, immediately quashed, as was the thought of what she would do once her baby was born. How could she think past this day?

Closing the doors again, she went back down the stairs. She would do something useful, have a meal ready for them, whenever they came back. Scrounging in the pantry, she found some canned chicken stock, a packet of dried peas, rice, and some spices: probably all well past their prime, but she might concoct a passable pot of soup.

She had put the peas on to soak when the doorbell rang. It must be Nick, she thought, and waddled – you could hardly call it walking any more – as quickly as she could to the front door. She swung it open anxiously, to find not Nick, but Inspector Greely and a woman in plain clothes.

'We'd hoped we might find you at home, miss.'

'Jack's not here.' Faith started to close the door.

'No, no, it's you we've come to see. Can we come in?'

When Faith hesitated, not sure if she could refuse, Greely said, 'Unless you would prefer us to interview you in the presence of your parents, of course.'

'I'm seventeen,' she retorted, bristling. 'I can speak for myself.'

'Then we'll have our little chat now.' The Inspector stepped inside, and Faith realized with a sinking heart that she'd backed herself into a corner.

She took them into the sitting room, and let them seat themselves on the worn velvet upholstery, surrounded by silver-framed photos of Jack's relatives.

'This is Detective Constable O'Toole.' Greely nodded towards the woman, who smiled brightly and didn't meet Faith's eyes. She had lacquered blonde hair and an abundance of make-up to match her false smile.

'And you are?' Greely continued. 'I'm afraid we

can't go on just calling you *miss*.' His companion slipped a notebook and pen from her handbag.

'Faith.'

'We'll have to have your surname, for the record. Unless, of course, you'd rather we had this little conversation at the police station.'

'Wills. It's Wills.'

'And your home address? That will be where you're registered with social security, that sort of thing.'

When Faith had reluctantly given them her parents' address, Greely settled back on the sofa and laced his fingers over his stomach. 'There, now that we have that out of the way, Miss Wills, we'd like to talk to you about your friend Nick Carlisle. He says that on the afternoon of the day Miss Todd died, he went to her house looking for you, but you weren't there. Is that right?'

Faith nodded warily.

'Now, that's all very well and good, except for one small thing. No one seems to have provided a satisfactory explanation as to where you were from, say, five o'clock, until you showed up on Mr Montfort's front porch a bit before midnight.'

'I – I went for a walk. Up Wellhouse Lane to the top.' Faith could see the disbelief written clearly on both their faces, but she persisted. 'But then I felt unwell, so I found a spot to rest. I don't know how long I slept, but when I woke up it was dark.'

'And then?'

'I walked back. Garnet's van was gone and the house was empty. I thought she must have been out looking for me, so I waited. But she didn't come.'

'What made you decide to give it up?'

'I . . . It was late . . . and I was . . . frightened.'

'So you went to Mr Montfort for help.' Something about the way Greely said it made it sound dirty.

'He's my friend, and I thought he'd know what to do. There's nothing wrong with that.'

'No, Miss Wills, there's not. If that were indeed the case.' Greely bared his teeth in a smile that held no warmth.

'What do you mean?' Faith felt her face flush with anger.

'It means I think you've left a few things out. I think you were there when Nick came. I think the two of you got into an argument with Miss Todd, a scuffle. Perhaps you didn't mean any real harm, but accidents happen, we all know that.'

Faith could only stare at him.

'Then, when you realized she was dead, you panicked. You helped Carlisle carry her to the van and put her in the back. Then he drove the van round the Tor, parked it, and walked back to pick up his bike.

'Oh, and then the two of you decided that you alone would go to Mr Montfort, pretending to be hysterical with worry because Miss Todd hadn't come home, when all the time you knew exactly where she was.' Greely rubbed his chin, then said, 'Unless, of course, Montfort was in on it too.'

Faith's hands and feet were numb with cold, her tongue stiff in her mouth. 'No. That's not true. None of that's true. That's crazy—'

'Did you and Carlisle confront Todd over the matter of Reverend Catesby's accident? Or was it something else? Miss Todd was jealous of you and Carlisle, wasn't she? Maybe you decided to put a stop to it.'

'No! I never saw Nick that day. And even if Nick *was* there, Nick would *never* hurt anyone.'

'Not even to protect you? What if *you* confronted Miss Todd over Reverend Catesby, and she attacked you to keep you quiet? Then Nick just happened to come along to the rescue.'

'I never spoke to Garnet! I never saw Nick!' Faith insisted.

Greely studied her, his expression suddenly sympathetic. 'Do your parents know where you are, Miss Wills?'

'No.'

'Well, now, that's a shame, isn't it? A young girl in your condition' – his glance raked her belly – 'needs her parents' support. But perhaps they don't approve of Mr Carlisle, is that it?'

'I . . . he— It's none of your business.'

'No? Well, my advice to you, Miss Wills, is that you might want to contact your parents. I suspect you're going to need some legal advice. And if I were your father, I'd tell you that it's not worth ruining your life – and that of your child – by protecting Carlisle. I'm sure we could come to some sort of arrangement with the prosecution service.' He stood. 'We'll be talking again soon. Don't get up. We'll see ourselves out.'

The policewoman, O'Toole, stood too, closed her notebook, and gave Faith another bright, false smile as she followed Greely out.

Faith sat where they had left her. The baby moved, kicking her repeatedly just above the pelvis, fierce little jabs. Placing her hands against her belly, Faith whispered, 'Shhh, shhh, it's all right,' and rocked mindlessly back and forth. Gradually, the kicking grew less frequent, then ceased. 'It's going to be all right,' Faith said again, softly, reassuring herself as much as the baby. *But how?*

Greely had made up his mind to pin Garnet's murder on her and Nick: he would keep looking for some sort of evidence to support his theory. It was her fault that Nick had got involved in all this; it was her responsibility to find a way to clear him.

If she could just search Garnet's things, and her papers. Surely Garnet had left some trace, some clue, as to who wanted her dead.

Tomorrow she'd insist on going back to work, and then she would find a way to get back into the farmhouse. And she would not let herself wonder what Nick might have done if he'd found her missing and believed Garnet responsible.

Nick stood outside the police station in Yeovil, stranded, without his bike and without a lift.

When he'd arrived at the bookshop that morning, Inspector Greely and a policewoman had been waiting for him in an unmarked car. 'Let's go for a little ride while we chat,' Greely had said. 'Unless you'd rather we talked in the shop?'

Nick had got into the car. But then they'd driven him from Glastonbury to the Yeovil station, and when Nick had protested, Greely replied slyly that they were just protecting his interests by doing things properly, tape recorder and all.

They marched him inside and into an interrogation room, Nick burning all the while with fury. After four hours of repeating the same questions in the bare, ugly room, they had let him go. With the smile Nick had begun to hate, Greely had assured him they would soon find something that would link him to Garnet Todd's murder. 'Oh, and don't leave town,' Greely added cheerfully, as if it were an afterthought.

Still running on anger and adrenalin, Nick stuck his hands in his pockets and started walking. By the time he reached the A37 going north, he'd begun to feel weak. He realized he hadn't eaten all day.

A lorry driver took him all the way to Glastonbury, dropping him at the Street roundabout. He started up Magdalene Street out of habit, but as he neared the shop it occurred to him that he had no idea what he would say to his boss.

Oh, just a bit of police grilling, a small matter of a murder. Nothing to worry about. Right.

Hurriedly, he crossed the street and, rounding the corner into the High, took refuge in the Café Galatea.

Now that he could get something to eat, he found he'd lost his appetite. Instead, he spooned sugar into a coffee and sipped it gratefully, warming his hands on the cup. It was a normal Saturday afternoon in the café; half a dozen customers relaxing over tea in the mid-afternoon lull; a middle-aged hippie in tie-dye and sandals hunched over the computer in the back; Melissa, the waitress who fancied him, glancing at him from beneath her lashes.

But in the space of four days his life had become a nightmare, and he had no guarantee that, for him, things would ever be normal again.

How the hell had he got himself into this mess? And what did he do now? Would he have been better off if he hadn't taken Superintendent Kincaid's advice – if he'd continued to deny that he'd been to the house? But Greely had told him they'd found his prints, and they would be doing a forensic match between his bike tyres and the tracks in Garnet's yard. When the test results came back, he'd look guilty as hell.

He could tell Greely some of the things he'd begun to suspect about Garnet, but it would only make his motive look stronger.

But there must have been others who had felt as he did about Garnet – there must have been someone who had wanted her dead. And if he could find out who, he might have a hope of saving himself.

Kincaid and Gemma pulled into Jack's drive just as he was getting out of his Volvo. They found Faith waiting for them in the kitchen, hands on her hips, furious spots of colour on her cheeks.

'Something smells good.' Jack wrinkled his nose in appreciation. 'We haven't had a proper meal in—'

Turning on Kincaid, Faith spat, 'How could you? You told Nick he should talk to the police, that it would be all right! So he did, and now they think he's a *murderer*.'

'Faith, I told him it was the best course, and I still think that's true. They've got Nick's prints in the house and his bike tracks in the yard. He'd only make things worse for himself by lying.'

'But you're a policeman. Can't you tell Greely it's not true, that Nick wouldn't—'

'I don't have any jurisdiction here. I can offer the Inspector my opinion, but I can't tell him how to run his case.' Kincaid held up his hand before she could interrupt again. 'I will tell you that I don't think he's got any solid evidence, so right now all he can do is try to get a response from Nick.'

'He thinks *I* helped. Did you know that?'

'Faith—'

'He said I needed legal advice.'

'Greely came here?'

Faith nodded.

'He interviewed you with no one else present?'

'There was a policewoman with him.'

Kincaid hesitated. It was a sticky situation, as Faith was legally an adult, but Greely could have found a better way to handle it. 'If he comes again, tell him that you will only talk to him if Jack, or one of us, is present. If he won't agree to that, tell him you insist on legal representation. That means he can't talk to you without your lawyer present. Got that?'

'But I don't have a lawyer!'

Kincaid turned to Jack. 'Is there someone you can call?'

'An old school friend. She's one of the best solicitors in the county.'

'Why don't you do that, just alert her to the situation?'

As Jack went to make his phone call. Gemma

guided Faith to the pot simmering on the cooker, and in a moment had the girl detailing the ingredients.

Crisis defused temporarily, Kincaid thought with relief, but what sort of idiotic thing had he just done? He had known even as he offered his support that he was placing himself in a precariously biased position. But something about this girl seemed to bring everyone's protective instincts to the fore. Except DCI Greely's, it seemed.

The doorbell rang. The murmur of Jack's voice came from the next room, so Kincaid went to the door, girding himself to do discreet battle with DCI Greely.

But it was a man he hadn't seen before, of middle age, dressed in cardigan and tweeds, with a rather unkempt mane of grey hair.

'Jack? Oh, sorry. Is Jack in?'

'I'm his cousin, Duncan Kincaid. Jack's on the phone just now, but if you'll come in, he'll be free in a moment.'

'Simon Fitzstephen.'

Kincaid shook his hand with genuine pleasure. 'Jack speaks very highly of you,' he said as he took Fitzstephen into the kitchen.

Faith looked up from her cooking and smiled. 'Simon! I've made some soup, if you can stay for a meal.'

'Yes, I'd like that,' Fitzstephen said, pecking her cheek, then he greeted Gemma as Kincaid introduced her. 'I've got some news for you all, when Jack's free. Is Nick coming?'

'He hasn't rung.' There was a quaver in Faith's voice.

'The police have been questioning Nick,' Kincaid told Fitzstephen.

Fitzstephen glanced at Faith. 'About Garnet?'

'I'm afraid so,' Kincaid replied. 'But they released him this afternoon. Not enough evidence to bring a charge.'

'Simon! I thought I heard your voice. Good to see you.' Jack searched his friend's face. 'Are you all right?'

'A bit of company wouldn't come amiss.' Fitzstephen's smile seemed strained. 'Faith's asked me to stay for a meal. But that's not the main reason I came. I've something to tell you. I wanted us all here, but I suppose we won't wait for Nick, as we've no way to reach him. And Garnet—' He shook his head. 'I've made some rather astounding progress in my research today. It seems that in 1082 Abbot Thurstan hired a mason called Hamlyn to do repairs to the Abbey church.' He had their complete attention. 'Very iffy, yes? A mere possibility of a connection. But twenty years later, one Alys Montfort made a fine gift to the Abbey, with a stipulation that it be recorded using her maiden name as well, which was Hamlyn.'

'Edmund's Alys?' breathed Jack.

'That would be my guess.'

'So there was a connection with my family – surely it *was* my family?'

'I think we can safely assume so,' agreed Simon. 'Although I haven't managed to trace all the links yet. And I think we can assume that Alys Montfort wanted someone at the Abbey to remember the girl she had been. What if we also assume that Edmund made a copy of his precious chant, and gave it to Alys for safe keeping?'

'You think the chant was passed down through my family,' Jack said softly.

'I think,' Simon answered gravely, 'that the chant might be in this very house.'

Winnie awakened to find Fiona Allen sitting by her bedside, watching her intently.

'Fiona!'

'You can't imagine how good it is to hear you speak. I couldn't just take Jack's word for it.'

'If it weren't for you . . .'

'I only did what I was prompted to do. There's no need for you to feel grateful to me.' Eyes twinkling, Fiona added, 'Maybe *your* God had something to do with it.'

'How *did* you happen to find me?'

'I was painting. When I got to a stopping point, I went for a walk, and there you were in the road.' Fiona shrugged. 'Simple enough, on the surface. But to tell the truth, it was a very odd night. I painted the Abbey, which I've never done in all the years I've been in Glastonbury. And when I went out, it was as if something were hanging in the balance.'

Winnie studied her friend. 'Fiona – there was something else, wasn't there?'

'I painted the child. Again. But it was different this time. She seemed protected, cradled by the Abbey itself. And,' Fiona went on, 'I heard singing. You know what a visual person I am . . . I don't hear things, I *see* them. But this – it's so frustrating, because I'm not musical, and I can't describe it. Even worse, I can't hear it in my head. I just know it was the most beautiful thing I'd ever experienced.'

'But Jack and I – we—'

'I know. Jack told me about your chant. What I don't understand is how I fit into it – or why you were coming to see me that night.'

'I wish I could remember!'

'Winnie . . .' Fiona's brow creased. 'I'm sorry about Garnet. I know you were friends.'

'I can see how people might have thought her difficult. She was . . .'

'Strong in her opinions.'

'Yes. There was something elemental about her. But you and Bram knew her too. I'd forgotten.'

'Garnet was passionate about issues even in those days – but of course it was more fashionable then to be radical. I suppose we should give her credit for remaining true to her convictions, unlike most of us. Bram and I gave up our causes for middle-class comforts.'

'I saw her that afternoon. In the café, but I only know that because I've been told it. I feel as though I've been robbed . . .'

'A last memory?'

Winnie could only nod.

'Let's try something,' Fiona suggested briskly. 'What's the very last thing that's clear in your mind before the accident?'

Winnie felt herself colouring.

'You can skip that part,' Fiona said, laughing. 'Did Jack stay the night?'

'I – I don't know.'

'Did he usually?'

'No. Not at the Vicarage. I thought I had to maintain some sort of propriety. But now . . . I wouldn't give a toss.'

'Well, we can ask him. He'll remember. What about the next morning? Was it rainy or clear?'

'Clear,' Winnie said instantly, then stared at Fiona in surprise. 'How did I—'

'What did you do when you got up?'

'Morning prayer. That's easy.'

'Okay. Then what did you have for breakfast?'

'Toast and tea.'

'Then you got dressed. Why did you take your bike instead of your car?'

'Because I – because it was a beautiful day.'

'So you got on your bike and started off. It was still cool, and the morning sun felt good. Where did you go?'

'Glastonbury.' Winnie laughed. 'This is amazing! I knew that without thinking.'

'From the Vicarage, you'd have come into the roundabout at the bottom of Wearyall Hill. Did you turn to the right, towards the Tor? Or did you continue on into town?'

'I went straight on, into Magdalene Street. The Abbey! I went to the Abbey. I – I – I can't bloody remember! There's just a blank after that.'

'Shhh. Don't force it. We've made some progress.'

Winnie sank back into the pillow. 'Why would I have gone to the Abbey?'

'Maybe we should back up again. What about the dinner party—'

'Andrew! You know how beastly Andrew was to Jack!' Winnie felt a cold weight in the pit of her stomach as the scene came flooding back. 'He's been behaving so oddly. He hasn't even been to see me since I got out of intensive care. And when he came before, when I was unconscious, he wouldn't come in. The nurses told me. He's changed, Fi.'

'Has he? Or could it be that you're just seeing things you've managed to ignore until now?'

'I – I don't know. I suppose he's always been a bit too attached to me, and easily hurt . . . When our mum and dad died, we went to live with my father's parents. But they were elderly – my father was a late only child – and they were so overwhelmed by their own grief they had no emotional room for us. I became mother *and* sister to Andrew. He was so lost.' How he had clung to her, begging for reassurance when he woke from the nightmares that plagued him for years—

'How old were you?'

'Thirteen. Andrew was eleven. After that, he was so terrified of losing anything he cared about – I suppose that's what sparked his interest in the past. It couldn't be taken from him.'

'You formed a very special bond,' Fiona mused. 'And neither of you married.'

'I never thought— We were such good companions, I never felt the need. I didn't know – I never expected Jack to come into my life. Oh, Fi! I've been so wrapped up in myself these past few months, with what I was feeling. And if I've given Andrew any real thought, it's been in a he'll-get-over-it way. But it goes much deeper than that, and I should have known it.'

'Winnie, you can't blame yourself for Andrew's shortcomings.'

'I thought I knew him, but I'm beginning to doubt even that. He went to Garnet's house the day after she died. Why would he do such a thing?'

'She was well known for her archaeological work—'

'He said he wanted to commission tile work for his kitchen. Andrew!' Winnie shook her head. 'It makes me wonder . . .'

'Wonder what?' Fiona prompted when her friend didn't continue.

'I've noticed things the past few months, around the Vicarage. Papers moved about, things missing. What if – what if Andrew's been . . . spying on me?' Reluctantly, Winnie met Fiona's gaze. 'Oh, Fi. What certainty is there in anything, if you can't trust those you love best?'

The rain that threatened all day had not materialized, but as night came on the air developed a soft fuzziness, hovering on the verge of fog. By the time Gemma and Kincaid arrived back at the B & B, the streetlamps and car lights were haloed with moisture.

As Gemma got out of the car, she was possessed by a sudden restlessness. 'Let's not go in just yet. It's such a beautiful night.'

'Shall we walk, then? See the sights of Glastonbury

by starlight?' Kincaid suggested. 'Unless you'd rather go down the pub for a pint.'

She laughed. 'You're such a romantic. A walk would be fine, and we'll see what strikes us.'

They let themselves out through the gate, and when they reached Magdalene Street, Gemma hooked her arm through his. 'I keep trying to imagine what it must have been like, eight hundred years ago. It seems such a long time, and yet people's emotions haven't changed that much.'

'Alys and Edmund?'

'Yes. And we don't even know if they were real.'

'You could get into all sorts of philosophical difficulties with that statement. There's the subjective approach: "Are they real if we believe in them?" But that's only the tip of the iceberg. There are worse dangers lurking. "Do we have souls? Is there life after death?" '

'How can you be so flippant?' Gemma scolded, pinching his arm.

'A defence mechanism, love. Those are places I'm afraid to go, even with my proper Anglican upbringing.'

She glanced up at him, unsure if he was still teasing. He never talked much about such things, but when she'd asked him once, point-blank, what he believed, he'd said he couldn't imagine a god that would let happen the things he saw every day on the job.

'What about this murder, then? Have you changed your mind about Nick since Greely seems so positive?'

Kincaid kept walking for a moment, then said, 'I just can't quite see Nick, or Nick and Faith, committing a deliberate murder. And in this case I think it would have been a bit hard to drown Garnet in a moment of fear or passion.' They had reached the Abbey car park. 'Is that Nick's bookshop?' he asked, pointing across the street. 'Jack mentioned his office was upstairs on the corner.'

'It overlooks the Market Square, then. Let's cross over. Earlier I saw a big second-hand bookshop down the road.' Continuing the thread of their conversation, Gemma asked, 'What about Andrew Catesby?'

Kincaid frowned. 'No motive. What possible reason could he have for killing Todd, a woman he apparently scarcely knew—'

'Unless he somehow got the idea that she was responsible for his sister's injuries. But he seemed genuinely shocked by the idea that someone might deliberately have hurt Winnie.'

'Maybe he's a better actor than we think, and he's the one who struck Winnie, out of some sort of warped jealousy. Then Garnet found out somehow, and he killed her to shut her up.'

'You're reaching on that one,' said Gemma. Then she went on more thoughtfully, 'When you were asking Winnie about Faith's parents today, there is a possibility you neglected to mention. Has it occurred to you that the reason Faith won't name the baby's father is that—'

'She was abused by her own father? That would certainly explain why she refuses to go home.'

'And it might explain why she's so set against seeing a doctor. Maybe she's afraid the baby may have genetic complications.'

'It wouldn't hurt to have a talk with her parents,' Kincaid agreed. 'I'll run it by Greely, make sure he doesn't object, and get their name and address. You can be sure he'll have got that out of Faith today.'

'If Faith was so secretive about her family, how did Nick get her address? Remember, he said he'd even gone looking for her at her parents' house in Street.' Then, in disappointment, Gemma added, 'Oh, the bookshop's closed.'

'A good thing. You have no room for more books in your flat. You're right about Nick, though – makes me wonder what else he hasn't told us.' He stopped and gave an exaggerated sniff. 'Is that fish and chips I smell?'

'Don't tell me you're hungry again?'

'It was only soup, and that was hours ago.'

'Two, maybe three,' Gemma corrected, smiling. Faith had done her best with Jack's meagre resources, but her pot of soup had not made a particularly generous meal for five people.

They had left Jack contemplating the ramifications of Simon's hypothesis. If there were even a possibility that a copy of the ancient manuscript might have been passed down through Jack's family, Jack would be faced with the enormous task of searching through the accumulated clutter in his parents' house.

The chippy was a bit further down, where the Market Square became a pedestrian mall. The shop's door stood open, serving as an enticement. It was a clean, well-lit establishment, with a proper restaurant in the back.

'Do you want to sit down?' Gemma asked.

'No. Let's keep walking. Somehow fish and chips never taste the same without the newspaper.'

Back in the street, with their steaming newspaper parcels in hand, Kincaid turned back the way they'd come. 'Let's walk up the High.'

They peered through the leaded glass windows of the ancient George & Pilgrims inn. The bar was full, the hum of conversation audible even through the glass. The building looked very old indeed, with its authentic black-and-white timbering and worn, blackened beams.

'Would Edmund have known this place?' Gemma asked.

'A century or so after his time, I think. Not that he'd have been allowed to frequent the inn. It was built to accommodate the pilgrims, and the abbot's high-ranking overflow.'

They walked on, past the Café Galatea and New Age shops, until Gemma stopped, transfixed, before a gallery window. A single painting, lit by a soft spotlight, stood against a black velvet backdrop. Luminous, winged creatures hovered over a moonlit city in which tiny humans went about their business, unaware. The vision was stunningly beautiful, the colours glowing like living jewels, but the creatures' faces were fierce and otherworldly. It made her a little uneasy. 'Are they protecting the people?' she asked softly. 'Or do they have their own agenda?'

'Fiona Finn Allen.' Kincaid was reading the artist's signature over her shoulder. 'That's Winnie's friend, the woman who found her after the accident.' He stepped back so that he could read the awning above the window. 'Allen Galleries.' Walking on, he remarked, 'I suppose it shows our self-absorption that we even think those spirits should be concerned with us. What if there are layers of reality we can't see that have nothing to do with human needs and desires?'

Gemma gave him a surprised glance. 'Now I think Glastonbury's getting to you too. Oh, look,' she added, stopping again to gaze through a bakery window at the empty trays, waiting for their early-morning baked goods. She felt a pang of longing for Toby, who was spending the weekend with her parents, 'helping', as he called it, in their bakery. Turning to Kincaid, she said, 'You know I'll have to go back tomorrow.'

'And I don't see how I can leave Jack in the lurch at this point. I hope Doug Cullen can manage a bit longer on his own.'

'What will the Guv say?' asked Gemma, referring to Chief Superintendent Denis Childs.

'I'll give him a ring at home tomorrow, explain the situation. Then you could drop me in Bath, and I'll hire a car.'

'No,' Gemma said, thinking it out. 'I won't need the car the next few days. After we've paid a visit to Faith's parents, you can run *me* to Bath, put me on the train, and keep the car.'

When he started to protest, she insisted. 'No, really. I want to take the train. I won't have to fight the Sunday trippers' traffic coming back into London.' That was true, and a valid enough argument to silence Kincaid, but it was the thought of those few hours on the train when she would have absolutely no demands that had decided her.

'You could do some background checks.'

'Along with three thousand other things on Monday morning. But make me a list tonight.'

They walked the rest of the way up the High in companionable silence. The New Age shops gave way to more pedestrian businesses: a launderette, a grocer's, a chemist, estate agents' offices.

When they reached the top, they turned and surveyed the street sloping gently down the hill before them. 'The mundane and the sublime, side by side,' Kincaid remarked.

'I'll miss you,' Gemma said impulsively, prompted by something deeper than thought.

Kincaid put a hand on her shoulder as they started back down the hill, matching strides. 'Glastonbury must have a salutary effect on you. I should bring you more often.'

Now, thought Gemma. She had the perfect opportunity. Just a sentence or two, and she would have put it behind her.

But she still wasn't one hundred per cent sure, not until she did a test, and she absolutely would pick one up at the chemist when she got back to London.

It had been so good between them this weekend, away from their responsibilities in London, working together on a case again, however unofficial. Why should she break the spell?

Especially when they had one more night alone together, under the rose-coloured canopy in the Acacia Room.

Chapter Fifteen

The Abbey did not languish and die from internal corruption; it fell as a great ship founders, at one moment going on its way, at the next plunging to destruction with all hands . . . Therefore it is that in the Abbey we have so clear a sense of our spiritual past, uncorrupted by decay. The spirit of the Abbey lives on, as it is said that the spirit of a man lives on who has died by violence before his time.

Dion Fortune, from
Glastonbury: Avalon of the Heart

Gemma studied the man sitting across from them in the tidy sitting room. Gary Wills looked to be in his early forties, trim, an executive with an electronics firm in Street. Add a wife with her own career, bright children, a well-located suburban home, and you had all the hallmarks of success. Why, then, had this family fractured so grievously?

Maureen Wills sat near her husband, without touching him. When she had reached out a hand towards him – to comfort or be comforted, Gemma couldn't tell – Wills had shrugged it off.

'We did everything for her,' he was saying. 'School

fees, sports, singing lessons, piano.' The piano sat against the far wall of the sitting room, its keyboard cover closed. 'How could she be such an ungrateful little tart—'

'Gary, please,' his wife entreated, with a pointed glance at the frightened faces of the two younger children, peering round the corner.

'You two.' Wills pointed at them. 'Go to your rooms. Now.' The boy and girl disappeared, but Gemma suspected they'd not gone far.

'She had a chance at the best universities,' their father continued. 'An abortion would have been the sensible solution, but no, she wouldn't hear of it. So I told her the boy and his family would have to do their part – why should *we* take on full responsibility for the little bastard? But she wouldn't tell us who it was!'

'So you suggested that she leave?' Kincaid asked, as if it were a perfectly sensible action.

'I only meant to make her see reason. I never thought she'd actually go . . .'

'You should have,' said his wife, as if their presence had given her the courage to speak up. 'You should have thought. You know how stubborn Faith is—' Maureen turned to Gemma and Kincaid. 'Since she was a toddler, she's been that way. And she was a hard delivery. I used to tell her she was stubborn even then . . . determined to come into the world in her own time.'

'But surely you must have had some idea who the boy was,' suggested Gemma. 'A regular boyfriend, or some gossip among her friends at school.'

'She didn't go out with boys.' Maureen said it firmly.

'Faith always looked down on girls who giggled and had crushes; she was far too serious for that. And her friends—'

'They didn't want to talk to us,' Wills interrupted bitterly. 'You'd have thought we'd done something terrible to her. And why should we go begging to anyone for information our own daughter wouldn't give us? If Faith is so determined to get on in the world without our help, she's bloody well welcome to it.'

'You!' Furiously, Maureen Wills turned on her husband. 'Why don't you admit all the hours you've spent driving round, looking for her? Or all the nights you've sat up in the kitchen until dawn? I've seen you – you can't deny it!'

Gary Wills gaped at her.

Maureen looked back at them, her face tear-streaked but resolute. 'I'd do anything to have Faith back. I don't care who the baby's father is, as long as our Faith is safe and well. You will tell us, won't you, where she is?'

'Mrs Wills,' Kincaid said gently, 'Faith didn't give us permission to do that. She—'

'But the child must be due any day! You say the woman who was looking after her is dead – someone's got to take care of her. Please—'

Gary Wills broke in again. 'I suppose Maureen's right. Faith needs to come home. Let bygones be bygones.'

'We'll talk to Faith,' Gemma promised. 'If she knows that you'll accept her without question, perhaps she'll agree.'

'You'll let us know about the baby, at least?' pleaded Maureen, and Kincaid assured them he would.

At the door, Gemma turned back to the couple. 'I know it must be hard to let your child go – they always seem to grow up before you're ready – but Faith has proved she has courage and determination. You should be very proud of her.'

When they reached the car, Gemma said, 'Do you think her father's capitulation will last if she comes home?'

Kincaid shrugged. 'Human nature being what it is, I rather doubt it. But I also doubt he'd have insisted on knowing the baby's parentage if he were responsible. I just hope I make a better job of it in the father department.'

Gemma glanced at him and said not a word.

'Have we time for another stop before your train?' Kincaid asked as they returned to Glastonbury. 'I'd like to see the scene of Winnie's accident.'

Gemma glanced at her watch. 'We should be all right. Let's leave the car at the café, shall we? I'd like to take the same route Winnie must have used that evening.'

They walked up Wellhouse Lane, its incline steep and slick, not suitable for any but the most expensive of mountain bikes, and Jack had told them that Winnie's was an old boneshaker. 'Faith said Winnie was pushing her bike – I can see why,' Kincaid grunted as they reached the turning into Lypatt Lane.

The smaller track was claustrophobic even at

midday – how much more so had it seemed at dusk? But Winnie could have squeezed the bike against the hedge if she'd heard a car approaching. Soon they reached the bend where the lane connected with the footpath.

'If someone struck Winnie deliberately, they waited here,' Gemma mused. 'But how could anyone have known she would be in this place at that time – unless she had had an appointment!'

'But that brings us back to square one,' Kincaid objected. 'If Winnie agreed to meet someone here, she has no memory of it. And unfortunately, an assignation in a dark lane isn't something she's likely to have put in her appointment book—'

'Hullo!' A woman had appeared in the lane and was gazing at them curiously. 'I'm sorry, but you looked a bit lost,' she added. A slight woman with untidy brown hair and brown eyes, she frowned as she studied Kincaid. 'You remind me a bit of someone I know.'

'Jack Montfort, by any chance? I'm his cousin, Duncan Kincaid. And this is Gemma James.'

'Fiona Allen.' Her smile faded as she realized just what they must have been doing. 'You're looking at the scene of Winnie's accident, aren't you?'

'You found her, I understand? And you live just up the lane?'

'The far end. Why don't you two come along for a coffee?'

As they followed her, Kincaid looked down into Bushy Coombe. 'I remember this from when I was boy. Jack and I used to climb in the Coombe, pretending to be monks – or cowboys.'

'An interesting juxtaposition,' Fiona commented with a chuckle.

'Both unwashed, and familiar with livestock?' Gemma murmured.

He gave her a quelling glance. 'We pretended we were fetching water from the spring, although I suppose the logical route from the Abbey would have been by Chilkwell Street.'

'Jack must have been interested in the Abbey as a child, then,' Fiona said as they reached an unremarkable stone house with a superbly tended garden. The interior of the house was clean and spare, and Kincaid imagined it must make a restful contrast to the garden's summer profusion. A small fire glowed in the sitting-room grate.

'I love this time of year,' Fiona explained. 'Any excuse for a fire.'

She seated them on the sofa and returned shortly with mugs of coffee on a tray. 'How is Winnie today, have you heard?'

Gemma accepted a mug. 'Jack went to fetch her home this morning—'

'She's not going back to the Vicarage, alone?'

'No, she's agreed to stay with Jack for a few days. You sound as if you're worried about her.'

'I am, a bit,' Fiona admitted. 'Although I'm not sure I can tell you why.'

'Something you saw or heard that night, perhaps?' Kincaid asked.

Fiona frowned. 'No, nothing that concrete. But I do know Winnie feels more uneasy about her brother than she may admit.'

'Do you know of any connection between Andrew Catesby and Garnet Todd?'

'No. It's odd, though . . . that two people so dedicated to preserving the past should be at such opposite ends of the pole. I don't think they could have liked one another.'

'Gemma found Catesby poking about Todd's house the day after she died.'

'Winnie mentioned that. It wouldn't have been difficult for Andrew to have learned of the connection between Garnet and Winnie, although Winnie didn't share much with him about her involvement with Jack's . . .'

'Experiment?' Kincaid supplied helpfully. 'But even if that were the case, what could Andrew have thought he'd find at Ms Todd's? It might help us if Winnie could remember what she did the day of her accident, or why she was coming to see you.'

'Oh!' Fiona brightened. 'When I visited Winnie yesterday, she remembered that she went to the Abbey that morning. But that's as far as we got, I'm afraid.'

'Jack said you painted the Abbey, the night Winnie was struck,' said Gemma. 'Was that unusual? I'd think you'd use Glastonbury scenes as a matter of course.'

'But I don't choose the things I paint. I suppose I could say they choose me. I just see them, and paint them, and that was the first time I've ever painted the Abbey.'

'We saw one of your works in town, last night, beautifully displayed. Allen Galleries – is that your husband's gallery?'

Nodding, Fiona explained, 'Bram's there today,

hanging some new pieces. It's difficult to change the displays when the gallery's open.'

'What are they – the creatures you paint?'

'I really don't know. It's like the settings – I just paint them. I suppose it's quite similar to what happens to Jack, with his messages from Edmund.'

'Might we see what you painted the night of Winnie's accident?' asked Kincaid.

'Of course.'

They followed her down a passage and into her glass-walled studio. She lifted a canvas from a stack against the wall and set it on an easel. In this painting, the creatures thronged round a human child cupped in a luminous bowl, within the great arch of the Abbey's ruined transepts. Unlike the work they'd seen in the gallery window, here the child seemed to be the focus of the creatures' attention, perhaps even their compassion.

'Edmund and Alys's child?' Kincaid murmured.

'Edmund's?'

Before Kincaid could explain, a man's voice called out, 'Darling?'

'In here,' Fiona answered. As her husband entered the room, she said, 'Bram, this is Duncan Kincaid, Jack Montfort's cousin, and his friend, Gemma James.'

'And how is Winnie?' Bram Allen asked.

'Jack is bringing her home from hospital today.'

'We'll pay her a visit then, in a day or two, when she's had a little time to recuperate.' Allen put his arm round his wife's shoulders and shepherded her back into the sitting room. 'Fiona's been working too hard,' he told Gemma and Kincaid. 'She had strict instructions to stay put in front of the fire this afternoon.'

'I only went out for a walk,' countered Fiona, 'and found our guests wandering about in the lane. I promise I haven't lifted a brush.'

Although Allen was pleasant enough, Kincaid sensed that Fiona's husband was uneasy, and his interest sharpened. 'Mr Allen, I understand it was you who found Garnet Todd's body.'

Giving his wife an anxious look, Allen replied, 'I'm just glad it wasn't Fiona. Her experience with Winnie was pretty dreadful – but then you'd know that.'

'Rather an odd coincidence, though, wasn't it? Mrs Allen finding Winnie and you discovering Ms Todd?'

'Winnie was only a few hundred yards from our house, and I walk round the Tor every morning,' Allen said with the air of a man keeping his impatience in check. 'Unfortunate, perhaps, but I wouldn't say *odd*.'

'Did you recognize Ms Todd's van?'

'No. To be honest, I'd had a bit too much coffee . . . I thought the van would make a good shield if anyone came along . . . I suppose I assumed someone had had a breakdown and left it to be collected later – until I looked inside.'

'Did you recognize Ms Todd, then?'

Allen paled. 'No. I'm afraid I wasn't . . . thinking very logically at that point.'

Kincaid remembered that they had found only Garnet Todd's and Faith's prints on the exterior of the van. 'You didn't try to get in? To see if she needed help?'

'It was obvious she was past that.' Again, Allen gave

his wife a concerned glance. 'I came home and rang the police.'

'But you knew Ms Todd?' pressed Kincaid.

'She was unique . . . one of Glastonbury's true eccentrics. The town won't be the same without her. I – Fiona?'

Fiona Allen stood and moved towards her studio. 'I'm sorry.' Feverish spots had appeared on her cheeks, and she seemed to have difficulty focusing on them. 'I'm sorry – I have to paint now. It's—'

'It's all right, darling,' her husband soothed. 'You go ahead. I'll see Mr Kincaid and Miss James out.'

With a last apologetic glance, Fiona disappeared into the passage.

'Does it always happen like that?' asked Gemma as Bram walked them to the door. 'It was almost as if she had no choice.'

'She doesn't,' Bram answered curtly. 'She becomes ill if she's kept from painting. And now I'd better check on her, if you don't mind.'

They said goodbye, and as they retraced their way through the garden, Gemma shivered. 'Has it struck you? Jack can't help writing; Fiona Allen can't help painting; and Faith says she had no choice but to climb the Tor. What *is* it about this place?' She looked up. The Tor seemed to hang above the treetops, a massive presence that dwarfed all other elements in the landscape. 'And what else might someone feel compelled to do?'

'You're sure about this?' Kincaid asked as he took

Gemma's bag from the boot in front of Bath railway station.

'Positive.' She kissed him, adding, 'You will talk to Faith about seeing her parents, won't you? I'll ring you tomorrow.' With a wave, she walked away.

He watched her until she disappeared into the interior of the station, then climbed back into the car and set about manœuvring his way out of the city. As a child, he had loved their summer visits to Bath, but these days it was so chock-a-block with tourists you could scarcely move.

Eventually, he found his way back to the A37 going south, towards Glastonbury. He took his time, enjoying the drive through the eastern edge of the Mendips. Gemma was right, it was lovely country, and he smiled, remembering how much she had disliked their trips out of London when they had first started working together.

Born and raised in busy North London, Gemma had been more than a bit agoraphobic. But she had changed, had adapted herself to new circumstances and surroundings. Her ability to do so was one of the things that made her a good copper, and would go a long way towards ensuring her success at her new job. Still, it was a hard transition, and he wished there were something he could do to make the process easier for her.

Of course, if he were totally honest, he'd have to admit he'd been more wrapped up in dealing with his own adjustment to working without her than with hers to her new posting. Even without the personal component of their relationship he'd have found replacing her difficult.

But he had been right to entice Gemma away for the weekend. She'd been more relaxed than he'd seen her in months, and he realized how much he missed that easiness between them. He would have to see what he could do to improve things in the future, but just now he had better turn his attention to Jack's predicament.

They didn't seem to be making much progress towards solving either Winnie's accident or the Todd homicide. Not that he would expect such a quick resolution on an ordinary case, but he was frustrated both by his limited time and his lack of control over the investigation. Greely's tactics were common enough – find the most likely suspect and bully him or her until you got a confession – but they certainly left much fertile ground unturned.

And to complicate matters further, Jack was bringing Winnie home from hospital today. If she were still in danger, how much more vulnerable would she be now?

He kept running aground on the same questions. Why had Andrew Catesby gone to see Garnet Todd? Why would someone other than Garnet have wanted to hurt – or kill – Winifred Catesby? If Garnet had not struck Winnie, where had she gone in the van that evening? And what had Winnie done in the hours she couldn't remember?

Some of the answers were undoubtedly locked within Winnie's mind and could not be forced. And some of the questions were undoubtedly connected, if only he had some clue as to which ones they might be.

Kincaid arrived at Jack's to find Winnie installed on the sitting-room sofa, her lap filled with a jumble of papers.

'That doesn't look a proper convalescent project,' Kincaid commented.

Winnie smiled up at him. 'I convinced Jack to start searching for the manuscript.'

'He told you about Simon's theory?'

Nodding, she said, 'And I think on this point Simon's judgement should be trusted. Unfortunately, I'm not much help yet.' She gestured at the papers in her lap. 'This is the best I could do. But it would be easier if I knew exactly what I was looking for.'

'How about a perfectly illuminated sheet of musical notation on parchment, with "The Lost Chant" at the top in Latin?'

'And why don't we have it rolled and tied with a red ribbon while we're at it? Seriously, though, *if* we're not all completely mad, and *if* Edmund did make a copy of such a thing, it would have been on parchment. And how likely is it that something like that would have survived all those centuries without special care and handling?'

'Simon seemed to think it was possible, and he's the expert. Where's Jack, then?'

'Up in the attic, covered with dust and cobwebs. And swearing a blue streak, is my guess.'

Kincaid grinned. 'I expect you're right. Why don't

you have a rest, and I'll bring you a cuppa in a bit. How's Faith?'

'Holding up, but terribly worried about Nick. No one's heard a word from him.'

'I'll go and have a chat with her.'

He found Faith in the kitchen.

'I see you managed to conjure up something to feed the masses,' he told her, and was rewarded with a smile.

'I made Jack run me to the supermarket this morning, before he went to collect Winnie. There's fresh bread and roast beef, if you'd like a sandwich.'

'I stopped on the way back from Bath, thanks.' He pulled out a chair. 'Are you not joining in the Great Treasure Hunt?'

'I'm going in to the café until closing time. Buddy rang – he's desperate for help. Sunday's a big day, with all the weekend climbers.' She watched him, her chin up, as if bracing to counter a negative reaction.

'Are you sure you feel up to it?' Kincaid asked gently.

'I'm fine. And it's only for a couple of hours.'

'I'll run you up to the café, then, and pick you up at closing—'

'I can walk,' she said acidly. 'I'm pregnant, not crippled.'

'Faith, it's your safety I'm thinking about. Until we know more about what happened to Garnet – and to Winnie – I'd just as soon you didn't go out on your own if it can be helped.'

'Don't tell me you think Nick—'

'I didn't say a word about Nick, and no, I don't

think it's likely that Nick had anything to do with Garnet's death. But why do you suppose he hasn't rung or come to the house?'

Faith grasped the back of a chair. 'I don't know. That day, when he came into the café and said I should check Garnet's front bumper . . . I was so furious. I told him to get out. But we've had rows before . . .'

'You don't think he's still angry with you—'

'And now, because of me, the police think he . . . I'd say he's got good reason to be narked with me.'

'I'm sure that's not the case. But if you like, I'll have a look for him after I drop you at the café.'

'Could you?'

'Any suggestions as to where, other than the caravan?'

'He likes to go to the Galatea, in the High Street. And the Assembly Rooms café.'

'Do you know anything about Nick, where he comes from, for instance?'

'Somewhere in Northumberland. He's got a first from Durham in philosophy or something. And I think his mum is well off.'

'So why is he working as an assistant in a bookshop?'

'I don't know. He's always on at me about finishing my education, but I can't see that it's done much for him.'

'What about Garnet? Do you know anything about her background?'

'Not much,' Faith replied. 'Her parents died when she was fairly young, and she didn't have any other family. She came to Glastonbury for the first Pilton

Festival, in seventy-one, and stayed. What do you suppose will happen to her house?'

'Did she leave a will?'

'She never mentioned one.'

'If she died intestate it will be a complicated process, but I'd imagine the property would eventually go to the state. Unless, of course, some long-lost relative comes out of the woodwork.' It was a remote possibility that some distant cousin had decided the property might be worth murdering Garnet for, but one they should check. 'Do you know anything about Garnet's friends?'

'She knew people in the Archaeological Society, because of her restoration work. And then there's Buddy, of course. They've been friends for ages.'

'Buddy's your boss?'

'Yes. And he'll be run off his feet if I don't get to work.'

Kincaid fished his car keys from his pocket. 'Faith, on the night of Winnie's accident, what exactly did Garnet say when she left the house?'

Faith snatched a shapeless cardigan from the peg on the kitchen door as they passed. 'She said . . . "I have to go. I'm late for an appointment." '

'And you assumed it was a delivery?'

'She'd said so in the café, when Winnie invited us to Jack's.'

A peep into the sitting room showed Winnie not waiting for the tea he'd promised, but fast asleep on the sofa.

When they reached the Escort, Faith said, 'I like your car. It's purple.'

'Wild Orchid, actually. But it's not mine. It's Gemma's.'

Faith gave him a sideways glance as she stretched the seat belt around her stomach. 'She's nice.'

'Very nice,' Kincaid agreed.

'She said she has a little boy, and she's raised him by herself since he was born.'

'That's right.' Kincaid answered cautiously, wondering where this was going. 'It hasn't always been easy, but she's done a terrific job.'

'What about his father?'

'He and Gemma divorced just after Toby was born, and he disappeared not too long afterwards. Didn't want to pay his child support.'

Faith digested this in silence as they drove to the café.

'Not all men are like that, you know,' Kincaid offered. 'Are you wondering if your baby's father will help you?'

'I don't need his help.' Her voice had grown steely.

'Faith, Gemma and I went to see your parents this morning.'

'But I— You didn't tell them—'

'No, we didn't tell them where you were. But we *did* promise we'd tell you how much they want you to come home.'

'That's the last thing my father would want!'

'I think your dad misses you. It's just hard for him to say so. Sometimes love and anger and worry get all tangled up, and the wrong thing somehow spills out.'

Faith was out of her seat belt as he came to a stop

in front of the café, but not before he'd seen the tears in her eyes.

'I've got to go. You can pick me up at five if you want.'

'I think I'll come in for a cup of tea,' Kincaid decided abruptly. 'I'd like to meet Buddy.'

'Charles Barnes,' said the café's proprietor, gripping Kincaid's hand. 'But most folks call me Buddy. What can I do for you?'

'Just a few minutes of your time, if you can spare it.'

'Sure I can. Any friend of Jack Montfort's is a friend of mine.' Buddy motioned Kincaid to a seat at a nearby table. 'He's been good to Faith. Garnet would have' – he cleared his throat – 'Garnet would have appreciated that.'

'Garnet was fond of Faith, I take it.'

'More than fond,' Buddy replied. Glancing at Faith, busy in the kitchen, he lowered his voice. 'There were times I wished I'd never told her about Faith, thinking to do a favour for them both. Garnet worried about her so, you'd have thought she'd brought that girl into the world herself. And now what's going to happen to Faith, with Garnet gone? I'll keep her on here, after the kid's born, but she's got no place to live.'

'Have you any idea why Garnet was so concerned about Faith's welfare?'

'She talked about the Tor, and about Faith being a magnet for the old powers, but there was nothing concrete. Garnet always had a bee in her bonnet about that stuff.'

'You knew her for a long time, Faith said.'

His weathered face creased in a smile. 'We were going to change the world, you know? Who'd have thought we'd end up old hippies, stuck to the side of Glastonbury Tor like burrs. Although I guess you could say Bram and Fiona made something of themselves, but they couldn't leave Glastonbury either.'

'You all knew each other?' Kincaid asked, surprised.

'Oh, we were tight, the four of us. Fiona and me, Bram and Garnet. But then things changed. They always do, don't they? Bram set his sights on Fiona, and Garnet and I . . . Well, we made the best of things. Garnet bought the old Kinnersley place for a song, and I suppose I thought we'd just go on for ever . . .' He lapsed into silence.

'Why did Garnet never have the old farmhouse modernized?'

'Habit, mostly,' Buddy said fondly. 'At first she couldn't afford it, then she just got used to it, I reckon. And I think she liked the reputation it earned her.'

'It can't have been easy for her, living there alone.'

'Not as hard as you might think. She had indoor plumbing, fed from the spring above the house, and the woodstove heated the water. And I don't think she missed things like television all that much. Garnet never had any trouble keeping herself occupied.'

So Garnet could have drowned in water from her own taps, Kincaid thought, but he said merely, 'But she was lonely, I expect, until Faith came along.'

'I expect she was.' Buddy said it quietly. His glance in Faith's direction made it clear that the girl's presence had filled more than one void.

*

There was no sign of Nick's motorbike outside his caravan, and no answer to Kincaid's knock.

Making the return journey to Glastonbury, Kincaid found a parking spot on the High Street. He and Gemma had lunched in the Café Galatea the previous day, and the pretty dark-haired waitress smiled in recognition as he came in.

He waited until she'd finished serving the nearest table, then asked her quietly if she knew Nick Carlisle.

'Nick who works in the bookshop down Magdalene Street? Yeah, sure.'

'Has he been in today?'

'No. Yesterday, though. Late. Moped over his coffee like he'd just lost his best friend,' she added, with an air of disappointment.

Thanking her, Kincaid crossed the street and ducked into the stone passageway that led to the Glastonbury Assembly Rooms. The doors stood open and he climbed the stairs to the café on the first floor. It was only semi-partitioned from the corridor and the meeting room, but it was an inviting, comfortable-looking space, if a wee bit scruffy. Ella Fitzgerald crooned Cole Porter over the sound system, and several tables were occupied by customers bent over books or newspapers, enjoying the Sunday afternoon lull. He went through the buffet queue and, when he reached the cash register, struck up a conversation with the cashier, a pleasant woman wearing a baseball cap. When they'd discussed the cake and the weather, he asked her if she knew Nick. 'Tall, slender chap, with dark curly hair?'

'Who could forget Nick?' she said, laughing. 'Comes in all the time.'

'Has he been in today?'

'As a matter of fact, he has.'

Kincaid pounced on the slight hesitation. 'Was there something odd today?'

'Nick usually comes in on his own, has a meal or a coffee – always chats me up – but today he was deep into it with a strange bunch, at the table in the corner there.' She nodded towards a table beside the worn sofa.

'Strange, how?'

The woman shrugged. 'Well, you know Glastonbury – you see all kinds. I've been here twenty years and nothing surprises me. But this bunch, they're *serious* pagans. Moonlight rituals on the Tor, that sort of thing. Gives me the willies, and I wouldn't have thought that was Nick's style.' She eyed him more critically. 'Is there some reason you're looking for Nick?'

'Just a friend passing through, wanted to say hello. He's not on the telephone, so he can be the devil to get in touch with.' Giving her a reassuring smile, he took his coffee and gingerbread to a table beside the disused fireplace, mulling over this latest bit of information. Who were these people? Druids? Witches? And just what was handsome young Nick up to now?

'Any joy?' Kincaid asked, sitting down on a tufted ottoman.

Winnie looked up from a thick batch of papers. 'No, but it's interesting reading. These are estate documents

– it seems the Montforts have owned property in this area practically for ever.'

'I suppose that follows. But Uncle John never talked much about his family.'

'What was he like?' Winnie nodded towards the silver-framed photos on the bookcase. 'I can see that Jack resembles him.'

'In looks, yes, but Jack's much more like his mother in temperament. Uncle John was terribly reserved' – he pulled a long face – 'and I always wondered how he and Aunt Olivia ended up together. When we went on holiday, he never joined any of our activities. He always had more important things to do.'

'Was it just you and Jack and your mothers, then?'

'And my pesky sister. And sometimes my dad, when he could get away.'

'It sounds lovely,' Winnie said a little wistfully, then looked back at the papers in her hand. 'Do you think Jack's father felt that family history and stories were frivolous?'

'A waste of valuable time, I'd guess. Uncle John read *The Times* from front to back every day of his life.' When Winnie laughed, he added, 'I don't want to give you the wrong impression. My uncle was a kind man, of good character, and I'm sure he was well respected – although I never thought about those things as a child. But he wasn't the sort to build stage sets in the back garden and help put on productions of *Peter Pan*.'

'And your dad was?'

'Always ready for an adventure, my dad. And speaking of adventures – I think it's time I see what

Jack's got himself into in the attic. Can I get you anything else?'

Winnie demurred, and was already immersed in her papers as he left the room.

Climbing the stairs to the first floor, he thought about his family, so taken for granted in childhood. He had assumed that everyone's parents were interested in their children's doings, and that all fathers participated in their children's lives.

The downside to possessing a creative and involved father, however, had been that his dad sometimes forgot to take care of mundane matters like the electricity bill, and he remembered more than one occasion when they had camped out in the house by candlelight until things could be put right. Fortunately, his mother had possessed a practical streak that he suspected his aunt Olivia had not shared, and she'd managed to keep things running smoothly most of the time.

It had been a while since he'd been home – he should take Kit to visit his grandparents, now that the boy had had a chance to get used to the idea. And he would ask Gemma and Toby too. They could make a proper holiday of it.

Jack had lowered the drop-down staircase at the end of the corridor. The creak of the springs as Kincaid climbed it brought back memories of childhood visits to the cavernous attic. As he emerged into the open space, he saw that Jack had rigged a work lamp on a flex, illuminating the space between the grey-filmed windows at either end.

Jack, on his knees in jeans and a very dirty sweatshirt, dug through a tin trunk. He looked up at Kincaid, wiping a hand across his forehead and leaving a large grimy smear. 'This is a bloody nightmare. I can't pass up anything, becausc I've no idea what might be important.'

Kincaid squatted and peered into the trunk. 'Probably not Great Aunt Sophie's petticoats.'

'Did we have a Great Aunt Sophie?'

'Undoubtedly.'

Jack grinned as he shook out the last bit of old-fashioned ladies' underclothing. 'Have you come to make yourself useful?'

'For an hour. Then I've promised to pick Faith up at the café.'

'Why don't you start over there, then?' Jack directed him to the eastern end of the attic, just out of range of the pool of lamplight.

Somewhat daunted, Kincaid said, 'Do we have some sort of system for separating the things that have been searched?'

'There.' Jack pointed to a section of boxes and oddments off to one side.

'Right.' Kincaid made his way gingerly along a pathway Jack had cleared across the attic floor, then whistled in dismay as he got a better look at the daunting task awaiting him. 'I think a bulldozer might be more appropriate,' he muttered, but bent to it.

First he transferred the large items – a wooden child's cradle; an ancient, rusted tricycle; a picnic hamper complete with dishes and accoutrements; a croquet set – to Jack's segregated area. 'All this stuff looks Victorian – it's probably worth a fortune.'

'I'll have to go on *Antiques Roadshow*,' Jack joked, without looking up from the pile he was sorting.

Kincaid moved a stack of framed pictures to one side and started on the boxes. To his delight, they held books. The volumes were dusty and musty, some with water stains or damaged covers, but nonetheless it was a treasure trove. After half an hour, he had come up with a handful of real finds.

'I'm no expert, but I think you'd do well to let my dad have a look at these.' He handed Jack copies of *The Moonstone, The War of the Worlds, Mrs Dalloway,* and *The Murder of Roger Ackroyd.* All were in good condition and, as far as he could tell, first editions.

Jack accepted the books with a discouraged sigh. 'And I've found three hideous lamps, a recipe collection from the twenties, some moth-eaten flower arrangements, and a box of ladies' hats.'

The first dozen of the framed pictures were obviously junk: cardboard reproductions of famous paintings in cheap frames. But there were three small landscape oils that Kincaid suspected might be valuable, as well as a nice watercolour of the Abbey ruins, and a larger oil portrait of a hunting spaniel that he thought Gemma might like, remembering her interest in Andrew Catesby's dog.

'Take it,' Jack said of the spaniel portrait, when Kincaid presented his latest haul. 'Give it to Gemma with my compliments.' He sat back on his heels and groaned. 'The light's going. We'll have to give it up for the day. I didn't expect the thing to jump out and bite me, but this really is like looking for the proverbial needle in the haystack.'

'What about Edmund?' Kincaid asked, rubbing his dusty hands against his jeans.

'No help there. I've tried.'

'Then I suggest sherry in the drawing room, when I've collected Faith. Maybe among us we'll come up with something.'

Faith stood watching for him outside the café, hands deep in the pockets of her cardigan. She waited until they had almost reached Jack's before she asked Kincaid, 'Any luck?'

'Some interesting things, but not what we're looking for.'

'No. I meant Nick. Did you find him?'

'I tried the caravan, and the cafés you suggested. No joy, but the woman at the Assembly Rooms says he'd been in earlier. If he doesn't show up this evening, I'll run out to the—' The sight of the car in Jack's drive instantly derailed his train of thought. A slightly battered white Vauxhall, unmarked. DCI Greely's.

'Ah . . . perhaps we'd better see what's up before we make plans. It looks as though Inspector Greely's come to call.'

'They won't put me in jail, will they?'

'Not if I can help it.'

Greely stood in front of the cold fireplace, hands behind his back as if warming them. Nodding, he said, 'Superintendent. Miss Wills.'

Winnie was still ensconced on the sofa, with Jack standing protectively by her.

'Inspector Greely,' Kincaid replied pleasantly, but it occurred to him that he was getting a good taste of being on the receiving end of things. 'What can we do for you today?'

'I just wanted to clarify a few things with Mr Montfort here.' Greely's smile was not reassuring.

Kincaid raised an eyebrow. 'Such as?'

Greely turned pointedly towards Jack, making it clear that he didn't intend to let Kincaid serve as intermediary this time. 'Mr Montfort, what time did you say you left the hospital last Thursday night?'

'I think it was about half past ten, but I really wasn't paying attention. Why?'

'The ICU nursing staff put it closer to ten o'clock. And it seems you told me it was near midnight when you arrived home and found Miss Wills on your doorstep. Is that right?'

'As far as I can remember. Look, what is all this about?'

'Well,' Greely drawled, 'it occurred to me that two hours was a very generous amount of time to make the drive from Taunton to Glastonbury, late at night with no traffic. And it also occurred to me that it takes a very *short* amount of time to drown someone – say three or four minutes.'

Jack gaped at him. 'Surely you're not accusing *me* of murdering Garnet? Why on earth would I do such a thing?'

Winnie reached up and took Jack's hand.

'Perhaps Miss Wills communicated her fears about

Miss Catesby's accident to you. At that time, I believe, Miss Catesby was still unconscious, her recovery quite uncertain. In such circumstances, you'd have wanted some answers very badly. Perhaps you merely meant to talk to Miss Todd, and it escalated into something much more serious – murder, in fact. And in that case, Miss Wills's story of coming back from her "walk" and finding the house empty is so much poppycock, and she either participated in the crime, or she acted as an accessory after the fact.'

Kincaid tried to catch Jack's eye, to caution him to say nothing, but Jack's gaze remained riveted on Greely.

'Number one,' his cousin shot back furiously, 'the first time I knew anything about Faith's suspicions was when she showed up on my doorstep around midnight. Second, the reason it took me longer than usual to drive from Taunton was that I was exhausted, and I had to stop several times in order to stay—'

'Give it up, Inspector,' Kincaid broke in. 'You're fishing. You've no evidence. And I've instructed my cousin to retain a lawyer.'

Greely rocked back and forth on his heels, placidly surveying them. 'I thought you might be interested in hearing my ideas, but as it seems you're not, I'll let you folks get on with your evening. Oh, by the way, Miss Catesby – I'm glad to see you making such a speedy recovery.'

'Thank you, Inspector.' She gave him a forced smile.

Kincaid gestured towards the door. 'I'll see you out, shall I?'

Greely nodded his farewells, then followed Kincaid into the hall.

'Do I take it no new evidence has presented itself, Inspector? Hence the stirring-ants technique?'

For once, Greely's smile looked genuine. 'Well, you know, Superintendent, when you stir an anthill with a stick, you generally get results.'

Kincaid returned the smile as he opened the door. 'Yes, Inspector, you do. But sometimes you get stung in the process.'

Andrew had rung the hospital, only to be told by a toffee-voiced receptionist that Winifred Catesby was no longer a patient there. After that he'd rung the Vicarage again and again, hanging up when the answering machine came on. He couldn't bear to hear her voice, and yet every time he felt he must.

After a while he took out the car, but the house on the Butleigh Road was dark, lifeless.

She was at Montfort's, then.

He knew Montfort's house, of course, he'd looked up the address in the telephone directory months ago. Now he could find it in his sleep, so often had he driven slowly by. Well, he would wait, and watch – he was good at waiting, and at watching – until the time was right.

When his own phone rang, he sat and stared at it until the ringing stopped.

Chapter Sixteen

The Tor is indeed the Hill of Vision for any whose eyes have the least inclination to open upon another world . . . There are some who, visiting Glastonbury for the first time, are amazed to see before them a Hill of Dreams which they have already known in sleep . . . Many times the tower is reported to have been seen rimmed in light; a warm glow, as of a furnace, beats up from the ground on wild winter nights, and the sound of chanting is heard from the depths of the hill.

Dion Fortune, from
Glastonbury: Avalon of the Heart

On the train from Bath to London, Gemma fell instantly into a heavy sleep, in which she dreamed jumbled, disjointed dreams, threaded throughout with the clicking and clacking of the train. When she woke, groggily, she felt there had been something she must do, but she could not remember what it was.

The memory nagged at her as she took the tube from Paddington to Islington, and as she rang her parents from the flat and asked them to run Toby home in their car.

When her parents arrived an hour later, Toby scrambled out of the car in a pair of brand-new, bright green wellies, shouting, 'Mummy, Mummy! I made sausage rolls! And we made special cakes for Halloween!'

Gemma swooped him up in a bear hug. 'You're going to take after your granddad, are you?'

'I'm a baker,' he announced proudly, wriggling until she put him down. 'Can I show Holly my boots?'

'All right. But knock first, okay?' She watched until he had closed behind him the gate that led to Hazel and Tim's garden, then ushered her parents into the flat.

'Has he been going non-stop all weekend?'

'More or less,' her mum answered, laughing. 'Cyn had her two over earlier, so he hasn't really touched down from that.'

Gemma rolled her eyes. Her sister's children were utterly undisciplined terrors, but if she complained, her mother would surely remind her of the things she and Cyn had got up to at that age. 'Stay for tea?' she asked instead.

'We'd best be getting back. I had ours just about ready when you rang. You look better. You should get away more often. How's Duncan?'

It was a loaded question. Her parents didn't approve of her unmarried state – or her 'pigheadedness' as they called it. Once, in a fit of temper, Gemma had retaliated, accusing them of not minding if she married an axe murderer, as long as they could tell their friends she was 'settled'.

'Depends on whether or not he was a good-looking chap,' her mother had rejoined promptly.

Now, Gemma smiled and answered, 'Duncan's fine. And his cousin's very nice.' She had told them only that they were making a social visit, and didn't intend to elaborate.

'Well, bring Duncan to see us. And let us know if you need us to mind Toby.'

When they had kissed her and gone on their way, Gemma wandered over to Hazel's, intending to practise her piano pieces while the children played. She filled Hazel and Tim in on the details of the weekend, then accepted a cup of tea and sat down at the piano and, with a sigh, attempted to concentrate on her music. But as she picked her way through Pachelbel's *Canon in D*, the immersion she sought refused to come.

Instead, her mind held an image of the worn stones of the Abbey rising from the emerald grass of the precinct . . . and the rocky flank of the Tor behind Garnet Todd's house on Wellhouse Lane, the broken tower on its summit like a finger stabbing at the sky.

Gemma sank back into her normal Monday-morning routine like a stone slipping into a pool, and yet there was an unreality to it, as if the hustle and bustle of her London life was merely surface noise. Wading through the accumulation of reports that had materialized on her desk over the weekend, she kept in mind the background checks she'd promised Kincaid, and when she had a free moment she put them in motion.

By late afternoon, information began to trickle in.

Garnet Todd had a record, for what it was worth. She had resisted arrest during an anti-war protest in London in the sixties and been found in possession of illegal hallucinogens. No surprise there. Garnet had always chosen the unconventional path.

Nick Carlisle, as Greely had mentioned, had been arrested and fingerprinted as a result of a pub brawl in Durham four years previously – a typical adolescent escapade. What surprised her was that his mother, into whose custody he had been released, was the famous North Country novelist Elizabeth Carlisle. Why would Elizabeth Carlisle's son choose to live in relative squalor in a Somerset backwater, working for practically nothing, when his connections would have guaranteed him a prestigious starting job? Principle? Or some sort of family trouble?

She put in a call to Durham CID and requested the number of the constable in Elizabeth Carlisle's small village. There was no answer when she rang, but she left her name and number on the constable's answerphone.

Kincaid had rung last night and brought her up to date on the negative results of their search for the manuscript, as well as Nick's apparent disappearance and DI Greely's sudden interest in Jack.

'What did the Super say when you rang him?' she'd asked.

'Officially, to keep my nose clean and be prepared to levitate back to London if anything breaks on this murder in Camden Passage. Unofficially, he was at school with the Chief Constable and will have my arse if Greely complains I'm interfering in his case.'

'Ouch.'

'I know. I hope I don't bugger this up.' Then, as he rang off – 'Oh, and by the way, I miss you.'

Gemma smiled at the memory, then went back to mulling over what he'd told her. It struck her that Faith had talked about Garnet's knowledge of Goddess worship, and now Nick Carlisle was looking up friends of the dead woman who had the same interest. Was it possible that Garnet's murder could be connected to her involvement in some sort of cult? Could her death have nothing to do with Winnie or Jack?

She typed 'goddess worship' into the search engine on her computer. The results were overwhelming, but she started through them resolutely, scanning articles and pagan sites. A name caught her eye. She ran the cursor back, highlighting a monograph on 'The History of the Goddess in Celtic Mythology' by a Dr Erika Rosenthal.

She had met an Erika Rosenthal a few weeks ago in the course of an investigation – surely the name was not that common. An elderly woman in Arundel Gardens had been burgled, and, concerned about the professional quality of the break-in, Gemma had gone herself to view the scene and interview the victim.

Erika Rosenthal had turned out to be in her nineties, sharp as a tack, and highly incensed at the theft of several valuable antiques. Gemma had been immediately taken with her – and with her home, a lovely place, filled with books and beautiful paintings and, most temptingly, a baby grand piano.

Today Gemma only had time to skim part of Dr Rosenthal's article before she was interrupted, and it was half past five by the time she cleared her desk for the day. On an impulse, she stuffed the report in her briefcase and rang Hazel, telling her she might be a bit late.

There was a fine mist in the still air and the wet pavement gleamed. She loved this weather, as she loved autumn in all its guises, and she took greedy breaths of the cool dampness as she walked to Arundel Gardens.

Erika Rosenthal's house wore its age gracefully. Its pale grey stucco was comfortably faded and it did not boast a satellite dish or an alarm system . . . though it was probably the lack of the latter that had contributed to Mrs Rosenthal's loss.

The old woman answered Gemma's ring, her face lighting up in recognition.

'Inspector James. You've found my things.' She was a tiny woman, with white hair swept into a smooth twist and bright shoe-button eyes in her finely wrinkled face.

'No, I'm sorry to say we haven't. I've come about something else entirely, Mrs Rosenthal, if you have a minute.'

'Of course. Come in, dear, and warm yourself by the fire.'

Gemma stood in front of the electric fire and looked round with pleasure. She resisted the temptation to go over to the piano, but for a moment she let herself imagine living in such a house. Then she chided herself for being unrealistic, and said, 'Thank you, that's lovely,' as she accepted a glass of sherry.

'Now, what can I do for you?' asked Mrs Rosenthal,

lowering herself into an armchair. There was a book open on the table beside her chair, an account of Mallory and Irvine's ill-fated expedition to Everest. Seeing Gemma's interest, she added, 'I've become an armchair adventurer, now that I no longer feel guilty for not attempting such things myself.'

'Are you the Dr Erika Rosenthal who wrote a monograph on pagan Goddess worship?'

Mrs Rosenthal chuckled. 'That I am. But why on earth would you want to know about that?'

Gemma noticed, as she had not on their first meeting, that Dr Rosenthal had the faintest trace of an accent – German or Eastern European. 'I've been, um . . . assisting in an investigation of a murder in Glastonbury. The victim seems to have had some knowledge of Goddess worship, and we're not certain whether this has any bearing on the case.'

'So you started researching and ran across my name. Clever girl. Or young woman, I should say,' the doctor apologized with a twinkle. 'But from my perspective, anyone under seventy is a girl.'

'I had the impression from your article that you were quite a respected authority on paganism,' Gemma said.

'I'm an historian, my dear, and I'm not sure that anyone is ever entirely respected in academe. But, yes, I have devoted a good deal of my life to the subject.'

'It seemed to me, from the things I read this afternoon, that for the most part Goddess worship is a fairly harmless – even positive – thing. All that getting-back-in-touch-with-the-earth stuff. And I can't say that men have done a terribly good job of running the world, so maybe the matriarchal society is not a bad idea either.' Gemma left the fire and sat in a small chair across from Dr Rosenthal. 'What I don't understand is why those beliefs could have motivated someone to kill this woman.'

'Ah, well, even the most benign aspects would provide motive enough. "Getting in touch with the earth", as you put it, usually evolves into actively opposing those who abuse our natural resources for their own ends, and there you encounter great greed. And there are men – and a few women – who cannot abide the idea of women in power. But I'm certain you know that from your own experience.' Dr Rosenthal studied her shrewdly. 'Paganism, like any system of belief that is world-shaping, can easily inspire fanaticism. You could say that Christianity is a basically benign belief, and yet it has been responsible over the centuries for enormous suffering in the world.

'But the worship of the Old Gods can go further. It has a dark side to it, an element of chaos, and there are those who aspire to tap that, to release it again into the world. And there are those who are caught up in it unawares. You say this murder happened in Glastonbury?'

'Yes, very near the Tor.'

Dr Rosenthal frowned. 'Glastonbury has always been a pivotal point, an energy focus. Dion Fortune understood that. Have you read her books? You should. Fortune was a practical woman with the soul of a poet, and she understood that the balance between the old forces and the new was quite a delicate thing. Some believe that the old powers give the earth its vitality, but that those powers must be kept in check, or chaos would overwhelm us.'

'But if that were true, why would anyone want to upset the balance?'

'Just as there are children who cannot keep their hands from the hot stove, there are always those who court the flames. It may be that your victim was one of them.'

Gemma thought of what Faith had told her about Garnet – and of the power she herself had sensed in the Tor. 'Do you believe such things are possible, then?'

'I am a Jew, my dear. During the war, I lost every member of my family to the camps. If you ask me what I believe, I can tell you that those atrocities were an incontrovertible example of the power of chaos, magnifying and abetting a very human evil.'

Kincaid was waiting outside the bookshop a half-hour before opening time on Monday morning, having dropped Faith at the café on his way.

After ten minutes of watching the passers-by, he saw Nick go past on his motorbike, then turn the corner into Benedict Street. A moment later, Nick came round the corner on foot, walking fast, but when he glimpsed Kincaid, his stride broke for an instant. Recovering, he came on, a determined expression on his handsome face.

Kincaid pushed away from the wall when Nick reached him. 'We need to talk.'

'I have to open the shop.'

'Then I'll come in with you.'

Nick hesitated, then shrugged and unlocked the door. Kincaid followed him in and Nick turned the 'Open' sign face-out.

'Jack and Faith have been worried about you.' Kincaid picked up a book on the Glastonbury Zodiac from the front table.

'I couldn't . . . after the police . . . I was bloody humiliated, if you want to know the truth.'

'Well, it seems you've lost first place on the suspect list, if that makes you feel any better. DI Greely has now moved Jack up in the running, but he still likes Faith as accessory.'

'You're joking!'

'I'm not. Perhaps if we all cooperated, we'd make some progress finding out who *did* kill Garnet, instead of working at cross-purposes. If you tell me, for instance, what you found out about Garnet yesterday, I might be able to put it together with something else. That's the beauty of an investigation.'

'How did you—'

'Faith had me look for you. I had a chat with the nice lady at the Assembly Rooms café.'

'Oh . . . Janet. I never thought . . .'

'It sounds to me as if you put your contacts and your knowledge of the town to admirable use.'

'It seemed a good idea.'

'Tell me why.'

Nick moved round the table, absently straightening books. 'I'd been worried for a long time that Garnet's intentions towards Faith weren't as altruistic as everyone seemed to think. But I knew anything I said, especially to Faith, would just be put down as jealousy.'

'So you kept quiet, and watched.'

'Listened would be more like it. I hear things in here.' Nick gestured around the shop. 'Gossip. Rumours. Bits of conversation. All pointing in the same direction – that this year is a window of power, a time when the forces of the Old Religion are near the surface.'

'Millennial hysteria?'

'Maybe. But I think Garnet meant to use Faith somehow.'

'And the people you talked to yesterday – did they corroborate that?'

'They wouldn't go that far, no. But they did mutter rather furtively about Samhain.' When Kincaid raised an eyebrow, Nick explained. 'That's the Celtic name for All Souls' Day, or Halloween.'

'And it's just a few days away,' Kincaid said thoughtfully. 'When you say you think Miss Todd meant to "use" Faith, are you talking about a sacrifice of some sort?'

'I – I don't know. But it can't matter now, can it?'

'I don't see how. But I wouldn't go broadcasting these theories to Inspector Greely.'

'Because he'll think I'm crazy?'

'Because it gives you a stronger motive to murder Garnet. You have to admit you've made no secret of your desire to protect Faith. Who else would go to such lengths—' Kincaid broke off abruptly, realizing that he knew.

'The Archdeacon is coming to lunch,' Winnie informed

him when he returned to Jack's. 'She says the Vicarage is going to overflow with covered dishes if we don't eat some of them. But I thought I could at least set the table.' She gestured at the clutter covering the oak surface.

'You direct; I'll clear,' Kincaid offered. 'Where's Jack?'

'He had to give some attention to his practice, poor man. He's done nothing for almost a week but run back and forth to hospital and wait on me.'

'No luck in the attic this morning?'

'No, but Simon stopped by to see how we were doing. What about you? Did you find Nick?'

'Yes. He's fine, just doing a bit of investigating on his own.' He had no intention of sharing Nick's suspicions about Garnet.

Seeing Winnie grasp a chair back as if for support, he suspected she was still more wobbly than she liked to admit.

'Okay, you sit,' he ordered. 'Now, where are the knives and forks?'

Suzanne Sanborne was an attractive, intelligent-looking woman, slender, with silver-threaded, curly hair. 'So you're the famous cousin from Scotland Yard,' she said, when she had hugged Winnie.

'Archdeacon.'

'Call me Suzanne, please. And help me with these casseroles.'

They were soon settled round the table for a convivial lunch, aided by the bottle of Bordeaux Kincaid had discovered in Jack's pantry. Winnie was anxious about her parish obligations, but the Archdeacon was quick to reassure her.

'The last thing you need to do just now is worry. I've asked Miles Fleming to fill in when he can, and I'll take some of your duties myself.'

'But I could at least—'

'Next week we'll talk about your taking the services,' Suzanne interrupted in a tone that brooked no argument. 'But you're going to have to be patient with yourself.'

'Suzanne,' Winnie said hesitantly. 'I know this sounds a stupid question, but have you any idea what I did on Wednesday? I had Jack bring my diary from the Vicarage last night, and I'd written in two sick visits for the morning, and a Deanery Chapter meeting after lunch. This morning I rang everyone up. It seems I kept the morning appointments, but I missed the Chapter meeting altogether.'

'Of course I know what you did!' Suzanne answered with a chuckle. 'Why didn't someone ask me sooner? I asked you to take a bereavement visit.'

'Did you?' Winnie said blankly.

'In Pilton. You know the vicar was on holiday last week.' Turning to Kincaid, she explained, 'I'd have gone myself but I had a Diocesan meeting, so at Winnie's party I asked her to take it for me.'

Winnie moaned. 'This is dreadful. Why can't I remember?'

'I'm sure you will,' Suzanne reassured her. 'My prescription for you is a rest. It looks to me as if you've done far too much today.' Glancing at her watch, she added, 'I've a meeting, but I can help get you settled, then Duncan can see me out.'

Very smoothly done, Kincaid thought as they escorted Winnie into the sitting room. When she was comfortably situated on the sofa, Suzanne gave her a last admonition. 'Now, don't you worry. Your parish will tick along without you for a few more days.'

'But I've a wedding—'

'We'll talk about it tomorrow. Get some rest.'

'But . . .' Winnie's protest trailed off as her eyelids started to droop. The wine and pasta had done their work well.

Kincaid and Suzanne stole quietly out and he walked her to her car.

'She really is doing remarkably well,' Suzanne said.

'Yes, but that's not what you wanted to talk to me about.'

'You don't miss a trick, Superintendent.' She gave him a quick smile, then sighed. 'I hate to be alarmist, but I'm quite worried about Andrew, Winnie's brother. He hasn't been to see Winnie since she left hospital, has he?'

'Not since she regained consciousness, as far as I know.'

'He refused to go into the ICU – were you aware of that? And every time I saw him in the waiting area, he seemed progressively overwrought. I'm afraid that his silence doesn't bode well.'

'You may be right. Can you see him? Have you any influence?'

'When I tried to reason with him in hospital, he only became more agitated. But we've been friends for a long time. Perhaps David and I should both talk to him.'

'I take it you're worried about more than Catesby's mental health. Do you think he would hurt Winnie?'

'Andrew cares for Winnie so much, I can't imagine . . . but sometimes love can get twisted.' Suzanne met Kincaid's eyes. 'Until we've at least tried to sort things out with Andrew, I'd feel better if you kept a close eye on Winnie *and* Jack.'

As soon as Fiona finished one canvas, another image coalesced in her mind, giving her no peace until she brought it to life.

She thought she had never worked so well, with such richness of colour or delicacy of detail, and for the first time in months the child had not appeared. But she was bone-weary, and when she'd put the final touches on the latest effort, she cleaned her brushes and left her studio.

Bram looked up from the book he was reading, his relief obvious. 'Finished, darling?'

Fiona stretched out on the sofa beside him. 'I'm knackered.'

'I wish I could help.' He stroked her forehead with his thumb.

'You do, just by understanding.' As a child, she had drawn on walls if no paper was available when the urge came on her – and had not understood when she'd been punished for it. At one point her baffled parents had tried to keep her from drawing altogether, and she had sunk into a state of depression so deep it bordered on catatonia.

'But I feel empty tonight,' she added, yawning and snuggling a little more firmly into his lap. 'This may be it for now.'

'Are they good?'

'Brilliant. You'll like them.' She smiled up at him. 'I think I'll go and see Winnie tomorrow, if she feels up to a bit of company.'

'Shall I read to you?'

'What are you reading?'

'William of Malmesbury's account of his visit to the Abbey in the 1120s. Listen to this. He's talking about the Old Church. " . . . *one can observe all over the floor stones, artfully interlaced in the forms of triangles or squares and sealed with lead; I do no harm to religion if I believe some sacred mystery is contained beneath them . . .*" '

Was that what Garnet had known? Fiona wondered sleepily, meaning to ask Bram, but the words began to stretch out like shining beads on a string, until they shimmered and faded away.

She woke on the sofa in a darkened room, with a blanket tucked round her and a cushion placed carefully under her head. It was late – or very early – she sensed that by the quality of the light filtering in through the blinds. She sat up, intending to go to bed for what was left of the night, and her dream came back to her in a rush.

The music – she had heard the singing again. Now it dissolved and slipped once more from her grasp.

And she had seen the Abbey, washed in a clear, pale light. But the heavily overgrown ruins had stood in an open, pastoral landscape, rather than their modern-day walled setting. A few thin cows grazed in the foreground, watched over by a man in old-fashioned dress who leaned picturesquely on a shepherd's staff.

Fiona lay back and pulled the blanket up to her chin, trying to make sense of the disparate elements floating about in her head: the music, Garnet, the beautifully coloured tiles in the Old Church, the odd view of the Abbey . . .

Her last thought, as she drifted off to sleep once more, was that the man with the shepherd's crook had looked remarkably like Jack Montfort.

Chapter Seventeen

But even St Michael was helpless against the Powers of Darkness, concentrated by ritual, and in the earthquake of AD *1000 the body of the church [on the Tor] fell down, leaving only the tower standing. Thus was the Christian symbol of a cruciform church changed into the pagan symbol of an upstanding tower, and the Old Gods held their own.*

Dion Fortune, from
Glastonbury: Avalon of the Heart

Faith felt very odd from the moment she woke on Tuesday morning. She wondered if any of the others sensed the heaviness, the oppression, in the air. She felt an urgency, as well, a sense that her time to take care of unfinished business was swiftly running out. And the baby, so violently active the past few days, was suddenly quiet, giving her only the occasional gentle nudge.

She felt her abdomen carefully, the way Garnet had taught her, but she couldn't be sure that the baby had dropped. Why wasn't Garnet here when she needed her? And how was she going to manage without her?

Fighting back tears of anger and frustration, she finished getting ready for work, then went looking for Duncan. She found him in the last bedroom, surrounded by opened boxes, his face already dirty and set in a scowl of discouragement.

Last night Nick had turned up at last, with a curt apology for his absence. He and Simon had joined in the attic search, carrying the smaller items down to Faith and Winnie in the sitting room. After a long evening's work, they had all declared the attic thoroughly sorted, with a disheartening lack of results. Now Jack and Duncan had begun working their way through the remainder of the house.

'Anything?' Faith asked Duncan, knowing what the answer would be.

'An old album with some photos of my mother as a child. But other than that, no. Are you ready for me to run you to the café?'

They had developed a comfortable routine in just a few short days, and Faith realized with a pang that she would be sorry to see it end. Nor did she like the idea of the deception she meant to practise today, but she could see no alternative. She must find proof that someone besides Nick had had reason to harm Garnet. And Duncan had told her that the police had sealed the farmhouse, so she couldn't very well ask him to take her to root through Garnet's things.

'I'll see you at five,' he said as she climbed out of the car at the café, and she lifted her hand in a wave as he drove away in Gemma's purple car.

It was a slow morning, much to her relief, because she grew progressively more uncomfortable as the day wore on. Her legs ached, and her pelvis felt as if her ligaments had turned to jelly. Buddy fussed over her, coming in from the shop to give her a hand as often as he could.

After lunch she waited, tidying and watching the clock. When the hands crept round to two, she gave the counter a last wipe and went into the shop.

Buddy looked up from his jewellery counter. His face creased instantly with concern. 'Are you okay, kiddo?'

'I'm not feeling very well. Would you mind if I left early today?' *It isn't a lie*, she told herself. *Just bending the truth a bit*.

'Is it the baby?'

'No, I don't think so,' she said uncertainly. 'But I think maybe I should take it easy.'

'Have you called someone to fetch you?'

'Yes,' she lied outright this time, forcing a smile. 'I'll wait outside.'

She slipped on her cardigan and went out into the light drizzle that had kept the climbers away. There was nothing for it but to walk, so she turned resolutely uphill and began.

The pavement grew more slippery and the rain heavier as she climbed. By the time she reached the farmhouse she was gasping, and a dull, heavy pain had taken root at the base of her spine. But she had done it! No one had passed her on her way up the hill, but still she looked round furtively as she ducked under the blue and white crime-scene tape that had been stretched across the gate.

She picked her way across the yard and unlocked

the back door with her key. All three cats trotted hopefully out from the shelter of the barn and she stooped to stroke them as they rubbed about her ankles, purring. 'Are you hungry, poor dears?' she said, and sang the silly little dinner song she had made up for them as she let them in the house.

Every surface in the kitchen was covered with a fine black dust, and the room looked as if a hurricane had raged through it, littered throughout with the objects from the shelves and cabinets. Faith grimaced as she lit the lamp and put food in the cats' bowls, trying to touch as little as possible. The sight of the casserole Garnet had made the day she died almost undid her.

The evidence of the police search was even more overwhelming in Garnet's office. There was fingerprint powder everywhere, and the room was a sea of papers. The drawers of Garnet's desk had been prised open, and all but one drawer was empty.

Lighting the lamp on the desk, she looked at the contents of the drawer they had left intact. It held a half-dozen spiral notebooks, and as Faith opened them, she saw that each was filled with technical notes on tile making. No wonder the police hadn't found them useful.

Garnet had been secretive to the point of paranoia concerning the recipes she used in the glazes on her tiles. She'd insisted that they were what made her work unique, and her restoration techniques possible. In a talkative mood, she had once told Faith that she used only natural materials available to medieval craftsmen, creating the authentic colours that made her tiles so prized.

But it seemed Garnet's secrets had not died with her. The journals held not only extensive notes, but accounts of formulas and experiments, failures and successes.

Faith was so fascinated that she forgot the time, until a glance at the darkening window reminded her that she must keep on. She had meant to be finished and back at the café when Duncan came to collect her, although what she would tell Buddy she had yet to figure out.

She put the journals back and thought for a moment. The office was a dead end. If there had been anything useful the police would have found it. Slowly, she returned to the kitchen. This was the heart of the house, where Garnet had spent her time when she was not working. Here she had sung while she cooked, she had read, she had rocked in the well-worn rocking chair.

Faith lowered herself into the rocker. Here she would have rocked her own child, if Garnet had not died. She looked round, trying to see the kitchen from Garnet's point of view. Garnet hadn't owned many things, but among her most treasured possessions had been her books, especially her cookbooks. They sat in the small nook above the cooker, apparently untouched by the police maelstrom.

With a grunt of effort, Faith stood and pulled out one book, then another, swiftly thumbing through them.

It was in a vegetarian tome Faith had seldom seen

Garnet use that she found the papers tucked inside the flyleaf: several sheets of foolscap filled with Garnet's spiky handwriting, pages torn from a book, and a newspaper clipping, yellowed and brittle with age.

First she unfolded the printed sheets, her eyes widening with shock as she read. The pages had obviously been torn from a primer on ancient magic, but these were not the gentle ceremonies Garnet had taught her – these were rituals that called the darkest and oldest powers up from the depths, rituals celebrating the Tor as the entrance to the Underworld, the home of the Great Mother. Participants began by walking the ancient spiral maze, the physical manifestation of the vortex of energy that would suck them up to the summit, and then down into the very heart of the Tor. Those who passed through chaos and death would emerge reborn, filled with the power of the Mother.

As she read, Faith knew with certainty that it was this force that had brought her to the Tor, and that Garnet must have known it too. With unsteady fingers, she opened the handwritten pages.

She might have been my daughter. She has come to me, a gift from the gods, redemption contained in her innocence. I will bring her child into the world . . . in return for the child lost, a life for a life . . . If only I can protect her from the power that awaits this birth.

So that was why Garnet had watched over her with such fierceness! She had known the thing that pulled and tugged at Faith for what it was; she had meant somehow to shield her from it. Fingers trembling, Faith opened the clipping, peering at the faded newsprint.

A photo of a child, a little girl, then a headline: TRAGEDY ON THE TOR, beneath which ran an all-too-brief story. *Four-year-old Sarah Jane Kinnersley was struck and killed yesterday evening in a hit-and-run accident on the slopes of Glastonbury Tor. The tragedy occurred at dusk in Wellhouse Lane, just below the Kinnersley farm. Sarah's parents realized something was amiss when Sarah did not—*

Faith looked up. A sound – she'd heard a sound. The clipping fluttered to the floor as she strained her senses to catch the sound again. But there was nothing but the spattering of rain against the windowpane, and she saw that the lowering sky had obliterated all but the last vestiges of daylight. She felt a rush of panic – was she late? Had she missed Duncan?

Looking at the clock above the stove, she breathed a sigh of relief. It was not yet five o'clock. She was all right. She would go down the hill and she would try to make sense of what she had read. But just now all she wanted to do was get out of the house, so empty without Garnet's presence, and back to warmth and light.

Her hand was on the kitchen lamp when the sound came again, this time unmistakable – a footstep, the groan of weight on the bottom step. Had Duncan discovered her missing from the café and come looking for her?

But surely she'd have heard the swish of the car on the wet tarmac, and the squeak of the gate. There was another creak, and a shadow against the curtained window.

The fear that gripped her was deeper than thought.

She looked round wildly for a place to hide, but it was too late. The door swung open and the last voice she had expected to hear said, 'Hullo, Faith.'

Gemma had slept fitfully, waking several times to check on Toby, tossing and turning in between. When the dull light that presaged dawn began to filter through her blinds, she gave up trying to sleep.

She sat at the half-moon table in the quiet flat, looking out at the garden, as the sky grew brighter. As she watched the familiar lines of tree and shrub take shape, she thought again about her conversation with Erika Rosenthal.

Dr Rosenthal was a rational woman, a scholar, and yet she had spoken of Old Gods and elemental powers without reservation. If she were right, Gemma's perceptions had been more than an overactive imagination, and Faith had indeed been in danger. Yet Faith had been drawn to the Tor before Garnet even knew of her existence; had the danger been not Garnet herself, but something else that had not yet run its course?

That thought made Gemma so uncomfortable that she stood and began to get ready for her day, but she worried at it restlessly throughout the morning. No matter how much she tried to rationalize it, she couldn't shake the instinct that Faith was still at terrible risk.

At noon, she called in her sergeant and informed him that she would be out for the rest of the day. Her superior was away on a training course – she'd have to explain herself to him when she came back. And Hazel! She would have to ask Hazel to keep Toby for the night.

But first, she rang Kincaid at Jack's.

'Andrew! What are you doing here?' Faith stared at the apparition in the doorway. His thin anorak glistened with rain, and his hair was plastered to his forehead. He looked different somehow, younger, and she realized he'd taken off his glasses.

'I've come to see you.' He stepped into the kitchen and shut the door. 'You're looking well.'

'Well?' She looked down at her distended abdomen, then back at him. 'Is that all you can say?'

'What should I say? That you're blooming? Or one of those other euphemisms people use to get round the fact that pregnant women resemble beached whales?'

His cruelty was shocking. Nor was there any trace of tenderness in his voice. What had she seen in him, all those months ago?

He had been impressed with her performance in his history classes, and with her knowledge of music. And she had been so flattered by his interest, intrigued by his boyish good looks and his air of vulnerability. When he'd begun asking her to stop by his office, she'd felt singled out, special. And then had come the casual touch, the hand on her shoulder, the stroking of her hair – so different from the fumbling of boys her own age.

The thrill of it had made her giddy with excitement, and when he'd said, oh, so nonchalantly, 'If ever you're walking up Wirral Hill, stop by my house for a cup of tea,' she had gone.

There had been a few charmed weeks of regular visits, of feeling so grown up, sleek with her secret and her superiority to the other girls in her class.

Then reality had struck – a missed period, the worry, the sickness, the inevitable acknowledgment of the truth. When she'd told him she was pregnant, he had wept in her arms like a terrified child, and she'd sworn to him she would never tell anyone the truth. And she'd believed that, once the baby was born and she was on her own, perhaps they could be together again.

Now she saw that she had been mad to think she had meant anything to him – or that she had ever been more than a dreadful mistake in his eyes.

'What do you want?' she asked.

'This can't go on, you know,' said Andrew, coming a step closer. 'This wondering, waiting for the axe to fall. I can't bear it any more.'

'I haven't told anyone!'

'Not Garnet?'

'No. I swear.' But she *had* confessed to Garnet, when Winnie had urged her to see her mum – and learned to her horror that Winnie was Andrew's *sister*! She had been introduced to Winnie only by her Christian name, and so had never made the connection.

'And you haven't told my sister?'

'I wouldn't tell Winnie!'

'I never expected that,' Andrew said dispassionately. 'That you would make friends with my sister. Did you think it would give you some hold over me?'

He shook his head. 'You should have known that was the one thing I would never tolerate.'

Too late, Faith realized her mistake. But if she had lied and told him Winnie knew, would it have made a difference? 'I've protected you. All these months. I had to leave home, because my dad would have killed you if he'd found out.'

'That doesn't matter now. But my sister . . . You have to understand. Winnie mustn't ever know. I can't take any more chances. I'm sorry.'

He was on her before she could move, his hands round her throat.

Faith felt the searing pressure of his thumbs, heard the rasp of his breath in her ear. She struggled, trying to pull his hands away, but she couldn't loosen his grip.

Even through the suffocating fog of her fear, she knew that if she lost consciousness she would be finished. She kicked at his ankles, but he merely tightened his grip on her throat. His face was contorted with purpose, unrecognizable. He pushed her backwards until she felt the cooker press against the small of her back.

Her vision blurred, sparking with luminous blue spots. In a last effort, she stopped scrabbling at his hands and reached behind her, groping for something, anything, that might hold him off.

Her fingers closed on the handle of Garnet's cast-iron frying pan. She lifted it, vaguely aware of a tearing in her wrist from its weight, then swung it with all her strength.

The blow caught Andrew in the temple.

She saw the flare of astonishment in his eyes, then his hold on her throat gave way and he crumpled, toppling back against the table. He grasped at it, pulling himself up; Faith swung the frying pan again.

Andrew slumped to the floor.

Faith stood over him, panting and trembling. There was no blood. If she moved, would he come at her again?

Then she gasped as pain gripped her, doubling her over, squeezing at her, and a gush of warm liquid ran down her legs. When she could stand upright again, she inched round Andrew's still form, whimpering in terror.

She had to get out, away from the house. Away from him.

Stumbling out the door and down the steps, she ran through the downpour across the mud-slick yard to the back gate, and, once through it, onto the rocky slope of the Tor.

Up. She must go up. Blinded by the rain, sliding and falling, then picking herself up again, she began to climb straight up the side of the hill, towards the ancient contours cut into the rock, the maze that led to the summit of the Tor.

Chapter Eighteen

History may tell us that Christianity came to these islands from Ireland, but legend, which enshrines the spiritual heart of history, declares that the Light of the West came to us straight from the place of its rising, and that we were indebted to no intermediaries for its transmission.

Dion Fortune, from
Glastonbury: Avalon of the Heart

'Hullo, love. Good journey?' Kincaid eased the car into the traffic exiting Bath station as rain began to spatter on the windscreen.

'Any luck with your search this morning?' Gemma asked.

'This has been a wild goose chase if I ever saw one. We've not turned up anything remotely resembling a lost Gregorian chant. I'm beginning to think we've all gone a bit soft in the head.'

'You won't be able to stay much longer.'

'No.' He concentrated on his driving for a few moments, then said, 'DI Greely is still sifting through the material from Garnet's house, but there are no phone records, no computer, no Caller ID – there aren't even any personal letters that he's been able to find, just business records.'

'And no help from those?'

'Only in the negative sense. He's checked with those customers who had tile-work commissions pending, but she made no deliveries on the night of Winnie's hit-and-run.'

'What about forensics?'

'No evidence of an assault or an abduction in the house, and although they did find a few of Nick's prints, they can all be accounted for by his story. The only other identifiable prints are Faith's and Garnet's, and there's nothing to indicate that prints were wiped, as they were on Garnet's van.'

'Not Jack's?' Gemma asked.

'Not a smudge,' he said with relief.

'Garnet Todd led a remarkably isolated life,' Gemma mused. 'Most of us have an accumulation of flotsam from our connections, our relationships. Faith told me that Garnet had been a midwife, so she gave up a job where she had regular, intimate contact with people for tile making, a solitary occupation.'

'She did have a few close friends. Buddy Barnes, for one.'

'Faith's boss?'

'I had a chat with him yesterday. It occurred to me afterwards that he's extremely fond of Faith, and that if there should be anything to Nick Carlisle's theories about Garnet preparing Faith for some sort of bloody ritual on the Tor, and Buddy found out about it—'

'You think Buddy might have murdered Garnet?'

'I've asked DI Greely to run a check on him, at least.'

'Then what about Winnie? What reason could Buddy have possibly had for hurting Winnie?'

'I haven't got that far. Did you realize they all knew each other, years ago? Garnet and Buddy, Bram and Fiona Allen. Buddy and Fiona were an item, apparently.'

'Well, perhaps it would all make sense if Buddy had murdered *Fiona*—'

'A long-simmering unrequited love?' Kincaid raised an eyebrow. 'At this point I'm open to anything.'

'What if' – Gemma gave him a sly glance – 'what if Garnet found out something about Nick that would ruin his chances with Faith for good?'

'Do I see cream on your whiskers? You've found something. Out with it,' Kincaid demanded.

'I told you I discovered that Nick's mum is the novelist Elizabeth Carlisle. This morning the constable in her Northumbrian village rang me back. It seems that our Nick left behind a baby he refused to acknowledge or support. His mum has done right by the girl, apparently, but Nick's name is mud.'

'And then he came to Glastonbury and fell in love with a girl pregnant with another man's child?' Kincaid snorted. 'Sounds like someone's idea of a cosmic joke. But I doubt Faith would find it amusing.'

'That might explain why Nick would kill Garnet, but not why he would have struck Winnie. Unless' – Gemma frowned – 'unless we've got it the wrong way round. What if it was *Winnie* who found out about Nick – isn't that more likely, with her connections? – then

Garnet saw Nick hit Winnie. So he was forced to silence her.'

'You're leaving out one thing,' Kincaid objected. 'Nick doesn't have a car. His bike could not have caused Winnie's injuries.'

'Perhaps he borrowed a car – or stole one.'

'That's a possibility we should check.'

The rain fell in sheets now, and the traffic ground to a halt behind a long tailback. Kincaid glanced uneasily at his watch.

'What is it?' Gemma asked.

'We're not going to make Glastonbury by five, in this downpour. But I asked Jack to pick Faith up at the café, if we weren't in time.'

'But she was expecting you—'

'Jack promised he'd be there at the stroke of five. She'll be fine.'

But as the minutes passed, Kincaid could sense Gemma's growing tension. She sat quietly, eyes fixed on the road, as if she could hurry the car. As they neared Glastonbury, the rain fell even more heavily and the sky grew black. He drummed his fingers on the wheel as they crawled behind a lorry.

But at last they zigzagged their way through the village of Pilton, and the final clear stretch of road lay before them.

Then his mobile phone rang.

It was Jack on the line, sounding frantic. 'She's gone. Faith's gone. She told Buddy she didn't feel well earlier this afternoon, that she was coming home. Then he began to worry about her, and rang me. No one's seen her since she left the café.'

'Where are you?'

'At the house. I rang Nick at the bookshop, but he hasn't heard from her either.'

'Wait there. She may ring you, or show up at the house any minute. And you don't want to leave Winnie alone. We're almost in Glastonbury - we'll find her.'

'It's Faith, isn't it?' Gemma said as he disconnected.

'Missing since mid-afternoon. Told Buddy she was going home.' He swore under his breath, but he knew it was his own lack of foresight he was cursing. Why the hell hadn't he been more careful? 'Where could she have got to?'

'The farmhouse.' Gemma said with certainty. 'Duncan, she's gone to Garnet's farmhouse.'

As Kincaid pulled the car over, Gemma grabbed her torch from the door pocket and jumped out. Fumbling open the gate latch in the rain, she ducked under the crime-scene tape and ran across the muddy yard. The sight of the kitchen door standing ajar made her blood run cold. She stepped inside and looked round, fearing the worst.

The butter-coloured cat sat on the kitchen table, blinking at her, and then, beyond that, in the midst of the chaos left by the police, she saw a huddled form on the floor.

'It's Catesby!' Kincaid exclaimed, behind her. 'Dead?'

Andrew Catesby had fallen on his back, half under the table, but even in shadowed light Gemma could see the ugly swelling on his temple. A heavy frying pan lay on the floor nearby, as if it had been dropped.

She could hear his breathing, raspy and laboured, and when she felt his wrist his pulse fluttered beneath her fingertips.

Kincaid was already dialling 999, and once he'd requested medical help he left a message with Control for DI Greely.

'Faith must have been the connection all along, not Garnet,' he said as he squatted beside her. 'Jack said she'd gone to public school – Andrew must have been her teacher. And the father of her baby. That day you found him here, he must have been looking for Faith.'

'She protected *him* all this time. Was it Andrew who tried to kill Winnie, then, because she'd guessed? And then murdered Garnet in case Faith had told her?'

'We may never know,' Kincaid said grimly. 'Unless Faith can tell us. Where the hell is the girl? If Andrew attacked her, she could be hurt. You stay with him. I'll search the house.'

Gemma glanced at the open door, thinking furiously. She knew with unshakeable certainty that Faith was no longer in the house. She knew, too, where she had gone, and that *she* must go after her.

She also knew that she could never explain her conviction to Kincaid, and that he would forbid her to make that climb alone in the dark. But they couldn't both leave Catesby. 'Right,' she replied. 'You have a look.'

It would take Kincaid a very short time to search the small house, and Andrew Catesby's breathing had not worsened. When Kincaid disappeared down the hall, she slipped quietly out of the back door.

The rain had diminished to a fine mist, a soft touch against her face. 'Bloody hell,' she muttered, realizing Kincaid must have the car keys. Looking up at the Tor's black bulk rising behind the house, she considered going straight up the hill, then dismissed the plan as more foolhardy than the one she was already contemplating. The lane it must be, then.

She jogged until cramp seized her, but pressed on to the Tor's north entrance. The path was undemanding at first, a fairly straight and gentle incline across a field, leading to a few stone steps and a narrow way through a copse of trees. Gemma breathed a sigh of relief as she came out the other side. Then she saw what lay ahead.

Jack prowled restlessly over the worn Aubusson carpet. 'Why would she do such a thing? I just don't understand it.' He stopped in front of the fire and warmed his hands automatically, not feeling the heat. 'If anything happens to that girl . . . I got her into this whole bloody mess—'

'Jack,' Winnie interrupted from the sofa, 'that's not true. Faith had met Garnet before you came in contact with either of them, and Faith has always made her own decisions, whatever her reasons.'

He knew she was trying to calm him – and perhaps herself – but he could tell from the pallor of her face how worried she was. 'I'm sorry, darling. You're right. She's managed well enough on her own until now. I'm sure she'll show up any minute wanting to know what all the fuss was a—'

The doorbell cut him off. He and Winnie stared at one another, but before he could move they heard Nick Carlisle's voice.

'In here!' Jack called, and Nick appeared in the doorway, dishevelled, his dark hair beaded with raindrops.

'Has she come back?'

'No. No word.'

'They've got Wellhouse Lane blocked off. They wouldn't let me through—'

'Who has it blocked off?'

'The bloody police. Something's happened. I'm going to see if I can get round on foot—'

'Nick. Duncan will ring if there's news. It might not have anything to do with—'

'That's bullshit. It's Faith, and you know it. I'm going up there. They can arrest me if they don't bloody like it.' The front door slammed a moment later.

Jack started after him, but Winnie put a restraining hand on his arm. 'Let him go. He's got to do *something*.'

Sinking down on the ottoman, Jack felt as if his bones had dissolved. 'Faith—' he began, but he couldn't go on.

Winnie had paled, but took his hand in a strong grip. 'She's fine, I'm sure of—'

The bell rang again. This time Jack stood and left the room without speaking.

He had feared the police, bearing bad news, but he was wrong. 'Jack?' There was a concerned expression on Fiona Allen's freckled face. 'Is everything all right?

I just saw a man run away from your house like the hounds of hell were after him.'

Jack ushered her in, explaining what had happened.

'Oh, I'm so sorry,' Fiona murmured. 'Listen, I can come back another–'

'No, don't go,' Jack and Winnie said in unison.

'There was something I wanted to tell you both,' Fiona said urgently. 'Last night, after I stopped painting, I had a dream.

'I heard the same music I heard the night of Winnie's accident, and I saw a painting of the Abbey. Seventeenth or eighteenth century, I'd guess, a watercolour. And the oddest thing was that there was a man in the painting who looked remarkably like you, Jack. And then there were Garnet's tiles–'

'A watercolour, did you say?'

'Yes, of the Abbey ruins, with cows in the foreground. Very nicely done too.'

Jack stood. 'I'll be back.'

But where the hell was the painting Duncan had found, he tried to remember as he took the stairs two at a time. He had only glanced at the thing, and had no recollection of what Duncan had done with it . . .

It proved easy enough to find, however, set carefully off to one side with the portrait of the spaniel Duncan had wanted for Gemma. Breathing a sigh of relief, he carried both paintings back down the stairs.

'That's it! That's exactly what I saw in my dream!' Fiona exclaimed as he held out the view of the Abbey.

'That *is* remarkable.' Winnie examined the small

figure in the foreground of the watercolour. 'It could be you in farmer's togs.'

'Look – there.' Fiona reached out to touch the bottom corner. 'Is that a signature? Have you a magnifying glass?'

Jack fetched the old glass from his mother's writing desk, and Winnie held it carefully over the small squiggle.

'It is a signature. *Matthew* – is that *Matthew*?' Jack heard the quick intake of her breath. '*Matthew Montfort.* It says Matthew Montfort!'

'But what does it mean?' Jack asked. 'We're looking for a manuscript, not a painting.'

'May I?' Fiona asked, and Winnie handed her the watercolour.

First, Fiona examined the front, and the frame, then she turned the painting over. The heavy paper neatly covering the back was discoloured, and had a spattering of water or liquid stains, but otherwise it was intact. Fiona ran her fingertip round the edge, checking the seal, then she smoothed her palm across the paper.

Once more, she repeated the motion, stopping at the same point. 'Have you a penknife? I think there might be something under the backing.'

Jack handed her his pocket knife, not trusting himself to speak.

Carefully, Fiona ran the tip of the knife under two of the edges. 'Yes, there is something. I can see it.' She loosened the third side and lifted the flap of paper away.

A sheet of paper covered in a graceful but old-fashioned hand lay beneath the watercolour's backing.

'Jack, I think this belongs to you,' Fiona said, awe in her voice as she transferred the painting to him.

He lifted the sheet, his heart thudding with excitement. Beneath it lay a flat, paper-wrapped package, tied with a faded silk ribbon. 'This appears to be a letter,' he said, struggling to decipher the handwriting. He read aloud haltingly:

'These papers have been passed from father to son in my family for seven hundred years, and we have preserved them to . . . our ability. But sadly, the original wrappings have disintegrated beyond my power to restore. I have devised a new place of safe keeping, as I have been instructed, in the hopes that this gift from Our Lord may be treasured and kept as it deserves.

'It is said that this is the Holy Chant of Glastonbury, brought by Joseph of Arimathea and his followers from the Holy Land in the First Century after the Crucifixion of Our Lord, perpetuated by twelve anointed choristers, as it had been since the days of the Faithful in Egypt. Thus when the Norman, Abbot Thurstan, sought to impose the form of worship practised in France upon the monks of our Abbey, they rose in protest against him and he shed their blood upon the Altar of the Great Church. So it is that this most holy of praises to Our Lord vanished from the sight and hearing of mankind, but was not lost.

'This I entrust to the care of' – Jack squinted at the script – *'descendants* – I think he says *descendants, and may the Blessings of Our Lord Jesus Christ be always upon you.*

Matthew Montfort, 1759.'

Jack looked up; Winnie's face was rapt. He had to clear his throat before he could speak. 'So it was true. I didn't really believe it . . .'

'I can't bear it,' Winnie breathed. 'Go on. Open the package.' When he hesitated still, she said gently, 'It's your right, Jack. This is what Edmund wanted.'

Fingers trembling, he untied the ribbon and folded back the wrapping from the tissue-thin folio beneath.

The path that had begun with such deceptive gentleness now switched back and forth up the steep north side of the Tor. The drop-off was sheer, the clay between the viciously sharp stones was slick as glass, and there was no railing.

Gemma made the mistake at first of trying to use her torch, but she found that while the circle of light lit the terrain immediately beneath her feet, it blinded her to the turns of the path and the nearness of the precipice.

She fell once, hard, cutting her hands and knees. She lay there a long minute, feeling the cold dampness seep through her clothing, letting her heart slow. It didn't matter that she was afraid of heights, she told herself, as she couldn't tell how far up she'd climbed.

After that, she used her hands as much as her feet, trying always to feel the rising ground on her right.

Still, she misjudged a turn in the path: her left foot slid over the edge, sending pebbles echoing down the hillside. She stood gasping, gathering her courage, but the prospect of the return journey was so terrifying she knew that even if it weren't for Faith, she could only continue upwards.

At last, her right hand reached into space, and as she moved gingerly in that direction she felt the ground level out beneath her feet. She had reached the summit. For an instant moonlight rent the clouds, illuminating the tower before her. Then the clouds blotted out the moon again, but the dark, squat shape remained imprinted on her brain.

How had she ever thought to find Faith in this desolate place?

She used the torch now as she inched forward, but it lit only the sparse turf, and once a startled sheep. When she called out Faith's name, the wind snatched the word from her mouth. She halted a few yards from the tower, unwilling to go any closer. Despair washed through her.

Then, in a lull in the wind, she thought she heard a cry.

'Faith!'

This time she was certain she heard a response – a moan? Or a sob? – and it came from the far side of the tower. Gemma hurried forward, stumbling.

As she rounded the tower, she saw a shape crouched against the base.

'Faith!' she called again, and heard something between a groan and a scream in reply. Gemma knew that sound, and the primal pain that prompted it. Faith was in labour.

The girl sat with her back pressed against the side of the tower, her feet spread apart, her knees up. Gemma knelt beside her and touched her cheek.

Faith turned her head towards Gemma's hand like a blind thing and whispered, 'Garnet?'

'No, love, it's Gemma. I've come to help you. Let's get you up and I'll take you down the hill.' But as she tried to raise the girl, Faith screamed again.

Panic bubbled in Gemma's throat. It had been less than a minute since the last contraction. They weren't going anywhere. Faith was going to have her baby right here, and soon. She was panting now.

'Breathe with it. Breathe with the pain,' Gemma urged. 'Remember what Garnet taught you.'

For a moment, she thought Faith hadn't heard her, then the girl obeyed.

'Good girl. Now just relax. Breathe again. That's brilliant.'

As the contraction eased, Faith whispered, 'I can't – without Garnet. *They* mean to take my baby . . . the Old Ones . . . I can't . . . I can't stop them by myself.'

'No one is going to take your baby. I'm here, and I'm going to help you. We're going to have this baby together. And the first thing we've got to do is get you out of these trousers.' The girl's clothes were sodden and she was shaking with chill – their removal could scarcely make her colder.

A litany of lack ran through Gemma's mind as she scooted Faith up the wall into a standing position. No towels, no gloves, no knife to cut the cord . . . and as her hand brushed against the tower she felt a numbing cold. She bit her lip to stop her teeth from chattering as the vicious wind scoured her back.

But there was no alternative, and at least she had done a brief midwifery course as part of her training.

She had the trousers down to Faith's ankles when the next contraction began and Faith slid into a squat, pressing against the wall.

'That's good, now. Breathe,' Gemma coached as she scrabbled for her temporarily forgotten torch. But it was useless and Gemma flicked it off with a mutter of frustration. She was going to have to do this by touch alone.

She reached down, feeling Faith flinch as her hand made contact. 'It's all right,' she soothed. 'I'm just checking the baby's progress. I won't hurt you.' Oh, God, was that the baby's head she felt, crowning already? Then the contraction eased. The baby receded, withdrawing into the safety of its mother's warmth.

Faith sagged against the wall, eyes closed.

'All right, love. You're almost there. Next time I want you to push, bear down with the contraction as hard as you can.' She pressed her palm flat against Faith's abdomen, breathing with her, and she felt the ripple of the muscles even before Faith moaned.

'Okay, here we go. Wait for the crest, then push.' She felt for the baby's head again as Faith bore down. There it was, the crown, then the entire head emerged as the contraction slackened off. 'Breathe,' she urged Faith. 'That's a good girl. The next one will do it.'

Gemma felt the groan resonating through the girl's body as the next contraction began. She tried to ease the baby's passage, but still Faith yelped at the unexpected pain of the baby's shoulders – and then Gemma held the infant in her hands.

It was wet, and warm . . . and still. 'Oh, dear God . . .' Desperately, she cleared the mucus from the tiny nose, then used the tip of her little finger to clear the child's mouth.

Silence.

Oh, God, please, Gemma prayed. What else had they taught her to do? Stimulate the baby's reflexes – that was it. She scraped her fingernail across the sole of the tiny foot. And again—

A cry split the air. Weak with relief, Gemma clasped the tiny form to her as a second wail followed the first.

'It's a girl. Oh, Faith, you have a little girl.'

'Let me – I want to hold her,' Faith whispered.

As Gemma inched forward, transferring the infant to her mother's arms, she felt a warm patch beneath her knee. She touched her fingertip to the spot, felt the dark pool in the grass. Faith was haemorrhaging.

She would not, could not, panic now. 'Faith,' she said quietly, 'you've got to get the baby inside your blouse, for warmth. Put her to your breast, let her suckle. And I need you to lie down, love. Now, put your knees up. There. Like that. Good girl.' Taking off her jacket, she covered mother and baby.

She had read somewhere that the mother's uterus would contract in response to the baby's nursing, a natural reaction that might slow the bleeding. She had no other recourse, and no means to warm them other than her own body.

Nor did she have any way to call for help, she realized as the dreadful enormity of her folly sank in. She had left her phone in her handbag, in the car.

Huddling against Faith to protect mother and infant as best she could from the wind, Gemma pointed her torch at the sky and began to flick it on and off.

Chapter Nineteen

> *Some of those who make the Glastonbury pilgrimage come to do reverence to the dust of saints in the serene green nave of the Abbey; some come to open their souls to the fiery forces going up like dark flames from the Tor. Who shall judge between them?*
>
> Dion Fortune, from
> *Glastonbury: Avalon of the Heart*

When Kincaid first returned to Garnet's kitchen and found it empty, he assumed that Gemma had gone out to meet the ambulance. A look out of the door, however, showed the yard deserted and quiet, the only vehicle Gemma's Escort parked in the lane. He crossed the yard and pulled open the gate, tearing the crime-scene tape loose.

But a look down the lane revealed no sign of activity. He went back into the house and knelt by Andrew Catesby. The man's skin had taken on an unhealthy tinge. Swearing, Kincaid rang 999 again and was assured by the dispatcher that help was on the way.

Standing, he called out for Gemma. There was no response. He checked the loo and the other downstairs rooms, fetching a rug from the sitting-room settee in passing. As he covered Andrew Catesby, he saw a scattering of papers on the floor beneath the table.

Gathering the sheets, he lifted them into the light of the oil lamp. He read Garnet's notes, then the book pages, with growing fascination. When he reached the newspaper clipping, he paused. *Kinnersley* . . . Where had he heard that name, and recently? It had been Buddy who'd mentioned that Garnet had bought the old Kinnersley place. The accident had happened here, then, outside this house. He read on . . . *Sarah Kinnersley's body was discovered by a neighbour, Charles Barnes, who informed her parents before ringing the police. No trace of the child's assailant has been found.*

Charles Barnes? Buddy, of course. Buddy . . . Garnet . . . two hit-and-run accidents, all connected somehow, if he could only see it. That didn't rule out the possibility that Garnet had seen Andrew strike Winnie with his car, but he was beginning to think that Andrew and Faith had played out a separate drama.

He was still puzzling over it when he heard the pulse of sirens.

'You didn't by any chance see Gemma down the way?' Kincaid asked, as he and DI Greely watched the paramedics load Andrew Catesby into the ambulance. He was now seriously worried.

'What, have you lost her, then?' Greely sounded amused.

'I thought she might have gone down to guide the ambulance,' Kincaid answered curtly.

'And you say the girl is missing as well? It would be my guess your partner saw, or heard, something, and went to have a look.'

'I'm very much afraid you're right.' With dismay Kincaid glanced round at the impenetrable darkness outside the farmyard. 'But how—'

A shout came from the officers in the lane; a moment later they appeared at the gate with a struggling and swearing figure between them.

'Let him go,' Greely ordered. 'How'd you get up here, lad?'

Nick Carlisle shook himself free and snarled, 'Across the foot of the Tor. Is she here? Is she all right?'

'Faith's not here, Nick,' Kincaid replied. 'But we found Andrew badly injured. And now Gemma's disappeared too.'

'I saw a light at the summit of the Tor, just one flash as I came across the field—'

'You think they've both gone up the blasted Tor, in the dark, in this weather?' Greely shook his head.

'Gemma had her torch,' Kincaid remembered. 'We've got to go after them. Have you a trained rescue unit? Faith may be hurt—'

'The baby,' interrupted Nick. 'It was due any day. She couldn't make that climb—'

'But if she did, it's very likely we've got another complication to consider. What about a stretcher?'

It seemed an eternity before Greely was running them down the hill in his own car, followed by his men in a panda. Leaving the cars near the bottom of the lane, they took the path that led up the southern face of the Tor, Greely having vetoed the north side as insane in the dark. The DI dispatched officers to search the lane leading to the north entrance and instructed them to go as far along the path as they deemed safe, and he had sent one constable to Chalice Well.

Nick, Greely, and Kincaid led, Greely having found torches for them all, while the three officers carrying lights, ropes, and the folding stretcher brought up the rear. Although the southern slope was considerably more gentle than the northern, it was still a difficult climb. Fortunately, the rain had stopped, improving the visibility if not the footing.

Although none of them had much breath for conversation, Kincaid heard Greely mutter, 'Mad. Bloody mad,' more than once.

'Likely as not they'll find the girl curled up somewhere along the lane again, like a bloody hedgehog,' Greely grumbled, when they stopped for a breather at the first plateau. 'And then I'll have a hell of a time explaining this' – he gestured at the officers – 'to my guv'nor.'

'I hope you're right,' Kincaid said. What had Gemma been thinking, going off without telling him? He knew she wouldn't have done such a thing lightly: that knowledge worried him even more.

They set out again, strung out single-file on the treacherous path. Suddenly Nick, who was in front of Kincaid, came to an abrupt stop and Kincaid teetered as he tried to avoid crashing into him.

'Look!' Nick exclaimed. 'A light. There it is again.'

Kincaid saw it then, a faint but regular flash from the summit in an SOS pattern. It could only be Gemma.

The sight spurred them to climb with renewed energy, Greely no longer grumbling. Kincaid shouted Gemma's name.

'Here!' As they reached the summit, she came running towards him. Kincaid gathered her to him, the fierceness of his hug part anger and part relief.

'I'm sorry,' she whispered. 'But I had to find her. The baby's fine, a little girl, but Faith's bleeding – badly, I think.'

Greely was on the radio, calling for another ambulance, and Nick had dropped to his knees by Faith's head, murmuring her name as the officers readied the stretcher. Kincaid squatted beside them and stroked her cheek with his fingertip. 'You should have waited for me. I'd have given you a much smoother ride home.'

Faith attempted a smile. The baby was nestled against her chest, her tiny rosebud mouth just showing beneath the edge of Faith's shirt. Kincaid found himself moved by the sight.

'We'll have you down this hill in no time,' he promised, stepping back, but Faith clutched at him.

'Andrew . . .'

'Shhh. Don't worry about that now. It's fine.'

The officers stepped in and strapped mother and infant on the stretcher, and they were soon caravanning back down the hill.

This time Kincaid and Gemma brought up the rear. He noticed that she was limping, and when he stopped to help her over a particularly difficult spot, he saw that her hands were cut and swollen. In the light from the torch, her face looked as pale as Faith's.

The ambulance was waiting when they reached the

lane. To Kincaid's surprise, Bram Allen paced nearby, his brow furrowed with worry. 'What's going on?' he demanded, hurrying towards them. 'They said an accident, someone badly hurt at the old Kinnersley place.'

'Andrew Catesby,' Kincaid replied.

'But the girl . . .' Bram's gaze followed the stretcher, now being loaded into the ambulance.

'Chose an odd place to have her baby.'

'I don't understand,' Bram said, a tremor in his voice.

'Neither do we, yet. She—'

'Duncan!' Gemma called to him from the rear of the ambulance.

'Sorry,' he murmured to Bram, then ducked through the milling officers to Gemma's side.

'Faith wants to speak to you before they go.'

He stepped up into the ambulance. 'You rang, princess?'

Faith's lips moved and he leaned closer. 'I wanted you to know . . .' Her voice was a thread of sound. 'Andrew . . . I didn't mean to hurt him. He – he said he couldn't bear for Winnie to know . . .'

'You did the only thing you could,' Kincaid assured her firmly. 'You protected yourself and your daughter.'

'Is he . . .'

'Don't think about that.'

'We're ready to go,' the paramedic urged.

Turning back to Faith, Kincaid said, 'You're going to be fine, sweetheart. We'll see you at the hospital.' He backed out and stood beside Gemma as the ambulance pulled away.

'She's so weak,' Gemma murmured. 'There was so much blood . . . And she's so very, very cold . . .'

The illuminations took Winnie's breath away. So rich were the colours, so intricate the details of the minute paintings that adorned the folio's alternate pages, that she could scarcely tear her eyes from them to look at the music itself.

The manuscript consisted of sixteen pages of tissue-thin, almost translucent vellum, folded to make a large, flat book. On the right-hand pages, the paintings filled the upper left corners, taking almost a quarter of the page, with the decoration continuing down the left-hand side and across the bottom. The text was in Latin, and above the text, the red, four-line staves bore the ancient, square notation of chant, drawn in black.

'It *is* in twelve parts,' she said. 'But I don't recognize the sequence. It's not an ordinary mass . . .'

'The Divine Office?' suggested Jack.

Winnie explained for Fiona's benefit. 'Traditionally, the Divine Office was made up of the services celebrated throughout the day in a monastery. Matins, Lauds, Prime, Terce, Sext, None, Vespers, and Compline. The chant repertory might have included recited Psalms . . .' Looking back at the manuscript, she struggled with deciphering the ornate text, murmuring the words as she translated – then the pattern clicked. 'It *is* a Psalm. Number 148! *Praise ye the Lord. Praise ye the Lord from the heavens; praise him in the heights. Praise ye him, all his angels: praise ye him, all his hosts.*

Praise ye him, sun and moon: praise him, all ye stars of light. Praise him, ye heavens of heavens, and ye waters that be above the heavens. It goes on, all the birds and beasts and creeping things are here too.'

'And look at the illuminations.' Fiona pointed with a fingertip, but didn't touch. 'There's the sun and the moon, and the stars, and here on the next page the birds . . . But look at the background in this one. It's Glastonbury. That's the Abbey, and that's the Tor behind it.'

'This is Edmund's work,' Jack told them. 'I'm sure of it. Look. That's Glastonbury again. And here. And this one, with the water flowing from the hillside, that's Chalice Well as it was then, where he met Alys.'

'But in the last days it shall come to pass,' read Winnie, *'that the mountain of the House of the Lord shall be established in the top of the mountains, and it shall be exalted above the hills, and people shall flow unto it.* That's Micah.' Turning several pages, she said, 'And after that, Revelation. It's Jesus' commandment to the Phildelphians. *Him that overcometh I will make a pillar in the temple of my God, and he shall go no more out; and I will write upon him the name of my God, and the name of the city of my God, which is new Jerusalem . . . Glastonbury* . . . the new Jerusalem . . .'

'Can you sing any of it?' asked Fiona. 'Do you know how to read the notation?'

'Yes, but . . . it needs a choir. I suppose I could try . . .' Winnie studied the new Jerusalem passage for a moment, then, hesitantly, sang a few syllables.

'Go on,' Jack and Fiona begged when she stopped.

Winnie sang another line of the verse, and as her

confidence grew, she felt the power of the music welling up within her, reverberating throughout her body. When she glanced up, the expressions of her audience told her its effect on them was as profound.

Fiona's eyes sparkled with tears. 'Just for a moment, I thought . . .'

'Was that the music you heard?' Jack asked Fiona.

'An echo of it, perhaps . . .'

'This' – Winnie's hands cupped the air round the folio – 'oh, Jack – how could this have been allowed to disappear?'

Jack went to the bookcase, returning with a worn Bible. 'This was my great-grandfather's, but he recorded as much as he knew of the generations before him. I think I remember seeing Matthew's name when I was copying the genealogical information for Simon. Here it is. *Matthew John Montfort, died 1762* – just three years after he wrote the letter. I suspect he never had the chance to pass the knowledge of the chant on to his son.'

'And by placing the manuscript in the painting, Matthew meant to take extra precautions. It's ironic, isn't it, that his actions caused it to be lost? Unless . . . You don't suppose . . . where he says, " . . . *as I have been directed*".'

'Edmund? Well, why not? There's no reason I should have been the only—' Jack stiffened.

They heard a murmur of voices, and a moment later Duncan and Gemma came into the room.

Winnie knew immediately that something was dreadfully wrong. 'Faith? Is she—'

'She's on her way to the hospital,' soothed Gemma. 'With her baby, a little girl.'

'How – what happened?' asked Jack, but Winnie saw that Duncan and Gemma were looking at her. She braced herself for a blow. If not Faith, then . . .

Duncan sat down beside her. 'Winnie, I'm sorry, but it's Andrew. He's been quite badly hurt. They've taken him to hospital in Taunton.'

'Oh, no, please. Not . . .' Searching his face, she said, 'There's more, isn't there? And worse. Faith—' The fragmented memory came back to her. 'We were talking, in the café, Faith and I . . . she said something about her archaeology class. It was only when I was walking up the hill afterwards that I realized she must have known Andrew – she was a Somerfield student – and in that case why had she never mentioned it, in all the time I'd known her? And Andrew, when I told him about the girl who had left school because she was pregnant, he never said he knew her . . . Fiona! That's why I was coming to see you. I needed to talk.' Winnie met Kincaid's eyes again. 'You said Andrew was badly hurt – how?'

'A head injury,' Duncan said reluctantly.

'Andrew tried to hurt Faith.'

Kincaid could only nod.

Winnie's face became expressionless. 'I must see him. Will you drive me to hospital, please?'

Gemma and Kincaid found Nick Carlisle haunting the corridor outside Faith's room. He hurried towards them.

'How is she?' asked Gemma.

'They think they've got the bleeding stopped, but she's awfully weak. She's resting now.'

'And the baby?'

Nick's smile lit his face. 'She's fine. Perfectly healthy, they say. Gemma . . . The doctor said you probably saved Faith's life – and the baby's. If there's anything—'

'You'd have done the same,' Gemma told him. 'I just got there first.' Somehow she understood that his gratitude was mixed with envy. He had wanted to be Faith's saviour, the hero of the day. 'Perhaps it's just as well, you know, that things worked out the way they did. Gratitude is a burden you'd not want to come between you two. You've a clean slate now.'

'I wish I did,' Nick said softly, his expression bleak, and Gemma recalled what she had learned of his past.

'Will they let us see her?' she asked.

'I'll find out.' Kincaid went to the desk, leaning over to speak to the dark-haired nurse. Gemma saw him flash his most effective smile, then he returned to them.

'Just one of us, for five minutes, and that's a special dispensation. You go in, Gemma. I'll stay with Nick.'

She eased open the door. The girl lay in the hospital bed, eyes closed, her dark lashes casting shadows on her cheeks. The baby lay in a cot beside her, only the top of her fuzzy head visible beneath a teddy-bear blanket.

Just as Gemma started to turn away, unwilling to wake her, Faith opened her eyes. Going to the bedside,

Gemma murmured, 'She's lovely. Have you decided what to call her?'

'Bridget.'

'Bridget . . . wasn't she a local saint?'

'Andrew . . . he always liked the story about St Bridget's Chapel at Beckery; that all who passed through the hole in the chapel's side would be forgiven their sins . . .'

'It suits her,' Gemma said softly. 'And you were very brave, you know.'

'Was I? I was so scared. I didn't know—'

'You can't know, until you've been through it. The nice thing is, you forget quickly.' Gemma smiled. 'Now, you get some rest—'

'I wanted to thank you. If you hadn't . . . Garnet knew what was going to happen, didn't she? On the Tor. Do you think somehow she knew about Andrew too?'

'I think Garnet loved you,' Gemma told the girl gently, 'and that's all that matters.'

Andrew had been rushed into surgery; there the haemorrhaging caused by the blows to his temple had been surgically evacuated to relieve the pressure on his brain. Now, his doctor had informed Winnie, they could only wait.

She had insisted that Jack stay behind in Glastonbury. Her undivided attention seemed a small penance for what she owed her brother. How could she have been so blind, so self-absorbed, that she had not seen his peril? As she sat beside Andrew's bed, her heart was gripped with fear for her brother – and for herself.

Could she bring herself to forgive him for what he had done? Even more difficult, could she find the strength to love him, knowing the secrets he had kept from her?

And if Andrew survived this, would he be able to live with his own terrible knowledge?

He stirred, his eyelids fluttering open. To her profound relief, he knew her instantly, and smiled. Then she saw the shadow of returning memory in his eyes and, with it, a recoil of horror and shame.

'Andrew, it's going to be all right, I promise. We're going to work through this together.'

He turned his face away.

Gemma and Kincaid found their way back to the ICU visitor's area and sat down to wait for Winnie. Kincaid fidgeted, frowning abstractedly as he studied a bright print on the wall.

'What is it?' Gemma pressed. 'Surely you don't think Faith is to blame for hurting Andrew—'

'Of course not. It's just that Greely's inclined to consider the case tidily wrapped up. Convenient for him, but I don't like it.'

'He assumes Garnet saw Andrew in the lane the night of Winnie's accident, and later confronted him.'

'Right. And that would fit nicely – except for the fact that Andrew's alibi for the time of Winnie's accident checked out. And if he were willing to *kill* Faith to keep his sister from finding out about their relationship, why would he have tried to hurt *Winnie?*'

Gemma thought for a bit. 'Andrew's affair with Faith must have started after Winnie met Jack, an act of emotional desperation, perhaps. When he discovered Faith was pregnant he cut her off, making her promise to tell no one. What a terrible irony that his rejection of Faith drove her to leave home, and led her to become friends with his sister.'

'If his motive in murdering Garnet was to keep her from telling Winnie, why would he kill Garnet the night *after* Winnie's accident, when he didn't know if Winnie would ever regain consciousness? Nor would it explain where Garnet drowned.'

'Bathtub? Kitchen sink?' Gemma offered.

'Then he cleaned up afterwards without leaving a trace? I suppose it's possible. But something's not right about this. Gemma, what happened up there on the Tor tonight? Was there something—' Kincaid broke off as the ICU door swung open.

Winnie came out and sat beside Gemma. Her face was bleak with exhaustion, and she closed her eyes briefly, seeming to gather strength.

'How is he?' Gemma asked.

'Resting comfortably, the doctor says. It's too early to know if the swelling will return, but they think the prognosis is good.'

'He's conscious? Did he—'

'No.' Winnie's eyes filled with tears. 'No, he didn't tell me anything.'

*

They drove back to Glastonbury in silence. Glancing at Nick, Winnie wondered if it had been loyalty to Andrew that had made Faith impervious to Nick's determined assault on her affections. Perhaps now she would be able to truly see this young man.

'Faith!' she exclaimed. 'I didn't even ask. Is she all right? And the baby?'

'She's doing fine,' Gemma answered. 'And the baby's lovely. Faith's called her Bridget.'

'St Bride,' Winnie said softly. It was a good name, and fitting. My *niece*, she realized for the first time, and that brought the tears she had held in abeyance. She let them slip unchecked down her cheeks, the salt on her lips tasting like blood. Something good *had* come of all this, and that thought comforted her.

But as they crossed over the River Brue, she said suddenly, 'I want to go to the Abbey.'

'But it's closed,' Nick protested.

'Take me to the Silver Street gate, then. Please. I can't explain—'

Duncan glanced back at her. 'It's all right. Just tell me where to go.'

'Past the Assembly Rooms, on the High Street. There's a turning to the right.'

The gate at the bottom of Silver Street was kept locked, but as it was made of wrought iron, it was the one place you could see easily into the Abbey grounds. Duncan pulled up next to the rubbish bins and Winnie was out of the car before it had come to a full stop.

She stood at the gate and looked through. The sky had cleared, and in the moonlight the ruined church cast a shadow on the greensward. Why had she come here? What had called to her so powerfully?

Closing her eyes, she saw a different vision. She'd stood there in the sunlight, beneath the great stone transepts, and she had heard the music rising round her. The chant . . . she had heard the chant, and she had known it for what it was. The elation and the certainty of her experience filled her once again.

Without turning, she said, 'Out of all the Grail mythology entwined with Glastonbury over the centuries, there is one legend that says the Grail is not an object – not a cup or a chalice – but a transcendent state of being, brought about by ritual and prayer. This chant that the monks of the Abbey were willing to sacrifice their lives for, that Edmund devoted himself to saving for future generations, is a part of that complex of rituals.

'I was *here*.' She turned to the others. 'On the day of the accident. I remember now. I saw everything, and I felt I would burst with the joy of it.'

'And afterwards?' Duncan asked.

She frowned. 'I went – I think I went to the Galatea. Then I rode to Pilton to make a bereavement call – Suzanne told me that. And then' – the scene flashed before her . . . the green of shimmering leaves and the sparkle of water – 'why, I stopped to visit Simon. We had tea in his cottage garden, by the river. But why didn't he say, when I couldn't remember?'

'Simon lives by a river, and no one bothered to mention it?' Aghast, Gemma exchanged a look with Duncan.

Nick said, 'But Jack's gone to see—'

Duncan quelled him with a glance. 'Let's get back in the car, shall we?'

He stepped away and made a call on his mobile phone. After a moment, he hung up with a mutter of frustration and climbed in with them. 'There's no answer at Jack's. Winnie, give us directions to Simon Fitzstephen's cottage.'

Kincaid caught a glimpse of the tower of the medieval church as they passed, then Nick instructed him to turn left into a steep lane that dead-ended after a hundred yards. Jack's blue Volvo was pulled up on the verge just past the cottage Nick and Winnie identified as Simon Fitzstephen's.

As Kincaid parked behind Jack's car, he told himself Jack was in no real danger; it was Winnie who was at risk. He debated whether to insist she stay behind with Nick, or to keep her in his sight, and decided on the latter.

The damp fronds of a willow brushed his face as he got out of the car, and in the darkness the rushing of the stream was as loud as a roar.

Kincaid rang the bell, then immediately opened the door and called out, not wanting to give Fitzstephen a chance to do anything rash – although there was no reason for the man to get the wind up. He had, after all, been in and out of Jack's house the last few days as calmly as you please: he had probably decided that Winnie was not going to recover any inconvenient memories.

Fitzstephen appeared in the hall and, when he saw

them all gathered on his doorstep, made a gesture of surprise. 'What is this, a delegation? Jack, look who's here.' His ascetic face seemed flushed, his hair more unruly than usual. 'This is delightful. Come in, come in.'

'Winnie! What are you doing here, darling?' Jack exclaimed.

'Do sit down,' said Simon. 'Jack and I were having a celebratory Scotch, if anyone would care to join us.'

The chant manuscript lay open on the sitting-room table, their glasses beside it.

'We haven't come to celebrate, Simon. There are some things we need to talk about.'

'Oh?'

'Everyone has been very ready to blame both Winnie's accident and Garnet Todd's death on Andrew Catesby,' continued Kincaid. 'A convenient solution, at least until he's able to defend himself.'

'If I know anything, it's that Andrew would never have tried to hurt me,' said Winnie.

'No,' Kincaid agreed. 'I don't believe he would have either. In fact, I don't think your accident, or Garnet's death, had anything to do with Andrew *or* Faith. I think it was something else entirely.'

Simon sat down and reached for his glass. 'Surely, Winifred's accident was just that, an accident,' he said reasonably.

'No. Jack's suspicions were quite valid. Someone deliberately struck Winnie that night. It was a daring move, and a foolhardy one, but there were tremendous stakes. You see, Winnie had realized that this chant' – Kincaid gestured towards the manuscript – 'was quite special indeed. And she had shared that knowledge with only one person.

'Don't you think it rather odd, Simon, that you neglected to mention to anyone that Winnie had come to see you that afternoon?'

'Why should I have mentioned it?' Simon sounded bewildered. 'She'd come to pay a visit in the neighbourhood, and stopped in afterwards for a cup of tea. What was so odd about that?'

'We talked about the chant, Simon.' Winnie stepped forward. 'The twelve-part perpetual chant.'

'What on earth is going on here?' Jack asked. 'What are you all talking about? Winnie—'

'I told Simon that I thought the chant was one of the rituals that makes up the Grail—'

'But the Grail is a myth,' protested Jack. 'And even if it were true, how could a chant be a cup?'

'I don't think the Grail *was* a cup. I think it was – is – a state of grace, and that this chant was one of the things used to create that state. When I asked Simon, as a fellow priest, what this meant for us, and for the Church, he said' – Winnie closed her eyes, as if trying to recall the exact words – ' "It isn't a valid construct, because our society is no longer theocentric." And then he suggested that I might be suffering from some sort of emotional hysteria as in, "middle-aged women in love have a tendency to become deranged".'

Watching Simon's face, she added softly, 'Oh, yes, I remember it all, now. You thought you could put me off it, but after I left, you must have realized that wasn't enough. So you came after me. You waited for a chance to make sure I wouldn't spread my theories any further.'

Fitzstephen lifted his hands in a helpless gesture. 'Winifred, I don't know what to say. We did talk about the chant, yes, but I never dreamed it was any more than a flight of fancy on your part. I can't imagine you think I'd—'

'Did you think that if this came out it would ruin your reputation as a Grail scholar? Destroy all your well-researched theories? Or did you think you'd somehow manage to take credit for the discovery? You've always been unscrupulous, Simon, willing to use other people's work as it suited you, but—'

'Has everyone forgotten Garnet Todd?' Kincaid asked. 'You and Garnet went back a long way, didn't you, Simon? Friends – maybe even lovers at some time?'

'What has my relationship with Garnet to do with this?'

'I believe that Garnet knew – or at least suspected – that your motives might not be in line with the rest of the group. Perhaps she'd followed Winnie that night, wanting to talk to her about Faith, or perhaps she just happened to see you coming out of Lypatt Lane, and once she learned of Winnie's accident she put two and two together.

'Did she come to see you the next night, determined to confront you about the attempt on Winnie's life? Did you have drinks in the garden? And when you realized what she knew, did you ask her to look at something in the stream? Did you—'

'No, wait,' interrupted Jack. 'I've just remembered!

We were looking for Faith that evening. I rang you and asked you to check the farmhouse, as Garnet didn't have a phone, and you said you would go.'

'I did.' Simon had stiffened in his chair. 'There was no one there, and I came home again. As for the evening of Winifred's accident, I had a speaking engagement in Bristol, in front of two hundred people, if anyone bothered to check. I left shortly after Winifred's visit and didn't return until midnight. You are all mad, utterly mad.'

'But—' Kincaid stared at him. 'Simon, when you went to the farmhouse that evening, was Garnet's van in the yard?'

'Yes, but there was no one in the house. I knocked *and* called out.'

'Bloody hell. I've been a fool. Simon, forgive me. Gemma – we've been blind. It was never Winnie who was in danger.'

Chapter Twenty

> *On more than one occasion, we who live upon [the Tor's] flank have been called upon to minister comfort and consolation to those who have actually seen what they went to look for.*
>
> Dion Fortune, from
> *Glastonbury: Avalon of the Heart*

It seemed to Gemma that she had never been so tired. She had listened to Kincaid's exchange with Simon Fitzstephen with a growing sense of unreality, as if she were becoming physically detached from her body. Now, as they sped back towards Glastonbury, she was having difficulty following Kincaid's logic. 'Are you saying you think Fiona Allen's husband might hurt her?' she asked.

'I don't know. But I do think Bram fits into this and somehow that it's connected to the death of little Sarah Kinnersley. When I saw her photo in that news clipping, I knew she seemed familiar – and then tonight at Simon's it came back to me: it was the face of the child in Fiona's painting.'

'The painting . . . it seemed almost as if the beings – angels? – were protecting the child . . .'

'Bram and Garnet were lovers at the time Sarah was killed. The Kinnersleys were so devastated by their loss that they walked away from their property – Buddy mentioned Garnet bought it "for a song". Buddy also said that after little Sarah Kinnersley died, everything changed. Bram left Garnet. He married Fiona.'

'Left Garnet because she knew the truth? Was Garnet an accessory in Sarah's death?'

'In the notes she left in the kitchen, she wrote that Faith was her redemption, and that bringing Faith's baby into the world would be a child's life for a child's life. But I think she came to feel that wasn't enough, that in order to counteract what was happening to Faith she needed to take some kind of direct action.'

'She confronted Bram—'

'I'd guess she told him she wouldn't keep his secret any longer, that it was time for him to make retribution by telling the truth.'

'And Winnie?'

'Garnet told Faith she had an appointment that evening. I think she'd set up a meeting with Bram, perhaps at the very spot where Winnie was struck.'

'And at the last minute Garnet found she couldn't go through with it – and Winnie just happened to be in the wrong place at the wrong time,' Gemma finished. 'The next day, when Garnet learned of the accident, she guessed who had been responsible.'

'Then did she go to him? Or did he come after her? Simon said that when he went to Garnet's that evening, her van was still in the yard. I'm guessing that Bram went to the farmhouse sometime after Nick left.'

'You think he drowned her in the house? But there was no sign.'

'No . . . Do something for me, would you? Ring directory inquiries, get the number for Buddy – Charles Barnes.'

Gemma complied and, when the number began to ring, handed the phone to Kincaid.

'Buddy? It's Duncan Kincaid. You know the spring on Garnet's property? Is there any standing water? A pool above the house. Right. Oh, and Buddy, one more thing: on the night Sarah Kinnersley was killed, do you know where Garnet was? Did she have a car?' He listened a moment longer, then said, 'Okay, thanks. I'll explain later,' and disconnected.

'She was with Bram Allen,' stated Gemma.

'And he would have been driving. Garnet had no car at the time.'

'I still don't understand why you're worried about Fiona . . .'

'Because I think that, like Andrew with his sister, there's one person Bram would do anything to protect from the knowledge of his crime.'

The lights still shone in the Allens' house, and when Kincaid rang the bell, Fiona opened the door immediately. 'Bram,' she said, ' – have you seen him?'

'He's not here?'

Fiona shook her head. 'When I came back from Jack's, I found him in the studio. He was – I've never seen him like that. My painting – he had my painting, the one of the Abbey, with the child. He'd cut it with his knife. And then he – he—'

'Slow down,' Kincaid said gently. 'What happened then?'

'He said things I didn't understand, something about stopping it once and for all, and he took the painting.'

'Bram left with the painting?'

Fiona nodded. 'Stop what? What did he mean? Where has he gone? Bram—'

Kincaid took the north path. More treacherous, yes, but faster, and if Gemma had done it, so could he. The setting moon provided enough illumination that he climbed without mishap, driven by fear of what he would find at the top.

Once at the summit he stopped, letting his breathing ease. Then he went forward quietly, scanning the silvered turf for a shadow of movement.

He found Bram Allen on the far side of St Michael's Tower, in the spot where Faith had lain. Bram sat huddled against the wall, Fiona's painting clutched to his chest, the knife in his right hand visible against the canvas.

'Bram,' Kincaid called softly, coming to a halt a few feet away.

Bram stood, looking at him without surprise. 'I'll give them blood, if that's what they want,' he said clearly. 'But not that girl and her baby. Not again.'

'Who wants blood?' Kincaid stood motionless.

'Old Ones. Garnet knew. Garnet always knew about

them. That night we danced, here, in the grass. It was Samhain, the time when the veil is thinnest. We called them and they came. We were wild with it, invincible, we possessed the world. But they wanted more – a life – and we were just the instruments.'

'Sarah.'

'I saw her face, for only an instant, above the windscreen. I've seen it every day of my life since. How did Fiona know?'

'The child in the painting.' Kincaid inched closer, aware of the glimmer of the knife.

'Why? Why did she come to Fiona?'

'That must have been terrible for you, when Fiona began to paint little Sarah.'

'Fiona didn't understand why I couldn't bear the sight of them. Then when she wanted to hang them in the gallery, I couldn't refuse.'

'But why kill Garnet, Bram?'

'It was building again, the old power. Garnet believed she could stop it – that we could stop it if I told. She came into the gallery. When she saw Fiona's paintings she said it was a divine judgement, that *Fiona* was my retribution. Fiona . . .' The despair in his voice chilled Kincaid to the heart. 'All these years I thought I could make amends by loving her, being part of her goodness. The only thing I couldn't do was give her a child . . . I hoped that grief might be punishment enough.'

'Did you agree to meet Garnet that night in the lane?'

'A customer came into the gallery. I had to get rid of her somehow. And then, waiting in the darkness, I thought how easy it would be . . . I didn't know it was Winnie until it was too late.'

And he had left her to die, Kincaid thought, *when he could so easily have called for help.*

'But Garnet knew, didn't she? So the next night you went to her house, and you convinced her to walk up to the spring.'

'I think she knew what was going to happen, at the last. Perhaps she thought her life would finish it. But it wasn't enough.'

'Bram, let's go home. It's over now. Your wife is frantic with worry about you.'

'You don't understand.'

'I know that Fiona will love you no matter what you've done—'

'No. I won't have her stained with this . . . this evil—' His gesture with the knife took in the Tor. 'Can't you feel it? Once it begins, only blood will satisfy their hunger.'

'Bram, there's nothing here. Let's go home to your wife. We'll get warm. Have a drink. In the morning, nothing will seem so terrible.' He shifted his weight, judged his distance from the weapon.

'I can't. Fiona—'

'Garnet was right, Bram. The only way to end this is to tell the truth. Give Fiona the chance to forgive you. She loves you – you owe her that.'

'I—'

'Give me the knife, Bram.' He stepped closer, held out his hand.

'But *they*—'

'It's over, Bram, the cycle's finished. They don't

need your life.' Kincaid tensed, ready to lunge for the weapon.

'I—' Bram put his hands to his face and sagged against the wall. 'You're sure?'

'I'm sure.' Kincaid took the knife from his unresisting fingers. 'Let's go home.'

He guided Bram away from the tower, leaving Fiona's mutilated painting abandoned against the cold stone.

They began the descent, Kincaid staying as close to Bram as the narrow path allowed. To one side was a sheer drop; mud and loose stones made the footing treacherous. The wind tore at them, tugging at their clothing like invisible hands.

At the first hairpin bend, Bram turned back. He spoke, but the wind snatched the words from his mouth. Then a shower of stones fell from above, striking him. Jerking away from the blows, Bram lost his footing and plunged over the edge.

'Bram!' Kincaid shouted, reaching for him, but his fingers grasped only air. He called out again and again, but no reply came from the impenetrable darkness below.

At last, exhausted, he continued downward, towards the help he knew would be futile.

It seemed that Bram had been right, after all. The Old Gods had been satisfied with no less than payment in blood.

All the way to Wells, huddled in the back of the car, Gemma could only think of how it had felt to hold

Faith's baby in her arms. And she found herself making a mute entreaty, again and again, that she would not lose what she had been given.

Chapter Twenty-One

. . . I often wonder whether the life of Avalon will ever stir again, or whether we shall be no more than a tourist show and a market town. Will these dead bones come together, bone to bone, as they did at Buckfastleigh? There is talk of a great new abbey to rise under the shadow of the old . . . and I . . . impenitent heathen though I am, [hope] that I shall hear Angelus from my high veranda.

Dion Fortune, from
Glastonbury: Avalon of the Heart

Kincaid waited alone outside the cubicle in the emergency ward for news of Gemma. When the doctor emerged at last, he stood. 'Is she—'

'She's fine,' the doctor informed him with abstracted cheerfulness.

'But what happened? Is she ill?'

'Um, not exactly. Why don't you go in and see her yourself.'

He found Gemma draped in a lilac-flowered hospital gown, her hair loose about her shoulders. Going to her, he sat on the edge of the bed and said only, 'Tell me what's wrong.'

Her smile was tremulous. 'There's nothing exactly wrong. It's just that I'm pregnant.'

'Pregnant?'

'It is a fairly common occurrence, you know, if you do the sort of things we've done.'

'But – how long?'

'Eight to ten weeks, the doctor thinks. I should have told you sooner. Only I wasn't sure . . . and I didn't know how you would feel . . . or quite how I felt.'

'The baby – is it going to be okay?'

'There's a bit of placental tearing, but it's not too severe. I'll have to see a specialist, and the doctor says I may have to take it a bit easier than I'm accustomed to. No more climbing mountains in the rain, or delivering babies, for a while.'

Gemma, pregnant? With his child? Kincaid shook his head, trying to take in the wonder of it. But what had she meant when she'd said she wasn't sure how she felt about it? 'Gemma – your job. I know how much it means to you. How will you—?'

'I don't know,' she said pensively. 'But tonight, when I thought I would lose this baby, I realized what mattered to me most.'

Unable to speak, Kincaid took her hand in both of his.

On the threshold of Faith's hospital room, Winnie hesitated. Kincaid had told her that Faith adamantly refused to press charges against Andrew, leaving the police powerless to prosecute him for his assault on her. Yet if her brother felt any gratitude, he had not expressed it – in fact, he'd refused to talk to her about Faith at all. He remained silent and unresponsive during her visits.

The doctors told her his physical recovery might be slow; Winnie suspected his emotional recovery would be even more difficult – if it were possible at all. But she must hope, and she had to begin by setting things right with Faith.

Taking a breath, she pushed open the door and went in. Faith greeted her with a smile, and Winnie gave silent thanks for the entry of this remarkable girl into her life.

When she had duly admired little Bridget, she asked, 'Your parents – how did it go?'

'Okay. They thought Bridget was gorgeous, didn't they, sweetheart?' Faith cooed to the baby at her breast. 'But I can't go back. I don't know how we'll manage, Bridget and I, but I know I don't fit in that life any more. Winnie— When I found out you were Andrew's sister, I was afraid you'd guess somehow about the baby, and I had promised no one would ever know—'

'It's all right, Faith. We have to think about the future now, and I have a proposal for you. I could use some help in the Vicarage. And even when Jack moves in—'

Faith's face lit up. 'You're getting married?'

'As soon as we can arrange it,' Winnie admitted. 'But even then, there will be plenty of room in the Vicarage, draughty old pile that it is, until you get on your feet. And we are, after all, family—'

'Andrew. He wouldn't – I mean I couldn't—'

'Of course you can. Andrew has no say over who lives in my home.'

'But—'

'My brother owes you a debt he can never hope to repay. But he can begin by providing support for little Bridget, and by getting used to the idea that we are all going to have to get on together.'

Faith slept after Winnie's visit, deeply and dreamlessly, and when she woke she knew what she was going to do. Garnet's legacy should not be allowed to vanish. She, Faith, with Winnie's help, could carry it on. She would learn to make tiles.

She was still mulling over the details of her plan when Nick knocked. He fussed over her and Bridget, but she sensed an awkwardness in his manner, and an unfamiliar chasm between them.

'Nick, what is it?'

He hesitated, then met her eyes. 'I've come to say goodbye.'

'What do you mean, goodbye? I'll be going home tomorrow, to Jack's, that is. And then Winnie's asked me to come and stay with her at the Vicarage.'

'I know,' Nick replied. 'She told me. But I'm leaving Glastonbury. I have to go back to Northumberland, Faith, and take care of some things.'

Faith stared at him. She suddenly realized that she'd foolishly assumed Nick would always be there, as constant as the sun and the moon.

'But . . . you'll come back, right?' she asked, making an effort to keep her voice steady.

'I don't know yet. But if I can get things sorted out, I think I may try to get into theological college. I thought – I thought that no one who had screwed up as badly as I have could possibly be a priest, but Winnie says you can't understand other people's mistakes if you haven't made some yourself. Seasoning, she called it.' He smiled. 'Don't look so shocked. It's what I've always wanted; it just took me a while to figure it out.'

'But . . . *Father Nick*?' She studied him as if seeing him for the first time. Nick, a vicar like Winnie? 'Well . . .' she said slowly, 'I suppose I could get used to it.'

Gemma and Kincaid had turned over all their information on the murder of Garnet Todd and Bram Allen's death to DI Greely. His team had already found Garnet's missing earring near the pool above her house, and a strand of Garnet's long salt-and-pepper hair snagged on a button on the jacket Bram Allen had worn the night she died.

Now, they sat in front of the fire in Jack's parlour, drinking tea and sorting through the events of the past days. Andrew's dog Phoebe, brought temporarily from the house on Hillhead, had curled herself up against Gemma's feet.

'Will Fiona be all right?' asked Kincaid.

'She's very strong,' answered Winnie. 'But this . . . I don't know. I've seldom seen two people love each other more.'

'Even though Bram wasn't what she thought?'

'I'm not sure,' Winnie said slowly, 'that it matters.

And are any of us ever entirely honest about ourselves?'

Gemma thought of her own failure to communicate with Duncan about what lay closest to her heart. 'What about Edmund? Do you think he knows now that his and Alys's child survived?'

'I hope so,' answered Jack. 'He deserves peace, after eight hundred years.'

'As does little Sarah Kinnersley,' Winnie said softly.

'What will you do with the manuscript?' Kincaid asked.

'Study, first,' Jack replied instantly. 'Consult with some of the experts on chant, and with conservators. The manuscript itself is remarkably well preserved, and we want to keep it that way.'

'You won't try to keep it hidden any longer?'

'I think almost a millennium is long enough, don't you? People should hear this – who knows what good might come of it?'

'It's quite a responsibility, isn't it, though?' mused Gemma. 'If it's what you suspect it is.'

'But there have always been caretakers in Glastonbury,' Winnie pointed out. 'Think of the monks, and Bligh Bond, and the Chalice Well Trust . . . We'll be following a well-established tradition. I think Edmund would have wanted that.'

'What about Simon?' Kincaid asked. 'I'm afraid we did him a disservice, regardless of any past indiscretions.'

'Perhaps . . .' Winnie smiled faintly. 'Although I did learn he'd contacted someone about publishing Edmund's communications, without consulting Jack.'

'So there's still a wolf under the sheep's clothing, after all.'

'I'm sure he meant to tell me,' Jack replied stubbornly, making it clear that he and Winnie would have enough differences of opinion to make life interesting.

'London is going to seem extremely dull compared to Glastonbury,' Kincaid said with a grin, 'but I suppose we'd better be getting back.'

'Wait.' Jack rose. 'I have something for Gemma.' He left the room, returning with a flat, paper-wrapped package.

'For me?' Gemma took it, curious. When she undid the twine and pulled back the paper, she found herself looking at an oil portrait of a hunting spaniel, who gazed back at her with eyes as soulful as Phoebe's. 'Oh . . .' she breathed. 'It's lovely.'

'See, I didn't forget,' Jack told his cousin.

'But he's not half as lovely as you, is he, darling?' whispered Gemma, who had leaned over to stroke Phoebe's silky ears. She thought of her flat, not big enough to swing a cat in, much less a dog. Owning a dog had seemed an impossible proposition, in spite of Toby's constant pleading. But now she faced challenges much more daunting than that, and she felt suddenly liberated, as if anything were possible, alight with excitement at the prospect of the inevitable changes to come. What had happened to her?

Could it be, she wondered, that Glastonbury worked its magic in more ways than they had imagined?

*

They stood beneath the great stone transepts of the Abbey Church. It was a perfect November afternoon, but the sun was sinking and the first hint of evening's chill had crept into the air. It was near closing and the precinct was deserted; soon they would have to leave as well.

'Here,' Winnie told Jack, moving through the nave into the Choir. 'I think it should be sung here, where it was meant to be sung.'

'And where the monks shed their blood to preserve it,' agreed Jack, gazing at the spot where the altar had once stood. 'Is that possible? Could it be done?'

'I don't see why not. There are choirs all over England – all over the world, for that matter – that would jump at the chance. But . . .'

'What?' he pressed, seeing her frown.

'I think the chant should be sung in Glastonbury, by ordinary Glastonbury folk. It's not perfection that matters, but intent.'

Jack pulled from his pocket the piece of paper he had brought to show her. 'I wrote this today, at the office.'

'Edmund?'

He nodded and started to hand it to her, but she shook her head. 'No, read it to me, please. I always imagine that his voice would have sounded like yours.'

Peering at the faint script in the fading light, Jack began to read haltingly. *'There is much rejoicing among the Company. The Spirit liveth still, and that which we dreamed we pass on to you, a Symbol of the great Truth which is to come.*

But ye must be ever vigilant, for although ye have

closed the door, the balance is ever in question, and the fall is perilous. Doubt not your worth, for this task is given you in good faith, and fear not, for we will Watch with you. May you grow in spirit and in joy.'

Jack looked up from the page. The western sky was washed with the rose and gold of the setting sun, and for an instant, he could have sworn he heard an echo of voices raised in song.